"Don't look at me li[ ]
"You're maki[ ]
a total [failure.]

"Bree!" Nessa's voice was shocked. "I don't think of you as a failure."

"Neither do I," said Cate. "I always envied you. Footloose, fancy-free and not chained by some mad notion of being a career woman like me."

"I didn't think you felt chained," said Bree. "I thought you were happy."

"I *am* happy," Cate told her forcefully. "I really am. But sometimes I feel pressurized. The company depends on me."

"I think I know what you mean," said Nessa. "Sometimes I'm rushing around after Jill and I wish that I had just a minute to myself only I don't because I know Adam will be home soon and that he's had a stressful day and he'll want to unwind and I suppose I feel pressurized, too."

"I thought you lived an idyllic life," said Bree.

"I'm very happy," said Nessa. "It's simply that occasionally it goes wrong. And you feel stressed by it."

"So," Cate said, "both Nessa and I get stressed in spite of the fact that we're both doing exactly what we want to do. Yet you don't, Bree. Why? What have you got that we haven't?"

Bree looked at them and scratched the back of her head. "Actually, it's what you both have that I haven't," she told them.

"What?" asked Nessa.

"Men in your lives," said Bree.

Also by Sheila O'Flanagan

Dreaming of a Stranger
Caroline's Sister
Isobel's Wedding
Suddenly Single
Far From Over
My Favourite Goodbye

He's Got To Go

Sheila O'Flanagan

down town press

New York London Toronto Sydney Singapore

DOWNTOWN PRESS
1230 Avenue of the Americas, New York, NY 10020

First published in Great Britain in 2002 by Headline Book Publishing

ISBN: 0-7434-7042-7

First Downtown Press trade paperback edition January 2004

10 9 8 7 6 5 4 3 2 1

DOWNTOWN PRESS and colophon are registered trademarks of
Simon & Schuster, Inc.

Manufactured in the United States of America

Designed by Jaime Putorti

For information regarding special discounts for bulk purchases,
please contact Simon & Schuster Special Sales at 1-800-456-6798
or business@simonandschuster.com

Acknowledgments

While I was doing some basic research into horoscopes for this book I discovered that, instead of being an Aries as I'd always thought, I'm actually a Pisces by about an hour. Maybe this explains why I started off working in a bank even though I always wanted to write. Fortunately, a lot of people helped me to change my life in spite of some occasionally dodgy horoscopes for Arians and Pisceans.

Thanks to:

My agent and friend, Carole Blake

My two U.S. editors, Amanda Ayers and Christina Boys, and everyone at Downtown Press

Louise Cox, a wonderful solicitor, who kept me focused on the important things

Sean and all at Sweeny & Forte, Ireland, who let me mess with their cars

Many thanks to my family who are always wonderful. Especially to my sisters Joan and Maureen who, whenever I write a book about sisters, have to put up with people asking them if we're like that

To Dish 'n Dren (aka Patricia and Brenda) for coming on the research trip

To Colm for everything that matters

And, once more, a very special thanks to all of you who've bought my books over the last few years and made the change from number cruncher to author so wonderful for me. I do hope you enjoy this one, too. If you have any comments or want to contact me you can do so through my website: www.sheilaoflanagan.net. I'd be delighted to hear from you.

1

♥

Cancer June 23rd–July 23rd

Protective, stubborn, moody, soft beneath a hard shell.

The day started badly but that didn't surprise her. Nessa's horoscope for the whole week had been the sort she hated, full of warnings about people being uncooperative, minor mishaps and things not going to plan. It was one of those horoscopes that made her check the signs either side of Cancer just to see if things would have been better if she'd been born a month earlier or later.

Gemini's were in for an exciting week, it seemed. Leos would see some new events taking hold—good for Adam, at least. But the predictions for Cancerians were dull and vague. Not like last month when she'd read about an unexpected windfall and had won five hundred euros on the Lottery the very next day. She'd scoured the pages of *The Year Ahead for Cancerians* for other potential money wins after that but hadn't come up with anything even vaguely promising. The next few weeks looked incredibly boring as far as she could see, filled with advice to focus on her resources and take time before making important decisions. She'd checked a few magazine horoscopes too on the off chance that they'd throw a better light on things but they'd been equally vague. The only thing for it, Nessa decided, was to try and make the week more interesting herself.

Because things hadn't started promisingly first thing (the alarm hadn't gone off and there'd been a big rush to get both her uncooperative husband and her equally uncooperative daughter out of bed) she hoped that they'd improve by tonight. She really didn't want minor mishaps to upset the assorted family gathering she'd planned for this evening. I don't know why I let myself in for things like this, she muttered, as she watched eight-year-old Jill eat breakfast by stuffing an entire warm croissant into her mouth. It's more trouble than it's worth.

But it always gave her a warm glow to have the people she cared about around her and to bask in their appreciation of an enjoyable evening. Typically Cancerian, her mother Miriam would say fondly, and Nessa knew that she was right. But she couldn't help herself. She liked filling her home with the people closest to her, and her parents' visit to Dublin from their home in Galway was a good excuse to have everyone around for the first time in ages. Miriam and Louis had moved back to their home county when Louis had retired the previous year. Nessa still hadn't got used to the fact that her mother was no longer a five-minute drive away. It wasn't as if she needed to call on Miriam that often, but it had been nice to know that she was there in a crisis. Not that there were too many real crises in Nessa's life. How could there be when Adam and Jill were part of it (even if they made it difficult in the mornings by refusing to get out of bed)?

And then she heard the crunch. She stood in the kitchen, coffee cup midway to her lips, while she processed the sound. She didn't really need to process the sound, she knew exactly what it was, she'd heard it often enough before.

"Oh, Mum!" Jill's blue eyes were wide with the knowledge too. "Dad's pranged the car again, hasn't he?"

"Sounds like it." Nessa put her cup on the breakfast counter. "Let's go and see."

They walked together into the front room and looked out of the bay window. Adam was getting out of the car, his face red and his eyes blazing with fury. Nessa could see clearly what had happened. In reversing the car out of the driveway, Adam had managed to clip the front wing of another car which was parked at the curb.

Shit, she thought, as she watched her husband stand and seethe. It was probably because he was eating the croissant as he drove. I should never have given it to him just to save time because he was late for a meeting. He can't drive and do something else at the same time. I should know that by now. I don't need a horoscope to tell me a mishap would result.

Of course, if he hadn't been a terrible driver, if he hadn't had trouble with, as he called it, spatial awareness, she might never have got to know him at all. They'd have passed each other by ten years ago instead of exchanging phone numbers in the less than romantic setting of the underground car park at Blackrock Shopping Centre. Parking was tight in the carpark at the best of times but, two days before Christmas, it was manic. Finding a space was difficult enough, parking in it wasn't easy what with all the other impatient drivers around, and getting out of it was even more difficult because spaces that had been a tight fit on the way in suddenly seemed to shrink on the way out.

But parking in difficult spaces held no fears for Nessa. Louis, a tanker driver, had taught his three daughters to drive and had taught them well. Unlike most relatives as teachers, Louis was good at instructing, good at staying calm and good at instilling confidence. Nessa, Cate and Bree Driscoll had all passed their test at the first attempt.

But, easy as it was for Nessa, Adam Riley was having terrible trouble. He'd just spent the past two hours in the shopping center, at least half of which had been spent trying to find somewhere to park in the first place; he was tired and bad-tempered and had spent much, much more than he'd meant to because he'd bought the first thing he saw for everyone and then, as he'd walked around a little more, had seen much more appropriate gifts and bought them too. He didn't mind spending money—in fact he enjoyed it immensely— but both his credit cards were up to their limits and his checking account was overdrawn. So he knew that as a result of today he'd be spending the next few weeks on some kind of drastic economy drive. And he hated economy drives.

He sat in his car and looked around him anxiously. The red car beside him was so close that only a couple of millimeters separated them. On the other side, a stone pillar seemed to be effectively blocking any possibility maneuvering. And there was a line of cars waiting to take the space which he should already have vacated.

Nessa was first in the line. She was listening to her Queen tape and singing along happily to "Bohemian Rhapsody" when she realized that the asshole who was trying to reverse out of the space she was waiting for was making a complete mess of it. She watched as he moved backward and forward and backward again without making any progress whatsoever. She was pleased that it was a bloke who was messing things up so badly; but she knew that most of the people in the line behind her would be thinking that some fool woman was making a mess of things.

Adam could feel his palms beginning to sweat. He knew that people were waiting. He knew that they were watching him. Most of the time he loved to have people watching him because he was a natural extrovert and enjoyed admiration but not here, not now.

He jumped as someone rapped on the driver's window.

"Let me."

The girl was tiny—no more than five feet two. Her dark brown hair curled around her oval face and two gray eyes peered at him from beneath a shaggy fringe.

He wound down the window. "Pardon?"

"We'll be here until New Year if you keep on doing what you're doing," she said. "And I want to get some shopping done. So, if you want to get out of that space, let me do it."

He was going to say no but something in her eyes made him say yes.

She slid into the car, pulled the seat forward as far as it would go and then reversed out of the space with the minimum of fuss. Adam couldn't believe it. The other cars in the line hooted their approval.

"Thanks," he said as she got out of the car again.

"Don't mention it."

"That was fantastic."

"You were doing it all wrong."

"Want to come for a drink?" He surprised himself. He hadn't had the slightest intention of asking the girl for a drink. He had a girl-friend. A tall, leggy girlfriend on whom he'd just spent a small fortune buying some very exotic lingerie.

"I don't think the people behind us would like that very much." She grinned at him. "They want you to move and move now."

"Sometime?" he asked.

"Maybe."

"What's your phone number?"

She gave him the number of the surgery where she worked as an office assistant and he gave her his number too. It went out of her head almost as soon as he told her because she wasn't good at remembering numbers. She didn't expect him to remember hers. Besides she wasn't looking for romance. She already had a very suitable boyfriend who worked in a bank and who was crazy about her.

She'd gone home and sat in the living room of the family house in Portmarnock where she read Cate's magazine, ate chocolate-covered raisins and drank the best part of a bottle of red wine. But when she got to the horoscope page of the magazine and read the prediction for Cancer, her eyes had widened in surprise. *"You love to help someone in a tight spot. Meeting new people in new places will have a surprising impact on your life. After this week, things will never be the same again."*

Things never were the same again. The man in the car, Adam Riley, had phoned the surgery the following day. He'd asked her for a drink again. This time she'd accepted.

He was very much a Leo, Nessa decided as she sat beside him in Davy Byrne's pub on their first date. He was tall, broad-shouldered with a slight tan despite his red-gold hair. He was witty and funny and he could laugh at himself and his parking predicament.

Nessa fell head over heels in love with him.

He dumped the leggy girlfriend although he cursed the three hundred euros worth of lingerie he'd left her with. She broke up with the banker—a Pisces, they should have been a perfect match. Six months later Adam and Nessa were married.

And in the past ten years, thought Nessa as she opened the front door and joined him in the driveway, he's managed to average at least one car-related mishap every twelve months. Which is kind of endearing but bloody annoying all the same.

"Didn't you see it?" she asked mildly as she surveyed the damage both to Adam's Alfa Romeo (it was a company car, Nessa always felt he should have asked for a Fiat Punto or something even smaller but Adam's sense of style wouldn't let him) and to the blue Mondeo.

"Of course I saw it," snarled Adam. "But I thought I had room."

"Oh, Adam!"

"Who the hell owns it anyway?" he demanded. "Bloody inconsiderate parking if you ask me."

He was winding up for some more invective when a disheveled looking girl with uncombed hair and mascara smudged eyes rushed out of the house next door.

Adam and Nessa exchanged glances. Their neighbors, John and Susie Ward, were away for a week. Their 22-year-old son, Mitchell, was alone in the house. More or less.

"Oh shit!" cried the girl. "Shit, shit, shit." She pushed her hair out of her eyes and stared at Adam. "You tosser," she said. "You had plenty of room."

"I wasn't expecting someone to park halfway across my driveway," said Adam hotly. "You should've been more considerate."

"You could've driven a truck through that space!" The girl's face was contorted with rage. "That's my dad's car. He'll fucking kill me."

Nessa glanced at her watch. Adam was late and getting later.

"Why don't you take my car," she suggested. "I'll sort things out here."

"Your car?" Adam looked at the little Ka. "But—"

"You'll make the meeting if you leave now," Nessa told him. "But not if you hang around here debating how well or how badly this girl parked."

"I—oh, all right." Adam looked at the two of them. "I'll ring you later, Nessa. But I'm not admitting liability. I'm not."

She stifled a grin as he folded his huge frame into the Ka. It wasn't his style of car at all but it would get him where he needed to be.

Jill, who'd followed Nessa out of the house, looked at the other girl with interest. "You're not wearing a bra, are you?" she asked.

"My name is Nessa Riley." Nessa shot Jill a warning look and held out her hand to the girl. "Would you like to come inside for a cup of coffee?"

The girl yawned, her anger suddenly dissipated. "I suppose so. Mitch won't be awake for hours anyway. I heard your hubby bang into Dad's car. I was probably waiting for some kind of disaster to strike." She followed Nessa and Jill into the house. "My name's Portia," she told Nessa.

"Like the car?" asked Jill. "Mum, she's named after a car!"

Portia grinned at Jill. "I don't think that was quite what was in my mother's mind. And, regretfully, I've never owned one."

"Mum would like a Porsche," confided Jill. "But she knows that Dad would want to drive it and Dad always pra— ouch, Mum!" She looked accusingly at Nessa who'd given her a tiny shove in the small of her back.

"Stop chattering and get your things together," Nessa told her. "As soon as I've finished talking to Portia we have to get you to school."

The only thing that Portia was really worried about was her father's fury. "He thinks I'm a crap driver," she told Nessa as they sipped the coffee which Nessa had poured. "He hates lending me the car. He only did this time because he's even more paranoid about me getting taxis on my own."

"I can understand that," said Nessa.

"Why shouldn't she get a taxi on her own?" asked Jill. "She's grown up, isn't she?"

"Listen, honey," said Portia to Jill, "you're never grown up as far as your dad is concerned."

"Dad told me he couldn't wait to have me grown up and out of the house," she informed Portia.

"That was after you spilt Coke on his keyboard," Nessa said.

Portia laughed.

"I'll phone your father," said Nessa. "Explain to him what happened."

"Thanks," said Portia. "I know he won't believe me when I tell him a bloke reversed into it. Dad doesn't believe that any man could possibly be a worse driver than a woman."

"If I ever see you again I'll tell you the story of how I met Adam," said Nessa. "In fact, I might tell it to your dad. That'll cure him of that sort of thinking."

"Mum had to unpark Dad's car," said Jill. "He was stuck in a carpark."

"Really?"

"Really."

"Sounds an excellent basis for a relationship." Portia stood up. "I'd better get back to Mitch."

"And we'd better get going too," said Nessa. "Otherwise Jill will be late for school."

Normally she walked Jill to the school which was half a mile away but, because they were running late, she drove Adam's car. It wasn't badly damaged at all and neither, it seemed, was the car that belonged to Portia's father which meant (hopefully) that they wouldn't need to claim on insurance or anything like that. Adam would pay for the repairs. He always did.

She drove through the town and along the estuary until she reached the doctor's surgery. She hoped that it wouldn't be a busy morning. But she knew it was a vain hope. Every day was a busy day. She also hoped that Adam would remember that he had to be home early because of the family gathering tonight. It was the kind of thing that, in his sense of injustice over the car incident, he was likely to forget.

2

♥

Aries March 21st–April 20th

Energetic, fiery, self-confident. Life's a competition.

The clock on Cate Driscoll's computer chimed and she realized that she'd already been in the office for three and a half hours. And it was still only ten o'clock. She rubbed her eyes then stretched her arms over her head. Coming in to work so early in the mornings held the advantage of being able to get loads of things done without any interruptions, but it also meant that she was already tired. Given the choice she probably wouldn't be in before seven any morning but with her current lifestyle it made sense. What was the point of lying in bed when she was already awake? Wide awake, thanks to Finn.

Cate hated her boyfriend's three-times-a-week early morning slot at the radio station where he worked because of the fact that she could never, ever get back to sleep after he left. Finn fondly believed that he tiptoed silently around the apartment in the mornings but he was totally unable to open or close a door without banging it and, of course, the buzz of his electric shaver was enough to banish all thoughts she might have of dropping off again. But she usually lay in bed with her eyes closed until after he'd slammed the apartment door closed behind him because there was no point in making him feel guilty about waking her. In reality she doubted that he'd ever feel guilty about waking her but she still felt that pretending to be asleep was better than telling him that the noise he made was something similar to a herd of elephants taking a stroll across the veldt. So as soon as he left she got up, which meant being in the office hours before anyone else. Some mornings when she was feeling particularly masochistic she'd pack her work clothes into a bag and drive to the gym. But things at the sports company where she was the sales director weren't exactly going according to plan this month and so the gym was the last place she wanted to be.

Finn would be finished with the radio program soon and he'd

have breakfast at the studio before sitting down with his researchers
and producer and chatting about next week's shows. Today, being
Friday, he'd also have to write his weekend column for one of the
newspapers and then—lucky sod—he'd go home to the apartment
and sleep for a couple of hours. So that when she arrived home at six
o'clock like a wet rag, he wouldn't be able to understand why she
didn't feel like going to Harry Byrne's pub for a few drinks and he'd
sigh and tell her that they didn't have to be up early in the morning
because it was Saturday and what on earth was the matter with her?

He was always asking her what was the matter lately. He'd tell her
that she was looking terrible and was in a foul humor and he'd mutter something about going out for a few drinks with his mates until
her mood improved. Cate shivered as she wondered whether it was
more than the fact that she was so stressed at work right now.
Whether it was simply that she and Finn were the matter and not
the fact that the Sales & Marketing Department was having the
worst quarter she could remember. She didn't want to think that
anything *was* wrong between them but sometimes she felt as though
she was losing Finn, as though the relationship they'd had was slipping away and there was nothing she could do to stop it. They'd
spent three wonderful years together since she'd come on his morning business program and talked to him about the new initiative
that the sports company she worked for had launched which would
help children in deprived areas become involved in sporting activities. She'd generated lots of interest for the project and it had
worked really well for the company too. She'd come back on the
program a few months later to talk about the things that had been
especially successful and had invited Finn to be guest of honor at a
dinner that the company was sponsoring for sporting achievement.
Finn had accepted and, after the dinner, she'd gone back to his
seafront apartment where they'd enjoyed a perfect night together.
She hadn't spent a night away from it ever since.

She sighed and rested her head in her hands. She wished she
knew why things didn't feel so perfect now. She didn't know exactly
what was wrong, she only knew that whatever she did these days she
didn't feel as though it was right. And she hated Finn having to ask
her what was the matter. Even worse was him telling her that she
looked awful! She didn't want him to think of her as a woman who
might have something that was the matter with her and who looked

awful. Finn didn't have time for that sort of woman, he'd told her that when she'd first met him. Life's too short, he'd said, to be gloomy and introspective and haggard. Which is all very well, thought Cate glumly as she lifted her head and looked at her computer screen again, but when you were responsible for sales and they'd fallen for two months in a row, it was damn difficult not to be gloomy and introspective and haggard. And bloody worried too. Her biggest worry was that Finn would simply get bored with her. After all, being a sales director wasn't exactly in the same league as being a media star. And Finn, even though his program was aimed at a business audience, was well on the way to becoming a media star. He was a panelist on two late-evening programs on the days when he wasn't doing breakfast shows. The evening programs covered more offbeat stories about commerce and had shot up in the ratings since he'd joined the panel.

Occasionally he guested on other presenter's programs too. Last week he'd been invited to the launch of a new brand of beer, ostensibly because the brewing company would be announcing its profits for the year soon and he'd be covering that news on his business program. But the beer launch had nothing to do with profitability. Cate had seen photographs of him in the paper afterward, flanked by two models from the ad agency which was promoting the brand. They were tall, thin and sultry and Finn looked as though he was having a truly great time at something he'd originally told her he didn't really want to attend.

She told herself that she was being silly. She was usually a successful, confident, go-getting kind of person who didn't have to be tall, thin and sultry to get on with her life. Not, she reminded herself, that there was anything wrong with the way she looked either. That was the stupid thing. She knew that she was attractive and that it was probably her face rather than her work for the sports company that had first sparked Finn's interest in her anyway. She was aware of her high cheekbones, decently proportioned figure and her smooth, clear skin. She spent a lot of time every morning ensuring that she was as perfectly made up as it was possible to be without appearing as though she was wearing any makeup at all. She was always prepared to buy the newest shades in foundations and lipsticks and eyeshadows so that her look was as understatedly up-to-the minute as possible. She had her nails manicured every week and her hair trimmed every fortnight. She wore expensive clothes from expensive shops and she wore them well. There was nothing wrong with the way she looked or the way she dressed. There was nothing wrong with the career she had. But, somehow, it seemed as if looking good and feeling good were two separate things these days when once they had been exactly the same.

She tapped her ruby-red nails on her desk and glanced at the clock on her computer again. Only five past ten. Yet it seemed as though she'd been sitting here thinking about things for hours. The door to the office banged and Glenda Maguire popped her head around Cate's office door. The sports company allowed staff to work flexible hours. Glenda, Cate's assistant, rarely came in before ten.

"How are you this morning?" Glenda was bright and cheery.

"Narky," said Cate.

"Oh, dear." Glenda looked at her sympathetically. "Out late with Finn-So-Cool last night?"

Cate gritted her teeth. The tabloids had named him Finn-So-Cool and the name—a pun on the name of the mythical Irish warrior Fionn MacCool—had stuck. Cate's Finn was a modern warrior. His golden hair flopped carelessly over his high forehead and his eyes were dark blue pools in an almost perfect face. But it was a strong face, a face with character. Finn oozed controlled charm. He knew when to smile and, when he was interviewing, he knew when to go for the jugular. Despite the topical nature of his programs he had the kind of ratings that chat show hosts would have died for. Both men and women tuned in to his soft, lyrical tones which could harden into cool authority whenever he wanted to make a particular point. Finn Coolidge was very, very popular. She was lucky to have him.

"We weren't out late," she told Glenda calmly. "But Finn gets up pretty early, you know, and he nearly always wakes me."

"It must be wonderful to wake up beside someone like him," said Glenda dreamily. "I only have Johnny. It's not quite the same."

"Can you get me the report that David McRedmond sent us last week?" asked Cate. "And some coffee, please, Glenda."

"Sure." Glenda withdrew from the office and made a face. Her boss really was narky this morning and she was going to steer well clear of her. She liked working for Cate Driscoll but she thought that the other girl sometimes took herself far too seriously for her own good. She'd been like a demon for the past two months. Everyone knew that sales were down because their competitors had beaten them to it with the release of another new trainer. That wasn't Cate's fault. If she wasn't careful, thought Glenda, as she filled the coffee machine with filtered water, Finn-So-Cool would go and fish in other waters. And Cate would have driven him to it.

Cate's phone rang and she reached out for it.

"Hi, it's me."

"Hello, Nessa." Cate made a face at the phone. She didn't feel like talking to her older sister right now. At thirty, she was only four years younger than Nessa but Nessa had a way of making her feel as though she were still a child. Cate didn't quite know how Nessa managed this given her status as a bloody part-time receptionist and almost full-time domestic paragon while she, Cate, had a career and not just a job. She knew she should be able to transcend being the second born but somehow she couldn't quite achieve it.

"I was calling about tonight."

"What about it?" asked Cate.

"You haven't forgotten, have you? Mum and Dad are coming around. So are you and Finn."

"No, I hadn't forgotten." Though I wish I didn't have to go, thought Cate. She could think of nothing more awful than sitting in Nessa's rag-rolled, chintzy house for the evening.

"I just thought that it would be nice if you could arrive early," Nessa told her. "So's we're all here when Mum and Dad call."

"Nessa, they're our parents, not some corporate clients of Adam's," said Cate irritably. "We don't have to impress them, you know."

"I'm not trying to impress," said Nessa. "Just make them feel wanted."

"Why?" asked Cate. "They already know that."

"You're hopeless when it comes to relationships and family things, Catey, you know that? It's a nice gesture, that's all."

"Fine, fine," said Cate. "We'll be there. D'you want me to bring anything?"

"No," said Nessa. "Everything's organized."

"Indeed," said Cate dryly.

"You don't sound very enthusiastic," complained Nessa.

"I am," Cate said. "Honestly."

"I baked a cake yesterday," said Nessa. "I've put chocolate icing on it. At first I was going to get lemon but I changed my mind. I think Mum prefers chocolate."

Why does she always manage to sound so smug, wondered Cate. So smug and settled and fucking secure about everything. I'm looking at our marketing budget and wondering where the hell I'm going to find another hundred thousand euros before the end of the quarter and she's making life and death decisions like lemon or chocolate icing.

Cate frowned. She didn't envy her sister's life even if it did seem to be completely devoid of pressure. Adam did all the worrying for her, allowing Nessa to concentrate on her lovely house and her precocious child and decisions on lemon or chocolate icing. Nessa was concerned with the domestic stuff and Adam was in charge of everything else and they both seemed to like it that way. Cate knew it would drive her mad. Although, she conceded, Nessa wasn't the one worrying about her bloody relationship, was she? She was happily cooking and cleaning and discussing various icing options. As though she was a Stepford Wife, thought Cate darkly. She flicked the computer mouse angrily across her desk.

"You'll never guess what happened this morning," said her sister cheerfully.

"What?" Cate didn't feel like guessing.

"Adam pranged the car again."

Well, thought Cate, at least that was one area where the Rileys weren't a perfect family unit.

"Again?"

"Backed out of the driveway into another car." She giggled. "He really is utterly hopeless."

"What did you do?" Cate frowned as she opened her e-mails. What was this garbage from Conrad Burton all about? How could the sale of their new sports shoe to a leading department store have fallen through? If it was because Nike had got one over on them again she'd kill someone. She knew she would.

"Oh, I sorted everything out. Adam had to rush off, he had a meeting in Loughlinstown. He took the Ka."

"The Ka!" Cate's mind was dragged back to the conversation. "I can't see Adam in a Ka somehow."

"He hardly fitted in it," admitted Nessa. "But he didn't have any choice. I drove Jill to school in the Alfa and I rang the garage about repairs but Bree wasn't in. I'll give her a call later on."

"Mornings aren't her strong point," said Cate.

"I suppose not," Nessa agreed. "Oh, by the way, I read your horoscope this morning. It was excellent, Cate. Apparently Mars is moving into Saturn or something which is very good for Arians. It was talking about great new opportunities."

"Really?" Cate's tone was skeptical.

"Really," said Nessa. "So I thought you'd better be prepared in case anything exciting presents itself. I know how you dynamic people like to seize every opportunity."

"It's a load of crap," said Cate.

"No it's not," protested Nessa. "Mine was right about this week, it's been one of those weeks where loads of little things go wrong and that's what it told me it'd be like. And what about last month? A windfall, it said, and it was right about that too. Five hundred euros on the Lotto. So don't tell me it's rubbish."

Cate was tired of hearing about Nessa's Lotto win. "Everyone born in July wouldn't have won five hundred euros on the Lotto," she said.

"But *I* did," Nessa told her triumphantly. "And that's all that matters. Look, Cate, got to go, can't hang around talking all day—a gang of patients has just walked up the path. See you."

"See you," said Cate although Nessa had already hung up. Honestly, thought Cate crossly as she scrolled through the rest of her e-mails, you'd swear that Nessa was the busy one, the one with the pressurized job, the way she carried on. Nessa had phoned Cate, not the other way around and yet Nessa had hung up as though she was keeping her from her work. It made her want to scream.

Glenda tapped at the door and placed a cup of coffee on Cate's desk.

"Don't forget you've a meeting with Jack Mullen at eleven," said Glenda. "And Barbara Donovan wants to see you sometime today. Plus the people from PhotoSnap are calling in about the brochure at twelve."

"Fine, Glenda." Cate took a sip of coffee. It tasted vile. She pushed it to one side.

"And Finn called," added Glenda. "But I told him you were on the phone."

"Finn called?" Cate was surprised. He hardly ever called her at work. "Did he say what he wanted?"

"Nope," said Glenda. "He said he'll call you back after lunch. It's not really important. He's at meetings all morning."

"Fine," said Cate. Me and Finn, she thought. Media star and businesswoman. Partners. Maybe we'll grab some brilliant opportunity between us and make Nessa's stupid predictions right. She took another tentative sip of the coffee and wrinkled up her nose at the taste. It was too disgusting to drink. She emptied it into the potted plant on the floor beside her desk. It was looking a bit dull. The caffeine might help.

3

♥

Sagittarius November 23rd–December 21st
Friendly, enthusiastic, optimistic. Fun-loving philosophers.

Bree Driscoll scrambled into her clothes, grabbed her backpack and clattered down the stairs of her flat in less than five minutes. Her hair was still damp from her thirty-second shower—her third rushed one this week—and it stuck to her head as she adjusted her black helmet. She was still pulling on her leather gloves as she revved up her brand-new Yamaha and roared down Morehampton Road to Crosbie's garage.

It was exactly a quarter past ten as she rushed into the workshop, grabbed her card and shoved it into the clock.

"I thought you were on the ten to eight shift," said Rick Cahill.

"Fuck off, Rick." She swept past him and up the stairs to the monkey room where she opened her locker and pulled on a pair of oil-stained overalls.

"Hey, Bree, Christy is looking for you." Mick Hempenstall threw

a filthy rag at her. "He found this under the bonnet of the nintey-
nine Romeo. Oh, and he mentioned that you were supposed to be
here by ten."

"I know that." Bree did up the poppers on her overalls. "I'm late.
I'll stay late this evening."

"Really?" Christy, the service manager, walked into the room and
Bree groaned under her breath. "That's very sweet of you, Bree, but
I'd prefer if you were here when you were supposed to be here. I had
you down for the red Punto this morning. I had to give it to Dave
instead."

"So what?"

"So it needed a hose replaced," said Christy. "You'd be able to get
at it better than Dave."

"Sorry, Christy." Bree knew there was no point in arguing with
him. "Really I am. I slept late."

"I gathered," said Christy. "Didn't anyone ever tell you that to do
a man's job you're supposed to have to work twice as hard?"

"Not when I'm three times as good," retorted Bree.

Rick snorted with laughter and Christy glared at him.

"Get going," said Christy. "The silver Alfa on ramp four. Full service."

"Yes, sure," said Bree. "Sorry again."

She clattered down the stairs and picked up the job card for the
Alfa. Then she pressed the button so that the hydraulics lifted the
car to the correct height. She stood underneath it and sighed with
relief.

In future she'd stick a piece of paper on her pillow to remind her
to reset the alarm clock in the mornings. It was something that she
tended to forget. She used to believe that her body was so in tune
with the rhythm of the sun that she'd automatically wake up when it
was bright outside. But it was a risky strategy when she'd been out
until after three in the morning and had drunk more beer than was
good for her.

It was just as well, she thought as she shook some powder into a
pair of surgical gloves and slipped them onto her hands, that she
really was twice as good as most of the other mechanics in the
garage. Otherwise Christy would give her the push. He wasn't
exactly known for his compassion.

She flexed her fingers in the gloves. She always wore them when she was working—they were the only true way of preventing oil and grease taking grimy hold beneath her fingernails as well as supposedly preventing the possibility of cancer from waste oil products— but only half the men wore them.

Real men don't need gloves, Rick had told her on her first day, and she'd laughed and told him that she wasn't a real man so it didn't matter. Bare hands were better for delicate work, he'd insisted, your sensitivity was compromised by wearing latex. She'd bought Rick a box of condoms for his birthday the following month. Everyone in the garage had got the joke except him.

She was gasping for a cup of coffee but Christy was standing beside the Cona machine and she didn't dare go near it yet. She yawned and pulled the brake fluid drainage unit under the car. Then she removed the plug and allowed the oil to drain out.

"Hey, Bree!" Dave beckoned her. She left the Alfa and walked over to him. "I forgot to tell you, your sister phoned earlier."

"Which one?" asked Bree.

"The nice one," said Dave.

"The nice one?" But Bree grinned at him. She knew which sister he meant. To the blokes in the garage, Nessa was the nice one and Cate was the crabby one. They all knew Nessa because of her periodic trips to get Adam's Alfa repaired and because she often popped into the garage when she was visiting her friend, Paula, who lived nearby. Cate, who also drove an Alfa, was a much less frequent visitor and, whenever she did call in, she simply dropped the keys at reception and asked them to phone her and tell her when the car was ready.

"Did Nessa say what she wanted?" Bree was keeping an eye on Christy who was talking to the manager of the parts department.

"She said it wasn't urgent but it was the usual."

"The usual!" Bree and Dave exchanged glances. "Don't tell me he's totalled it again."

"A man like her husband shouldn't have the top-of-the-range model," said Dave in disgust. "That's the car you should be driving, Bree."

"I like my bike," she told him. "I'm too young for a car."

Christy had finished talking to the parts manager and was turning back into the workshop. "I'll call her later," said Bree and she hurried back to the service job. She stood beneath the car again and checked the brake hoses, the tires and the driveshaft boots. It was only a year old. She would've been surprised if there had been any leaks or rips.

Then she pulled the air gun from the wall and removed the nuts from the tires. It was the simplest thing in the world to do and she did it every single day but each time it gave her a thrill. From the first time she'd seen the McLaren team doing it in a Formula One race on TV she'd decided that that's what she wanted to do herself. And although she never made it onto a Formula One pit team, she'd loved every moment of the four-year apprenticeship she'd done to become a qualified mechanic. There'd only been one other female apprentice when she started, although Bree was sure that there'd be more soon. Since car engines had become more tightly packed and more dependent on electronics it wasn't necessary to be able to lug heavy bits of equipment around the workshop anymore. In fact, being familiar with the diagnostic computer was more of an asset.

"Why were you late?" Dave watched as she lifted a wheel from the car.

"Out late last night," said Bree. "Hit the sack around four. Not a good idea."

"A new lover boy wearing you out?" asked Dave.

"I wish." Bree grinned at him. "Maybe one day I'll find a decent man!"

"I keep asking you but you keep rejecting me," said Dave plaintively.

"I've no interest in sharing my life with another grease monkey." The banter between them was regular and familiar. "We'd find fan belts in the bedroom."

"I was kind of hoping for suspender belts," said Dave and she made a face at him.

When she'd finished checking the wheels and the brake pads she peeled off her gloves and went to the phone.

"Dr. Hogan's surgery." Nessa had a sing-song voice when she answered the phone which was quite unlike her usual speaking voice.

"Hello, hello," said Bree. "I've got suppurating sores all over my body and I think my leg has become disconnected from my hip."

"Where were you earlier?" demanded Nessa. "You're always telling me that you start at eight."

"I usually start at eight," said Bree. "I wasn't due in until ten this morning."

"I rang at ten past and there was no sign of you."

"I was on the way," said Bree.

"On the way isn't exactly good enough, is it?" asked Nessa. "I mean, if you're meant to be there at ten, being on the way ten minutes later isn't what your employer wants. You could—"

"Shut up, Nessa." Bree interrupted the tirade. "I know I'm the worst employee in the world but, guess what, they think I'm good at my job. They haven't fired me yet."

"Don't bet on it," muttered Christy as he walked by her.

"Why did you ring?" asked Bree.

"Two things," said her older sister. "The first is that I wanted to remind you about tonight. I was hoping you'd be here by half seven."

"I can't," said Bree. "I'm working till eight and I'll probably have to stay a bit later because of my late start this morning."

"That's my point exactly," said Nessa. "If you were more conscientious about getting to work on time then you wouldn't have to stay late to compensate and you'd be able to fulfil your other obligations properly."

"Nessa, it's only Mum and Dad."

"That doesn't mean that you shouldn't be here on time," said Nessa.

"I'll be there as soon as I can," promised Bree.

"I'm cooking dinner," said Nessa.

Bree sighed. She liked the idea of a cooked dinner because she hadn't had a decent meal in weeks.

"I'll be there by nine," said Bree.

"You're not on the bloody continent now," snapped Nessa. "Nine is way too late."

"I'll see what I can do," said Bree.

"OK." Nessa sounded partially mollified. "Secondly I wanted to know when you could look at Adam's car."

"So he's done it again," said Bree.

"Very, very minor," Nessa told her. "It's just the light on the rear passenger side."

"How good is your sex life?"

"What?!"

"With a husband like him I wonder that you ever manage to—"

"Bree!"

"We're really busy at the moment." Bree looked around the workshop. There were cars on all of the ramps with another dozen in the waiting area. They usually got through twelve to fifteen full services a day as well as some of the other maintenance jobs that they had to do. Repairing Adam's car could take a few minutes or a few hours, depending on how bad the damage actually was.

"It's only superficial damage, I think," said Nessa. "But I want to be sure. In any event the cover for the brake light needs to be replaced. I wanted you to check that there wasn't anything else."

"I'll bring a cover with me tonight," said Bree. "And I'll give it a quick look then see how long repairs would take."

"Great."

"So, I'll see you tonight."

"Yes. Fine. Oh, and listen, I told Cate about hers earlier because mine was so uncannily accurate but according to your horoscope you're going to be showered with good fortune this week," said Nessa.

"I hate to burst your bubble," Bree said. "But so far the only thing I've been showered with this week is abuse."

"If you were in on time you wouldn't be," Nessa told her. "All the same, it might be worthwhile buying a scratch card or something."

"You're my older sister," said Bree. "You're nine years older than me, in fact. But sometimes you act as if you're a teenager. You don't seriously believe all that star stuff, do you?"

"It works for me," said Nessa. "And you know that it foretold—"

"I know, I know," interrupted Bree. "Your massive Lottery win last month."

"Absolutely," said Nessa. "So you shouldn't be skeptical or dismissive."

"Right," said Bree. "Now I'd better go before I really do get fired."

She hung up and grabbed a cup of coffee, walking back to the Alfa with the Styrofoam cup in her hand.

The oil feed line was beside the air line on the wall. She pulled it toward the car and began filling the oil tank. She yawned again and wished that the coffee would kick in soon. She was still feeling terribly sleepy.

"Oh, fuck!"

Her words reverberated around the workshop and the other mechanics stopped to see what was the matter with her. Then they started to laugh as they saw the black, viscous puddle which had formed around her feet. She'd forgotten to replace the plug in the oil sump. The oil which she'd been pumping into the car had gone straight through the tank and onto the floor. It was a mistake that first-year apprentices didn't even make. Her boots were ruined.

"Way to go, Driscoll!" Rick waved at her.

"Nice one, Bree," said Dave.

"Shut up, shut up," she said urgently. "If Christy sees this he'll flip altogether. And I really can't afford for him to fire me," she muttered frantically. "Not when I'm paying back the loan on my new bike."

She looked at the spreading oil slick in disgust and then smiled wryly. She'd been showered after all, although hardly with the good fortune that Nessa had predicted. She tore some paper towels from the dispenser and mopped ineffectually at her splattered clothes. Nessa would doubtless tell her that she should think laterally about horoscopes. But the only thing she could think of was that it was going to cost her a fortune to replace her damned boots!

4

♥

Moon in Cancer

Very instinctive, emotional, affectionate.

It was amazing, thought Nessa as she watched her father and her husband chatting in the living room, how well they got on together given their totally opposite natures. Louis was a conservative man at heart who believed in keeping your head down and holding something in reserve for a rainy day. Adam liked showing off and enjoyed spending money on the latest gadget just so that he could say he owned it first. Louis watched Gaelic football. Adam was a rugby supporter. Louis was good with his hands. Adam was good with his brain. But both of them needed to feel wanted. Miriam had looked after Louis for forty years in such a way that he hardly realized he was being looked after at all. Nessa looked after Adam too. He worked very hard and she liked to think that his home was an oasis of peace for him.

Nessa knew that some people would see her as being hopelessly old fashioned. But she didn't care. Women who said they wanted it all—women like Cate—just hadn't got it yet. It was impossible to have it all. Life was about making choices. What those women needed to do was to make the decision that they'd be happy with. Only some of them didn't know how.

"Jill and I will have to visit you during the summer." Nessa turned from Louis and Adam's discussion about tiling bathrooms (there was no way she was going to allow Adam to have a go at tiling the bathroom, they'd get in a proper, professional tiler like they always did) and smiled at her mother.

"Sure," said Miriam easily. "We've plenty of room."

The house they'd bought on their retirement was a three-bedroom dormer bungalow in Salthill. Miriam had been brought up in Salthill and she'd always wanted to go back.

"I liked being there last year," said Jill who was sitting at Miriam's feet. "You've a much nicer house than us, Nan."

"Thanks a bunch, Jill." Adam had heard her comments. "That's the last time I waste money buying you all that Lara Croft stuff for your bedroom just so it's exactly how you want it."

"Dad!" Jill wailed and Nessa giggled.

"Don't mind your father," she told Jill. "He's not in the best of humors today."

"Because of the car."

"What happened to the car?" asked Louis while Adam glared at both Jill and Nessa. He gave an edited version of events to Louis. He hated having to admit to his lack of prowess as a driver. Even though he joked about it to most of his friends, he wasn't able to joke about it with Louis.

The doorbell rang and Nessa heaved a sigh of relief. The arrival of one of her sisters would deflect the conversation. She answered the door and returned to the living room followed by Cate and her boyfriend, Finn.

It's not fair, thought Nessa, as her sister kissed both parents. We share the same genes. We have the same bone structure. But how the hell does she manage to look the way she does when I have to work so damned hard just to look average? And why is it that she's still a size eight while I constantly fight with the twelves? Actually, Nessa mused as she continued to appraise her sister, Cate appeared even thinner than usual tonight with her dark hair pulled back from her face and her black linen dress emphasizing the slimness of her frame. She wasn't sure that such leanness really suited her sister. She looked as though a puff of wind would blow her over. But nothing would blow her over because everyone knew that Cate was the tough one, the business one, the one who would one day be somebody. Who was somebody already only maybe not enough of a somebody in her own eyes. And, continued Nessa to herself while she smiled at her sister in welcome, it might be hard to think of yourself as somebody wonderful in your own eyes when you're constantly on the arm of a man like Finn.

"Hi, Nessa." Cate sat elegantly on the sofa beside her mother while Finn accepted a glass of wine. "We're a bit late. The phone went just as we were leaving. You know how it is. How're you?"

"Great, thanks."

Nessa was looking at Finn, not at Cate. It always took a couple of minutes for her to accustom herself to his good looks. If she looked at him for long enough she became used to the golden hair falling over the suntanned forehead, the high cheekbones and the warm, kissable lips. She didn't fancy Finn, he was actually too good-looking to be true and besides she loved Adam far too much to fancy anyone else, but Finn was almost hypnotically attractive.

"How are things in the business world?" she asked him.

Finn smiled at her. "Who knows?"

"I thought you did," said Nessa. "I thought that Finn-So-Cool and his early-morning topical radio show knew everything there was to know about what makes the country tick."

"Oh, please." He sighed. "I hate that tag. And I know as much as the next person. Not that it matters," he looked around triumphantly, "because I'm changing jobs."

"Changing jobs?" Miriam looked from him to Cate. Her daughter smiled faintly.

"Yes," she told Miriam. "Finn has been lured away from doing the dry economic and business show in the mornings to the dog-eat-dog world of evening chat shows. On television, not radio."

"Really?" Miriam looked at him in delight. "A chat show? That's wonderful news, Finn."

"Isn't it?" said Cate. She was still in shock about it herself. Finn hadn't told her that he'd been approached about the possibility of doing TV, he hadn't mentioned the discussions he'd had with the TV producers, he hadn't said a word, not even dropped a hint, about any of it. Until today when he'd phoned her to tell her it was a done deal. She'd clenched the receiver, listening to his excited tones spilling down the line as he told her how brilliant everything was going to be while a hollow feeling of jealousy and fear spread through her. Finn was going to be a TV star. He was going to be even more famous than he was already. And she was nothing at all.

"When will you start, Finn? Are you part of the summer or autumn schedules?" asked Nessa.

"Autumn—that's much better," Finn assured her. "It'll be on Friday nights and I've already had a lot of talk with them about how we want it to go."

"Taking over where the *Late Late Show* left off?" suggested Louis.

"Better than the *Late Late*," said Finn confidently. "Let's face it, chat shows have moved on from that tired old format. I know I can make a real go of it."

"Congratulations." Adam lifted his wineglass.

"It's so exciting!" Jill clapped her hands. "You'll be on the telly, Finn. Can I be on the telly?"

"I'm sure I can get you into the audience of one of my shows," said Finn.

"So they won't be topical shows?" Adam said. "If you can get kids on them."

Finn flashed a glance at him. "Of course they'll be topical. But some will be more light-hearted than others. I'll get her on a light-hearted one."

"It's wonderful news, Finn," said Miriam. "I'm already a minor celebrity in Salthill among the people who know you're going out with my daughter. I'll be a real celebrity when you start appearing in gossip magazines!"

"We won't be in gossip magazines," said Cate.

"Finn might," Nessa told her. "Let's face it, Catey, he's Ireland's most photogenic man."

Finn laughed. Adam looked slightly disdainful. Louis grinned.

"Let me check on dinner," said Nessa. "It's beef in Guinness. I decided to do some one-pot cooking since Bree said she was going to be late."

"Why?" asked Cate.

"Late into work today meant that she had to stay late tonight," said Nessa disapprovingly. "Really, that girl needs a kick in the behind. How she expects to hang on to her job I'll never know."

"Maybe because she's good at it," suggested Finn.

"Their patience will run out," said Adam. "I always advise my clients to get rid of maverick staff, no matter how good they are. And Bree is a maverick."

"What's that?" asked Jill.

"Not something you need to bother with, sweetheart," said Miriam. "And we shouldn't be talking about your auntie behind her back."

"You're right, Miriam," conceded Adam. "Can I get you another drink?"

It was nearly half an hour later and Nessa was getting very edgy about the state of her food before the doorbell rang.

"I'm sorry, I'm sorry," said Bree as she catapulted into the room. "I know I'm late. I asked Christy if I could go early even though I was a bit late in and he said yes but this stupid old bat came in to get her car fixed just as I was leaving. *And* they were digging up the road outside the flat so I couldn't even get the bike into the house. And, even on a bike, traffic through town was just awful . . ."

"It's OK," said Miriam. "We haven't started without you."

"I knew you wouldn't." Bree turned to Adam. "I brought the light cover for your car, Adam. I'll do it later."

Bree has the same genes as me too, Nessa mused as she observed her youngest sister, but even though her hair is the same color as mine and Cate's, she always manages to have that artful just-got-out-of-bed look, whereas you'd think that Cate had stepped out of the hairdresser and I—she touched the back of her own head—maybe I need to change my style for something a bit more up-to-date. Only I never seem to have time to go to the hairdressers. Even though I *know* the girls think I have plenty of time to do whatever I want.

Bree wriggled onto the sofa between Cate and Miriam while Finn stood behind them.

"New system?" She nodded at the Bang & Olufsen CD player.

"Absolutely," said Jill. "Daddy blew an absolute fortune on it. Mum nearly had hysterics."

Nessa looked at Jill despairingly while Adam laughed. "That's condensing the story somewhat," he told them all. "It's a great system. Nessa had hysterics because she doesn't like the way the CD player hangs on the wall."

Bree nodded. "You used to have a painting in that spot, didn't you?"

"Yes," said Nessa. "I preferred the painting."

"Oh, I don't know," said Cate. "I rather like the CD player. It's elegant."

"It'd look good in your shrine to simplicity and modernity," said Nessa. "But I think it's a bit austere for this house."

"Austere is nice," Finn told her.

"I like comfort," said Nessa.

"Comfort us all by dishing up some food," suggested Adam. "I'm starving. I had a toasted sandwich at two o'clock and nothing since then, given that you wouldn't let me raid the fridge when I got home." He smiled at the rest of the family. "This was on the basis that it'd ruin my appetite. I ask you! A starving man doesn't ruin his appetite by having a quick snack two hours before he eats."

"Oh, shut up, Adam," said Nessa tolerantly. "Come and make yourself useful and open a couple of bottles of wine."

It was over a year since the entire family had been together. Nessa had to admit that her parents were looking better than ever—retirement to Galway obviously suited them. The trip to Dublin this weekend was part of a package to see the ballet at the Point (Miriam loved ballet) which included a two-night stay in the Conrad Hotel. Miriam and Louis had taken lots of weekend breaks around the country in the last year and, Louis informed the family, they were going to spend a month in the States in October.

"You're really getting the most out of life, aren't you?" Finn looked at the older couple admiringly. "You're an absolute advertisement for active retirement." He scratched the side of his cheek thoughtfully. "Maybe I could do a show about that. Life for the over-sixties. How it doesn't all have to be about incontinence and immobility."

"Finn!" Cate was outraged. "How can you say that sort of thing?"

"Lots of people think it," said Finn.

Louis laughed indulgently. "You come up with the show, Finn. We'll appear. A modest fee is all that's required."

"What show?" asked Bree, and looked at Finn in admiration as he told her. "Omigod," she squeaked. "You'll get to meet all sorts of celebs. Are you going to ask a Formula One guy on? You must, Finn, you absolutely must. And then I can meet with them afterward! Schumacher would be good."

Finn laughed and told her he'd do what he could. But that he was dead keen on the over-sixties idea. He wanted to appeal to everyone, he told Bree. Not just airhead twenty-somethings like her.

He's so happy, thought Cate, as she watched him. He's delighted with this new job and his confidence just radiates on his face. He looks even more damned attractive than ever. Which means more stupid fan mail letters, thought Cate. From silly women who should know better. Who should know that a person isn't just how they look. He's so much more than that.

She bit her lip. She wished she could feel better about Finn's job but she couldn't. All she could think about was the fact that he was becoming more and more successful and in demand while she was still doing what she'd been doing for the past three years, trying to make her sports company's stuff look better than anyone else's in an already overcrowded market. And failing miserably right now. She realized suddenly that nobody had tried to headhunt her in ages. Maybe she was yesterday's news. Maybe the word had already got out. She shivered then smoothed back a nonexistent stray hair from her face.

They sat around the dinner table and tucked in to the beef in Guinness. Finn, still enthusiastic about the idea for his show, asked Miriam and Louis what had made them decide to move back to Galway after spending their adult lives in Dublin.

Louis shrugged. "I think everyone thinks about going back to their roots when they get older. When the chance came we took it."

"I would've stayed if my girls weren't settled," said Miriam. "But they are. More or less." She looked archly at Cate and Finn.

"I'm as settled as I'll ever be," said Cate hastily.

"Well, you've got a good job anyway," her mother conceded. "And, of course, Nessa is as settled and as happy as anything, aren't you, darling? I know that Bree will never settle so there's no point in me waiting."

"I might," said Bree. "There's nothing to say that I won't."

"Bree, you've been in your current job for a year. Surely you must be thinking of moving on by now?" Cate looked skeptically at her younger sister.

"I still like it there," said Bree. "Though who knows?" She was tired of this conversation which happened regularly whenever her mother was around. Miriam was like Nessa, a settling down sort of person. Bree was like—well, no one she knew in her family because she hated the idea of settling down anywhere. Whenever she heard Nessa talking about decorating or adding an extension to the house or doing the garden she felt shivers run up and down her spine and she wanted to get up and go that very instant. Cate was as bad in her own way, thought Bree. Cate might think that she wasn't a settling sort of person either just because she was living with Finn rather than married to him, but Cate was settled in her career and in her life. Cate wasn't happy unless she was working to some stupid deadline, attempting to do too much in too short a space of time while always trying to look cool and groomed as though she'd just stepped out of a fashion shoot. Bree couldn't see the point of living like that. She liked to have time to herself, to immerse herself in restoring old motorbikes, while thinking about the next place that she'd like to visit. Given the rather dismal weather so far this year, she rather thought it might be somewhere warm. Her new bike, a Yamaha YZF-R6, was sleek and cool and sporty, but like all motorbikes, it was better fun to ride it in decent weather.

"Any chance of second helpings?" she looked pleadingly at Nessa. "I'm absolutely starving."

"Sure." Nessa went into the kitchen and returned with the pot. She ladled some more food onto Bree's plate. "Why are you so hungry?"

"Busy today. Didn't get time to eat. Although that's probably not a bad thing really."

"Why?"

Bree made a face. "I've put on half a stone in the last few months. It's those breakfast baps we normally get in the garage in the mornings. Impossible to resist."

"Bree!" Cate looked at her in horror. "They're probably so high in cholesterol that they register off the scale."

"I know." Bree swallowed a mouthful of beef. "That's why they're so utterly gorgeous."

"What's in them?" asked Finn.

"Sausage, bacon, egg and beans," replied Bree. "You can get 'em with black and white pudding too but that's gross."

"Black and white pudding is gross?" Cate's eyes were wide. "The whole concoction is disgusting, Bree. You should be eating healthier foods than that in the morning. Why don't you have a muesli bar or something?"

"Because I'm hungry in the morning," said her sister easily. "And muesli is God's most revolting food. Anyway, I'll lose the weight again once I go back to the gym. I haven't had time because I've been working on the old bike before I sell it. And if you don't mind me saying so, you could do with a bit of larding yourself, Cate. I nearly mistook you for a black Biro when I came in."

Nessa stifled a giggle while Cate looked at her sister in outrage.

"I have a perfect height to weight ratio," she told Bree frostily.

"But are you happy?" asked Bree. "Let's face it, Catey, none of us in this family were built to be sylphs. And it suits us. Nessa isn't thin but she's pretty. You're thin but you look permanently pained."

"I do not!"

"Yes, you do."

"Girls, girls!" Miriam's voice held a warning. "No disagreements at the table."

Bree grinned but fell silent. There was something about her mother's tone of voice that could still stop all three girls in their tracks. Nessa has it too when she's talking to Jill, Bree thought. It's clearly a skill that comes with motherhood.

"Tell us more about the new job, Finn." Adam changed the subject. "How much control will you have?"

"Quite a lot," said Finn enthusiastically. He began to outline his ideas for the show while the others listened to the soft, lilting voice that he used to such effect when he was interviewing anyone. A few months earlier there had been some talk of putting him on the drive home slot but the station wasn't sure that it would be the best use of his talents because he would have been competing with the hottest broadcasters on the opposing stations and that would've been a gamble—a gamble Finn was perfectly prepared to take but the station wasn't. And now things were even better because he reckoned that TV would turn him into a megastar. Finn wanted to be a megastar, even if it only lasted for a short time. He wanted the name Finn Coolidge to be instantly recognizable, for people to know who he was and to think that his show was essential Friday night viewing. He couldn't wait for the series to start.

Nessa cleared away the plates then brought in the cake that she'd made earlier, as well as a cafetiere of coffee. Both Finn and Cate declined the cake.

"I'm watching my weight too now," said Finn. "You know all this thing about the TV adding ten pounds. I don't want to overindulge."

"It's only a slice of chocolate cake," said Nessa.

"Laden with calories," said Cate. "I'll pass too, if you don't mind."

"Fine by me," said Nessa. "But Bree is right. You're beginning to look more like a Biro every day."

"Give me a break," said Cate.

"You look fine." Finn put his arm around her and hugged her.

Cate was surprised at how good it made her feel. Maybe she was being paranoid about Finn these days.

"I want to do an experiment," announced Nessa suddenly.

"What sort of experiment?" Jill (who'd been very quiet as it was past her bedtime and she didn't want to draw attention to herself) couldn't help asking the question.

"You know how you guys give me such stick about horoscopes and everything?"

The family groaned in unison.

"Exactly," said Nessa. "So I thought I'd try something out. I read everyone's horoscope this morning. Adam's was particularly accurate—it said he'd meet some bumps along the way—and he did." She grinned while Adam looked annoyed. "And mine was a messy onc this week all about delays and things which happened."

"It wasn't my fault dinner was delayed if that's what you're getting at," said Bree.

"I didn't say it was. But lots of little things went wrong for me this week," Nessa told her.

"So what's the experiment?" asked Finn impatiently.

"I bought eight scratch cards at the supermarket today," said Nessa. "According to all of the predictions I read, today is Mum's lucky day. So if any of the cards are going to pay out, she should pick it."

"Nessa, that's not an experiment, that's ridiculous." Cate was scathing.

"Do I get to keep my winnings?" asked Miriam. "You won't try to nab them from me or anything?"

"Of course you can keep them," said Nessa impatiently.

"Then it's a great experiment," Miriam said robustly.

"So we all keep any money we get on the cards?" Finn looked at Nessa quizzically.

"Sure," she said. "Not that you need it, Finn, with fame and fortune just around the corner."

"OK, I'm in."

Nessa fetched the scratch cards from the kitchen shelf. "Mum should have first pick," she said. "See if her lucky vibes are working."

"If they are, it shouldn't matter whether she goes first or not." Bree grumbled. "If the 'fluence is there, it should stop us picking the unlucky cards."

"Oh, shut up, Bree," said Nessa impatiently. "Mum, pick first."

They all picked their cards. Then they began to scratch them.

"Nothing for me," said Cate. "You told me this morning that I'd be having great opportunities or something, didn't you?"

"This isn't an opportunity," said Nessa. "Finn's show is an opportunity."

"Absolutely." Finn blew the debris from his card. "And just as well because I'm not making any money on instant gambling."

"Me neither," said Louis.

"Mum?"

Miriam was carefully scratching her card with a five-euro piece. "Wait a moment," she told them. "I've uncovered two one hundred panels."

"Really?" Despite herself, Cate moved so that she could see what Miriam was doing.

"A fiver," said Miriam in disgust as she uncovered the second last panel.

"This is actually getting quite tense." Bree giggled. "If she uncovers a hundred euros, we'll all do the washing up, Nessa."

"Oh my God!" Miriam stared at the card in disbelief. "A hundred euros."

"You're joking!" Adam looked at her in astonishment.

"I'm not," said Miriam. "I was going to say it as a joke because I thought it was a tenner, but it's a hundred. I actually won."

"You don't have to do the dishes." Nessa sounded so self-satisfied that Bree wanted to hit her. "But you can stack everything in the dishwasher for me."

"That's unbelievable," said Louis. "Did you know, Nessa? Was it a trick?"

"No trick," said Nessa. "There's always a chance of winning when you buy a few scratch cards. I thought maybe someone would uncover a fiver. But I did believe that Mum's aura was lucky this week."

"I feel like I should apologize to you," said Bree. "But that'd break my heart."

"I feel that I should give you the money," said Miriam.

"No," said Nessa. "You've given me credibility. That's worth a lot more."

"Are horoscopes always right?" asked Jill. "Do they really tell you the future?"

Nessa shook her head. "Not always," she told her. "But they can help you be prepared. So that nothing can take you by surprise."

"Bullshit," said Cate.

"Well, maybe," admitted Nessa. "But it's nice to have them on your side all the same."

5

♥

Moon in Aries

Quick to react, impulsive, sometimes selfish.

Miriam sent Nessa a bouquet of flowers with a note thanking her for the dinner, the company and especially for the winning scratch card. The bouquet arrived early on Monday morning, another morning of late rising in the Riley household, which meant rushing around in a flap again. Although this time Nessa told Adam to get breakfast at work. She wasn't giving him the opportunity to ram another car while he was eating a croissant.

Nessa was disappointed to think that this might be another week of inconveniences and disruptions but, when surgery ran exceptionally late, she knew that it would be. Late surgery meant a problem in picking up Jill. Last year it had been less of a problem because Nessa had been able to phone Miriam who would happily drop anything to meet her granddaughter from school. Nessa had never felt that she was imposing on Miriam when she asked her to do things. But phoning Adam and asking him if he could help was a different proposition entirely.

It had been a vain hope that he'd be available to pick up his daughter anyway. He wasn't even in the office when Nessa called his direct line and his mobile phone was switched off. He was probably at some other stupid meeting, she thought. For all that Adam talked about his importance in the management consultancy business, where he gave companies advice on how to run their own firms more efficiently, his time never seemed to be his own. Nessa couldn't remember the last occasion he'd been able to nip out and deal with some domestic difficulty and, deep down, she understood it. But it would've been nice, she thought as she listened to his message telling her to leave a message, if he had the sort of job where he could walk out for an hour or two, no questions asked.

Adam expected her to be able to walk out of the surgery any time. As far as he was concerned, her job was trivial in the scheme of things, something to keep her occupied in the mornings when Jill was at school and a way for her to have money that she could spend on herself without talking to him about it.

Nessa also knew that her job wasn't important and it didn't bother her. At first she hadn't expected to stay working because she'd assumed that there'd be more than one child. There was no biological reason why that hadn't happened, as her gynecologist told her when she'd asked him why she hadn't got pregnant again after Jill. If they were relaxed about it, it would happen of its own accord, he assured them. But it didn't and now Nessa couldn't imagine getting pregnant again. They'd stopped talking about a brother or sister for Jill a long time ago. It never cropped up in conversation and it was something that had been relegated to things that might have been. Only once did she think that it might be about to happen again, the day that her horoscope had told her that a new event would cause significant changes in her life. She didn't know why she'd thought it would be a baby but she did. And, afterward, when she realized that the new event was merely Dr. Hogan setting up a once-a-week asthma care clinic and asking her if she'd be able to help out, she knew that she never would have another baby. And she stopped thinking about it. She stopped regretting it too. Life was perfect the way that it was, with her and Adam and Jill as a tightly knit unit where everyone slotted neatly into place together. Adam the carcrasher, Nessa the carer and Jill the daughter that they were both crazy about.

She scratched the top of her head with her pencil and sighed. Without Miriam to rely on, Nessa's own life had become more difficult. And, unlike her friend Paula whose younger sister lived a stone's throw away and had two kids of her own, neither Cate nor Bree were ever available for emergency pick-up duty. In fact, thought Nessa grimly, by the time either of her sisters got to the children stage themselves, Jill would probably be a teenager and they'd be looking for her to baby-sit for them.

She picked up the phone and rang Jean Slater, the mother of Jill's current best friend, Nicolette. She hated having to ask Jean who, unlike Nessa, had produced a clatter of children as easily as dealing a deck of cards and who seemed to spend her days in a whirlwind of child-related activities. Nessa felt that Jean was far too busy to worry about Jill as well as her own brood. But she was stuck.

"No problem," said Jean when she phoned her. "Jill would probably be here playing with Nicolette anyway. Don't worry."

Nessa, who could hear the wails of the latest Slater baby over the phone, promised Jean that she'd get there as soon as possible. She replaced the receiver and buzzed the next patient. Cate and Bree thought she had it easy. How little they knew.

Bree was standing in the service reception area when the owner of the bright yellow sports edition Punto arrived. She raised her eyebrows in surprise as she saw him because he was at least forty if not fifty, had dark hair grizzled with gray and carried a briefcase. In Bree's experience men like that drove heavy saloon cars—Mercedes or BMW or Volvo if they were well-off enough, Toyotas or Fiats or Fords if they were in the second layer of management. This man looked wealthy enough to be a Mercedes man so his ownership of the Punto was even more of a surprise.

"What the hell is all this about?" He was scanning the itemized list of the service and repair works they'd carried out. The work that she'd carried out, actually, because she'd taken the Punto job card and spent more time than she'd expected working on it.

"All the work was authorized," said Christy calmly.

"But—replacing the power-steering hose and fluid, and all of the brake pads—the car isn't that old, surely you didn't need to do that. And the clutch too?"

"That clutch wouldn't have got you to the end of the road." Bree walked over to him. "And if you didn't drive the car like a seventeen-year-old boy racer then half of what we had to do wouldn't have needed to be done at all."

"Excuse me?" He turned to look at her while Christy shot her a warning glare.

"My name is Bree Driscoll," she told him. "I'm the mechanic that worked on your car. And it was a long haul." Her eyes glittered. "The engine is frequently revved at far too high a level. From the wear on the tires you're clearly taking corners too quickly. And you're driving it through fields at speed too, which is why we had to replace some additional hosing and why, eventually, you'll have even more problems."

He stared at her.

"It's not my place to criticize the driving of our customers," she continued, "but, honestly, what do you expect when you're clearly pretending to be a rally driver?"

Christy groaned softly as the client continued to stare at Bree.

"Anyway," she said as she dropped her empty Styrofoam coffee cup into the black refuse sack, "if you want to spend less on servicing and repairs I suggest you drive the car as though you were a middle-aged suburban man instead of David Coulthard."

He started to laugh then and Christy sighed with relief.

"It's not my car," he told Bree.

"Pardon?"

"It's not my car," he repeated. "It's my son's."

She made a face. "Makes more sense now," she admitted. "I didn't think you were the go-faster stripes type when I saw you."

"Declan Morrissey." He held out his hand. She shook her head and indicated her oil-smeared glove.

"Better not shake on it," she told him. "But I'm glad you understand."

"I'll pass on your comments to my son," said Declan. "I'm not sure how effective they'll be."

"They won't be effective for as long as you foot the bill for the repairs," said Bree.

"I promised," said Declan bleakly.

"You'd want to start reneging on that promise fairly soon," suggested Bree. "Otherwise he'll bankrupt you! You're going to be back with it again in a few months, you know, and all the problems will be the same." She shrugged. "It's up to you, though. How old is he?"

"Who?"

"Your son."

"Michael's twenty-one," said Declan.

"I know it's not for me to say," Bree said while Christy winced at the thought of what she was going to tell one of their very best customers now. "But he needs driving lessons. I don't want to cast aspersions on your entire sex, Mr. Morrissey, but most men are terrible drivers when they're younger. It's the penis thing, you see. So you all drive around the place like lunatics, terrified to be beaten away at the lights by anyone else but particularly a woman, feeling that driving slowly is something for old ladies in ten-year-old Fiestas and generally believing that everyone on the road is looking at you in whatever it is you're driving."

Declan chuckled and Christy looked relieved.

"It was a birthday present for Michael," Declan said.

"Wow. Wish my parents could've bought me birthday presents like that," she told him. "I think I got a pair of gloves for my twenty-first." Actually, she remembered guiltily, Louis and Miriam had bought her a set of motorbike leathers including heavy gloves for her birthday and she'd felt absolutely great going out in all the gear.

"You're right, though," said Declan. "Maybe it was an overindulgent gift."

"I guess if you were getting him a car you might as well have bought him something that really does go fast," said Bree. "Otherwise he'd be trashing Nissan Micra's around town and probably doing even more damage. Try and get him to drive in the right gear, that'd help. And slowing down at corners would be good too."

"I'll tell him," said Declan.

"Suggest to him that he should pay the bill if it's over a couple of hundred," added Bree.

Declan looked at the invoice in his hand again.

"Good idea," he said.

"Anyway, I'd better get back to the workshop." She glanced at Christy. "Otherwise my manager will fire me."

"I'd hate to be responsible for that!" Declan smiled at her. "Thanks for the advice."

"No problem." She waved lightly and pushed open the door to the workshop.

"Sorry about that," said Christy to Declan. "She's a nice girl but her mouth does kind of run away with her sometimes."

"I didn't know that you had women mechanics." Declan handed his Visa card to the service manager.

"She's the only one," said Christy.

"Is she any good?"

"She did that service in half the time it would've taken most mechanics," said Christy. "And—though it pains me to say it—she probably did it better than most of them."

"Really?"

"She's got a way with cars," said Christy. "She loves them. I've seen her do a complete service in two hours and then suggest we check out something else completely and she's usually right. Very annoying."

Declan grinned. "Has she been with you long? Only I haven't seen her before."

"A year, I think." Christy furrowed his brow. "I can't remember, to tell you the truth. Seems like she's been here forever. Apparently she's had two job offers since she joined so I'm not actually expecting her to stay."

"That good?"

"Oh, there's a shortage of qualified mechanics at the moment," Christy told him. "It's not entirely down to her, all of my guys have had offers. But she's most likely to take one."

"Why?" asked Declan.

"Because she's flighty," said Christy. "Can't stay in the one place for too long. I don't think she's stayed anywhere else as long as this but she always has brilliant references. She spent a year traveling around the world too. Not the settling down sort."

"Pretty," said Declan noncommittally.

"Cleans up well." Christy grinned at him. "But she also packs a mean punch. Did karate or something as a kid. Nobody messes with her."

"I've certainly no intention of messing with her." Declan laughed. "I've enough trouble at home already." And more trouble, he said to himself as he took the Visa card, when I talk to Michael about what he's doing to that car.

Cate stood in front of the wardrobe mirror and looked at her reflection. Her makeup was perfect—honey-beige foundation, natural glow blusher and smoke-gray eye shadow set off by her favorite extra-lash mascara. Her lips were cherry red and glossy. Her navy dress was almost perfect too, neatly cut, not too low yet showing enough cleavage to tell people that she wasn't afraid to flaunt her best assets. It was Finn's personal favorite of all her dresses and she wanted to wear something that Finn liked because she knew that he didn't really want to come to the drinks party tonight. It wasn't a media affair, just the sports company and some of its clients to celebrate five years' successful business in Ireland. Maybe in a few months' time, she thought, when the major awards dinner for the sports scheme they'd recently launched was under way and the kids from the KickStart Initiative won their awards, he might feel it worth his while to drop in. Because in a few months' time there'd be a glitzy media night and, by then, she had no doubt that Finn Coolidge would be a big star and he'd want to be seen at an event organized for kids. But not tonight when it was just business and it wouldn't do his career any good.

"Bitchy," she said out loud as she turned to check how she looked from the back. He's not really like that. He doesn't weigh up things according to how helpful they'll be to his career. And he's coming tonight, isn't he? So what's the problem?

The problem was that she wished he wanted to come instead of knowing that he'd be turning up out of a sense of duty. But, she muttered to herself as she fastened her silver necklace, whoever wanted to go to a boring drinks reception anyway? Especially when it was for something as mundane as the sports company and not glitzy and important like one of his media events.

She went into the living room and poured herself a glass of wine.

She'd only drink water at the reception but wine was a nice option now. Then she sat down on the ultra modern but surprisingly comfortable leather couch and waited for Finn to come home.

Why hadn't he told her about the TV program sooner? she asked herself as she ran her finger around the rim of the glass. There had been a time when they talked about absolutely everything, a time when he wouldn't have kept something so important a secret from her. He'd said it was because he was afraid to talk about it. That if he actually spoke the words it might not happen at all. That was the kind of woolly thinking that Nessa, with her horoscopes and predictions and "feelings" about things, would come up with. It wasn't the way Finn and Cate had led their lives.

But she couldn't fight with him about it. He was so thrilled and so absolutely sure that she was thrilled too that she didn't have the heart to argue with him. Besides, she *was* thrilled. Even if it meant that Finn was so close to realizing all his dreams while she wasn't even sure what hers were any more.

When she was twelve she'd wanted to be a model. She'd overheard two adults talking about her and had been pleased to hear them say that she was exceptionally attractive. Not pretty in a conventional way, one of the women had said, but an arresting face nonetheless. Cate had been proud to have an arresting face. She'd wondered then if she should send in photographs of herself to model agencies and see what they had to say but she wasn't altogether convinced that Miriam would approve. And then a few days later—like a warning from God or something—she'd seen a program on TV about supermodels and diets and drugs and all sorts of things and Miriam had clucked and said that it was no life for a young girl and that it was the most sordid business she'd ever come across. In some ways, Cate had been relieved. She wasn't sure she had the stamina to become a supermodel. Besides, she wasn't tall enough yet. But the whole episode had sparked an interest in looking her best which had stayed with her ever since.

It was in secondary school that she'd discovered her aptitude for business. The teachers encouraged it. Looks may come and go, the careers guidance teacher had told them one day, but a good business head stays with you forever. And Cate had a good head for business. Most of the time.

She looked at her watch. Finn was late. That wasn't exactly a surprise because, unless it had to do with his radio program where Finn was pathologically punctual, he was late for everything. Like she was, unless it was anything to do with work. We're a sad pair, she murmured under her breath, when we can be on time for total strangers but late for each other.

She tapped her fingers on the side of her wineglass and frowned. Too much later and they'd be late arriving at the party which she couldn't do. She was meant to be there before anyone else, smiling at their clients and welcoming them as they arrived. Not turning up half an hour after them, breathless and red-faced.

She reached for the phone and dialed his number.

"Finn here," said the recorded message. "I can't take your call right now but do leave a number and I'll ring back as soon as I can."

"Why haven't you got the phone switched on?" she said. "Finn, we'll be late for the reception. Ring me as soon as you listen to this."

She walked around the living room impatiently, her heels tapping her annoyance on the wooden floors. If he didn't ring in the next five minutes she'd have to leave without him and she knew that would lead to a row later. He'd turn up at the reception a couple of minutes behind her and he'd ask her if she didn't trust him to be on time and she'd say but he hadn't rung and he'd say that he didn't need to ring, hadn't he told her he'd be home on time?

Only he wasn't on time, was he? On time would've been five minutes ago. Come on, Finn, she urged. Don't make me have to go without you.

She expected the phone to ring as she was leaving the apartment but it didn't. She checked that her own mobile was switched on as she ran down the stairs to the underground car park. And she left it easily accessible so that if he rang while she was on the way to Brown's she'd be able to grab it without panicking. But it still hadn't rung by the time she got to Drury Street car park and she had to clamp down on a mixture of rage and worry as she hurried across the street to the hotel where the reception was taking place.

"Thought you weren't going to make it, Cate." Ian Hewitt, the managing director, frowned at her.

"Sorry, Ian. Got held up in traffic," she lied. "Everything looks great, doesn't it?" She looked around the room and noted the corporate logo strategically placed in all the locations she'd demanded.

"Actually, yes." Ian smiled at her. "I guess you do know what you're doing."

"Some of the time anyway," she said as she accepted a glass of Ballygowan. "Oh, look, Gerald Mannion has arrived. I know that we're really hopeful about their order for the HiSpeed shoe. Let me go and grab him."

She cut across the room and welcomed the client, flashing her brilliant glossy smile at him and leading him toward Ian. Then she went to meet and greet the other arrivals, always saying something different to each one, always trying to make every single person feel individually welcome.

Her phone was set to vibrate rather than to ring. At this point, almost an hour into the reception, she wouldn't hear it over the buzz of conversation unless it was set to loud. And she wasn't going to ruin the carefully created ambience with the strident tones of her phone bleating around the room.

But where the fuck was he, she wondered. She was anxious, but only a little anxious. She knew that he really wouldn't have crashed the car or done anything terribly stupid like that. But what if someone had plowed into him? She wished she hadn't thought of that. She wished she could just think that the bastard was late or that he'd forgotten about the reception so that she could be properly mad at him. Now, she knew, she'd be relieved when he turned up because that'd mean that nothing awful had actually happened. But she didn't want to be relieved, she wanted to be annoyed.

And then she saw him walking into the room and she was both relieved *and* annoyed. Particularly when Ian made a beeline for him and began pumping his hand in congratulations about the TV program.

"Where the hell were you?" she demanded when he finally made it to her side.

"Sorry," he said. "Got caught up in a meeting, had to have a few drinks afterward, you know how it is."

"You should have rung me," she said furiously. "I was worried about you."

"Oh, for heaven's sake, Catey!" He looked at her in amusement. "What's there to worry about? What awful thing did you think could've happened to me?"

"How should I know?" she asked. "A crazed fan might have stabbed you, I suppose!"

He laughed. "I haven't got to the crazed fan stage yet," he said. "I'll let you know when."

"You still should've called," she told him.

"I know. Sorry."

"I thought you'd forgotten."

"I don't forget," he said. "You know I don't."

"Hello, it's Finn Coolidge, isn't it?" The buyer for a small chain of sports shops interrupted them. "I listen to your show in the mornings. It's great. Very insightful. And now I believe you're doing TV?"

There had been a big press announcement about Finn's TV show. And the radio station, panicking at the loss of their star, had renegotiated a package with him for a current affairs program three days a week in the drivetime slot that they originally hadn't wanted him to do. But now they reckoned that Finn would pull the listeners in anyway.

Finn grasped the buyer's outstretched hand. "Yes," he said. "I'm hoping I don't fall flat on my face on TV. You know how it is, some of us do great on radio but end up being absolutely crap on the tube."

"I'm sure it'll work out really well," said the buyer. He looked at Cate. "I didn't make the connection," he said. "I remember you telling me that your boyfriend worked in the media, and I read something about Finn's girlfriend being a businesswoman too, but it was only when I saw you together that it clicked."

"Oh, I try not to let him hang on to my coattails." Cate smiled.

"And I try to keep her locked in the kitchen," added Finn.

"It was nice to meet you," said the buyer to Finn. "And any time you're looking to do sports-related stuff on either of your shows just let me know."

"Sure," said Finn easily, taking the man's card. "Nice to have met you too. Bit of a plonker," he said in aside to Cate. "How do you put up with people like that?"

"He's quite a good customer," she told him. "Small chain but in good locations. And I put up with him the same way you put up with people kissing you on both cheeks and calling you darling."

Finn looked at her. "You're really quite ratty tonight, aren't you?"

"Oh, sod off!" She was tired of talking to him and she wished now that he'd never agreed to come in the first place.

"OK," said Finn. "I will."

He walked across the room, spoke for a couple of minutes to Ian and to another of the directors and then disappeared. For a moment, Cate thought that he'd gone to the men's room and then she realized that he'd actually left. He'd sodded off, just like he'd said. She'd been narky, he'd been bored, now he was gone.

"Bastard," she muttered as she reached for a glass of wine despite her rule about drinking only water. "Fucking bastard."

After Finn's desertion, the night was very successful. Ian told her that it was a pity Finn had another obligation, only not terribly surprising. And she smiled and said that his life was very busy at the moment and they hardly got a minute to each other but she was sure he'd enjoyed the time he'd spent at the party. Ian suggested that Finn might be able to give them a certain amount of publicity in the future and Cate gritted her teeth and said that possibly he would. She hated the way everyone went weak at the knees over someone who was only fairly well known. But they all did with Finn, even the bloody men!

It was late by the time she got back to the apartment. From the coast road she could see that it was in darkness and she supposed that Finn had already gone to bed. She regretted having argued with him but, honestly, he could be so annoying. And he was certainly getting a bit big for his boots these days.

She opened the door quietly so as not to wake him. She slid off her shoes and padded into the kitchen where she poured herself a glass of water. She'd ended up drinking wine at the reception after all and was now raging with thirst. Fortunately she'd been too annoyed with Finn to get properly drunk. She yawned and finished the water. Then she went into the bathroom and took off her makeup.

It was almost one o'clock before she opened the bedroom door. She stopped in the doorway and clenched her fists. Finn wasn't home yet. She could have clattered around the apartment in her damned high heels and he wouldn't have known anything about it. Where the hell was he?

For the second time that day she rang his mobile phone and got his message minder. But this time she didn't bother leaving any message.

•   •   •

She couldn't sleep. Her body was tired but her mind was racing. She visualized Finn in a nightclub, meeting people, having fun without her. And it made her angry because she didn't want Finn having a good time without her and she didn't want to think that he was out there not even thinking about her while she was lying, rigid, in the bed worrying about him.

Why do I always worry about him? she asked herself. He's perfectly capable of looking after himself and he never gets so drunk that he can't find his way home, so what, exactly, am I worried about? She rolled over and pummelled the pillow, trying to make herself go to sleep. But she was alert for the sound of footsteps in the hallway and his key in the lock.

She'd drifted into half-sleep when he finally arrived home. The sound of the apartment door clicking closed woke her properly and she glanced at the bedside clock. Nearly four in the morning. She gritted her teeth.

He moved around the apartment with his usual lack of quiet. She heard him open the fridge door and she knew that he was drinking a litre of water—his surefire hangover prevention exercise. She heard the buzz of the electric toothbrush as he cleaned his teeth and his muffled exclamation of annoyance as he dropped something (probably the chrome mug) onto the bathroom floor.

She didn't open her eyes when he came into the bedroom and she sensed him undressing and hanging his clothes in the wardrobe. Wherever he'd gone and whatever he'd done, he wasn't that drunk. When Finn was really blitzed he didn't hang his clothes up, he simply stepped out of them, leaving them in a jumble at the side of the bed.

He moved to the center of the bed and flung his arm over her.

"Where have you been?" she asked.

"Nng."

"What?"

"Out," he said more clearly.

"I know that," she said sharply. "Out where?"

"Friends." He sighed deeply and his breathing was suddenly regular and even. He was asleep.

Cate removed his arm from across her body and nudged him. But Finn slept on, oblivious to her movements. She propped herself up on one elbow and looked at him—the face that launched a thousand front pages. Well, almost. He still looked strong and athletic and, somehow, authoritative, even in sleep. He murmured again and then started to snore gently. Cate clamped down on her feelings of rage. Whenever he had too much to drink, even just one can of beer too much, Finn snored. The snores started off gently and then grew louder and louder until they reached a crescendo, when suddenly he'd stop. The snoring drove her mad but the sudden silence was even worse. She always thought he'd choked when he was silent.

She slid out of the bed and went into the kitchen. She made as much noise as she could as she filled the kettle and switched it on. She hoped he'd wake up but in her heart she knew he wouldn't. Finn liked to sleep. He was good at sleeping.

She made herself a cup of tea and stood at the huge window overlooking the bay. The string of lights curved into an enormous semicircle from Howth to Bray. It was a view that never ceased to enthral her.

It was Finn's view. She swallowed a mouthful of tea and thought about it. She was living in Finn's apartment looking out of Finn's window and drinking tea from Finn's blue and white mug. Of course there were plenty of joint mugs she could be drinking from. They'd bought loads of damned mugs and cups over the past three years but right now she was drinking from Finn's mug.

She turned back and looked at the living room. It was furnished exactly as it had been three years ago too. Finn's choices. Which would have been her choices too if she'd been around to make them at the time—pale wooden floors and units complimented by the black leather couch and matching chairs. Masculine. Not flouncy or pretty or Nessa-like in their domesticity. Clean lines to fit in with the kind of life they led.

But still, mostly Finn's stuff. She'd bought the painting by an artist who was still displaying his work on the railings of Merrion Square on Sunday mornings. It was an abstract oil painting of a bright red fish on a dark blue background. Not pretty, either, but striking. She'd also bought the big mirror in the pewter frame. And the big pewter vases filled with pale dried flowers which were decorative but not in the slightest bit girly.

She drained the mug and shivered. She was Finn's girlfriend living in Finn's place. Just because things had been rough the last few months didn't mean that it would all go horribly wrong. But she suddenly felt very insecure.

"You should get married." Nessa's words came back to her. Conventional, boring Nessa who probably hadn't even slept with Adam before she'd married him. Cate twirled the ends of her hair as she remembered the conversation with her older sister a year or so after she'd moved in with Finn.

"You should get married to him if you love him," Nessa had said. "And if you don't love him then you should think about how much of your life you're prepared to waste on him."

She'd tried to tell Nessa that marriage didn't matter—for God's sake, she'd said, this was the new century, she wasn't going to get trapped in the moral straitjacket of the 1950s. But Nessa had shrugged and told her that it was all very well to say that marriage was only a bit of paper and that it didn't matter but, when it came to who owned what, it did.

Cate remembered being shocked at Nessa's mercenary attitude.

"I thought you believed in true love," she'd said sarcastically and Nessa had smiled and said that of course she did but a little bit of realism never hurt either.

We do love each other, Cate told herself as she got back into bed a few minutes later. We love each other and we'll get through this. Being married or not being married doesn't make the slightest bit of difference.

6

♥

Moon in Sagittarius

Enjoys freedom, travel and a challenge.

B ree opened the heavy front door of the house in Marlborough Road and leaned against the crumbling brick wall. It had been an effort to get up the steps in the first place and now she needed to catch her breath. She looked at Steve, slumped into a disheveled, drunken heap beside the door, and sighed deeply.

Why had she agreed to let him come home with her? It wasn't as though she had room for him, as though her flat was big enough to allow stray men to spend the night. She pushed her untamed hair behind her ears and looked at him again. She'd felt sorry for him. As she always did. A sucker for a bleeding heart.

"Come on, Steve." She shook his shoulder. "Time to wake up."

He groaned softly, opened his gray-green eyes and looked blearily at her.

"I'm tired," he said. "Leave me here."

"Don't be ridiculous," she told him. "You'd probably be arrested or something. Come on up to the flat and you can flake out there." She reached out to him and pulled the collar of his cotton shirt, forcing him to stand up.

"You're a real friend, Bree, you know that?"

"Yes," she said wryly. "I know."

"The others—they despise me."

"No they don't." They'd had this conversation already and she didn't want to have it again.

"They don't respect me."

"Steve, you're being silly."

"I'm not." His voice was despairing.

"You need to sleep it off. Then you won't feel like this. It's the bottle of vodka talking."

"I didn't drink a bottle of vodka," protested Steve.

"The Bacardi Breezers then," she said.

"You can be a right bitch sometimes," he said. "But you're my best friend."

"Thank you." She draped his arm around her shoulder. "Now come on, it's two flights up."

They staggered up the stairs together and into her apartment. Steve immediately fell onto her double bed and closed his eyes again while Bree filled the kettle and made herself a cup of tea.

Another night of being someone's best friend. She was beginning to be tired of being best friends to an assortment of men. And yet many of them considered her to be a real mate. They asked her advice about presents for their girlfriends, they chatted to her about secret worries (like being scared of getting incurable diseases or being hopeless in bed) that they didn't feel that they could talk to other men about. They treated her like another bloke. And that was all right by her. Most of the time.

She sat down, propped her feet on the table and sipped her tea. I'm a modern kind of woman, she told herself. I don't need to have deep, intense relationships with men. I can be friends with them without thinking of every man I meet as a potential life mate. I'm not like Nessa who trawled through pages and pages of magazines checking to see what sort of man she'd be most compatible with and trying to make herself into the sort of woman they wanted her to be. Or like Cate who, before Finn, had had a succession of men who were clearly some kind of trophy boyfriends but who were certainly not her friends. I, on the other hand, have a much healthier attitude toward relationships. Even though some of them go horribly wrong. Well, she admitted, really all of my non-platonic relationships have gone horribly wrong.

She scratched the side of her nose as she thought of them. There had been a pattern to them, one which she'd identified and tried to eliminate although not always successfully. She fell for weirdoes. Attractive weirdoes. Handsome weirdoes even. But weirdoes all the same.

Like Gerry, who'd spent most of his time sitting in his flat smoking joints and listening to sixties songs. She'd been attracted by his effortless good looks and lack of ambition but it had stopped being quite so charming after the first month. It was fortunate that she usually came to her senses fairly quickly. Because there had been others—like Enrique whom she'd met while she was working for a couple of months in Spain and who'd kept a scrapbook of photos of his previous girlfriends in various states of undress (she'd left the town of Villajoyosa as soon as she'd discovered the scrapbook and before he'd had a chance to add her to it); Fabien, the French guy, another absolute movie star in the looks department but possibly the worst mechanic in the world and full of the particular arrogance that attractive Frenchmen always had—she'd discovered that he had two other girlfriends as well as an ongoing "relationship" with the married woman in the apartment across the road from the garage. After that discovery it was adieu to Fabien and to the little town of Carbonne.

And in England there'd been Terry—fair-haired and unlike her usual ideal man in the looks department, but attractive in a muscle-bound way nonetheless—with whom she'd lived for two months before he told her that he was leaving England and joining the

Foreign Legion. She hadn't thought that people actually joined the Foreign Legion but apparently they did. After he'd left, the police had called around to the flat to ask about him. She hadn't wanted to know why. She'd decided then it was time to come back to Ireland.

The weirdoes in Ireland weren't as weird (although there'd been a brief fling with Marcus who kept pet snakes). In reality, she hadn't found time to fall for anyone in the last few months. The job at the garage, as well as the occasional nixers that she did, took up a lot of her time and she was quite happy to revert to meeting men simply as friends rather than as potential soul mates.

But now, looking at Steve sleeping on her bed, she wondered whether or not she should think of finding someone for herself. Not a weirdo, not a friend, just an ordinary sort of boyfriend. Someone who'd stick around long enough for her to buy them a birthday present or a Christmas present. Someone she could share things with.

She shuddered. She didn't really want to be dependable and dull and someone's girlfriend instead of someone's best friend. Did she? Besides, she never fell for the sort of bloke who wanted a common-or-garden girlfriend. Maybe being best friends was a better option.

She glanced at Steve again. She was, of course, currently Steve's best friend. It was almost a cliché to be best friends with a gay man but she was. She'd met him shortly after she'd come back to Ireland and they'd hit it off immediately. He'd just finished a relationship with a bit of a weirdo too. So they'd exchanged weird bloke stories while buying each other drinks and before she knew where she was they'd become friends.

Bree liked Steve and enjoyed being with him. But he'd fallen for an out-of-work actor a few weeks earlier, had a brief but passionate affair with him and had phoned her earlier in the afternoon to tell her all about his broken heart.

What is it about me, she wondered, that makes me great friend material but not good girlfriend material? Why am I so different to Nessa and to Cate when we've both got the same genes in our bodies? How is it that they're so good with men while I'm not? Despite the fact that I try to pretend to them that I don't give a stuff really, I have a horrible feeling that I'm getting slightly jealous.

She shivered. This definitely wasn't the way to think. She looked at her watch. It was late but she was too tired to figure out exactly what time it was. It was the lateness of the hour and the drink and the struggle of getting Steve back to the flat that was getting to her. She'd feel better in the morning. She knew that she should take off the little bit of makeup that she wore before getting into bed but she just couldn't be bothered. She put her empty cup into the sink, flopped fully clothed on the bed beside Steve and almost immediately fell asleep.

Cate stood in the shower and thought about what they'd say when she told them it was over. Nessa would be full of gushing sympathy while at the same time managing to let Cate know that Nessa herself had the most perfect relationship; Bree would shrug and tell her that she was better off without him; and Miriam would blame herself. Cate squirted moisturizing foam wash onto the white puff and squeezed it over her shoulders. Miriam would think that because she wasn't around to look after her second daughter, Cate had managed to mess things up. Without Miriam's steadying influence, Cate had allowed Finn to become the kind of bloke who didn't arrive home until four in the morning, who drank himself into a stupor at the slightest opportunity, who treated her like a mere possession. The kind of bloke who'd rolled over in the bed when she'd got up and made herself some coffee and who hadn't even bothered to respond when she poked her head around the door and asked him if he wanted any himself.

He wasn't interested in her any more, that much was painfully clear. And it hurt Cate more than she wanted to admit that his interest had waned from the moment he'd been offered the TV show. It was as though she was suddenly an unimportant part of his past, an inconvenience to be dealt with. She felt her tears mingle with the jet from the shower. She'd believed in the relationship, trusted him, allowed herself to care about him. And in the end she was left with the bitter feeling that she'd soon be looking for another apartment in the city and she'd be out there as a single thirtysomething all over again. She shook her head. She hadn't even wanted to acknowledge how great it had been to be part of a couple, knowing that there was someone to share things with, knowing that she didn't have to sleep alone at night.

And I'm pathetic, she thought as she rubbed the puff over her body angrily, if I can only value myself in terms of not having to sleep alone at night. I'm a successful woman. I don't need a man beside me to make me feel fulfilled. She wished she could believe what she was telling herself.

The apartment was empty when she stepped out of the shower. Finn had been asleep—at least she'd thought he'd been asleep—when she went into the bathroom, but maybe he'd just been waiting for her to get out of the bed so that he could sneak out without having to talk to her. She felt the hot tears sting her eyes again and clenched her jaw. I will *not* let him make me cry, she told herself as she wrapped the snow-white bath towel around her. I will not let him make me cry and I will be cool and poised and grown-up about everything. I'm thirty years old, for God's sake. Thirty-year-olds don't need to cry over mere men.

She pulled on a pale pink T-shirt and a faded pair of jeans. She sat on the couch in the sun-washed living room and stared out at the languid movement of the sea. It was strange to feel as though everything was over when they hadn't even talked about it yet. But she knew that they would. Finn had never walked out of the apartment without even saying goodbye before. Doing it this morning had changed their relationship forever.

Her stomach rumbled. She was hungry but she didn't feel as though she could eat anything. Why was it that falling in love and falling out of love had the exact same effect? When she'd first gone out with him she'd been so enraptured by him that she hadn't been able to eat a thing even though he'd taken her to the Halo at the Morrison Hotel which was the ultimate in chic food and even décor. She massaged the back of her neck. Nessa would have a great time telling her that she'd told her so, reminding her that she should have married him while she had the chance.

But I never had the chance, she told herself. He didn't want commitment. Neither did I.

She heard the door of the apartment click open and her heart fluttered. Remember, she told herself, no tears. Just be cool.

"Anyone home?"

She saw the flowers before she saw him, an enormous bunch of deep red roses, far too many to fill the two John Rocha vases that they had.

"Finn?"

"Who were you expecting?" He lowered the massive bouquet until she could see the glint of his blue eyes.

"Nobody." She stood up. "What's all this?"

"This," said Finn as he thrust the flowers at her, "is my way of saying that I'm sorry."

"Sorry?"

"For being such a shit," he told her. "And I have been a shit this last while, haven't I? Since I got the TV program. Since before then. Since I started to talk to them about it."

Cate bit her bottom lip. "I guess."

"You were meant to say that I wasn't." Finn grinned at her. "So that I could actually feel quite good about myself! You were meant to say that you hadn't noticed I was behaving like a total asshole."

"Well . . ." She grimaced and blinked to hold back the tears.

"But I know I have," he said. "I should've told you about it before, Cate. I should have talked to you when they first approached me. But I was afraid to count my chickens before they'd hatched. Afraid it mightn't come to anything after all and I'd end up looking stupid."

"I understand," she said.

"You don't," said Finn. "Not really. It's my dream, Cate. You know that. And it was so close to coming true. I thought that saying it out loud might break the spell."

"You sound like Nessa," she told him.

He laughed. "I'm Aquarius," he said. "According to your sister I'm supposed to be objective and unemotional—"

"Maybe that's why they've picked you for the chat show," said Cate.

"Well, a lot of the time I know I *am* objective and unemotional," he told her. "But I shouldn't let my head rule my heart all the time."

"And do you?"

"I think so."

"It doesn't matter," she said.

"It does." Finn stepped closer to her and took the flowers away from her. He placed them carefully on the floor, allowing a small puddle of water to form on the polished wood. "I should've shared it with you, Cate. The good or the bad part. I felt terrible about not saying anything but the longer I didn't, the harder it got. Then when it happened I was just so relieved I blurted it out on the phone! I should've told you properly, face to face. But I couldn't seem to connect with you about it the way I expected and I thought that maybe you weren't very happy about it."

"I was surprised," she told him. "I was hurt that you didn't tell me sooner."

"I know," he said. "Although it took me a while to work it out—maybe I won't be such a hot-shot chat show host if I can't work things like that out myself."

"Maybe you won't," she said.

"But the thing is," he said urgently, "whether it works or not, whether this time next year I have another show or not, the important thing is that you're with me."

She stared at him.

"I love you," he told her. "I've loved you for ages. I can't say since the day we met because that day I just lusted after you. But then I loved you."

She smiled.

"And I'll keep on loving you, Cate. No matter what."

"Will you?"

"Success means nothing unless you've got someone to share it with."

"You think?"

"Of course," he said passionately. "It's one of the topics on my show. The fact that people really do price happiness and love ahead of everything else."

"Ahead of a Mercedes Benz Kompressor?" She named his favorite car.

"Miles ahead."

"Ahead of an around-the-world holiday?" He'd always wanted to do that.

"Absolutely."

"Ahead of—"

"Ahead of everything," he told her firmly.

She looked into his eyes, an even deeper blue than the sea outside, and then she touched him gently on the side of the cheek.

"Marry me," she said.

The words had come out before the thought had properly formed in her head, words that she thought—hoped—that one day she might hear but never that she would actually say herself.

He grinned at her. "That's my Cate."

"Pardon?"

"It's what I love about you. You want something, you ask."

"I was joking," she told him hastily.

"Really?"

"Sort of." She didn't know how to act now. She'd asked him to marry her, a really naff, so unfeminist type of thing to do. A few minutes ago she'd been telling herself that she didn't need commitment for God's sake! They'd been happy living together without that tie, it was totally unnecessary now. But she'd been feeling vulnerable because of his sudden career change and his unexpected behavior and she'd allowed Nessa's warnings to take root inside her head. And she'd had a horrible feeling that, despite all his talk about how much he loved her, he'd never pop the question himself.

"Do you want to get married?" he asked.

She shrugged. "It's not essential."

"Do you love me?"

She rested her head on his broad shoulder. Of course she loved him. She'd always loved him. Half of Ireland loved him. It was bloody hard not to love him.

"I guess I do," she told him.

"Getting married would be fun," he said.

"It's not supposed to be fun!"

He laughed at the tone of her voice.

"You know what I meant," she said.

"I suppose I could do a show on marriage," he mused. "Get people who've been together for years as well as some newlyweds . . ."

She raised her head and looked at him doubtfully.

"I'd love to marry you, Catey," he told her. "It's time we got married. Really it is."

She rested her head on his shoulder again.

"Only don't let's do the Nessa thing just yet."

"Pardon?"

"You know. The suburban house. The pink curtains. The screaming child . . ."

"Don't worry," said Cate. "I'm nothing like Nessa."

"I know." He kissed the top of her head. "You're much, much sexier."

7

♥

Sun in Aries, Moon in Capricorn

Rise to the task with courage, enthusiasm and commitment.

R ed suited her, thought Cate, as she surveyed herself in the long mirror. Red brought out the color in her cheeks and the darkness of her hair and made her look altogether more healthy and vibrant than she'd done in ages. She should go with it more often instead of the blacks and navys that she so often wore. And the latest Dior skin-smoothing foundation she'd bought yesterday looked great too. It was supposed to have a lifting and firming action and she felt lifted and firmed. She daubed some iridescent Terra Bella on her cheeks to increase the healthy glow effect and then pushed her fingers through her hair again. She did that mainly so that she could see the sparkle of the diamond on her engagement finger as the light from the bedroom window caught it. She felt very silly at exulting in her ring, very unprofessional woman, but she couldn't help it. It was a real cracker of a ring.

They'd bought it together from a jeweler in the Powerscourt Townhouse Centre and it had been specially made for her. Finn wouldn't even let her look at the prices, he insisted that she choose something that she really wanted. Part of her had wanted to be understated and elegant but another part, a part that she didn't even know existed, wanted glitz and glamor. Glitz and glamor won out in the end and now she found it almost impossible not to wave her left hand around at the slightest excuse.

"Aren't you ready yet?" Finn burst into the room and Cate put her hands down by her side as nonchalantly as she could.

"Yes," she told him.

"Red suits you," he told her.

"I know." She smiled. "I was just thinking that myself."

He leaned his head to one side and looked at her critically. "You know what else suits you?"

"What?"

"You've put on a bit of weight."

"D'you think so?" Her voice was anxious. "I thought the zip was a bit tighter than usual."

"Yes, but it's fine," he assured her. "You were getting awfully skinny, Cate."

"I wasn't."

"You were! Even Bree noticed it the night we went to Nessa's house."

"She called me a Biro." Cate grimaced. "Bitch."

Finn laughed. "She's outspoken, is Bree."

"She's an idiot." Cate opened the wardrobe and took out her light tan shoes. "She doesn't give a toss about her job or her life or where she's going."

"That's not fair," said Finn. "Just because she has different priorities to you."

"She has loads of potential," Cate said. "She was really brilliant at math and science at school. She could've done anything."

"But what's wrong with what she's doing now?" asked Finn. "She's good at it—and it's very handy to have a mechanic in the family."

"Maybe." Cate smiled. "Especially if you're Adam Riley."

"Oh, Adam." Finn shook his head. "I've never met anyone with as rotten a sense of space as Adam."

"If it wasn't for Bree, Nessa and Adam would probably have a lot more rows in that marriage," declared Cate. "She's saved them a fortune in car repairs." She looked at her watch and shrieked. "God, you're right! I'm really late. They'll have my guts for garters!"

"I'll get you in on time," Finn told her. "Don't panic."

"I'm not panicking." Cate picked up her bag and hurried out of the room. Then she turned and went back again for her keys.

"You always panic when you meet your sisters," said Finn in amusement. "You'd think you'd be relaxed about it but you're not."

"It's just . . ." Cate tucked an imaginary hair behind her ear and looked at her fiancé. "I'm the one in the middle, Finn. Nessa's always been the one that tells me what to do and Bree has always been the one who I had to look after and sometimes I feel as though I don't know who I'm supposed to be with them."

"Corny as this sounds, how about being yourself?" suggested Finn.

Cate giggled. "You learning all that for the TV show?"

"Come on." Finn put his arm around her shoulder. "Let's go throw you to the wolves."

Nessa and Bree were already sitting in Il Vignardo's. Cate had chosen it, she enjoyed the atmosphere of the cellar-like restaurant with its low ceiling covered in sculpted vine leaves and attentive, friendly waiters. Nessa, as always, had arrived a little early but Bree was almost exactly on time. They ordered a bottle of red wine and waited for Cate to arrive.

"I don't know why she's always late," said Bree. "You'd think that with that job of hers she'd be one of those people who measured out their time to the second."

"You're one to talk." Nessa leaned back in the chair. "You're never on time for anything. I didn't think you'd be here before her."

"You expect me to be late," said Bree. "The scatty younger sister."

"You're not scatty," Nessa said.

"But you expect me to be," repeated Bree. "You used to say that all the time, Nessa."

"What? What did I say?"

"You'd say, oh, we can't expect much from Bree. She's the scatty one."

"No I didn't."

"Absolutely."

"Crap," said Nessa decisively.

"So what do you think about Cate and Finn?" Bree changed the subject.

"I think it's great," replied Nessa. "Don't you?"

Bree shrugged. "Sure. Once she's happy."

"Why don't you think she'd be happy?" asked Nessa.

"It's what we said at dinner at Mum and Dad's," Bree told her. "I just don't see her as a celebrity chick."

"She's not," said Nessa.

"Did you see the piece about them in the entertainment section of the newspaper?" demanded Bree. "It was so naff I nearly puked."

Nessa nodded. "I read it last week while Jill and I were staying at Mum's. She says to give her a call, by the way, she hasn't spoken to you in ages. We had a good old laugh at it together. But they were simply using it to publicize Finn, weren't they? It's not real fame."

"It was gross all the same," said Bree. "And I can't see Cate sticking it even though she does enjoy slapping on the face stuff and prancing around in new clothes."

"She loves him," said Nessa. "She's stuck with it for three years."

"Not the fame bit though," said Bree seriously. "She's stuck with him while things have just been OK. But when they change—maybe he'll change too."

"I doubt it," said Nessa. "Finn's a nice guy. He's Aquarian so he's pretty sensitive."

"You think that'll save them?" Bree giggled.

"They should get on reasonably well," said Nessa. "They complement each other even though they might think differently about some things."

"I'm Sagittarian," said Bree. "Who's best for me?"

"You're difficult," said Nessa.

"Why?"

"Because your moon is in Gemini," Nessa told her.

"And?"

"You crave a soul mate," said Nessa. "But you're always looking out for something better than you have already."

"That's total rubbish," said Bree. "I have loads of friends."

"And none of them good enough to be boyfriends?"

This was so near the thoughts that she'd had so recently herself that Bree nearly choked on her red wine.

"I'm supposed to be a kind of philosopher," said Bree. "Maybe that's why."

"You look for answers by traveling around the place," Nessa told her. "But you won't find them that way."

"I'm not looking for answers," said Bree. "I'm not looking for anything. Except, perhaps, something to eat sooner rather than later."

"Why do you have to make a joke out of everything?"

Bree sighed. "I don't. I just don't want to spend the night listening to you lecturing me."

Nessa looked at her younger sister and frowned. "Is everything all right?" she asked. "Nothing's bothering you, is it?"

"Of course not," said Bree impatiently.

"Sure?"

"Nessa, stop doing the big sister act! I'm fine. My job's fine. My life is fine."

"So everything's fine, then," said Nessa.

They sat in silence. Bree picked at a spot of candlewax on the table and wished that Nessa didn't always try to dig into her mind. There was something about Nessa that wouldn't allow her to leave things unchallenged. It was impossible to use throwaway remarks with a woman who picked up on them and worried them to get to the bottom of them.

Bree sighed. Everything *was* fine, there was nothing in her life that had changed to make things different. Byt that, she admitted to herself, was the problem. As she'd dressed for tonight's celebration dinner with her sisters she'd suddenly felt once again as though they'd found something that she hadn't. Nessa and Adam, utterly crazy about each other. And no matter how much she protested to herself about Cate's role in her relationship with Finn, at least he was ready to make a commitment.

How do you know, she wondered, who the right man for you really is? How do you know when you're both ready for commitment?

"What the hell is keeping her?" Nessa's irritated tone broke into Bree's thoughts.

Bree looked at her watch. It wasn't like Cate to be quite so late, she realized. Cate normally arrived just late enough to let them know that she was a busy person and that they were lucky she'd managed to find the time.

"Maybe Finn is making mad, passionate love to her," she suggested. "P'raps he couldn't stand the idea of her coming out with us and he's tied her to the bed and is already beating her into submission."

Nessa giggled. "What a thought! Nobody could beat our Cate into submission."

"She might like it," suggested Bree.

"Would she?" Nessa screwed up her face. "D'you think so?"

"God, how would I know?" Bree sounded horrified at the idea.

"I just wondered," said Nessa thoughtfully. "I think he's a domineering kind of bloke and—"

"But Cate's not the sort of woman who'd let herself be dominated," said Bree.

"Not in the usual sense," agreed Nessa. "She might like it in bed though."

"I doubt it," said Bree. "And I'm not entirely sure we should be sitting here talking about our sister's sex life!"

"You're right," agreed Nessa. "It's not something I want to explore either. I'm glad, though, that they've finally decided to get married."

"So you're not the only one?" asked Bree.

"I don't care about that," said Nessa. "But I'm pleased to see them publicly expressing their feelings for each other. I like to think of Cate as a person with feelings as opposed to a career girl automaton."

"She's not an automaton!" cried Bree. "And of course she has feelings."

"Oh, I know." Nessa sighed. "It's simply that she seems to freeze them over sometimes. Don't you think so?"

Bree shrugged. "I don't think about it that often, to be honest."

"I'm being silly," said Nessa. "I don't know what's got into me today."

"Dodgy horoscope?" Bree's eyes twinkled at her and Nessa laughed.

"Boring horoscopes actually." She rummaged in her bag and took out three sheets of paper. "I brought them with me."

Bree took a page from her. "Where did you get this from?" she asked.

"Internet," said Nessa. "I found a really good site."

"Was it the one that predicted your Lotto win?" asked Bree.

"Yes." Nessa looked at her triumphantly. "Only it's not predicting anything at the moment."

"Certainly not for me." Bree scanned the page. "What does 'you need to get in touch with your inner feelings' really mean, Nessa?"

"Maybe you do need to," Nessa told her. "Maybe you're not listening to what you really want."

Bree looked at her watch. "What I really want is food," she said. "If Cate doesn't show up in the next five minutes we're ordering without her. Celebration or no celebration."

Nessa chuckled. "No reason why we can't celebrate her engagement without her. But we don't have to. She's finally decided to grace us with her presence." She waved to the doorway where Cate was standing. The tall, willowy girl waved back at her and strode confidently to the table.

"Where the hell were you?" demanded Nessa as Cate pulled out a chair and sat down. "We've been here for ages."

"Sorry." Cate looked at her repentantly. "I was swanning around and lost track of the time."

Bree's eyes opened wide in amazement at this admission. Very unlike Cate to admit to losing track of anything, she thought. Maybe her engagement had changed her completely.

"So," she said. "Show me the ring!"

Cate had phoned her sisters the day that she and Finn had bought the ring. She'd been afraid to do it earlier in case, somehow, he'd change his mind. She knew that she was being a little silly about it but she didn't see the point in telling the girls until she actually had the ring on her finger. And it had taken all her powers of persuasion to prevent Nessa (who'd been visiting their parents with Jill) from driving back from Galway straightaway to look at it.

Now, a few days later, she extended her hand and they gasped in admiration at the large solitaire on her finger.

"It's fabulous." Nessa sighed and glanced at her own engagement ring, a simple gold hoop with three small diamonds. "It must have cost him a fortune."

"He can afford it!" Cate smiled confidently. "He wouldn't let me look at any of the prices in the shop, he told me to pick the one I liked best."

"It's a lovely choice," Nessa told her. "Really striking."

"It's certainly eye-catching," said Bree as she caught hold of Cate's hand and scrutinized the diamond. "If he ever leaves you, you'll be able to flog it and pay for a couple of comfort eating binges."

"Bree Driscoll! That's a horrible thing to say." Cate drew her hand back.

"Sorry." Bree grinned at her. "But you know me, Cate, jewelery was never my thing."

"What about ordering some food?" suggested Nessa quickly. "We've been here ages and my stomach thinks my throat's been cut."

"Good idea." Cate opened one of the menus and glanced over it.

When the waiter arrived they ordered salads, lasagne, garlic bread and a bottle of Chianti.

"I'm really glad for you, Catey," said Nessa once her glass had been filled. "Here's to a long and happy marriage with Finn-So-Cool."

"Thanks," said Cate as they clinked their glasses together. "Only, do me a favor, don't call him that. He hates it."

"Does he?" Bree looked surprised. "I rather thought he liked it."

"He doesn't," said Cate.

"I brought your horoscope, Cate." Nessa filled the sudden silence. "Only it's not very exciting."

"Why should it be?" asked Cate as she took the paper from Nessa and glanced over it. "I've already done my exciting thing. Though I thought you'd know in advance."

"Actually your horoscope last week did say something about stunning events but I thought it was something to do with your work."

Cate grinned. "For once maybe it was right. We got a massive order for our new shoe which has put us right back on track for our sales targets."

"Brilliant!" cried Nessa.

"Imagine that," said Bree. "An engagement and a shoe order all in the one week!"

"How did he propose?" Nessa made a face at Bree and turned to Cate. "Did he go down on one knee or did he just look at you and say how about it?"

Cate felt herself blush and she put the page on the table. "Neither."

"How then?" asked Bree.

"Well, he—"

"You were having mad passionate sex and he shouted marry me, marry me, and you said, oh, OK, anything to get you off me," suggested Bree.

"Bree!" But Nessa was choking back the laughter.

"Actually, I asked him," said Cate coolly.

Bree and Nessa stared at her.

"You asked him!" squeaked Nessa. "You didn't, Cate, did you?"

"I just said I did."

"Wow." Bree looked at her admiringly. "You truly are a liberated woman, aren't you?"

"It's no big deal," said Cate.

"What made you ask him?" Nessa looked at her curiously. "I thought neither of you would ever bother."

"I knew the time was right," said Cate. "And he'd just brought me home a magnificent bunch of roses . . ."

"If you'd waited, maybe he would've asked you," said Bree.

"Maybe."

"But you just jumped in there like you always do," said Nessa.

"It was one of those now or never moments," Cate told her.

"I'm impressed." Nessa filled their glasses. "To Cate. May nothing ever hold her back."

"To Cate!"

They clinked their glasses together vigorously and Nessa mopped up the splash of wine that had ended up on the table. They fell silent as the waiter arrived with their food but resumed the conversation as soon as he'd left.

"How did Adam propose, Nessa?" Bree looked at her older sister. "Or are you another sister who caught her man and brought him kicking and screaming to the altar?"

"No," said Nessa dreamily. "He proposed to me. Romantically."

"Naturally," said Cate.

"He's a romantic sort of person," Nessa told her.

"So, how, Nessa?"

"In the car," said Nessa. "At Howth Summit."

"Don't tell us what you were doing at Howth Summit." Bree giggled. "I've seen cars parked there with the windows all steamed up."

"We didn't steam up the windows," said Nessa primly. "We were looking at the view."

Cate and Bree guffawed.

"We were!" protested Nessa. "And he said something like me being more lovely than all the flowers on the hillside or the stars in the sky or something like that and he asked me to marry him."

"You're joking," said Bree.

"Why should I be joking?"

"Adam never struck me as a swooning romantic sort," she said. "I thought it'd be more pragmatic with Adam somehow."

"Oh, no," said Cate. "Adam is a gesture kind of man, isn't he? Although I'd have thought he'd propose to you over a candlelit dinner."

"Yes, well, he's not as clichéd as you think," said Nessa pertly.

"Obviously," said Cate.

"And he did propose to me," said Nessa.

"You mean, I had to force Finn?" Cate's voice was dangerously calm.

"Of course not," said Nessa. "Let's face it, you can't force anyone to marry you."

"Oh, I dunno," said Bree. "What about all those shotgun weddings?"

"They don't happen anymore," said Nessa dismissively.

"Finn would've asked me," Cate said. "But, like I said, the time was right so I just did it."

"And you were right," said Bree firmly. "Finn is one of those guys who probably waits around for everything to happen. Adam is a businessman. Makes a decision, gets the job done. Even though he probably would prefer to think of himself as a laid-back type of person."

"I don't think he cares," said Nessa.

"Oh, absolutely." Bree shook her head. "Your husband would like to be seen as the young, trendy type."

"Trendy?" Nessa laughed. "Adam?"

"He's not so much trendy as a connoisseur," said Cate. "He likes the good things in life, doesn't he, Ness?"

"I suppose so." Nessa nodded. "He prefers to spend the money and buy something good than make do with an inferior product."

"You can tell by his clothes," said Cate. "Always expensive."

"So are yours," said Nessa.

"Only because I like to dress well for work," said Cate.

"That's not a work dress." Nessa nodded at her sister's red outfit. "It's far to clingy."

"Is there something wrong with it clinging to me?" demanded Cate.

"Of course not!"

"Girls, girls!" Bree did a passable imitation of their mother's voice.

"I like nice clothes too," said Nessa. "I just can't afford them all the time."

"Oh, come on!" Cate said. "You're not exactly impoverished."

"No, but we don't always have loads of money to splash around," said Nessa. "You wouldn't believe how expensive a kid is. And it's all very well to tell me that I should say no to her ever-increasing demands but if the other kids have stuff I feel bad if she doesn't."

"Either way you've a lot more than me," said Bree. "I think I've got a leak in my bank account or something. No matter how much money goes in, more seems to go out."

"You're not organized," said Cate. "Anyone who says that they can't manage money is simply not organized."

"You're far too organized!" complained Bree. "Anyway, since I don't have a bloke to spend money on me I have to look after myself."

"Isn't there anyone in your life?" asked Nessa. "You should have someone, Bree."

Bree shook her head. "There was Steve. He was living with me for a couple of weeks."

"You never said anything about a Steve before!" exclaimed Cate.

"We weren't an item," said Bree.

"Sounds to me like you were," Nessa said. "You don't let any stray bloke live with you, do you?"

"He's gay," said Bree.

The sisters stared at her.

"Oh, for heaven's sake!" Bree looked at them in frustration. "I was just leading you on! He was sharing with me for a while because he broke up with his boyfriend."

"How do you meet these sort of people?" asked Cate as she poked her fork into the still bubbling lasagne and released an aromatic waft of garlic.

"Steve isn't a 'sort of person'," said Bree indignantly. "He's very nice."

"Though not exactly boyfriend material," suggested Cate.

"I'm not looking for a boyfriend," said Bree.

"You know, I can't remember a time when I didn't have a boyfriend," mused Nessa.

Cate giggled. "I can. When Tom McArdle broke it off with you and you pined after him for weeks."

"I didn't pine," said Nessa tartly.

"Yes you did!" Bree was relieved they'd got off the subject of her love life. "I remember that too. You kept scribbling his name on bits of paper."

Nessa made a face. "He was an Aries, like Cate. It never would have worked. We didn't agree on anything."

"You surely don't think that your star signs had anything to do with it," said Cate.

"Not really," admitted Nessa after a pause. "It was really because he'd met someone with a smaller bum and bigger tits."

The two younger sisters dissolved into laughter at the outrage in Nessa's voice.

"What upsets you more?" asked Cate. "The smaller bum or the bigger tits?"

"The smaller bum, I suppose," said Nessa. "Since Jill my tits have turned into Tom's dream chest."

"What about you, Cate?" asked Nessa. "Did you have a boyfriend-free zone in your life?"

"Oh, sure," replied Cate. "When I was at college, much to my regret. I know I should've had loads of them then but I went through my very serious phase. I was thinking about starting my own business and making pots of money so men would've been a distraction."

"You were really into it at one point, weren't you?" asked Bree. "Are you still?"

"Into what?"

"Starting your own business? Making pots of money?"

"Oh, I'm happy doing what I'm doing now," said Cate dismissively. "And as for making money, everyone thought you should be coining it in a few years ago and that there was something wrong with you if you weren't. Times change."

"Have you?" Bree picked up the last slice of garlic bread.

"I think so," said Cate. "I'm mellower."

Nessa snorted.

"Don't you think I'm mellower?" demanded Cate.

"Mellow is a state of mind," said Nessa. "I'm not sure you've reached it yet."

"I must be mellow." Cate sounded anxious. "I'm engaged to be married."

"And that's mellow?" Nessa laughed.

Bree refilled their wineglasses while Nessa and Cate continued to debate whether or not Cate was a more relaxed person than she used to be. They were both more relaxed than her tonight, thought Bree. She'd always believed that she was the relaxed one, the chilled-out one, but right now she didn't feel like that. Tonight she felt like the left out one although she told herself over and over again that she was being ridiculous. She was only twenty-five, for heaven's sake.

She was young. She didn't need to be engaged or married. She needed to do exactly what she had been doing for the past five years. Living her life. Having fun. Being single.

Nessa pushed her almost empty plate to one side and sighed. "I'm stuffed. It's so good to get out and eat something without having to worry about washing up."

"You have a dishwasher, don't you?" demanded Bree.

"That's not the point," Nessa told her. "The whole cooking, cleaning, tidying thing is a package. Even stacking plates in a dishwasher takes away the enjoyment of a good meal."

"Unstacking the dishwasher is just as bad," Cate pointed out.

Bree looked at Cate in disgust. "You sound married and settled already! It's as though your entire lifestyle has changed in a week! And you haven't even danced up the aisle yet. What'll you be wearing?"

"I haven't decided yet," said Cate. "Something stylish, though."

"You couldn't be anything but stylish." Nessa tried and failed to keep a note of envy out of her voice.

"So have you decided on a definite date?" asked Bree. "What's the delay? Given that you two have been shacked up for three years why don't you just pop into the registry office and have it done right away?"

"I want to make a day of it," said Cate.

"And does Finn want to sell the exclusive rights to a gossip magazine?" asked Bree.

Cate flushed. "Don't be stupid."

"Maybe the TV station will pay for it," continued Bree. "Turn you both into an item."

"That's even more stupid," said Cate uncomfortably. "It's a private thing."

"All the same," mused Nessa, "I suppose there's a temptation . . ."

"No, there isn't," said Cate. "Nobody's paying for the wedding and nobody's selling photos and it's not some bloody media event, Nessa!"

"Keep your hair on," said Nessa mildly. "We're just having a bit of fun with you."

"Well, don't," snapped Cate. "It's my wedding day we're talking about not some bit of fun."

"It's supposed to be fun," Bree pointed out.

"It will be." Cate stood up. "I'm going to the loo. I'll be back in a minute." She walked across the room while Nessa and Bree watched her.

"Touchy," said Bree.

"Very." Nessa raised her eyebrows. "She doesn't seem in the slightest bit relaxed about it at all, despite what we were saying about being mellow."

"Cate'll never be mellow," Bree said.

"D'you think she's doing the right thing?" asked Nessa. "I mean, I know she's been living with him for ages but maybe it's just not right for them to get married."

"Maybe." Bree shrugged. "How does anyone know?"

"I knew," said Nessa.

"Oh, you." Bree shrugged again. "You were always going to live happily ever after with Adam Riley, weren't you?"

"Not necessarily," said Nessa. "We didn't rush into it."

"Come on!" exclaimed Bree. "I remember the day you brought him home, Ness. You were like the cat with the cream. You positively oozed proprietorial charm."

"Yes, well, I knew he was the one really," admitted Nessa. "Once he phoned me, I knew." She signaled the waiter and ordered another bottle of wine. "How about you?" she asked Bree. "Anyone on the horizon other than gay friends?"

"Oh, you know me," said Bree dismissively. "They're on the horizon for a day, they're in sight for a day and then they're on the other horizon."

"You'll find someone."

"Please!" Bree made a face. "Don't sound so patronizing, Nessa. I may find someone. I may not."

"What may you not do?" Cate sat down at the table again.

"Find someone," Bree told her. "Now that you're about to get hitched, Nessa's turning her attention to me."

"I'm not," said Nessa. "I just asked."

"And have you found someone, Bree?" asked Cate.

"No!" Bree waved her hands in exasperation. "But I'm sure we're going to discuss it. Or Nessa will lecture me about it."

"I'm not going to lecture you," protested Nessa.

"You don't need to settle down," said Cate. "You're only a kid."

"I am not!" cried Bree.

"But you're still living in a grotty flat and staying up till all hours."

"I like my grotty flat," said Bree. "Honestly, you two are going to be impossible if you gang up on me." She sighed. "Look, maybe one day I might want to be with someone for a while but not yet. OK?"

She groaned as she saw the sympathetic looks that her sisters gave her.

"Don't look at me like that!" she cried. "You're making me feel like a total failure!"

"Bree!" Nessa's voice was shocked. "I don't think of you as a failure."

"Neither do I," said Cate. "I always envied you, Bree. Footloose, fancy-free and not chained by some mad notion of being a career woman like me."

"I didn't think you felt chained," said Bree. "I thought you were happy."

"I *am* happy," Cate told her forcefully. "I really am. But sometimes I feel pressurized."

"How?"

"The company depends on me," she said. "I'm an essential person there. If I don't perform, we lose sales. I think about it all the time. And sometimes it makes me feel sick."

"If it's bothering you, you should leave," Bree said. "Nothing's worth feeling sick over."

"Absolutely," agreed Nessa. "Cate, you'll get an ulcer or something if you worry too much. No wonder you look pained and thin sometimes. Does Finn know?"

"You're blowing it up out of proportion," said Cate. "I like feeling this way. All I'm saying is that sometimes it'd be nice not to have to care. I'm not saying that I don't want to. Besides, we got the shoe order last week. The pressure's off again."

Bree looked at her doubtfully. "If you're sure . . ."

"I think I know what you mean," said Nessa. "Sometimes I'm rushing around after Jill and I wish that I had just a minute to myself only I don't because I know Adam will be home soon and that he's had a stressful day and he'll want to unwind and I suppose I feel pressurized too."

"I thought you lived an idyllic life," said Bree.

"I'm very happy," said Nessa. "It's simply that occasionally it goes wrong. And you feel stressed by it."

"So," Cate said. "Both Nessa and I get stressed in spite of the fact that we're both doing exactly what we want to do. Yet you don't, Bree. Why? What have you got that we haven't?"

Bree looked at them and scratched the back of her head. "Actually, it's what you both have that I haven't," she told them.

"What?" asked Nessa.

"Men in your lives," said Bree.

They ordered another bottle of wine and their conversation became more giggly. Bree told them more about Steve and they said he sounded really nice and very sweet. Nessa related a story about the night that Adam had come home out of his tree with drink from some office function and had pissed onto the gas fire. Cate told about the day when she'd really and truly lost it in the office and had screamed and roared at everyone and then one of the guys had muttered "time of the month" and she'd hurled a bottle of Tippex at him. The bottle had split open and covered him in the sticky white solution and she'd been horrified. She'd also footed the cleaning bill.

Nessa talked too about having to accept that she'd probably never have another child and how hard that had been. For Adam's sake, she told them, she didn't want to make a big issue of it and so she never had, but sometimes it got to her. Rarely, now, but sometimes.

Cate said that the thought of being pregnant absolutely terrified her but that she and Finn had already agreed that children weren't on the agenda for quite a while. Especially not with Finn's great new job.

And Bree said that it was OK being twenty-five and a mechanic without a permanent love interest except that people were so bloody judgmental and that she was certain that some men thought that she was a lesbian only she absolutely wasn't. She knew that she wasn't. And just because she preferred jeans to Dolce e Gabbana it didn't mean that she had any problems with her sexuality. And, to set the record straight in case they needed any reassurance, she wasn't a virgin.

They left the restaurant after midnight, drunk and silly, their arms around each other.

"Will you be OK in a taxi on your own?" Nessa asked Bree.

"Of course I will." Bree tried to look witheringly at her but only succeeded in squinting. "I'm grown up."

"I know," said Nessa. "It's just that when you've changed someone's nappy you have a certain view of them."

"You sure do!" Cate giggled and got a fit of hiccoughs.

"Here's a cab." Nessa stood out on Amiens Street and hailed it. She bundled Bree into the backseat. "Take care. See you soon."

"Cheers." Bree sat back and gave her address to the driver who headed south of the river.

It was another five minutes before Cate and Nessa managed to get a cab going northside.

"I enjoyed myself tonight," Nessa told her sister. "We don't get out much, do we? We used to meet at Mum and Dad's but that's not an option anymore."

"I was thinking that myself," said Cate. "We definitely should do it more often."

"Once a month maybe?"

"Maybe."

"I'll organize it," said Nessa. "We could come to my house next time."

"No!" Cate's tone was more vehement than she intended and Nessa looked at her in surprise. "When we go to your house it's different," said Cate. "It's you and Adam and Jill and you're a family. Being out tonight, it's the three of us who are the family."

"I never thought of it like that," said Nessa. "But you're right."

"That's me." Cate yawned. "Philosophical after a few glasses of wine."

"Aren't we all," said Nessa ruefully. "I'm really glad about you and Finn, Cate."

"So am I."

"Though surprised that you were the one who asked."

"You shouldn't have been," said Cate. "Don't you always say I'm the one who gets what she wants?"

"I wasn't sure that was what you wanted."

"I wasn't sure myself," admitted Cate. "Not until I asked."

"At least he said yes."

"I know." Cate sighed and closed her eyes. "But for one horrible minute, Nessa, I thought he was going to say no."

8

♥

Sun in Cancer, Moon in Libra
Generous of time and heart.

It was a long time since Nessa had woken up with a hangover. In fact, as she opened one eye and tried to focus on the alarm clock, she couldn't even remember the last time she'd had a hangover. She'd been surprised at the amount she'd managed to consume in Il Vignardo's last night but it had seemed right at the time because they'd been having so much fun. Now she wished she'd been a little less girly and a little more motherly because Jill's voice, calling her from outside the bedroom door, was like a dentist's drill going through her head.

"Get up, Mum!" Jill hollered. "It's really late."

Nessa blinked a couple of times then dragged herself upright in the bed. It was nearly ten o'clock—very late in Jill's scheme of things. She looked at the empty space in the bed where Adam should be. He didn't normally get up before her, but she was usually out of bed by nine at the latest on Saturday mornings. And awake long before then, listening to Jill getting her own breakfast and pottering around the house.

"I'm awake," she called out and Jill pushed open the bedroom door.

"Dad said not to wake you," she told Nessa. "But someone knocked on the door. I didn't answer it 'cos I'm not allowed but I thought it was time you got up anyway."

"Where's Dad?" Nessa couldn't even remember him getting out of the bed earlier. Either she'd been even more zonked than she'd thought or he'd been especially quiet.

"He got a phone call," explained Jill. "He said he'll be back for lunch."

"Oh good." Nessa moved her head experimentally from side to side. The bricks she felt were inside it slithered around and banged off her skull.

"Dad said that you went out with Bree and Cate and got drunk," said Jill accusingly.

"We had a few drinks," Nessa admitted. "Cate was celebrating."

"Because she's going to marry Finn. I know," said Jill.

"That's why we had a few drinks," Nessa told her.

"Dad said that you were senseless when you got home."

"I wasn't," said Nessa crossly. "I was tired. It was late. And your father has no right to say I was senseless."

I never tell him he's senseless, she muttered under her breath as she eased herself out of the bed. Even on the nights when he's been out with the lads and comes home absolutely rat-arsed. Those nights were few and far between, she conceded, but that wasn't the point. They had a rule that they never criticized each other in front of Jill.

"I was watching *One Hundred and One Dalmatians* on video," said Jill. "But it's finished. I want to go out and play with Nicolette."

"You're speaking to Nicolette again, are you?" asked Nessa.

"I was always speaking to her," said Jill.

"I thought you'd dumped her for Natalie in Galway," Nessa said.

"Oh, Mum!" Jill looked at her pityingly. "You're so not with it."

Nessa laughed and groaned as the pain ricocheted around her head.

"Do you feel really awful?" asked Jill. "Are you totally hungover?"

"It's not that bad," said Nessa. "I'll survive."

"Miss Fitzgerald says that alcohol is a drug. And drugs are bad for you. Like cigarettes," Jill informed her piously.

"Yes, drugs are bad for you," said Nessa. "So are cigarettes. Sometimes people do things that they know are bad for them anyway. Too much alcohol is certainly bad for you."

"So why do people do it?" asked Jill.

"Why do you eat two ice creams one after the other even though you know it'll give you a tummyache?"

"Because it's nice," said Jill.

"So's wine," Nessa told her. "But not the morning after."

She went downstairs and watched from the porch as her daughter crossed the road and knocked on Nicolette's door. Jean Slater opened the front door, waved at Nessa and ushered Jill inside. Nessa was relieved that Jill was playing in Nicolette's right now and not the other way around. She couldn't have coped with two eight-year-olds running around the house today.

God, she felt dreadful. There had been a time, she knew, when she would've been able to drink wine and not feel utterly wrecked the next day but that time belonged to a different Nessa, the unmarried Nessa, Nessa before she became a mother.

Being a mother changed everything. Even though everybody told you how different things would be it was impossible to absorb the enormity of it. The way your life suddenly became someone else's. The way nothing was more important than the welfare of your child, no slight to them too small for you to be up in arms about, no concern of theirs too trivial for you to ignore. And, of course, it was impossible to have hangovers with children because you didn't have time to wallow in pain and misery in your bed when someone was demanding your attention.

It had been good of Adam to get up so quietly and to have ensured that Jill was washed and dressed all without waking her. Nessa considered making him his favorite meal, chicken dopiaza, for dinner that night but the thought of the spices made her feel ill.

She made herself a cup of tea and sat down at the kitchen table. He'd left the newspaper open at the horoscopes page, which amused her. Like everyone, he laughed at her for reading them and, like everyone, he loved it when they were right.

"You've been burning the candle at both ends," she read as she sipped her tea. *"You need time to recharge your batteries. A quiet day would be a good idea."*

Bree pressed the button which lowered the Fiat Brava down to ground level. She got into the car and drove it to the concourse outside the workshop, glad that this morning's jobs had all been fairly straightforward. The Brava had needed its brake discs replaced, and all of her earlier jobs had been just as simple.

She got out of the car and brought the keys back to reception.

"You look the worse for wear today," said Christy. "Where were you last night?"

"Out with my sisters," said Bree. "Cate got engaged."

"Cate—the cool one?"

Bree grinned. "Yep."

"Didn't think she was the sort who believed in marriage," said Christy. "I thought she was one of those career woman feminist types."

"You can be a career woman and still believe in marriage," said Bree mildly.

"Oh, I don't know." Christy looked wistful. "It's not that I don't think women can do a good job—sure, you're a great little worker, Bree—but things were easier when they stayed at home."

"Christy Burke, you're a chauvinistic old sod," said Bree. "D'you really think I'd be better off in the kitchen?"

"Only if you could cook," he told her and ducked as she threw an empty Styrofoam cup at him.

The phone rang and Christy picked up the receiver. Bree poured herself another cup of coffee and sipped it slowly. Because she'd been feeling a little fragile this morning she'd worked twice as hard as she normally did. She couldn't understand why she was feeling fragile—unless it was the fact that she normally drank spirits rather than wine. But she'd even felt a little woozy in the taxi last night, surprising herself by closing her eyes until the driver had decanted her outside the flat.

Usually she liked getting home to the flat after a night out. But last night it had felt strangely unwelcoming. For the first time she'd noticed how drab the curtains were and how threadbare the carpet in the living room was. She'd opened the tiny fridge and taken out the only item in it—a half-carton of milk—which she drank in one go. She'd looked at her tiny shower room and sighed at the grubby tiles and then she'd crawled into her unmade bed and lain there quite unable to get to sleep.

She felt inadequate. Until yesterday she'd always felt superior to her sisters but suddenly she'd felt inadequate. She'd rationalized the marriage thing but she couldn't rationalize her sudden feeling that maybe they also had a point about possessions. She'd jeered them, of course, when they got on to the topic of houses and apartments and interior decorating. She'd laughed when Cate and Nessa had held a fifteen-minute discussion on the merits of net curtains versus venetian blinds, roller blinds and roman blinds. Bree hadn't even known there were so many different ways of covering your windows. And she'd laughed even more when Nessa talked about the way that she persuaded Adam that converting the garage had been his idea when he'd been so opposed to it at the start.

Manipulative, she'd said. And not worth the effort.

She didn't want to think that she'd quite like to try her hand at converting a garage into a study. Surely, she thought, her talents would lie the other way around. She should convert the entire house into a garage.

"I'll send someone to see it." Christy's words suddenly reached her and she turned around as he replaced the receiver.

"Want to do a job on site?" he asked.

"What sort of job?"

"Tires," said Christy.

"Tires!" Bree looked at him in disgust. Changing tires wasn't exactly a mechanic's job.

"Do you remember Declan Morrissey?" asked Christy.

Bree frowned.

"You did the service on his son's Fiat," Christy reminded her.

"Oh, of course." She nodded. "The lunatic young driver syndrome."

"That's the one," said Christy. "He's had a visit from some vandals, it seems. They've slashed the tires of his car and his son's car. He wondered whether he'd be better off getting a tire place to come around and deal with it but I said we would. Do you want to do it?"

"Sure, why not." Bree drained the cup and threw it into the refuse sack. "Does he want a full set for both cars?"

"Plus a spare," said Christy. "He drives the Alfa, the son drives the Fiat."

"I remember," said Bree.

"We'll send him a bill," said Christy. "You don't have to get a check or anything."

"OK." Bree yawned. "It'll be nice to get out."

"Don't spend all day at it," warned Christy. "You've a few other things to finish here too, you know."

"Give me a break," said Bree. "You know I've done loads already."

"Oh, all right." Christy looked at her consideringly. "When you've finished the tire job and you drop the van back, you can go home."

"You're all heart, Christy," said Bree as she pushed open the door to the huge storeroom. "Absolutely all heart."

Declan Morrissey lived near the RTÉ studios in Donnybrook. Bree indicated left as she drove down Nutley Lane and found the small turn that led to the Morrissey house. Big houses, she thought, as she looked for number four. Big houses, big money, no wonder Declan had bought a car for his son and was footing the bill for the repairs. Despite his comments about the size of the bill, it probably didn't make the slightest bit of difference to him.

She parked the van outside a detached house with a cobbled driveway where she recognized the yellow Punto she'd worked on previously.

The house was double-fronted, two windows either side of the door and three windows along the front at the upstairs level. The door was painted in olive green with a heavy brass knocker shaped like a lion's head. There were two terracotta urns on the step, overflowing with brightly colored flowers which scented the air. Despite the grandeur of the house, it looked welcoming. Bree lifted the lion's head and knocked on the door.

The man who answered the knock was a younger, entirely sexier version of Declan Morrissey. He was about six feet tall with olive skin and black hair which fell into his huge brown eyes. Bree felt her body tingle as she looked at him.

"I'm here about the tires," she said. "I'm Bree Driscoll. From the garage."

"Hi." He smiled at her and she felt her heart flip over. "I'm Michael. Are you the girl that told Dad I was compensating for a small penis?"

"Of course I didn't say that!" She felt her face flame with embarrassment. "I just said that you drove too fast."

"He lectured me," said Michael. "I take the corners too fast and I drive like a rally driver—a bad rally driver, he told me. I didn't take much notice because he said that some girl in the garage had told him all this but," his brown eyes flickered, "maybe you do know what you're talking about."

"I know what I'm talking about," said Bree. "You're driving that Punto into the ground. What's the point?"

"What's the point in having a fast car if you don't drive it fast?"

"There's laws about how fast you should drive," said Bree. "Why don't you spend a day at Mondello if you want to drive fast?"

"Mondello?"

"You can hire out a Formula Ford and drive it around the track. You can hire a rally car too."

"It wouldn't be the same," said Michael.

"It's great fun," Bree told him.

"Have you done it?"

"Of course."

"How fast?"

"What d'you mean?"

"Your lap time?"

"Pretty fast," she said.

"I bet I'd beat it."

"Perhaps." Her look was challenging.

"I thought I heard voices. Hello again." Declan Morrissey strode into the hallway and smiled at Bree in recognition. "You've been sent out to do the tires, have you?"

"Hello, Mr. Morrissey. Sorry about your bad luck."

"Bastards," said Declan. "You read about this sort of thing but you don't think it'll happen to you."

"Why did it happen to you?" she asked.

"I don't know," said Declan.

"Intimidation," said Michael.

"Don't be stupid." His father looked at him in irritation.

"Dad's involved in a fraud trial at the moment," said Michael. "He thinks someone might be trying to upset him."

"A fraud trial?" Bree looked at them in surprise.

"Dad's a barrister," Michael told her.

That explained the expensive house and the extravagant twenty-first present, thought Bree.

"It's not intimidation," said Declan irritably. "It was just some blokes coming home from the pub drunk or something."

"Either way, I guess I'd better get on with it," said Bree.

"Do you want a hand?" asked Michael.

"I can manage," she said.

"It'd be easier with two of us," said Michael.

She grinned at him. "Actually, no. You'd be in the way. But you can chat to me if you like."

"OK. But I can help you get the tires out of the van."

"Sure."

They rolled the tires into the driveway and Bree jacked up Michael's Punto.

"So why do you do this?" he asked curiously as she slid the front passenger tire into place.

"Why not?" she asked.

"It's not a job you'd expect a woman to do," said Michael.

She looked at him. "I'll pretend you didn't say that."

"Well, it's not," he protested. "You can say all you like about women doing men's jobs but most of them don't want to get their hands dirty."

"Did you just meander out of the jungle or have you learned to be so sexist?" she asked.

"OK, I've never met a girl who likes getting her hands dirty," he said.

She laughed. "I love getting my hands dirty."

"I don't," admitted Michael. "Even though I like to drive fast. I think I take after my mother. She wasn't a hands dirty kind of woman."

"Wasn't?" Bree glanced at him.

"She died," said Michael.

"I'm sorry."

"Thank you."

Bree liked the way he said thank you instead of muttering that it didn't matter like so many people did. She liked his calm acceptance of her condolences.

"It was five years ago," said Michael. "She had cancer."

"That must have been difficult." Bree moved around to the back of the car.

"Not nice," admitted Michael. "And, of course, more difficult for her because she was away from home."

"She died abroad?"

"Ireland was abroad to her," said Michael. "She was from Spain. Valencia."

That explained the dark good looks, thought Bree.

"Have you any brothers or sisters?" asked Bree.

"Two sisters," said Michael. "Marta and Manuela. They got the Spanish names."

Bree grinned. "She liked the letter M, your mum."

"I guess so." Michael grinned back at her. "My sisters are both younger. Marta is eighteen. Manuela is fourteen."

"I'm the youngest in my family," Bree told him. "I've two older sisters." She lowered the Punto and tightened the bolts. "OK, now to your Dad's car."

Declan Morrissey drove the same top-of-the-range Alfa as Adam.

Bree and Michael brought the wheels into the driveway and she began the task of fitting them.

"And your sisters, how old are they?" asked Michael as he watched her.

"Nessa is thirty-four. Cate is thirty."

"And you?"

"I'm twenty-five," said Bree. She looked up at him. "Getting old!"

"You look very young," Michael said. "I thought you were a kid when you knocked at the door."

"The overalls might have been a giveaway." Bree glanced down at her blue working clothes with the Crosbie's garage logo emblazoned on the pocket.

"A little," said Michael.

"Michael! Phone!" Declan stood at the front door and called his son. Bree continued to work in silence. Pity he was younger than her, she thought as she fitted the last tire. He was very, very attractive. But probably a weirdo like all the others.

She checked the nuts on the tires, stood up and wiped her hands on the seat of her pants. Then she knocked on the front door again.

"Finished?" It was Declan who answered it this time.

She nodded.

"That was quick."

"It's not difficult," said Bree. "Pain in the neck for you, though."

"Oh well." Declan shrugged philosophically. "These things happen." He smiled at her. "Would you like a cup of tea or anything before you go?"

Bree wrestled with her conscience. A drink of anything would be nice, she was still feeling dehydrated from the previous night. But she really only wanted to say yes because it might mean seeing Michael again. Which was pathetic.

"I'd love a cup," she said.

"Great," said Declan. "This way."

He lead her through an elegant tiled hallway into a bright, sunny kitchen. The enormous pine table was covered in newspapers and magazines. Michael was leaning against the wall and talking fast and fluent Spanish on the phone. Bree liked the liquid sounds of the Spanish words. She understood a little of his conversation, the Spanish that she'd learned during her time in Spain coming back to her. But Michael was talking about Ireland, about the U2 concert he'd been to at Croke Park. Bree had been to that concert too.

Declan filled the kettle and placed two china mugs on the table. "Milk?"

Bree nodded.

"Sugar?" asked Declan. "Are you like all tradesmen—loading up your tea with sugar?"

"You're supposed to call us tradespeople." Bree grinned. "And sometimes I take sugar but not always."

"So—this time?"

She shook her head.

He took a bright yellow teapot from the shelf and poured hot water into it. Bree felt as though she should be doing something to help but she didn't quite know what.

"Of course I miss you!" Michael had switched to English and Bree felt his words like a dagger through her heart. Typical, she thought. I see a man, I like him but he's involved with someone else. Someone Spanish, it seems. Maybe he met a girl the last time he was there.

Declan saw her eyes flicker in his son's direction.

"He's talking to his sisters," said Declan. "They're staying with Monica's parents for a few weeks."

"Monica?"

"My late wife," said Declan.

"Yes," said Bree. "Michael told me about her. I'm sorry."

"Thank you."

The same polite acceptance. The same clear, candid eyes. Declan was nearly as attractive as his son.

"They're having a great time." Michael replaced the receiver and sat down at the table with them. "But Mannie is feeling a little homesick." He looked at Bree. "She was the one who'd spent the least time in Spain."

Bree nodded in understanding although she didn't really understand because she'd never felt homesick in her life. Even when she'd lived in Spain. She'd lived for the moment, never thinking about life anywhere else.

The kettle boiled and Declan filled the teapot. He placed a plate of scones on the table. Bree eyed them hungrily. She hadn't eaten earlier because of her hangover but she was starving now.

"Take one," said Michael. "If you don't, Dad'll be very hurt."

"No I won't," said Declan. "Don't feel obliged to eat anything if you don't want to, Bree."

"Actually, I will have one." She took a scone and cut it in half. "I'm ravenous."

Michael laughed. "If only the girls ever said that!"

"Marta and Manuela are always on diets," explained Declan. "I try to tell them that they don't need to be but I know I'm wasting my time."

"I've never been on a diet." Bree spoke through a mouthful of crumbs. "I can't see the point, really. I know that I'm a biggish girl and I honestly can't see myself being happier if I was existing on lettuce leaves all day."

"You need muscles to lift those tires around the place," said Michael.

"You didn't let her lift them!" Declan looked shocked.

"It's my job, Mr. Morrissey," said Bree. "If Christy had come out to do it, you wouldn't have had Michael lifting tires for him."

Michael laughed but Declan looked uncomfortable.

"I'd better be off." Bree drained her cup. "Thank you very much for the tea. And the scone was absolutely delicious."

"It's Dad's secret talent," said Michael.

"What?"

"Baking." Michael told her. "Didn't you realize they were home-cooked?"

"They tasted really good," said Bree. "But I didn't imagine . . ."

Declan grinned. "You lug tires, I bake scones. Equality in action."

"Absolutely," she said.

Michael walked with her to the door.

"Will we see you again?" he asked.

"I hope not," said Bree. "I don't like to think that your tires would be slashed two nights in a row."

"Will *I* see you again?" amended Michael.

She looked at him, feeling a long-dormant thud of excitement in her heart. He was only twenty-one though. Young for a potential boyfriend. Too immature? Twenty-one-year-old blokes were babies really. But he seemed different. And he'd spoken of his mother with regret but not in the uncomfortable way that many men did when they talked about bereavement.

"How?" she asked.

"A drink?" he suggested. "At the weekend if you're free?"

"Sounds good."

"Will I phone you?" he asked.

"Will you?" She grinned at him.

"Of course."

"OK then." She reached into the pocket of her overalls and took out a dog-eared business card which she handed to him.

"I'll phone," he promised.

"Great."

She climbed into the van and switched on the ignition. She wasn't feeling ropey anymore. The vestiges of her hangover had disappeared. She glanced over her shoulder as she eased out of the drive. He was still standing at the doorway of the house and he waved as she drove away.

Cate didn't have a hangover. She hadn't drunk very much the previous night although she'd made sure that both Nessa and Bree's glasses were always filled. But she hadn't felt like drinking, hadn't even felt very hungry which, she told herself, was an excellent development.

She stood in front of the full-length mirror in the bedroom and looked at herself. Despite the constant dieting, she'd put on weight in the last month. Cate hated carrying extra pounds, she felt as though her body had betrayed her whenever she stood on the scales and realized how much she was over her target 112 pounds. She was always over her target, it was impossible for someone of her height and build to weigh any less than 119 pounds without starving herself to death. According to her height/weight ratio graph her ideal weight was actually 126 pounds. But she liked the idea of being underweight. It made her feel more self-confident.

She didn't weigh herself very often because she didn't want to disappoint herself. Not hopping on the scales every day made her feel proud—she wasn't a food junkie or a weight junkie or someone who couldn't look at a slice of cake without mentally adding up how many calories it contained. She was simply a woman who could regulate her eating habits.

But she knew that if she stepped on the scales this morning it would tip closer to nine stone than to eight. Much closer. If not over. She could see it in her shape. Less Biro, more blancmange, she thought. She wondered if people actually ate blancmange anymore. She couldn't remember having ever eaten it herself.

She studiously ignored the scales and looked at her reflection in the bathroom mirror. Even if (and despite last night's excesses) her skin looked good and her hair hung in a glossy sheen around her face, it meant nothing if she wobbled her way through the day.

She pulled the fawn towel tighter around her.

She couldn't remember when exactly the thought hit her but she felt the sudden surge of panic and bile rise in her stomach. She swallowed hard and exhaled slowly to quell the rapid beating of her heart.

That wasn't possible, she told herself. It just wasn't.

She opened the bottom drawer of the bathroom unit and peered inside. She pulled out a box of Tampax and looked inside as she frantically started to do some mental arithmetic. The box was nearly empty. She remembered buying it—an emergency dash from the office to the chemist down the road one Monday afternoon. But which Monday afternoon? A warm Monday because she remembered wishing that she wasn't in such a rush to get back into the office. It had been a difficult morning and she'd been bad-tempered and irritable and she'd had a row with Finn the night before. But that was ages ago. Before they'd got engaged. She frowned. Surely she'd had a period since then. Surely.

She sat on the edge of the toilet seat and turned the box over and over in her hand. The sunlight streaming through the bathroom window reflected off the diamond ring on her finger.

She stood up and let the towel drop at her feet. She stood sideways in front of the mirror and looked at her body. Were her breasts fuller? They'd ached a little last week but she hadn't given it any thought. She cupped one in her hand and wondered if it actually felt bigger. Her stomach. Well, it was certainly rounder. But it did that whenever she ate too much. Which was why she didn't. She rubbed it gently. Her skin was soft.

She'd definitely missed a period. Definitely. She'd worked it out now. There hadn't been one since the day she'd started it in the office. How could she not have noticed?

Of course it didn't have to mean that she was pregnant. Besides, birth control was part of the fun for them. Finn told her that the way she rolled a condom onto him was almost a sex act in itself. And she enjoyed the sensation of the extra-ribbed versions that they often used. Was is possible that one of them had been damaged and they hadn't even noticed? She shook her head. Surely not. Her heartbeat steadied a little as she took a deep breath and rewrapped herself in the towel. She'd been under pressure lately and everyone knew that stress could knock your cycle out of sync. Feeling bloated didn't have to be because she was incubating a child, for heaven's sake! That could probably happen if you were under stress too. And the last few weeks had been stressful, what with thinking that it might be all over with Finn and then suddenly, joyously, realizing that it had only just begun. They hadn't been able to keep their hands off each other since they'd decided to get married. They'd made love every single night and occasionally during the day too. Instead of feeling settled and familiar with him now that they were engaged, the whole thing had raised the level of excitement they felt with each other. She'd surprised herself by waking up at 3 A.M. a couple of nights earlier and reaching out for him, pulling him closer to her, then suddenly rolling on top of him so that his eyes opened wide in surprise. And he'd grinned at her and taken her breast in his mouth, his tongue playing around her nipple until she was almost frantic with pleasure. It had been the best sex ever. They hadn't forgotten protection that night either. Although, she remembered, they'd used an older packet of condoms that had been lying in her bedside locker for a couple of months because with all the extra sex they'd run out of the ribbed ones.

She couldn't be pregnant, she told herself again. She couldn't be. Being pregnant would ruin everything. And things had only just started to go right.

9

♥

Sun in the 7th House

Relationships with others extremely important, guard against emotional dependence.

*T*he Year Ahead for Cancerians had promised a quiet week and that was exactly what Nessa was getting. It was the week when Jill went to the summer camp organized by the school, which meant that Nessa had five almost full days to herself. She'd looked

forward to this week ever since the beginning of the far too long
summer holidays and she'd made lots of plans for her freedom days.
She'd promised herself some time walking along the coast and simply chilling out but, in fact, she'd spent most of the week visiting the
different shopping centers in the city and spending money that she
didn't really have. Monday had been Blackrock and Dun Laoghaire,
Tuesday she'd gone to Blanchardstown, Wednesday had been the
turn of Liffey Valley, and on Thursday she'd gone into the city center where she'd strolled up and down Grafton Street, a treat which
she hadn't managed to have in months. Usually when she went
shopping, Jill came with her, dragging out of her hand and complaining that she was bored. The only times she perked up were
when they went into HMV or Virgin where she demanded the
newest CD by whatever happened to be the latest hot boy band or
girl band, but the rest of the time she dragged her heels and scuffed
her toes and drove Nessa crazy. Jill liked nice clothes but she wanted
them to be brought home to her. She made lists of things she liked
and the shops that they had to be bought in. Malahide was a hotbed
of designer one-upmanship as far as eight-year-olds were concerned.

It had been wonderful to wander around the shops all by herself,
Nessa thought wistfully. Especially when she could sit in a café afterward for a cappuccino and doughnut without having to keep an eye
on her squirming daughter. On Monday, her oldest friend, Paula
Trelfall, had come with her on the shopping expedition and they'd
giggled their way through Next and Principles, looking at clothes
that were far too young for them but wanting to buy them anyway.
Paula had married John the year before Nessa and Adam had married
but, after six years and three children, John and Paula had split up.

Now Paula worked full time in the insurance company she'd left
when she married and earned twice as much money because they
were desperate to get experienced people and because they realized
the value of employing women with children who weren't likely to
rush off and change jobs on a whim. It had taken Paula two years to
sort out her life after John but she'd done it.

"I admire you." Nessa said it every time she met her friend.

"There's nothing to admire," Paula told her. "I just got on with
things. That's what women do, Nessa. We get on with things."

"You hardly had a choice," Nessa pointed out.

"That's why." Paula grinned wryly. "You have three kids depending on you—well, you don't have time to sit around wallowing in misery. At least, not when they're up and about. You have to carry on. Pretend that everything's all right. Even when it's not."

"But everything is all right now?" Nessa beckoned the waitress in the café where they'd stopped for coffee and cakes and asked for refills.

"Nessa, nothing is as perfect as you want it to be," said Paula. "There are times when I'm fucking miserable! I look at myself and think that I'm thirty-four and I have three kids and what chance do I have of another serious adult relationship? Who takes on a woman with three kids? Who wants to? Besides," she sighed as she added lumps of cane sugar to her coffee, "I don't want to be 'taken on' by anyone anymore. I've worked things out for me and the kids and I'm happy about it. I'm not sure I could cope with some bloke tramping home and putting his size elevens on our brand-new sofa."

Nessa smiled at her. "Maybe when the kids are older?"

"Don't be daft, Nessa." Paula withered her with a look. "By then I'll be in my late forties and no man is going to look past my fine lines and wrinkles and think that underneath beats the heart of a twenty-year-old."

"It doesn't seem fair, does it?" asked Nessa.

"Of course it's not fair," agreed Paula. "But it's the way things work out!"

Nessa mulled over the conversation as she packed her bag for the gym. This was her last day of freedom and she'd mapped it all out. A session (not too long) on the bikes and the ab crunch machines, followed by a couple of lengths of the pool, then a sauna and jacuzzi. Finally, a trip to the hairdresser to get her low-lights done and some shape on her untidy locks.

And after that, she thought, as she zipped the bag closed, it was back to being Adam's wife and Jill's mother and she was so, so happy to be Nessa Riley, still married and still loved. Poor old Paula, she thought. It wasn't easy for her and, of course, she had to live with the knowledge that her shit of a husband had found someone new. Paula hadn't met the replacement woman in John Trelfall's life and she didn't want to. Bad enough to know that the bitch existed, Paula said, even though the bitch hadn't actually been the cause of them splitting up. That had been the result of John's brief but torrid relationship with his secretary.

"I hadn't thought that things like that still happened," Paula had told Nessa miserably when she found out. "His fucking secretary, Ness! Don't you think he could've been more inventive?"

The sun was shining as Nessa opened the boot of the car and threw the bag inside. I should go to the beach, she thought, not the gym. I should jog barefoot along the strand and then plunge into the sea instead of the pool. She shivered at the thought. It didn't matter how glorious the day was, the sea was always freezing.

The gym was a ten-minute drive from the house. She swung into the car park and left the car near the entrance. Then she grabbed her bag and ran up the steps. My warm-up, she thought. It was months since she'd last worked out. She swiped her card and waited for the receptionist to laugh at her for even daring to show her face. But the raven-haired beauty behind the desk simply smiled a corporate welcome smile and waved her through.

I should come more often. Nessa always had the same thought when she stood in the changing rooms and looked at the tanned and toned bodies of women who weren't embarrassed to be seen in a bra and thong. Nessa knew that she'd never have the nerve to wear a thong, not with her cellulite. She'd long since decided that she was approaching an age when gravity starts to take hold and where she shouldn't expect everything to stay in the same place as it was before. I need to work at being the sort of woman I used to be, she thought, as she pulled on last year's support top and shorts. And even then I'll never quite manage it. Not after giving birth to a ten-pound baby girl. After a few months of fruitless effort she'd accepted that it was impossible to get her body back to the exact shape it had been before, absolutely impossible. She didn't know how actresses and models actually did it—even with their armies of personal trainers and macrobiotic diets. There were bits of you that had just changed beyond recognition and she couldn't see how you could haul them back into shape no matter how hard you tried.

But Adam liked her like this. He'd said so one night when she'd been feeling a bit down because Jill had a cold and had been fractious all day and because she hadn't had time to wash her hair or even to brush a little bit of bronzer over her face like she normally did. When they'd gone to bed, she'd lain beside Adam and asked him, straight out, whether or not he fancied her anymore. Whether it was possible to fancy a woman with baby food in her hair and boobs which had tripled in size but which weren't round and firm like the Baywatch babes.

"I love you like this," he'd said as he pulled her toward him. "I love to snuggle up to you and hold you tight and know that there's actually something to hold on to."

"Why don't you then?" she'd asked and was rewarded by him hugging her fiercely and making love to her with the same kind of passion that he'd shown on their first night together.

Maybe I'll take the initiative tonight, she mused, as she slung her towel around her neck and headed for the treadmill. I'll cook him a nice meal and shove a bottle of Chablis in the fridge and later on, when Jill is in bed, I'll jump on him. She giggled aloud at the thought. Actually, she told herself, much better if she didn't do any cooking and they just sent out for pizzas as they had done when they were first married. They never did that anymore; in her quest to become the domestic goddess of his dreams she'd invested in every celebrity cookbook ever written and had even learned to make her own pizza dough.

Her breathing grew more labored as she increased the incline on the machine. I'm so out of condition, she muttered as she gritted her teeth. I used to be more able for this.

Ten minutes later she'd had enough and wandered down to the pool where she swam a lazy couple of lengths before heading into the sauna. She poured water over the coals and lay down on the top bench, using her towel as a pillow as she let the dry heat penetrate her bones.

The door opened but she didn't bother opening her eyes. She wasn't in the mood for casual chit-chat today, she simply wanted to relax and recharge her batteries. A whole week of shopping had taken it out of her although she had to admit that her tiredness was pleasurable rather than the drained exhaustion she often felt by Friday afternoons.

"So tell me what happened?" The sound of a girl's voice broke the tranquility of the sauna. For a brief moment Nessa thought that the girl was talking to her. She half turned but before she'd even opened her eyes, another voice answered.

"He just told me it was over." The second girl's voice was flat and emotionless, though vaguely familiar.

"What a shit."

"He didn't even try to deny it!" She raised her voice slightly. "I mean, Terri, you'd think he'd at least try to deny it, wouldn't you?"

"How could he?" asked Terri. "I'd seen him with her, hadn't I? He knew you'd believe me."

"I didn't want to believe you. I wanted to think that everything was great."

"They're all the same," said Terri sympathetically.

"I know." The other girl sighed. "You trust them. You invest a whole heap of emotion in them and they still let you down." She sighed again, even more heavily. "But I thought that this was going somewhere. Six months, Terri."

"Portia, you're far too young to get that involved."

Nessa's eyes flickered open. She remembered that name. The name of Mitchell Ward's girlfriend. The girl whose father's car Adam had reversed into. She'd called Mr. Laing after talking to Portia in the kitchen and had explained everything. They'd sorted things out without having to resort to the insurance companies. Was this the same girl? She sounded like the same girl. Honestly, thought Nessa, if she was, then Mitchell hadn't behaved awfully well if he'd two-timed her!

"I know I shouldn't be thinking about serious involvement," said Portia gloomily. "But he was so gorgeous, Terri. And why couldn't he have told me it was over before I found out about the other girl?"

"They're all the same," said Terri resignedly. "Want to have their cake and eat it too. All of them."

"You're right, I suppose." Portia sighed. "I saw his next-door neighbor the other day. Remember I told you about the incident with him? Lovely wife, lovely daughter. But there he was in the Old Stand with his tongue down some woman's throat."

There was a moment's silence while Nessa felt as though she'd just been thumped in the chest. A wave of nausea washed over her.

"What a shit." Terri sounded indignant.

"I know," said Portia. "And she was so nice to me and everything. Gave me a cup of coffee, phoned Dad."

Nessa released the breath she realized she'd been holding. It couldn't be the same Portia, could it? It sounded like her, she knew it sounded like her, but if it was . . . That would mean that she, Nessa Riley, was lying in a sauna listening to two girls talking about her husband kissing another woman. A bed of sweat trickled down the side of her face.

"Do you think she knows?" asked Terri.

"Who?"

"The wife."

"It didn't seem like it at the time." Portia's tone was dismissive. "But how could she not? It's sad, isn't it, that if she does she's still happy to play the dutiful wife and mother."

That's because I *am* a dutiful wife and mother, screamed Nessa silently. And there's no reason for me not to be. You're not the person I thought you were. I made a mistake. And you're certainly not talking about my husband!

"What would you do?" asked Terri. "If your husband cheated on you?"

"Mitch cheated on me and I drank about a hundred vodkas with Red Bull," said Portia. "Hardly the best thing to do."

"But helpful."

"Helpful enough," said Portia. "At least it gave me the courage to laugh at him."

Mitch, thought Nessa frantically. Christ, it is the same Portia.

"They all need to be laughed at," said Terri. "Shower of shits, the lot of them."

"Yeah." Portia didn't entirely sound convinced.

"He was a jerk anyway," said Terri loyally.

"Stop trying to jolly me out of it." Portia sounded irritated. "It's over. I know it's over, he knows it's over. Just let me wallow in the misery at having split up with yet another boyfriend."

"I don't know why you should feel miserable about that," said Terri mischievously. "Variety is the spice of life and all that sort of thing."

"Yes, but I don't necessarily want it to be!"

"You didn't want to split up with Derek last year either but it was all for the best, wasn't it?"

"I suppose so."

"And this is too. Come on, Portia, you're miles too good for him."

"You think so?"

"I know so."

"Same as that bloke's wife is miles too good for him too?"

"Poor woman." Terri's voice was suddenly sympathetic.

"She seemed so nice. Laughing and joking with me," said Portia. "And she wasn't angry with him for smashing up the car or anything. Maybe she puts up with it for the sake of her daughter. For the lifestyle too. She has a lovely daughter. And those houses can't come cheap."

Nessa felt as though her head would explode. She was lying in a sauna listening to a woman telling her that she was only staying with Adam for the sake of her daughter and because she had a nice house. But she wasn't. She was staying with Adam because she loved him and was married to him and because she believed, she really and truly believed, that he felt the same way. And he just couldn't be the person that Portia was talking about because Adam would never kiss someone in public. Not the way that she was describing. Adam was self-conscious like that. He didn't even like holding hands in public. He certainly wouldn't—Nessa shuddered—shove his tongue down someone's throat. Especially not if he was having an affair! He'd be far too discreet to do that if he was having an affair. Adam wasn't having an affair. Somehow she was getting everything mixed up. So this girl was going out with someone called Mitch. It didn't have to be the Mitchell Ward she knew. And her name was Portia. It was an unusual name, certainly, but not as unusual as it once was. She'd mentioned an incident with a car. She said that the man who stuck his tongue down women's throats had smashed his car. Adam hadn't smashed the car. He'd barely dented it. She wondered if she was going to throw up.

"Come on, Terri," said Portia. "I'm warm enough. Let's hop in the plunge pool and head off."

"OK."

Nessa heard the other girl pick up her towel and slide her feet into her flip-flops. The door of the sauna opened, allowing a cool draft of air to lower the temperature a little.

She lay there for a few minutes, unable to move. It was as though someone had thrown a lead weight over her. Her breath came in short gasps and her head spun alarmingly. She was afraid that if she tried to sit up she'd faint.

I'd know, she told herself. I'd know if he was seeing someone else. I really would. It'd be impossible not to know. There'd be giveaway things, like him rushing to pick up the phone or having to go out late to work or coming home reeking of perfume.

He never rushed to pick up the phone. But, she thought, he had a mobile. He worked late sometimes, even occasionally at weekends, but he'd always done that. It was part of his job. She bit her lip hard. Maybe he'd had affairs ever since they were married. Maybe he never worked late at all. She shook her head. She'd often phoned him in the office. Often. And he was there, just as he said. Unless, of course, he was having it off with one of the girls from the company. She traced her finger across her bottom lip which had started to swell from the force of her teeth. He never came home reeking of perfume though. Never. She'd have remembered that. So it couldn't be an affair. It absolutely couldn't.

Even if Adam had kissed another woman (she shivered again at the thought) it might have simply been a platonic sort of kiss, not at all the type of kiss that Portia had described. The girl was probably exaggerating. She'd sort it out. Somehow those girls had got it all mixed up and given her the most momentous fright. But it wasn't true. It couldn't be true. She'd definitely have guessed.

Besides, she thought, as she eventually pushed open the door of the sauna and stepped outside, her horoscope hadn't said anything remotely like this. No upheavals, no disasters, nothing about being deceived. A quiet week, it had said, for recharging batteries. It wouldn't have let her take this blow without warning. Out of nowhere.

She couldn't remember having a shower although she knew that she must have. She couldn't remember drying her hair or smoothing her anti-aging cream into her skin. She couldn't remember getting into the car and driving home. She forgot about her appointment with the hairdresser. She sat at the kitchen table, where not that long ago she'd sat with Portia and with Jill after Adam had pranged the car, and she tried to think of how she might have got things wrong. Only it was difficult. Portia had been so clear.

She got up from the table and picked up *The Year Ahead for Cancerians*. She turned to her page for the day. She'd glanced at it already this morning and it hadn't said anything awful which was why she was so sure that she'd got the wrong end of the stick.

"*Positive planetary activity has you in an equally positive frame of mind,*" it said. "*Unseen hands are helping you. Move swiftly. It's time to make the decisions you've been avoiding until now.*"

Nothing awful. Nothing. She *was* in a positive frame of mind. Certainly she'd been feeling very positive when she set off for the gym. And she remembered the bit about making decisions. She'd thought it was the decision to go to the gym. She'd been putting that off for weeks!

She exhaled slowly. There was no point in getting into a state about things. Not yet. Not until she'd worked out what was really going on. If anything. There couldn't be anything. Could there? Really?

She reached out for the phone and dialed Adam's number. She listened to the ringing tone for a moment then hung up. What could she say to him? Is it true that you're having an affair? Oh, hi, Adam. Listen, just wanted to check—are you being unfaithful to me? When you said that you were out with Mike or Liam or Tim or Jeff, is there any chance that you were actually sitting in a bar with your tongue down someone's throat? She couldn't talk to him. Couldn't speak to him. She needed to see him face to face. Reassure herself that everything was all right. Everything *was* all right. She knew it was. It had to be.

She leaned her head on the kitchen table. Calm. She needed to be calm.

Later, she sat bolt upright and looked at the kitchen clock. It was four o'clock. Jill's camp ended at four. Her daughter would be waiting for her, worrying about her, fretting that she'd forgotten about her on her last day. Nessa grabbed her bag and her car keys, ran her fingers through her badly dried hair and rushed out of the house.

"What happened to you?" Jill's eyes were accusing. The teacher didn't look too happy at having to wait either.

"I'm terribly, terribly sorry," said Nessa. "Something cropped up and I couldn't—"

"Children must be collected by four o'clock, Mrs. Riley," said the teacher.

"I know. I know," said Nessa. "And I really do apologize." She smiled faintly. "Just as well that it's the last day. I wouldn't want her victimized because of me."

"We would never dream of victimizing children!" The teacher sounded shocked.

"I didn't mean it like that." Nessa knew that she was babbling. "I just—I thought—look, come on, Jill, time to go." She took hold of her daughter's arm and steered her toward the car.

"What's wrong?" asked Jill.

"Nothing." Nessa started the car and stalled the engine.

"There must be something wrong."

"There isn't," said Nessa.

"You were late," said Jill.

"I said I'm sorry."

"But you're never late."

"Well, I was today." Nessa realized that she'd snapped at Jill and turned to look at her. Her daughter was staring straight ahead. "I'm sorry," said Nessa. "I got delayed and I was worried that I was late and that's all that's the matter."

"Are you sure?" asked Jill.

"Sure, I'm sure." Nessa smiled at her as she turned onto the coast road and pulled down the visor as the afternoon sun blazed straight into her eyes. She drove faster than usual while all the time telling herself to slow down because Jill was in the car and even though she wouldn't care if she crashed herself she certainly wasn't going to have an accident with her daughter. But it was hard to concentrate on the road ahead, hard to listen to Jill's excited chatter about her day and to answer as though she'd really heard what the little girl said.

She swung the car into the driveway.

"Mum!" Jill cried out in fright as Nessa scraped against the gate which wasn't properly open. "You've pranged the car!"

"It doesn't matter." Nessa unbuckled her seat belt.

"But—but—you never prang the car! Dad prangs the car!"

"Just for once I thought I'd copy your father," said Nessa shakily.

"But Auntie Bree can't fix your car. It's not her make." Jill scrambled from her seat, opened the door and surveyed the ugly gash on the passenger side.

"I'll fix it," Nessa told her. "It only needs a lick of paint."

"But why?" asked Jill. "Why did you do it?"

"Because I wasn't thinking properly," said Nessa. "And that'll teach you to think properly yourself."

Jill stared at her. "And you were late as well," she said accusingly. "Are you having the change of life?"

"What?" Nessa was startled out of her anguish.

"Dorothy's mum is having it," Jill explained. "She goes all hot and cranky. It happens when you get old."

"Thanks," said Nessa. "I didn't realize I was that old."

Jill shrugged. "Dorothy said that her mother does stupid things but her father says it's because of the change."

"I'm not having a change of life," said Nessa. She bit her lip as she opened the hall door. "At least, not that sort."

10

♥

Saturn in Aries

Determined and strong, especially
in difficult circumstances.

Cate opened her bedside locker and took out the pregnancy testing kit. She'd had it for nearly two weeks, since the day after her engagement celebration with her sisters when the horrible thought had struck her and she'd rushed out to buy it. When she got home she changed her mind about using it, feeling suddenly convinced that she couldn't possibly be pregnant and that her missed period was entirely down to the fact that she'd been so stressed at work. Knowing that they'd got the order for the new HiSpeed shoe and that sales figures were going up again, she was certain that her period would come and so she'd hidden the test in her bedside locker beneath her boxes of Tampax and Veet where she knew that Finn wouldn't accidentally discover it. The last thing she needed was Finn questioning her about being pregnant if she wasn't.

Once she'd bought the test and hidden it she'd carried her tampons in her handbag every day, waiting for the moment when she'd need them. She tried to push the whole idea out of her head, knowing that worrying about it could make things worse. Nessa had told her that she often felt it was her own worrying about not getting pregnant a second time that had prevented it. The doctors had advised her not to think about it, to be more relaxed. It would happen of its own accord, they'd told her.

Only it hadn't. For the first time ever Cate wondered how Nessa really felt about her inability to have a second child. Had there been days, she asked herself, when Nessa prayed just as hard that she was pregnant as she, Cate, was now praying that she wasn't? And was there a little part of Nessa which felt cheated? Jill was still an only child and nothing that Nessa had done had changed that.

Cate slowly peeled the cellophane wrapper off the box and looked at it again. She'd come home early from work so that she could do the test when she knew that Finn had a meeting with the TV producer and wouldn't be around to find her. But she was still reluctant to do it. The longer she remained uncertain the longer she could be herself. If she did the test and it was positive then she would become someone different. Right now, as far as she was concerned, she wasn't pregnant. Right now that possibility was still something remote. But once she did the test then it wasn't a possibility anymore. Then it would be a fact. *Could* be a fact, she reminded herself sternly. She'd actually skipped a period once before and she hadn't been pregnant then so she didn't have to be this time.

I don't want a baby, she whispered as she threw the cellophane into the bin and then retrieved it in case Finn saw it and wondered what it was from. I'm not ready for a baby yet. I don't have any maternal feelings. My biological clock hasn't started sounding alarm bells. And my relationship certainly wouldn't be helped by having a child. The last thing Finn and I need right now is a child. Besides, I don't want the pain and the tests and all of the things that go with being pregnant. I'm definitely not ready for that. Finn isn't ready either. He's too caught up in his career and he's right to be caught up in his career. If we had a child now he'd be one of those fathers who, in years to come, would regret that they didn't have time to spend with their kids. She laughed shortly. Maybe he'd be interviewed with his second wife, his young wife, just pregnant with their first child and he'd say that he hoped he'd be around more for this one because he'd been too busy the first time. That was the standard second family interview, wasn't it?

She shivered. Why was she even thinking about him with a second wife? She was going to marry him and she was going to be his only wife and everything was going to be fine. They'd have kids but not yet. They'd talked about it before in a very general way. He believed that you had to establish yourself before you brought anyone else into the world. That you had to have done at least some of the things that you really, really wanted to do. Otherwise you'd resent them afterward for holding you back. You'd be the sort of parent who yelled at your kid with words like "after all I've done for you" while remembering all the things you'd given up just so that you could be there when they needed you. You had to be ready for kids, Finn had told Cate. And then he'd laughed and wondered would he ever be ready. Would he ever get to do all the things he really, really wanted to do.

She opened the package and took out the instructions. He was so close. So very close to doing the thing he wanted to do most. Having a baby wouldn't stop him. But it would cramp his style. And she knew, without a shadow of a doubt, that he would resent it. And her. Which would make her resent it too.

She rubbed the bridge of her nose. Nessa would think that these were selfish thoughts. Nessa would think that Cate didn't want a baby because it didn't fit in with her lifestyle. And it was perfectly true. A baby *couldn't* fit in with a cool, modern apartment on the coast. A baby couldn't fit in with people who worked twelve hours a day. A baby needed time and attention but she and Finn didn't have the time and attention to give it. What would be the point in them having a baby that didn't fit in with their lifestyle? They weren't ready to change. They'd worked hard to get where they were. They didn't want to give it all up now for a baby they weren't ready for. If she was pregnant, people would expect her to be pleased. And, even if she wasn't, they'd expect her to become pleased. But she wouldn't be pleased. Maybe most people would think that being Cate Driscoll and being pregnant by mistake wouldn't be as awful as being an unmarried sixteen-year-old with an unplanned pregnancy. But why wouldn't it? As far as she was concerned, it would be just as awful. Bringing someone into the world when you didn't want them was awful no matter who you were.

She smoothed the instruction sheet and stared at the print but it was blurred and hard to read through the tears that had suddenly filled her eyes.

"I'm not pregnant," she said out loud as she stood up and took the kit to the bathroom. "I'm not."

She'd thought it would take longer. Even though the test had said that she only had to wait a couple of minutes for the blue line to appear she never dreamed it would be so quick. It seemed to her that one second she wasn't pregnant and the next second she was and there was no time in between while she was simply thinking about it. And it wasn't as though it looked uncertain or unclear. It was the most definite blue line she'd ever seen in her life. She put her hand onto her stomach and started to cry.

Nessa felt as though she was outside of herself. She could see herself doing the things that she normally did—tidying up Jill's room, unpegging the clothes from the line, pulling up a few desultory weeds from the flower bed in the back garden—but it was as though a different person was moving through the house, another Nessa walking through the garden. She was still operating on autopilot, suddenly finding herself in the bathroom without remembering even having come up the stairs, or standing at the sink without knowing why. And all the while nothing could rid her head of the thought of Adam and the unknown woman and his tongue down her throat.

It was such a disgusting image. It wasn't Adam. That was the only thing that she had to cling to, the only thought that sustained her. Adam was a man who liked the fine things in life. Being in a situation like that with a woman was crude. The last thing that Adam was was crude. He was magnetic and charismatic and attractive— even if not a patch on Finn Coolidge in the animal charm school— and he certainly wasn't crude. So he wouldn't, couldn't, behave in public like that with a woman.

Unless she had him under her spell. Unless there was something about this woman that had changed him completely. Only, thought Nessa despairingly as she sat on the edge of the double bed, he hadn't changed. Not with her. Not with Jill. Not at all.

She got up and opened the wardrobe door. She felt guilty as she slid her hand into the pockets of his suits. She didn't know what she expected to find there but she had a vague notion that maybe there would be something. But there wasn't. No carefully folded up love letters. No unexplainable Visa card receipts. No gift-wrapped bottles of perfume. Everything was exactly the way it always was. Nothing had changed at all.

Jill and Nicolette were playing in the back garden. Nessa called her daughter and handed her some money.

"Pop down the road to the newsagent's," she told her. "Get the latest copies of *Woman's Way, Woman and Home, New Woman* and *She.*"

Jill looked at her in astonishment. "All of them?"

"All of them," said Nessa.

She read the horoscopes for the month ahead. *Woman's Way,* which had a weekly horoscope, told her not to be distracted by other people's emotional issues. *Woman and Home* said that she would regret rushing into certain decisions. *New Woman* told her that she had been putting other people's feelings ahead of her own for too long, and *She* suggested that her imagination was working overtime.

"Exactly," she said out loud as she closed the glossy magazine. My imagination is working overtime.

He arrived home at seven-thirty. Nessa felt her heart thud even harder in her chest as she heard the car pull up in the driveway and the beep of the alarm as he locked the doors. The effect of reading the horoscopes had worn off. She'd remembered that Portia's comments weren't figments of her imagination. She'd heard the words, spoken by someone who didn't even know she was listening. And they were fact. Adam had stuck his tongue down some woman's throat. She hadn't imagined hearing that. So she'd spent two hours oscillating between hope and despair until she didn't know how she felt anymore.

"What on earth happened?"

She spun around at the sound of his voice and water from the kettle, which she'd been filling for no reason, went everywhere. She grabbed a cloth and began mopping the floor.

"What do you mean, what happened?" Her voice was muffled as she leaned down.

"To your car!" Adam was shocked. She could hear it in his voice. She'd forgotten about the car. "My car?"

"Yes," he said. "There's a bloody big gouge along the side of it."

"Oh, yes." She straightened up and wrung out the cloth. "I scraped it."

"You what?!"

"Scraped it," she said. "You know. What *you* do on a regular basis."

"I know *I* do it," he said jokingly. "But a Driscoll woman? Scraping a car? Unheard of, I would've thought."

"Not anymore." She didn't know how she was saying these banal words when the ones she wanted to use were so different. She didn't know how it was that he was talking to her as though nothing had changed between them. His expression was one of surprised concern. It wasn't the expression of a man who was cheating on his wife. As if she knew what that should be!

"Did you call Bree?" he asked.

"No," said Nessa.

"I'm sure she'll be able to sort it out," he said confidently. "I know it's not her make but all those colors are pretty much the same, aren't they?"

"She can buy Ford paint anyway," said Nessa.

"Sure. Of course." He put his arms around her and hugged her. "Never mind, honey, at least you know what it's like now."

She wanted to lean back into his embrace but she couldn't. She wriggled out of his hold. "What would you like for dinner?"

"You haven't started it yet?" He looked downcast. "I'm starving!"

"Are you?"

"Ravenous," he assured her. "I didn't have time for lunch today. Too busy."

Doing what, she wondered. Meeting women and sticking your tongue down their throats?

"What would you like?" she asked.

"What about you?"

She shrugged. "Pasta?"

He made a face. "It's not exactly what I was dreaming of after the day I've had," he said. "Any chance of steak?"

"It's too warm for steak," she said. "And it's not quick."

"We could barbecue it and eat outside," said Adam.

"Don't be stupid." She opened the kitchen drawer and looked aimlessly inside. "It takes ages to heat up the barbecue."

"No it doesn't," said Adam. "It's gas."

"Even still."

"Oh, what's the matter with you?" he asked in exasperation. "I thought you liked eating outdoors. I was trying to be helpful."

This was her opportunity. To tell him what she knew. That he'd been seen with another woman. But the words froze on her lips and she wasn't able to speak them.

"Headache," she said.

"Probably the effect of the car scrape," said Adam cheerfully. "It gets us all different ways. I don't mind what I eat. Pasta's fine if that's all you feel up to."

If you really want steak you could make it yourself, she thought. Only you don't, do you? Not ever. You come home and you expect me to have things ready for you like some kind of fifties housewife. And I've let you expect it. Because I thought that way you'd always love me.

Adam opened the fridge and took out a tin of beer.

"I'll sit in the garden for a while," he told Nessa. "Do a bit of unwinding. The traffic was brutal on the way home. I was stuck at the village for ages."

"OK," she said.

What kind of person am I, she asked herself as she watched him relax into the comfortable lounger, what kind of person am I that lets him carry on as though nothing has happened? And what kind of idiot does he think I am?

Only he doesn't know that I know something. He thinks everything is exactly as it was this morning. Perfectly in its place. She opened the cupboard and took down the packet of pasta shapes. Her eyes were filling with tears again and she blinked them away as she shook the pasta into a saucepan.

If I hadn't heard the girls in the sauna I'd have said yes to the steaks, she realized. I'd have agreed straightaway and allowed him to fire up the barbie and I'd have made some coleslaw—I would have entered into the spirit of it and enjoyed it and done what he wanted because when he's happy, I'm happy. It's another Cancerian trait, of course, wanting people to be happy. I always thought that it meant I was a warm, caring person. But is it simply pathetic instead? It must be. Portia thinks I'm pathetic and she hardly knows me. And surely it's pathetic not to say anything to him. Because I'm afraid. Afraid to know. I'd prefer to pretend that I didn't know.

Which was what Portia had said. Nessa remembered the younger girl's words, that she probably knew about Adam and the other woman only she put up with it for the lifestyle and for her daughter. If it's true, she asked herself suddenly, could I pretend that I didn't know? After all, not knowing hasn't done me any harm so far. It hasn't affected my marriage—how he's treated me or how he's treated Jill. Anyway, maybe it's just a kind of seven-year-itch thing.

Something brief and torrid that he'll get over, which will leave us stronger afterward. She wiped some mushrooms with a damp cloth. But will I be stronger, she wondered. Will I get over it? If it ends and he's still with me and nothing has changed, will I be able to forget it? To go on living as though nothing has happened? As though I never knew?

Her headache was getting worse. She looked out of the kitchen window. Adam was talking on his mobile. She felt her mouth go dry.

Was he talking to her? The other woman? Was he saying that he was at home and his stupid, compliant, silly, useless wife was making him something to eat? Was that the kind of thing they talked about? Did they discuss her? Did she ask him about her? Did they laugh about her and her ignorance of their affair and did they hold each other tightly and wrap themselves into their own world, excluding her?

Or did the other woman even know he was married? Was she as stupid in her way as she herself was? Did the other woman believe him when he told her that he loved her and that he wanted to be with her? Did she dream of the day when he'd ask her to marry him, unaware of the existence of his wife and daughter and the detached corner house in Malahide who could screw it all up for her?

Did she love him?

Did he love her?

Was it just sex?

Nessa heard him laugh suddenly and she wanted to be sick. He laughed like that with her sometimes. When they were sharing a private joke, a piece of silliness that only the two of them understood. He must be talking to her. He must. Then Jill ran into the back garden and threw herself at him. He hugged his daughter, said something to the person on the phone, then put it to one side and got up out of the lounger. He lifted Jill into the air and made a face at her, indicating that she was too big and heavy for this sort of lark. Then he sat down on the grass beside her and listened as she told him about her day at summer camp and, undoubtedly, about how the car had got scraped. She heard him laugh, then hug Jill again.

He couldn't be seeing someone else, thought Nessa. He just couldn't. He wouldn't jeopardize everything that he had for someone else. Why would he bother? What would be the point?

• • •

"Do you want to join us?" asked Finn over the phone to Cate. "We're in La Finezza."

She shook her head even though he couldn't see her. But she wasn't quite able to speak. She hadn't done anything except shake since she'd seen the blue line on the pregnancy test.

"Cate? Are you there? Do you want to join us? It'll be fun."

He'd phoned to say that the producer had invited him and one of the researchers to dinner and they'd love it if Cate could come too. But she couldn't. Obviously. She wasn't fit to go to dinner with anyone.

"I'd love to." She was surprised at how she managed to get the words out. "But I'm really whacked tonight, Finn. I've been doing loads of paperwork and I've just run a hot bath."

"Are you sure?" Finn sounded disappointed. "They really want to meet you."

"And I'd like to meet them too," lied Cate. "But not tonight, Finn."

"Have it your way."

"Honestly, I would like to," she repeated. "But—"

"It's OK," he said. "Don't worry about it."

"I'll see you later," she told him. "Have a good time."

"Sure."

Fuck, she said as she put down the phone. Fuck bloody fuck. Now he was annoyed at her and the last thing she wanted or needed was for him to be annoyed at her. They'd often argued before about how he would suddenly go out to dinner with one of his media buddies and forget all about her. And now, the first night he'd thought of asking her, she'd refused. He'd think it was some kind of revenge on her part. Getting him to ask her and saying no. He'd think she was being petty.

She sighed and sat down on the leather couch again. She drew her knees up underneath her chin and wondered how she could still do that when she was pregnant. And then she thought that maybe it would harm the baby and she stretched her legs along the seat.

The baby. It was such a small word for something so monumental. Of course, it was hardly a baby yet, was it? Only the size of her fingernail or her finger or something, she supposed. Which meant that it wouldn't do it any harm if she did whatever she liked with her legs while she was able to. She drew her knees back under her chin and thought about getting fat. She didn't want to get fat. She thought pregnant women looked gross—there was no way that it was attractive even though loads of magazines tried to pretend that you could look gorgeous carrying a huge lump in front of you. They fobbed gullible women off with stories about their hair being shinier or their nails being stronger or some kind of crap like that, as though it could compensate for not being able to see your own feet! And, worst of all, was the whole birth thing. Nessa had told her a little bit about it after Jill was born and Cate had stopped her because she'd thought that she was going to be sick. She couldn't, she absolutely just could not go through what Nessa had gone through. She didn't want people poking and prodding at her body. She didn't want to have blood tests at regular intervals. Blood tests made her faint. And the idea of a baby forcing its way out of her made her shake with terror.

I do *not* want to be pregnant, she said out loud, her voice trembling. I do *not* want to have a baby. I do *not* want to have *this* baby.

She got up and stood by the huge window. The sea was calm today and the water still sparkled with the light of the evening sun. There were hundreds of people walking along the seafront—in couples and families and groups. There were joggers, cyclists and skaters too, all taking advantage of the warm summer. And there were women and men walking side by side as they pushed buggies containing loved and wanted babies.

Cate put her hand on her stomach again. I wouldn't be able to do that with this baby, she thought. Because I'd resent every damn minute of pushing it along the seafront when I could be doing something else. They told you that you changed, that you'd do anything for your child. But she didn't want to change. She didn't want to do anything for somebody that she'd never asked to have.

If I had an abortion, she allowed the thought to form in her head, nobody would ever know. And then I wouldn't have to go through with all of the things that I never wanted to go through with. I wouldn't have to tell Finn or Nessa or Bree or Mum. She shivered. Her mother would disown her if she thought Cate was even thinking about an abortion. Nessa or Bree probably wouldn't think too much of her either. But it was easy for other people, she thought hotly, easy for them to say that you should make the best of it and get on with things. She could see how they'd think it would be right for her to have this baby when she was getting married to the soon-to-be most popular man on TV. But they'd be wrong. She knew Finn. She knew herself. She knew what they both wanted. And she knew that a baby wasn't on the cards. Not now. Maybe not ever.

The more the evening went on the harder it was for Nessa to say anything at all to Adam. As they sat in front of the TV and watched a succession of half-hour sitcoms, she formed sentences in her head but wasn't able to say any of them out loud. Adam was slouched on the sofa, his legs stretched out in front of him, another beer on the small coffee table beside him. It was the way things always were on Friday nights and she simply wasn't able to ruin it all by bringing up a subject that she didn't even know how to deal with. So she allowed the time to slip by and suddenly they were in bed together and he was reaching for her as he always did on Fridays. He drew her close to him and slid his hand along the inside of her thighs and she was sure, at that point, that he must know there was something wrong with her. But he didn't seem to notice and she felt the pressure of his hand increase. She couldn't quite believe that she was making love to him as though nothing had changed. And she couldn't quite believe that she was holding him tightly and telling him she loved him when, right then, she thought that she probably hated him.

Afterward she lay beside him and listened to his steady breathing as he slept. She wanted to fall asleep herself but, every time she was on the brink, every time she felt herself drifting into semi-consciousness, she would suddenly feel herself begin to fall and would jerk awake, her heart thumping, her nerves jangling.

She wondered if she'd ever be able to sleep properly again.

Cate couldn't sleep either. Finn had arrived home from La Finezza just after midnight in good humor and slightly drunk.

"You should have come," he told her. "It was fun."

"I'm sorry," she said. "I had things to do and I knew that I wouldn't be good company tonight. I didn't want to spoil things for you."

"I love you." He kissed her haphazardly.

"I love you too." She watched him go to the bathroom, heard him clean his teeth and then stumble toward the bedroom. She waited until she could hear his snores before going to bed herself.

"I'm pregnant," she whispered in the darkness as she lay beside him. "But I don't really think we want this baby, Finn. Do we? If you say that we do then I won't think about the abortion anymore. But if you don't say anything, can I assume that you're OK with it?"

She knew he wouldn't answer. He was deep in slumber, untroubled by the fears and worries that assailed her. But she knew what he'd say to her. That she was right about the baby. That it wasn't a wanted baby. That she should do something about it. And he'd hold her in his arms and kiss her on the forehead as he always did when they'd come to a disagreeable decision. But he knew that she'd do what was right. For her. For him. For both of them.

11

♥

Venus in Sagittarius

Emotional freedom is the key.

While Nessa and Cate were both lying awake in bed, Bree Driscoll was powering along the Morehampton Road. She could feel the pressure of Michael's arms as he clung on to her while she slipped along the inside lane and past the line of traffic that even at this hour clogged Donnybrook village.

She'd had a good time with Michael tonight. Their first date, the session at the Point Theatre, had been OK although they'd met up with a gang of Michael's friends and suddenly it wasn't really a date between them but a kind of group thing where everyone knew everyone else and they ended up going for drinks together. Bree had felt a little out of things as they'd joked about their college days and the fun they'd had and what a pain it was to be in the real world and having to earn a living. She'd felt out of things, too, when she realized that for them earning a living meant being involved in high-profile careers in law or media or design, not slogging it out in a garage. She'd never been ashamed of working in a garage before—

she still wasn't ashamed of it—but the girls, in particular, had made her feel totally inadequate.

Afterward one of the guys had given her and Michael a lift back to Donnybrook but that had meant her getting out of the car first and simply giving Michael a peck on the cheek and telling him she'd had a good time. He'd call, he said, and she really wasn't sure whether or not she believed him. So she'd been relieved when the phone had rung and he'd invited her out again.

Their second date had been better. They'd gone to the movies, a horror one that he'd chosen, especially, he said, to have her shrieking and cowering beside him. In fact, horror movies always made her laugh and she did hardly any shrieking and cowering which disappointed him. Afterward they'd had coffee and Michael had told her—as so many men did—that she really was quite unique and that he'd never met anyone like her before. He'd asked, again, about her motorbike and about her love of cars and all things mechanical and he'd wondered, aloud, whether or not she'd let him ride the bike.

"Are you mad?" She'd grinned at him. "I know how you drive a car." But she'd suggested that the next time they went out together he could call to her flat and she'd bring him for a spin on the bike. He'd shared a taxi home with her and once again dropped her at the flat before continuing on to his own house. Bree had always thought that twenty-one-year-old men were a seething mass of hormones only waiting to pounce so she was torn between frustration and hurt that he didn't seem to want to jump on her and tear the clothes from her body. She'd fondly imagined that she'd spend her time with Michael Morrissey fending him off and it was disconcerting to think that he could so easily allow her to kiss him on the cheek again and say goodbye.

So for their next date she brought him along the coast road out as far as Howth on the back of her bike and up to the summit of the hill where they'd sat and watched the sun going down while he told her about the new job that he was starting in September in the sales and marketing department of a large retail company. Great prospects, he'd said, and a brilliant step-up from his current temporary job simply answering phones in a market research organization. She'd listened and nodded but had remembered, quite suddenly, that it was Howth summit where Adam had romantically proposed to Nessa. Yet despite watching the sunset with Michael (which should have been laden with romance, she thought) the atmosphere between them was simply friendly. He was fun to be with, she enjoyed his company and he was very, very attractive, but she wasn't sure that there was a spark between them. Not the kind of spark that she'd hoped might be there—that she supposed would be there if he was the one that suddenly turned her into decent girlfriend material. She didn't want to push it but she rather felt as though he saw her in the role of an older sister rather than a potential bedmate. She wondered if it really was because he was a bloke four years younger than her but she tried to dismiss that idea. If she were to think like that she'd be no better than the people who tried to stereotype her and say that it was odd for a woman to be a mechanic and to ride fast bikes. Just because Michael was twenty-one didn't mean that he couldn't be as mature as any of the other blokes she'd gone out with in the past. More mature than half of them and, at the very least, not a weirdo!

She eased back on the throttle as she turned onto the road where he lived. Then she glided to a halt outside the house.

"That was brilliant!" He took off the helmet and, in the light of the streetlamp she could see that his eyes were shining. "You are the coolest girl I've ever known. The way you weaved in and out of traffic. The way you took corners. Fan-bloody-tastic."

She grinned and took off her own helmet. "Glad you enjoyed it."

"I would've liked it if we could've gone even faster," he told her. "There's something about speed on a bike . . ."

"You shouldn't get excited about speed," she said. "If you do, you let it conquer you instead of you conquering it. Speed is just something to keep control of."

"Oh, but belting along faster than anyone else is magic," said Michael. "Knowing you can piss all over people at the lights . . ."

She laughed. "I try not to think of you as a bloke like any other bloke," she told him. "I try not to think of you as someone who's turned on by engine revs and driving fast. But you are, aren't you?"

"Not always."

They hadn't kissed before. Not properly. But now he leaned toward her and she knew that he was going to put his arms around her and kiss her here, outside his house, and kiss her in the way she needed to be kissed.

A car pulled up and caught them in its headlights. Michael loosened his hold on her and turned around. Declan Morrissey got out of the car and waved at them.

"How are you?" he asked Bree.

"Fine thanks." She was flustered. She knew that he must be aware that she was dating his son but she hadn't expected to see him like this, her face flushed with the anticipation of Michael's kiss.

"Do you want to come in for a coffee?" he asked.

She glanced at Michael who nodded.

"Nice outfit," said Declan as she stood in the kitchen and unzipped her black leather biker's jacket.

"Thanks." She wished she didn't feel so uncomfortable in front of him. It was as though he was looking at her, assessing her and, somehow, finding her lacking. Maybe it was because of the leathers. Maybe he didn't think that a girl who worked in a garage and wore leathers was exactly the kind of girl he wanted for his attractive son.

"We went to Howth." Michael sat down at the table while Declan spooned coffee into a cafetiere. "Bree is the most brilliant girl on a bike I've ever met."

"You've never met a girl on a bike before," Declan pointed out.

"Yeah, well." Michael grinned. "She's still something."

"I wish she could teach you to drive better," said Declan.

"I don't teach anything," said Bree hastily.

Declan smiled. "Would you like something to eat?"

"Will you be hurt if I say no?"

Michael laughed. "She remembers things too."

"I said I wouldn't be hurt if you didn't have anything to eat the last time you were here and I won't be hurt this time either. But, knowing my son, if you've been on a date with him you haven't had anything to eat. He's not known for wining and dining his girl-friends in style."

Girlfriends. Bree wondered how many girlfriends Michael might have had. He was so gorgeous and attractive to look at, she supposed he'd never be short of someone wanting to throw herself at him. And, of course, all those girls in college would have looked at his lean, tanned face and soulful brown eyes and melted at the knees. As she had.

"Have a slice of apple pie." Declan took a half-finished pie out of the fridge and put it on the table with the coffee.

"Thanks." Bree was ravenously hungry. Declan was right, after they'd watched the sun go down they'd gone for a few drinks. She'd stuck to mineral water and Michael hadn't drunk that much either but the only food they'd had was a packet of Bacon Fries each.

"Next time we go out I'll bring you for a meal," promised Michael. "And you won't have to come back here and stuff yourself on Dad's apple pie." He looked at her empty plate. "Were you hungry?"

"Not really," she lied. "But it was a nice pie."

Declan laughed and refilled her cup. "Make him bring you somewhere nice," he warned Bree. "Otherwise you'll end up at Pizza Hut."

"What's wrong with Pizza Hut?" demanded Michael.

"I like pizzas," Bree assured him. "Especially with extra chilli topping."

"I told you she was something else," said Michael admiringly. "None of my other girlfriends liked extra chilli topping."

It was an hour later when she arrived back at the flat. Declan had gone to bed and Michael had walked outside with her. But he hadn't tried to kiss her again and she couldn't figure out whether it was because he felt uncomfortable knowing that Declan was so near or whether it was because he just didn't fancy her enough. He enjoyed being with her, that much was clear, but was this relationship, like so many others, a "just good friends" kind of thing? Did he see her as a mate who happened to have a size 34B chest? Was she, as Nessa had once scornfully told her, totally lacking in feminine charms?

She peeled off her leathers and got into her unmade bed. She sat in it and looked around her. She was certainly lacking in feminine touches. The flat was, as always, a mess. Maybe I should make more of an effort, she thought. Tidy things up a bit. Shove some flowers into a vase. Let people know that I am, actually, a woman.

She shuddered. She hated being thought of as a woman. Hated being categorized as someone who ultimately would get married and settle down and have children. And she wondered how many women had hated the idea too until, one day, they'd met someone who'd changed their minds about it all.

It would be funny, she thought, if the man who changed her mind about it all turned out to be a twenty-one-year-old speed freak from down the road.

12

♥

Sun in 3rd House

An active mind and a good communicator.

It was chaotically busy. Cate sat at her desk and wondered how she was going to hold three meetings, attend a lunch seminar at the Sports Council, interview a potential new accounts clerk and have a set of figures ready for Ian Hewitt for five o'clock. It wasn't possible. She knew it wasn't possible even if she'd had a full compliment of staff today—which she didn't because apparently four people were down with some kind of stomach virus and had phoned in sick that morning. The only thing about being so frantically busy was that it didn't give her time to worry about her own life and how terrible everything was and what on earth she was going to do about the baby. The baby that she didn't want to know existed. The baby that nobody else knew about yet because she still hadn't said a word to Finn. She wasn't going to say anything to him either. Not until she knew what she wanted to do.

He'd taken her out to Wong's on Saturday night and for a couple of hours she'd been able to pretend that everything was fine. She'd pushed the whole baby issue to the back of her mind as she chatted to him about his listener figures for the radio show (up by three percent last month) and the agenda he now had for the first few TV shows—some good guests with interesting stories as well as some celebs to reel in the viewers. She'd managed to pretend that she wasn't pregnant at all, that the whole thing was a figment of her imagination, and somehow the evening had been better than any they'd spent together since she'd asked him to marry her. But later that night, before they'd made love and while Finn was trailing his fingers from her throat to the top of her legs as he always did, she wondered frantically whether or not he'd realize that she was fatter and whether he'd suddenly put two and two together and ask her straight out about being pregnant.

Only he hadn't, of course. He'd kissed her and touched her and then entered her just as he always did and nothing, absolutely nothing was any different.

"Hey, Cate, your taxi's here!" Ruth Pearson stuck her head around the door. "Lucky you, managing to skive off to the Sports Council for a few hours. Wish I could get out of this madhouse."

"Wish I could stay," said Cate ruefully. "I've a ton of work to do." She opened her bag and took out her makeup. "What time is that girl coming in for her interview?"

"Half-two." Ruth watched as Cate expertly refreshed her look and reapplied her creamy red lipstick.

"If I'm late back, stick her in my office and give her a couple of newspapers."

"Sure."

"If Ian comes back, tell him that I'll have the figures for him by this evening."

"OK."

"And if Finn rings—" Cate broke off. He might ring, they were supposed to be going out again that evening even though she dreaded it. She snapped her compact shut again. "Oh, if Finn rings just tell him I'll see him back home."

"Right you are." Ruth was still nodding as Cate grabbed her bag and hurried down the stairs.

Nessa was weeding the front garden when she saw Mitchell Ward walk by. She straightened up and waved at him.

"Hi, Mrs. Riley." He smiled at her. The Wards had lived next door since Mitchell was fourteen. He'd never dream of calling her by her Christian name.

"Hi, Mitchell." She pushed a strand of hair out of her eyes. "Quick question for you." Her heart was beating very fast.

"Yes?"

"Remember the girl you had staying with you earlier in the summer?"

Mitchell's face flamed red. What the hell did Mrs. Riley want to know about his girlfriends? Was she planning on telling his mother something? He'd always thought that Mrs. Riley was an OK sort of woman but you could never be sure about parents.

"Portia? What about her?" He tried to keep the worry out of his voice.

"I was wondering if you had a phone number for her," said Nessa.

He looked at her in surprise.

"She had tea with me the morning Adam bumped into her car," Nessa said. "And we were chatting about something—I just wanted to give her a call."

"I haven't seen her in ages," said Mitchell. "I'm sort of going out with someone else."

And she's heartbroken only you don't know that, thought Nessa. Probably even if you did you wouldn't care because you're a bloke and why the hell should you.

"I only want her phone number," she told him. "Not to talk to her about you."

He grinned suddenly and Nessa could see why Portia had fallen for him. Although he wasn't conventionally attractive—he had a bump on his nose and probably sported too many freckles for most women—his smile was arresting and lit up his face.

"She wasn't awfully happy about us splitting up," he confided. "But, to be honest with you, she was getting far too clingy, Mrs. Riley. She wanted to know where I was all the time and what I was doing and why I couldn't be doing it with her. You know? I'm only twenty-two. It's not like I'm ready for the whole commitment thing."

"I understand," said Nessa dryly.

Mitchell took his mobile from the pocket of his cargo pants. "I still have her number in this. Hadn't got around to erasing her yet." He read it off to Nessa who memorized it.

"Thanks," she said.

"No problem." He pressed a few buttons on the phone. "She's consigned to the trash can now anyway. Frees up another place in the Mitchell Ward directory of available women!"

"I suppose that's a good thing?" Nessa tried hard to smile at him.

"Absolutely," he assured her.

Bree had four services to do, plus an investigation into a strange noise from the engine of a navy blue Alfa Spider. She wanted to get on with the job on the Spider but she had to do the services first.

"Hey, Bree!" Rick Cahill waved at her. "Any chance you could try and loosen this nut for me? It's tight to the block and I can't quite get at it."

"Sure." She wiped her hand on a cloth and peered into the engine. "Give me the wrench."

"What it is to have dainty little hands," said Rick when she'd done the job and handed the tool back to him.

"Thanks," she said.

"You'll make someone a wonderful husband one day," he told her.

She looked at him. "Will I?"

"Absolutely. Handy around the home, handy in the garage— what more could a man ask for?"

"Someone who wears sexy dresses and high heels maybe?" she suggested.

"Do I detect a slight bitterness in your tone?" he asked lightly. "Isn't the course of true love running smooth for you, young Bree?"

She sighed. She rarely talked about her personal life in the garage. Working with a bunch of men didn't really present many opportunities for intimate conversations and she wasn't the sort of person who liked having them anyway. But she was feeling dispirited about Michael Morrissey's apparent lack of interest in her other than as someone who could ride a motorbike very fast. It might have been different if his father hadn't shown up, he might have given her the passionate kiss that would have changed everything, but by now she doubted it.

"The course of true love never runs smooth," she told Rick equally lightly.

"You're going out with Declan Morrissey's son, aren't you?" he asked.

"How the hell did you know that!" She stared at him in astonishment.

"I heard Christy talking about it," he said.

"Christy!"

"He knows Declan socially," Rick told her.

"I didn't know that." Bree glanced toward the tiny office where Christy was talking on the phone. "He didn't say. He told me that Declan was just a good customer."

"Oh, they're not friends," said Rick. "As such. Declan's in the same golf club as him."

"Fuck." Bree wrinkled up her nose. "I don't really want them talking about me over their gin and tonics."

Rick grinned. "Doubt that they do."

"But he's talked about me already!" she wailed.

"If the course of true love is giving you a bit of gyp then maybe he won't be talking about you for much longer."

She groaned. "I don't know how things will pan out between me and Michael," she told Rick. "He's nice but a bit juvenile, you know."

"Good-looking, though," said Rick.

"You know him?"

He nodded. "He was in here last year when his Dad bought the car."

"OK, so he's good-looking," conceded Bree. "And there's a lot to be said for looks, as all of you guys know only too well." She cast a disparaging look at the Pirelli calendar which hung on the far wall.

"But we all know that looking is one thing and loving is something else," said Rick.

"Please don't get all sensitive on me," she said. "I come in here so that nobody gets sensitive on me."

Rick laughed. "Go and drain a few oil sumps," he told her. "That'll take your mind off things for a bit."

"Thanks." She smiled back at him. "You always know how to get things into perspective."

The interviewee was sitting in Cate's office when she arrived back, twenty minutes late, from the Sports Council meeting. Cate pushed open the door, smiled briefly at her and took her CV from an intimidatingly high pile on her desk.

"Anita Reid," she said.

"Yes." Anita looked at her. She had auburn hair, clear skin and sparkling blue eyes. She was, thought Cate, extremely pretty.

"So," Cate said. "Perhaps you'd like to run me through your experience to date."

She looked attentively at her as Anita gave a rundown on her career but she wasn't really listening. She was wondering whether or not she could download some information on abortion clinics in the U.K. from the internet. She'd looked up Clinics in the Golden Pages first thing that morning and found a variety of women's health clinics sandwiched between Cleanrooms and Clocks. There were numbers in Ireland—where abortion was illegal and where, even if it wasn't, she'd be sure to meet someone she knew in the damn waiting room—and numbers in the U.K. too. But she hadn't been able to pick up the phone and call. She might have done if Ruth hadn't barged into the office to tell her that Glenda and the other girls were out sick. But the moment had passed. Maybe there would be more information on the Net. Then she wouldn't have to talk to anyone. She really didn't want to talk to anyone.

"And that's how I'm here." Anita Reid smiled brightly at her. Cate exhaled slowly. Anita could've told her that she was an ax murderer for all that she'd heard. But the girl seemed nice and capable and enthusiastic.

"Where do you see yourself in two years' time?" asked Cate.

Anita raised an eyebrow. That was a rather old chestnut in the interview stakes, she'd expected more from the professional-looking woman sitting opposite her.

"Hopefully I will have progressed in the company," she said. "I like responsibility. I like working to deadlines. I enjoy challenges."

So do I, thought Cate. I was just like you when I joined the company first. I wanted responsibility and deadlines and challenges and I worked so hard to get all of those things. And I can't, I just can't throw it all away for the sake of smelly nappies and baby sick.

Even though she now had Portia Laing's phone number, Nessa knew that she wasn't going to call her. Asking for the number had been a sudden impulse but Nessa knew that she wouldn't be able to phone the girl up and say that she'd overheard her talking about her husband. It was too unbelievable. Portia would think she was some sad, mad cow. She thought that anyway.

The more intelligent thing to do, thought Nessa, was to systematically go through the house and see if she could find the faintest shred of proof that Adam was cheating on her. Nobody could cheat on somebody else without leaving some kind of evidence lying around. After all, if he was seeing someone, maybe she'd given him a token, something to keep. When she'd been going out with him she'd sent him little cards. Maybe this other woman had sent him little cards too. And maybe he'd been stupid enough to leave one somewhere.

She poured herself a cup of coffee and opened *The Year Ahead for Cancerians*. She hadn't looked at it in two days. She was disillusioned by the fact that the biggest blow in all of her life had happened without any warning from her book. It wasn't as though she believed everything, she told herself firmly, but the horoscopes had been fun and helpful in a light-hearted kind of way. If she couldn't trust them anymore then what was the point of believing in anything at all?

"*By now you've made important decisions about your future,*" she read. "*You should be able to make progress from here although it won't be easy. Getting information about the things you're dealing with may prove more difficult than you imagined. Have faith. You are headed in the right direction.*"

So what's that telling me, she asked herself. That if I dig deep enough I'll find something that'll confirm my worst bloody suspicions? That Adam will deny everything? Or that I'll discover that Portia was the one who was telling lies? She leaned her head on her arms and sighed deeply. Things had been so great a few months ago. How could they have turned around so horribly now?

She sat up and pushed her coffee to one side. She'd find out the truth. And it wouldn't be as bad as she imagined. Things were rarely as bad as anyone imagined, she was sure of that.

Cate looked at the printed sheets in front of her and felt sick. She'd now read about surgical abortions and medical abortions and what she should do in order to get either of them. The site she'd visited had given information for people who lived in the U.K., overseas and Ireland and she wondered just how many women had to travel for abortions. How many women were so desperate that they booked their tickets to the U.K. and saved for the operation because to do anything else would ruin their lives?

She rubbed her eyes. A baby would ruin her life. It would. Really. But she wasn't desperate. She could afford the operation. She could afford the trip to the U.K. Hell, she could even put it down as a business trip if she wanted. She wasn't getting an abortion because she was too young to have a baby, or because she had so many other children or because some bloke she hardly knew had got her pregnant and abandoned her. She wanted an abortion because she was afraid that a baby would come between Finn and herself, because she had other priorities in her life and because she was terrified of being pregnant. Surely those reasons were as good as any others. Her reasons mightn't be as desperate as some women's but she was desperate in her own way.

She looked at the pages again. Everything was dealt with in a matter-of-fact manner. Nobody was preaching at her or making judgments about her or telling her that she was a foolish woman for getting pregnant in the first place. They talked about helping her, not lecturing her. They offered counseling to her and they told her that it was entirely her choice.

But she didn't need counseling. She didn't need sympathy. She just needed to get rid of the damn baby.

She began to shake. It sounded so final. It sounded so awful. It hadn't seemed like that before but now it did.

Those people who said that women used abortions as a kind of contraceptive didn't know what they were talking about. They didn't know how terrible it felt. To be the one who had to make the decision. To be the one who had to think about it. To be the one who tried to pretend that she was thinking of a simple surgical procedure when all the time she was feeling guiltier and guiltier about what she was proposing to do. She'd always wondered why girls who found themselves pregnant by mistake didn't rush off and get the abortion straightaway. Why there were women who waited until it began to get dangerously late. But now she understood. It was a final decision. It was a terrible decision. It was a decision she didn't know how she was going to make.

Bree was on her break in the monkey room when her mobile rang.

"Hi," she said.

"Hello, it's me."

"Michael." She couldn't keep the pleasure out of her voice. "How're you?"

"Great," he said. "I wondered would you like to go out on Friday night."

"Sure. Where to?"

"I was thinking about what Dad said," he told her. "So maybe to a restaurant? For a meal?"

She laughed. "You don't have to bring me for something to eat just because of your father," she told him. "I'm quite happy to go into town and have a few beers."

"No," he told her. "I need to treat women a bit better!"

Bree grimaced. She was being lumped in with a collection of women again. It wasn't exactly confidence-building.

"Where would you like to go?" he asked.

"Oh, Michael, I don't mind."

"I'll surprise you," he said.

"OK."

"Wear something slinky," he told her.

"What?"

He laughed. "Only if you want to. I haven't ever seen you in anything other than jeans."

"Haven't you?" she frowned.

"Nope."

"And you'd like to?"

"Dad asked me if you had legs," said Michael.

"Oh."

"I said I reckoned you had. I said I reckoned you had the best legs in the business. I want to be proved right."

"Oh," she said again.

"So—seven on Friday?"

"I'll be ready."

She replaced the phone in her pocket. She didn't have anything slinky. She'd never possessed anything slinky. But if it moved her relationship with Michael from being some kind of platonic friendship into something more romantic then maybe slinky was what she needed. It couldn't be that hard to find slinky clothes. Cate wore them all the time.

Maybe, thought Bree, as she strolled back into the workshop, she could give Cate a call. She hadn't talked to her in ages and it would be nice to get her sister's view on what would look good on her. Bree was a great believer in asking the experts for help on things. She always sighed whenever people came into the garage with the results of their DIY tinkering on their cars which had only made the problem worse. So it made sense that if she was going to move into a new area of her life she should get a bit of expert advice herself. And Cate was the very person to ask. She'd phone her later.

Cate sat in the empty office building and thought that she was going to have a breakdown. She could feel it in the way her mind would race first one way and then another. Abortion. Have the baby. Could she live with herself if she went to the clinic and said that she didn't want this child? Could she live with herself if she didn't? Why had this happened to her now? Why not in a year, two years, when she might be ready for a baby. When she might want a baby.

She needed to talk to someone. She'd never been much for talking to anyone before, she'd always believed she could solve her own problems. But this time she knew she couldn't.

Only she really didn't know who she wanted to talk to.

Nessa sat and stared at the postcard. She'd found it in the middle of a book about time management. It was hardly pulverizing evidence of an affair, it was a simple postcard with a picture of a blue sea, bluer sky and white beach. And it just said "Wish you were here xxx A." It could have been anyone sending him postcards. A colleague perhaps. And he might have been using it as a bookmark. Anything like that. But she didn't think so. She thought that she'd found the proof. And she didn't know what to do.

She could phone Paula. Her friend had gone through exactly the same thing and had survived it. Paula would know how she felt, what it was like to have your world collapse around you. But Paula would give her the pep talk, Nessa knew that. Paula would tell her that men were worthless shits and that what she needed to do was to get her hair cut, buy a new wardrobe, get a new job and start drinking red wine. It had worked for Paula. Nessa wasn't sure that it would work for her.

But she had to talk to someone. The pain was building inside her so that she was actually clutching her stomach. Everyone said that grief was an emotion. But it wasn't. It was so physical that it actually hurt.

She was still clutching her stomach, her body rolled forward so that her head was almost touching her knees, when the phone rang.

13

♥

Leo July 23rd–August 23rd
Naturally buoyant, loves to be admired.

"Hi," said Adam when she picked it up. "How're things?"

"Fine." Why had she said that, she asked herself. Why had she given him her automatic response when things weren't fine. They were as far away from fine as it was possible for them to be. They were nowhere near fine.

"I'll be a bit late tonight," he told her. "Couple of things on. We're meeting the management of a company we took on earlier in the summer. They wanted to talk about our report."

"OK," she said.

"It's likely we'll go for something to eat afterward," said Adam. "So don't bother with anything for me. If we don't get food I'll grab a takeaway on the way home."

"Sure."

"How's Jill?" he asked. "Making the most of the good weather?"

Nessa glanced out of the window. Jill, Nicolette and their other friend, Dorothy, had rediscovered the Barbie dolls which they'd rejected as too childish a few months earlier. She supposed that she should be slightly concerned that all of the Barbies were stark naked and therefore flaunting their enormous plastic chests but, right now, she didn't care what awful game they were playing.

"I guess so," she said.

"Tell her I'll try and be home before she goes to bed," said Adam.

"OK," said Nessa.

"Are you all right?" he asked.

She felt her throat constrict and hot tears flood her eyes. "Yes."

"You sound a bit funny," said Adam. "Hope you're not getting a cold. Summer ones are the worst."

"I'll see you later," she told him.

"I'll try not to be too long," he said.

She replaced the receiver slowly. Rage and hurt still battled

within her. The rage was as much at herself now, for not saying
something to him. But what was she going to say over the phone?
Women didn't accuse their husbands of having affairs over the
phone. You waited until he was home and relaxed and not expecting anything and then you laid out the facts in front of him and
waited for the denial. Because he was sure to deny it. John Trelfall
had denied it when Paula confronted him even though she had the
incontrovertible proof of the message that the stupid other woman
had left on the answering machine. Silly bitch had thought she'd
got John's mobile. Paula had been devastated, of course, but at
least she had something tangible with which to back up her accu-
sations. All Nessa had was a postcard with three x's from someone
called A.

The only person that Nessa could think of whose name began
with the letter A was Alicia Kearns who lived at the top of the road
and, in her wildest imaginings, she couldn't see Adam with Alicia
Kearns who was almost masculine in her build, had short wiry hair
and (as Adam had remarked himself) legs like tree trunks. Alicia had
been walking down the road wearing a pair of Bermuda shorts and a
long T-shirt while Adam had been cutting the grass at the front of
the house. He'd come inside and asked Nessa for a tin of beer—to
get over the shock, he'd said, of seeing the Kearns woman striding
past the gate. It wasn't Alicia, thought Nessa. It couldn't be.

She knew the sort of woman Adam liked. Slim—slimmer than
she was, even though he told her that he liked her like this—with
dark hair and big eyes. Adam preferred brunettes and he loved big
eyes. Nessa knew that she'd scored heavily with him because of her
huge gray eyes.

Where was he going tonight anyway? Was it really a business
meeting? Or was that a lie so that he could be with his A woman
where he could behave with her in a way that he'd never behaved
with his wife.

Was it her fault? she asked herself. Had she done something
wrong? Had she turned into a different Nessa to the Nessa he'd married? Had she driven him away?

Cate wasn't answering her phone. Bree had left a message on the
phone in the apartment and on her mobile but Cate hadn't called
her back. Bree supposed that her older sister could be too busy to

return her calls but she felt miffed all the same. It couldn't be that
hard to pick up the phone, she grumbled to herself, no matter
how high-flying and busy her sister wanted to make herself
appear. She wondered whether or not she'd be better off getting
some advice from Nessa instead. Nessa could look quite nice
when she put her mind down to it. But her eldest sister lacked
Cate's sophistication and style. All the same, Nessa did a lot of
shopping and she could probably point Bree in the right direction. It was a terrible indictment of her fashion sense, thought
Bree, that she really didn't have a clue where the best shopping
was in Dublin these days.

She stretched out her denim-clad legs in front of her. Jeans were
great. Simple, easy and they could look very stylish. She'd dressed up
her jeans on a number of different occasions and she thought that
she looked pretty good. In fact she was sure that she'd look a damn
sight better in her Levi's and top than she would in any slinky dress
that Cate or even Nessa might recommend. But Michael wanted to
see her in a dress and she wanted to make the effort for him. She
wanted to think that it was worth making the effort for him.

I'll try Cate once more, she decided, and if she doesn't answer
then I'm going over to Nessa's. She hit redial on her phone and was
connected to Cate's voicemail again.

"It's about the millionth time I've called," said Bree. "But it
doesn't matter, it wasn't important. You can call me later if you like.
I'll be in Nessa's." That'll intrigue her, she said to herself as she slid
the phone into her bag. I'm not at Nessa's so often that she won't
wonder why on earth I'm there!

It was only when she was stopped at the traffic lights that she
realized she hadn't phoned Nessa to tell her she'd be over. She'd
phoned Cate so many times that she'd actually forgotten to call
Nessa. But, she decided, it didn't matter. Nessa was bound to be at
home. And Nessa would surely be delighted to see her.

Cate and Finn were having dinner in the apartment. Cate had
shoved a Marks & Spencer meal for two in the oven and the fragrant
aromas of the Indian selection wafted through the air.

"First show next month." Finn beamed at Cate.

"I truly think you'll be brilliant," she told him.

"Do you?"

"Of course," she said. "People like your voice. People like your face. People like *you*, Finn."

"They don't know me." He shrugged. "They think they do but of course they don't. You know me, Catey. You know what I'm really like. But everyone else, they know the image that the TV station is making for me."

She was amazed that she could laugh. She hadn't thought anything could possibly make her laugh but the expression on Finn's face did. "You're beginning to sound like someone out of a boy band."

"Ugh! Sorry." He took some naan bread from the bowl in front of them. "Am I taking myself a touch on the serious side, d'you think?"

"Not really," she said. "I know what you mean. I see ads in the paper that say you're the voice of the nation but I know that's horseshit really."

"That's why I love you," he told her. "You tell it like it is."

"I bet all the megastars say that." She sighed. "They tell someone that they love them because they don't treat them like a mega-star but, in the end, they leave them because of it."

"Cate!" His voice was horrified. "I'm not going to leave you."

"Aren't you?"

"We've only just got engaged! Why on earth are you thinking like this?" He stared at her. "Is something the matter?"

She knew that this was the time to tell him. While they were on their own together and while he was ready to talk to her. But she simply couldn't. She didn't know why except that telling him would make it more real even than telling Nessa. And the urge to tell her older sister (a foolish urge, Nessa couldn't possibly understand how she felt) had evaporated since a few hours earlier when she'd picked up the phone to call her and got the engaged tone. Nessa was probably talking to one of her married-with-kids friends. Yakking away about the price of children's clothes or the hassle of getting them back to school. She'd told Cate once that when you had kids your entire social circle changed and that all of your without-kids friends faded into the background while you bonded with people who knew what it was like to walk out of the house with baby sick on your jumper and a kitbag full of baby essentials that weighed a ton.

"Cate?" He was still looking curiously at her.

"I'm sorry," she said. "I had a busy day today myself. I guess I'm not entirely with it."

"I love you, Cate," he told her. "You know that. I'm not going to leave you just because I have a job on the telly!"

She smiled wryly. "I never thought you'd leave me just because you got a job on the telly."

"We suit each other," he said. "We like the same things. Holidays in the sun. Spicy food. Adult company. We dislike anywhere it rains. Roast beef and veg. Snotty nosed kids."

She swallowed. "At some stage do you think we'll have kids? I mean—would you like to?"

"Not unless your hormones kick in and you can't do without them," he told her cheerfully. "I know it happens with some women, it's like some desperate urge you have to give in to, isn't it? But you're not the sort of girl for desperate urges. If, in the future, you decide that it's what you want then we'll talk it over. But not until after my first season. I can't imagine what my first season would be like if I was up half the night listening to a crying baby."

"You wouldn't be." She didn't look at him as she poked casually at the Rogan Josh. "Your first season would be spent waiting for my waters to break."

"Oh, God, Cate—don't talk about things like that while we're eating." He made a face. "It's utterly disgusting."

"I know." She looked up and smiled brilliantly at him. "You'd wonder why any woman puts herself through it at all."

Nessa and Jill were watching *Thunderbirds*. Nessa felt it was rather criminal of her to allow Jill to watch TV when it was warm and sunny outside but *Thunderbirds* was the must-see children's program of the summer and Jill was going through a wanting to be an astronaut phase. Posters of Thunderbird 3 were stuck all over her bedroom wall, along with those of the Starship *Enterprise* and Jeri Ryan as *Voyager*'s Seven of Nine.

Jill chewed the ends of her hair as the Tracey brothers winched someone to safety just in the nick of time. The roar of an engine in the driveway made her look up from the TV program.

"Hey, Mum, it's Bree!" She stood up and rushed to the window. "She's here. On her bike."

"Bree!" Nessa got up more slowly. "What on earth does she want? Is something wrong?"

Her horoscope hadn't said there would be anything wrong. But what the hell did it know about anything!

"You let her in, Jill. I'm just going up to comb my hair," she said.

She hurried up the stairs and into the bathroom before Jill opened the hall door. She heard Jill chattering excitedly to her sister and informing her that Nessa was doing herself up but would be down in a minute. She looked at herself in the bathroom mirror. Her eyes were red from her tears of earlier and although Jill hadn't noticed anything Nessa thought that Bree might be a different proposition altogether. She looked for Optrex on the shelf but couldn't find any so she simply splashed her face with cold water and patted it dry. Then she dabbed some foundation over her blotchy cheeks. This had the effect of making her lips disappear so she hurried into the bedroom and applied some pale pink lipstick. It wasn't exactly great, she decided, but it'd have to do. She pulled the brush through her hair and sprayed Estee Lauder's Sunflowers around her throat.

"Why are you honoring us with your presence?" she asked as she opened the door and walked into the living room.

"Look, Mum. Bree gave me her helmet." Jill's voice was muffled.

"Very cool," said Nessa.

"Suits you," said Bree. She looked at Nessa. "Are you OK? Jill said you were getting yourself done up. Not on my account, I presume?"

Nessa shook her head. "Of course not. I was busy today and I needed to comb my hair. But I hadn't time earlier."

"You've put on lippy." Jill lifted the visor. "And stuff on your face."

"Thanks, Jill. Why don't you go out for a while?"

"No!" cried Jill. "I want to stay here and play with Bree."

"Bree wants to talk to me, I think," said Nessa.

"I won't get in the way," Jill assured her and sat down on the floor.

Nessa shrugged and looked at Bree. "Is everything all right?" she asked.

Now that she was here, Bree felt silly. Other sisters might spend time exchanging fashion tips but it hadn't really been a Driscoll kind of thing. And Nessa looked far too hassled to want to talk about dresses. She wondered what the matter was. Knowing Nessa it wasn't really a crisis. Nessa didn't have crises. She got frazzled over silly things but never anything important.

"I was coming to you for advice," said Bree sheepishly. "I know that sounds silly."

"No." Nessa was kind of relieved to have something new to think about. "What sort of advice? Why me?"

"Actually, it *is* rather silly," Bree said. "I—well, I'm going on a date and I wanted to ask you about clothes."

"A date!" Jill put her arms around Bree's neck. "With a boy?"

"Yes," said Bree. "A date with a boy."

"I thought you'd gone on hundreds of dates," said Nessa slowly. "Why do you want to know about clothes for this one?"

"He wants to see my legs."

Jill laughed and Nessa, despite the heavy feeling that hadn't gone away, couldn't help smiling too.

"I know, I know!" cried Bree. "It's silly."

"Seeing your legs isn't silly," said Nessa.

"Does he not believe you have any?" asked Jill.

Bree sighed. "Every time he's seen me I've been wearing jeans or a boiler suit," she said. "This time we're going to a nice restaurant and he wants me to wear a slinky dress."

Nessa smiled again.

"Obviously I don't have a slinky dress," said Bree. "Thing is, I don't even know where to look for a slinky dress. I know that sounds stupid."

"Bree, you can get a dress anywhere," said Nessa. "The shops are crammed with slinky summer creations. Reduced in the sales too, now," she added.

"I know. But I want something that I feel comfortable in. And that looks OK." She made a face at Nessa. "I thought maybe you could give me hints about the style it should be. If I go into a shop and try something on I'm sure the sales assistant will say it looks fine even if I resemble a walrus in drag. I haven't got an eye for dressy up clothes, Ness, you know I haven't. I can tell when a pair of trousers looks like an elephant's arse on me but, to me, every dress looks like that."

Nessa grinned. "You should be talking to Cate, not me."

"I know," said Bree. She looked apologetically at her sister. "I rang Cate. But she wasn't picking up her phone."

"So I'm second choice?" But Nessa sounded faintly amused.

"Better than nothing," said Bree. "And I really do need the advice."

"Is this a serious kind of date?" asked Nessa. "When we went out celebrating with Cate you didn't have anyone in your life. Except the gay bloke living in your flat."

"Steve isn't living in the flat anymore," said Bree. "He's found a place of his own."

"So who's the slinky dress man?" asked Nessa.

Bree felt her face go red. "His name's Michael."

"And you really fancy him?" Nessa had noticed the color in her sister's cheeks.

"He's lovely," Bree told her. "Incredibly sexy "

"Oh, Bree! That's a rude word." Jill looked disapproving.

"Sexy is rude?"

Nessa grimaced. "Depends on the context as far as eight-year-olds are concerned." She turned to Jill. "Look, why don't you bring Nicolette over and you can play in the garden until it gets dark." She glanced at her watch. It was nearly eight o'clock which would give them an hour.

"But I want to talk to Bree about sexy," said Jill.

"And Bree and I want to talk to each other," said Nessa firmly. "I don't sit in on your chats with Nicolette, do I?"

"Nicolette's a friend," said Jill mutinously. "Bree's my family."

"I'll stay until after dark," Bree promised. "I won't go without playing with you for a while."

"Oh, OK." But Jill wasn't altogether pleased about the turn of events. "Can I show Nicolette your helmet?"

"Of course," said Bree. She grinned at Nessa as Jill ran out of the house. "She's cute."

"She's a bloody terror," said Nessa. "So tell me about this sexy man."

She listened as Bree talked about Michael's sultry good looks courtesy of his Spanish mother and attractive father but she couldn't concentrate. She wondered how long it took for the looks to fade and for the relationship to mean nothing at all. If it was based on his sex appeal and Bree's sudden willingness to wear dresses then it

surely didn't amount to much. But her marriage had been based on
so much more and suddenly it wasn't amounting to much either. To
her horror she felt the tears sting her eyes again.

"Nessa!" Bree stared at her sister. "What on earth's the matter?"
Nessa shook her head and said nothing.

"I didn't know there was something wrong. I wouldn't have come
if . . ." She looked at Nessa helplessly. "Tell me," she said eventually.
"Maybe I can help."

"Of course you can't help," snapped Nessa.

Bree bit back the retort. Nessa was upset and she couldn't blame
her for being snappy. She watched as her sister scrubbed at her eyes
with a tissue. It was hard to know whether or not this was important, thought Bree. Although she didn't have crises, Nessa had
always been the crying one, the one who could turn on the water-
works equally effectively whether she was happy or sad. Any time a
weepie had been shown on the TV Bree and Cate had giggled as
Nessa worked her way through a box of Kleenex. Bree remembered
Nessa watching Elaine Paige and Barbara Dixon singing "I know
him so well" on *Top of the Pops* with tears streaming down her face
(Nessa had, apparently, broken up with a boyfriend the week before
the song hit the charts). And, of course, when their pet rabbit Doe
had died Nessa had been almost inconsolable.

"Maybe I *can* help you," said Bree eventually. "Sometimes talking
about things puts them in perspective. You told me that yourself."
Actually, she thought waspishly, Nessa had told her that when she
was trying to find out about Bree's own love life just after she'd come
back from the U.K. Nosy bitch, Bree had thought then, and hadn't
told her anything.

How could Bree understand, Nessa asked herself. She was footloose and fancy free despite the slinky dress man. What did she
know about real love, about partnerships and commitment and the
things that mattered?

"I think Adam's having an affair." She could hardly believe she'd
said it. The simple words didn't do justice to the enormity of what
he might have done.

Bree could hardly believe she'd said it either. Adam! The almost
perfect man. The husband that Miriam had told them was the
benchmark for what all husbands should be. Adam Riley having an
affair! Bree couldn't have been more shocked if she'd heard that the

Pope was having an affair. No wonder Nessa was plowing through the tissues.

"Are you sure?" she asked.

"Of course I'm not sure," said Nessa sharply. "If I was sure I wouldn't only *think* he was having an affair."

"Take it easy," said Bree. "I'm trying to help."

Nessa blew her nose noisily. "I know."

"Well, why do you think . . ."

"I overheard someone say so," she told Bree.

"Who? How?"

It was a relief to tell the story. Nessa couldn't quite believe that she was telling it all to the sister who wouldn't know a stable relationship if it camped on her shoulder but it was definitely a relief to share her fears with someone.

"You poor thing." Bree put her arm around Nessa and hugged her tightly. "You poor, poor thing."

Tears flooded down Nessa's cheeks again. She hadn't expected sympathy from Bree. She'd expected her to tell her not to get so worked up about it. And to say that she was probably imagining it, that Portia had clearly known she was there and was just winding her up.

"It mightn't be true of course," she said through her sobs. "But it's hard to imagine a way that it couldn't be." She looked hopefully at Bree.

"I know," said Bree.

This was definitely wrong, thought Nessa. She'd given Bree the cue to come in and tell her how she could be wrong but Bree hadn't taken it.

"And the postcard could be from anyone," she added.

"I suppose loads of things have innocent explanations," agreed Bree. "Where is he tonight?"

"Out," said Nessa flatly. "With clients."

"Which clients?" asked Bree.

"I don't know." Nessa frowned. "Some company that they've got business from. He told me but I wasn't listening."

"It isn't an excuse, is it?"

"Oh bloody hell, Bree, I don't fucking know!" Nessa covered her face with her hands. "It might be true, it might be a lie. I don't know anymore. I can't guess when he's being honest and when he isn't because I always thought he was! So if he's lying to me now I can't tell."

"He's a shit," said Bree.

"We only think that." Nessa blew her nose again. "It might be OK."

"You honestly believe that?" asked Bree skeptically. "You're crying your eyes out because you *think* things are OK? That girl said that the bloke crashed into her and that his wife gave her coffee and rang her father. Nessa, it's pretty damning, don't you think?"

Nessa said nothing.

"But maybe not certain," Bree conceded. "Maybe it wasn't such a passionate kiss. Maybe there is a reasonable explanation—she might be a business acquaintance that he's trying to be especially nice to and he's just turning on the old Adam Riley charm a bit too much. It doesn't have to be a full-blown affair. As for the postcard—that could be from anyone. You need to be sure."

"Yes." Nessa sniffed loudly.

"So why don't you ask him?"

"Ask him?" Nessa looked at Bree in horror. "I can't ask him."

"Why not? At least if you ask him you'll know."

"If I ask him and he says he's having an affair I don't know what I'll do," said Nessa miserably. "I'm not ready for him to tell me it's true. And if he denies it—well, I'll have stirred things up for nothing and I don't know if I'll believe him anyway."

"You have to do something," Bree said. "You can't sit around thinking about it and getting yourself more and more worked up." She looked at Nessa thoughtfully. "You could hire a private investigator. Someone to follow him around the place for a while."

"I couldn't do that!" Nessa looked aghast. "He's my husband."

"He's your potentially cheating husband," said Bree.

"People like me don't hire private investigators," Nessa said firmly.

"People like you do," said Bree.

Nessa was silent. This was more the Bree that she was used to. The practical, do something about it Bree. The girl who didn't take any nonsense from anyone.

"I'll think about it," she said finally.

"I could do it for you," suggested Bree.

"He'd recognize you," said Nessa scathingly. "He does actually know you."

Bree grinned at her. "I know. But I could do a bit of following on the bike. He doesn't know the bike. He should, of course, but he doesn't. He hardly knows the difference between a Vespa and a Harley."

"I think he does."

"He doesn't notice cars or bikes," said Bree patiently. "If you want I can follow him for you for a couple of days."

"What about work?" asked Nessa.

"I can take some time off."

"I don't know." Nessa picked at her thumbnail and split it. She bit the jagged edge.

"Think about it," said Bree. "Let me know."

Nessa nodded. "OK."

"He's a shit," said Bree again.

"Maybe not," said Nessa. "I could be totally overreacting. He's good to me, Bree. He's always been good to me. And to Jill."

"I know," said her sister. "But sometimes that's not enough, is it?"

Nessa exhaled slowly. "No." She wiped her eyes again. "But what about you?" she asked. "What about you and the slinky dress?"

"Forget about me and the damned slinky dress," said Bree. "I'll give Cate a buzz tomorrow. Maybe she'll come shopping with me." She smiled at Nessa. "Can you imagine Cate and me in a clothes shop? The poor girl will be having hysterics."

Nessa smiled faintly too. "Probably." She stood up. "Come and have a look in my wardrobe anyway. I don't really have slinky but I do have dresses."

"Nessa, I don't want to hang around while you're upset. It doesn't matter about the dress."

"Please," said Nessa. "I want you to look."

"OK." Bree nodded. "Then I'll leave you in peace."

"I don't know about that." Nessa sighed. "It was cathartic having you here and spilling my guts."

"How long have you known?" asked Bree curiously.

"It seems like forever," said Nessa. "But only a few days."

"And you've kept it to yourself."

"I didn't know who to talk to about it," said Nessa. "I didn't know who to call. I thought you and Cate would laugh at me. And I didn't want to shatter Mum's illusions—" She covered her mouth with her hand.

"What?" asked Bree.

"I just wondered," said Nessa slowly, "when me and Jill were in Salthill. Staying with Mum and Dad. Was he with her then? Did he have her back to this house?"

"Don't think like that," Bree told her. "You'll go crazy if you think like that."

"I'm going bloody crazy anyway," said Nessa tautly as she walked out of the living room and up the stairs.

14

♥

Neptune in 4th house

Chaos can rule at home both in organization and looking after children.

It was nearly ten o'clock when Bree got back to her flat. Adam still hadn't arrived home by the time she left Nessa's, having looked at some dresses and then helped put Jill to bed. For the first time, Bree had realized that Nessa's clothes—while not as up-to-the-minute as Cate's—were clearly expensive and that slinky dresses didn't exactly come cheap.

She took off her leather jacket and flung it onto the bed. Tomorrow, she thought, I'll tidy up the flat. Definitely. After all, if I bring Michael back here and I'm wearing a slinky dress I really don't want to have him take it off me and drop it in a pile with my oil-stained T-shirts and grimy socks.

She was looking forward to her date with Michael. She'd never gone to an expensive restaurant with anyone before, she'd always preferred quantity to quality and so had her other boyfriends. This was going to be very different. More grown up. Maybe it's time, Bree mused, that I began to think of myself as grown up.

Her mobile phone rang and she retrieved it from her jacket pocket.

"It's me," said Cate. "You rang a million times. And then you went to Nessa's. What's wrong?"

"Nothing," said Bree. "At least, nothing when I called you."

"There's something wrong now?" Cate's voice was anxious.

"Not exactly," said Bree. "I was ringing because I wanted your advice about—"

"My advice!" Cate interrupted her. "What do I know about six-stroke engines or whatever it is you work on?"

"Don't be stupid," said Bree. "Clearly I was looking for your advice as a fashion guru. But—"

"I don't believe I heard that," said Cate. "Fashion. You?"

"You don't have to sound so surprised," Bree said irritably. "I wanted to ask you about dresses. But you weren't available so that's why I went to Nessa's."

"Nessa!" Cate's voice was scathing. "What would she know about fashion?"

"Not a lot about the sort of gear you wear sometimes," agreed Bree. "But she has some nice clothes, Cate."

"Money will always buy you nice things," said Cate scornfully. "But not style."

"I never realized before how patronizing you could be," said Bree. "Well, not true, because you were always a patronizing sort of cow, weren't you?"

"I'll pretend you didn't say that."

"Oh, you were," said Bree. "Looking down on me for being your grubby little sister."

"You are little. You are grubby."

"Still?"

"You said it."

"I don't think I want to talk to you." Bree was annoyed.

"Fine," said Cate. "I only rang back because you sounded so urgent. But I didn't realize it was just to get at me."

"Actually things are different now. I do need to talk to you despite the fact that you're a bit of a bitch," said Bree slowly. "It's about Nessa."

"What's wrong with Nessa?" asked Cate. "Did she discover that her next-door neighbor got new curtains and now she has to get new ones too?"

Bree couldn't help smiling even though she knew that it wasn't a very sympathetic thing to do. "It's nothing to do with curtains," she told Cate.

"What, then?"

"She thinks Adam is having an affair."

Cate was silent. Bree could hear occasional static on the line but nothing else.

"Are you still there?" she asked.

"Adam having an affair?" Cate couldn't keep the shock out of her voice. "You're joking."

"Clearly not," said Bree. "And if you'd seen the state Nessa was in you'd know that she was taking it seriously too."

"But what makes her think he's having an affair?" asked Cate.

Bree told Cate about the conversation between Portia and Terri that Nessa had overheard in the sauna, as well as the discovery of the postcard from "xxx A."

"Jesus wept." Cate could hardly believe it. "Poor old Ness."

"She doesn't know whether it's true or not," explained Bree. "She keeps thinking that maybe these two girls were talking about someone else even though she knows deep down it couldn't possibly be. And she's also wracking her brains to think of someone whose name begins with A that they both know."

"What makes her think she knows this person anyway?" asked Cate.

"Nothing," said Bree. "I think she just wants to feel that she might know them. Although why she'd want to feel like that is a mystery to me."

"What's she going to do? Confront him?" asked Cate.

"She hasn't decided yet," said Bree.

"Will I phone her?"

"I don't know." Bree was doubtful. "If you call her now she'll think that I hardly had time to get home before ringing you with the lowdown. You know what she's like. She'll think I couldn't wait to ring up and gloat about the fact that her perfect marriage isn't so perfect after all."

"Probably."

"So perhaps you could leave it until tomorrow at least."

"Might be best," agreed Cate.

"Let me know how she is," Bree asked her. "I said that if she wanted me to trail Adam and spy on him I'd do it."

"Spy on him?"

"Nessa fondly imagines he'd spot me if I followed him on the bike but you know Adam, Cate. He hasn't a clue. So I could check it out next time he tells her he's going to be late home."

"Presumably he wasn't at home earlier?"

"He was meeting clients allegedly," said Bree. "God knows how many times he's used that excuse."

"Poor Nessa," said Cate again. "She must feel terrible."

"She didn't look great," admitted Bree. "She'd put on makeup because she'd clearly been crying like mad but it made her look worse, if anything."

"Why would he do it?" asked Cate. "He has a good family. Nessa loves him. I thought he loved her."

"See what thought did."

"Oh, Bree. Don't be so bloody cynical."

"It's hard not to be."

Cate sighed. "Is it just a dream?" she asked. "The whole idea of getting married and living happily ever after?"

"You're asking the wrong person," Bree told her. "I'm still waiting for Mr. Might Be Right. And you should know, Cate. You're engaged."

"You wanted to ask me about clothes?" Cate changed the subject back to Bree's original reason for phoning her.

"It doesn't really matter," said Bree dismissively. "I was looking for a place to buy a slinky dress."

"What!"

"Why does everyone sound so surprised when I ask about dresses?"

"You know perfectly well why," said Cate crisply. "I'd say you were about four the last time you wore a dress."

"The red one," said Bree.

"You even remember!"

"Only because it was so uncomfortable. Every time I bent down you could see my knickers."

"Sometimes that's the point of a dress," Cate told her.

"Not when you're four," said Bree.

"Well, no," admitted Cate. "That used to be my dress, didn't it?"

"Yes," said Bree. "Bloody hand-me-downs. Why on earth Mum kept it that long I'll never know."

"Of course you do." Cate sounded amused. "Mum always liked the idea of being thrifty about clothes."

"That's probably why I've been scarred for life about dresses," said Bree glumly. "Anyway, I'm going out and I need a dress and I wanted to know was there anywhere good I should check out."

"What sort of dress?"

"Slinky," repeated Bree. "And preferably one that doesn't show my knickers."

"I'm sorry," Cate told Bree when her laughter had subsided. "I just don't see you in slinky."

"At least Nessa made the effort," said Bree irritably. "Even though her heart is broken."

Cate was silent. For a moment she'd forgotten her own trauma. She loved the moments when she forgot, when everything seemed OK again.

"I'm sorry," she said. "What do you want it for?"

Bree explained about her date with Michael Morrissey and his desire to see her legs.

"You don't really want slinky," said Cate. "Slinky is what you think you should wear but it's really not you. You want something less sophisticated than slinky."

"You mean I'm not elegant enough to carry it off?" demanded Bree.

"Slinky is Catherine Zeta Jones," said Cate. "You're more Kate Winslet."

"Great," said Bree. "Is that before or after she went down with the *Titanic?*"

"Oh, don't be silly," said Cate briskly. "You've got to be realistic. Wear a dress, certainly, you'll look great in a dress. But not something that clings."

"Cate, I'm a size ten and a bit," said Bree. "You're making me sound like a mountain. What the hell size are you?"

"Eight," said Cate dismissively. "But a small eight."

"I'm a ten, Nessa is a fourteen and you're a small eight." Bree sighed. "That probably means six. You're too thin, Catey."

"You've said that before."

"I know but—"

"Look, do you want my advice or not?" asked Cate impatiently.

"All right."

"It's summer," said Cate. "It's still warm. Wear something reasonably loose because then you won't keep checking it to see if it's gaping anywhere. When you're a bit heavier—"

"I—am—not—heavy." Bree enunciated every word.

"OK," amended Cate. "When you're not a stick insect you can't afford to swan around in diaphanous stuff. I think you should get a nice cotton dress. And go for a definite color. A warm one with your complexion. Actually a deep pink or purple would be nice."

"Pink!"

"You did ask."

Bree sighed. "And where should I shop?"

"Anywhere," said Cate. "There are loads of places. Do you want to spend a lot of money? Is he that important to you?"

"I don't have a lot of money to spend," said Bree.

"Try somewhere like Mango," suggested Cate. "They're not bad. Or Oasis."

"Thanks," said Bree. She sighed. "I feel really guilty talking about getting dressed up when Nessa is so unhappy."

"Don't," said Cate. "She wouldn't want you to feel guilty."

"I know," said Bree. "But I can't help feeling it all the same."

"I'll phone her tomorrow," promised Cate. "And I'm really looking forward to hearing about your date."

Bree laughed. "It'll probably be a complete disaster. Anything I plan always ends up a complete disaster."

"Not everything, surely," said Cate.

"You'd be surprised," Bree told her.

Cate replaced the receiver slowly and turned toward Finn who'd been pretending not to listen to her conversation with Bree but whose eyebrows had shot up when the word "affair" was mentioned.

"Nessa thinks Adam is having an affair," she told him.

"I gathered as much."

"The bastard!" Cate was surprised at how angry she felt.

"Maybe you're all jumping to conclusions."

"It sounded pretty definite to me."

"It's not your problem, Cate. You have to let them work it out."

"I know," she said impatiently. "But Nessa's my sister and if that fucker has upset her—"

"There's two sides to it," Finn reminded her.

Cate looked at him. "You're saying it might be her fault?"

He shook his head. "Only that nothing's clear cut."

Tell him now, she urged herself. Tell him while he's caught up with looking at two sides to an argument. While he knows that nothing is clear cut. Tell him that he's going to be a father.

He yawned. "I feel bloated after all that nan bread," he told her. "And tomorrow's an early morning. I'd better get to bed."

"I'll follow you," said Cate.

"Sure." He kissed her on the lips. "Goodnight."

"Goodnight," she said.

Nessa was in bed when Adam came home. She pretended to be asleep when he slipped under the sheets beside her. Once his breathing became regular and even, she slid out of the bed and took his shirt out of the laundry basket. She sniffed it. Cigar smoke and Chinese food, she decided. And Polo aftershave, which she'd bought for his birthday. She couldn't smell perfume. So maybe tonight had been a night with clients after all. Cigar smoke and Chinese smelled like a business thing not an illicit liaison.

Oh, what the hell would I know, she asked herself despairingly. I'm only the fool of a wife.

15

♥

Moon/Saturn aspects

Cautious, possibly pessimistic in outlook, lacking self-confidence, difficulties with relationships.

Cate was already awake when Finn's alarm clock went off the following morning. She listened as he did his usual thump around the apartment, banging into things, letting doors slam shut and actually singing (if that was what you could call the noise he was making) in the shower. Doesn't he know by now how bloody loud he is, she asked herself. Does he actually do it deliberately? But she didn't move as he came back into the bedroom and adjusted the blinds so that pale early morning light filtered into the room before he got dressed. Unlike many people who presented radio programs and who sat behind the mike in faded woolly jumpers or slogan-emblazoned T-shirts, Finn liked to wear a suit on his show. He felt that it set him apart, as someone who took the issues seriously. Businessmen come into the studio, he told Cate once, and they're wearing the corporate image. I want to make them feel as though they're talking to a person who understands what it's like to be running a big company.

He swore under his breath and Cate knew that he'd messed up his tie. Despite wearing the suits, he actually hated ties. He knocked against the side of the bed as he left the room and she gritted her teeth. One day she was going to tell him that he always knocked into the side of the bed. And that if all the previous noise he made didn't wake her, that certainly did.

She opened her eyes as he closed the bedroom door. Five minutes and he'd be gone. She'd get up then, she thought. Lying here awake was driving her crazy. The hum of his voice through the closed door made her frown. Was he on the phone to someone at this hour? She propped herself up on her elbow and strained to listen.

"Finn Coolidge. The voice of a nation."

He was saying the words, she realized. The slogan from his TV show. Repeating them with a number of inflections so that each time he said them the emphasis was different. She felt a lump in her throat. It meant so much to him. It was his dream and it was coming true.

His voice stopped and she heard the apartment door open then bang shut behind him.

She lay in the bed for a while, unable to move. Then, suddenly, she sat up. She rushed into the bathroom and only barely made it before she threw up, violently, into the sink.

She leaned against the wall and closed her eyes.

"Changes have been in the air for some time now but you haven't felt deeply enough to make any decisions," read Nessa. *"The conjunction between the Moon and Saturn can make you feel pressurized. Gradually you realize that you must shift your focus. Discussions with others will enable you to recognize opportunities for what they are."*

I don't want to shift my focus, she thought miserably. I like my focus the way it is. And does this mean that if I start talking to him about his other bloody woman it'll give him the opportunity to tell me it's all over between us?

I don't want it to be over. She looked at the magazine again. I don't want everything I've worked for to be swept away.

"*No matter how much you've pondered on recent decisions, be prepared to reassess your position,*" said Adam's horoscope. "*You're chafing at delays and situations where other people make decisions. Discussion is vital.*"

Talk. Discussion. Communicate. As if I don't know all that crap already. But I don't want confrontation. She rubbed her arms. I hate confrontation. I always have. I don't want to tell Adam I need to talk to him and suddenly have a row about his other woman.

She took another biscuit from the barrel and nibbled on it. Then she opened the Golden Pages.

She was surprised at the number of detective agencies operating in the country. Nearly all of them undertook what they called marital and family law investigations. Some of them even specialized in marital and family law investigations. As well as discreet covert surveillance. Nessa found it hard to think that she was even contemplating having Adam watched, discreet or otherwise. The agencies promised photographic evidence too. She smiled grimly at the thought of someone taking photos of Adam engaged in a spot of tongue shoving down the postcard woman's throat.

But it was an idea. Better than accusing him and allowing him to tell her that she was losing her marbles and that there was no other woman. She had so little to go on that it wouldn't be difficult for Adam to tell her that she'd got it all wrong. And for him to somehow cover his tracks (if that was what he wanted to do) afterward. He could say that Portia Laing didn't even know him and that she was clearly mixing him up with someone else. Nessa wouldn't be able to prove anything different. She'd have caused trouble for nothing.

Nessa felt another spurt of hope. Maybe Portia *was* mixing him up with someone else. She said she'd seen Adam with this woman but how could she be sure it was him? She'd hardly spent more than a minute cursing and swearing at him for banging into her father's car before he'd gone to work. She might, in fact, have made a simple mistake.

Nessa felt a wave of relief sweep over her as she reassessed what she'd heard Portia say. She had no doubt that the girl had seen someone and that the man was Adam's age, maybe even looked like Adam but, with the memory of the car incident still in her mind, Portia could have imposed Adam's face on the actual man concerned. So she'd told a story about Adam which really related to someone else. That made sense, reasoned Nessa, after all, she still didn't have any evidence with which to accuse Adam. Except for the postcard. But the postcard meant nothing.

She walked into his tiny study and opened the book on time and management studies again. The postcard was exactly where she'd left it. "Wish you were here, xxx A."

"Lots of innocent explanations," she said out loud. "Lots."

The phone rang and she nearly jumped out of her skin. She looked at it warily, half expecting it to be "xxx A" although she realized immediately that she was being silly. But she reached out for it as though it was radioactive.

"Hello." Her voice was tentative.

"Hi, Nessa." Cate's voice was equally tentative.

"Hi, Cate." Nessa didn't say anything else.

Cate wasn't sure exactly what she wanted to say either. She took a deep breath. "Bree phoned me yesterday," she told Nessa. "She said she was in your house."

"Oh, yes."

"She'd been looking for me earlier," explained Cate. "But I was at meetings and I couldn't phone her back. Then Finn and I were having dinner so I . . ." Her voice trailed off.

"I showed Bree some dresses," said Nessa. "She has a hot date apparently."

"She said you had some lovely stuff."

"Not your kind of thing, though."

"Different styles," said Cate. "We always had different styles."

"She's going shopping," Nessa said. "Late-night opening tonight so she's bound to get something."

"I gave her some tips," said Cate.

"It's funny, isn't it, thinking of her in a slinky dress."

"I told her not to go for slinky. I said that loose cotton would be nicer."

"Cotton!" Nessa sounded disgusted. "She wants to look gorgeous, not sensible."

"She can get something really nice in cotton," said Cate. "It doesn't have to look like day wear."

"Bree has a lovely figure," protested Nessa. "She could wear voile or satin."

"But she can't carry it off," stated Cate. "She'd clump around the place in satin and look uncomfortable. I wanted to help her look glamorous and feel OK at the same time."

"It's up to her," said Nessa tiredly.

"Sure."

There was silence. Nessa picked at the corner of the "xxx A" post-card while Cate, who was doing up some accounts figures on her Excel spreadsheet, accidentally cleared a row of numbers.

"I'd better go," said Nessa. "I promised Jill I'd bring her swimming later."

"Bree said that you might have a problem." Cate's words tumbled over each other. "With Adam."

"Did she?"

"Yes," said Cate.

"What sort of problem?"

"She said you thought that he might be seeing someone."

"Elegantly put." Nessa closed the book on the postcard before she ripped it to shreds.

"If there's anything I can do, Nessa . . ."

"Like what?"

"I don't know."

"It doesn't matter anyway," said Nessa. "I've been making a fuss about nothing. That girl was mixing Adam up with someone else."

"How d'you know?" asked Cate. "Have you talked to him?"

"No," said Nessa. "But I thought about it again and, you know, she hardly even saw Adam. So I don't know how she could be sure it was him."

"Why would she say it if she wasn't sure?" asked Cate.

"She was talking to a friend," explained Nessa. "She was telling a story. How much better for her to make it someone she'd met recently than any old bloke."

"I suppose you might be right," said Cate doubtfully.

"I was upset last night," said Nessa. "I overreacted to something. Bree happened to be here and caught the brunt of it. It's nothing."

"Well, if you discover that maybe it's more than you think . . ."

"It's not," said Nessa firmly. "Absolutely not. Me and Adam are rock solid. Just like you and Finn."

Cate said nothing. She thought she was going to cry. She didn't want to cry, certainly not in the office and absolutely not in front of her sister. But she could feel the lump in her throat and the sting of tears in her eyes. Is it my hormones, she wondered? Is this what happens to pregnant women? Do they all cry at the drop of a hat? Do *we* all cry at the drop of a hat, she amended.

"Cate?" Nessa broke the silence. "Are you still there?"

"Yes." Cate cleared her throat.

"I'd better be going," said Nessa again.

It wouldn't be fair to burden Nessa with her problems when she had problems of her own, thought Cate. Besides, Nessa would be terribly judgmental. Not that she could really blame her. Nessa had wanted a second child so much that Cate couldn't see her sister sympathizing in the slightest with her horror of finding herself pregnant now. Pregnant and engaged. Where would be the problem, as far as Nessa was concerned?

"Can we meet?" Cate surprised herself by asking the question. She rubbed the back of her neck. She hadn't been able to stop herself even though she'd made a decision not to tell Nessa anything. What the hell was wrong with her?

"Meet?"

"Meet," said Cate impatiently. "You and me."

"What for?"

"I want to have a chat with you."

"What about? I've told you, me and Adam are sorted out."

"It's nothing to do with you and Adam," said Cate. "The world doesn't only revolve around you and Adam."

"If you're going to talk to me like that—"

"I'm sorry, I'm sorry," said Cate. "I didn't mean it."

"Just like you didn't mean it the night you borrowed my blue angora jumper and spilled Malibu and orange down the front?"

"Nessa, I spent months apologizing to you for that!"

"The one item of clothing I had that you liked so you borrowed it and then ruined it."

"I paid you back."

"It wasn't the same."

"Do you want me to say sorry all over again?" demanded Cate.

"No." Nessa sighed. "What do you want to talk about?"

"Not on the phone," said Cate. "I don't want to talk to you on the phone."

"Is everything all right?" Nessa frowned. This didn't sound like Cate at all.

"I don't know," said Cate.

"You're not sick are you?"

"Of course not," said Cate. "I just—I wanted your advice on something."

"My God!" Nessa laughed shortly. "You and Bree both. Given that she was talking about fashion—a subject that we've already established I know very little about—what do you want to discuss? Piston rings?"

"No," said Cate. "Just some stuff, that's all."

"Well, OK," said Nessa. "What do you want to do? Drop around?"

"No." Cate's tone was vehement. "Let's meet for a drink. How about tomorrow night?"

"I'll have to check and see if Adam is in," Nessa warned her.

"God Almighty, Nessa, you're as much entitled to be out as he is," snapped Cate. "Just tell him to be in."

"I don't just tell Adam anything," said Nessa.

"Maybe you should."

Nessa shrugged. "Perhaps. Let's assume he'll be in. Where d'you want to meet? Can you come out to Malahide?"

"Sure," said Cate. "Smyth's? Say about eight?"

"Sounds OK to me," said Nessa.

"See you then," said Cate and hung up.

Nessa stared at the handset and listened to the dialing tone. She'd never known Cate to be so abrupt. But if Cate thought that she was going to Smyth's tomorrow to talk about Adam, she had another think coming. She wasn't going to let Cate pick at her marriage and tell her what she should and shouldn't do. Cate might have said that she was looking for advice but Cate was the girl who spent most of her youth dishing out unasked for advice herself. Usually, Nessa conceded, rather good advice about makeup and clothes and boyfriends. But not advice that Nessa bothered to heed.

Anyway, she can't give me advice about my marriage, Nessa decided as she walked out of the study and closed the door behind her. I love Adam. I trust Adam. We have a good, strong relationship.

• • •

She told him about her drinks date with Cate while they were watching the evening news. He'd arrived home early that night with a box of Terry's All Gold.

"I wish I could confess that I'd rushed out and bought them for you in a fit of mad passion," he told her, his eyes twinkling. "But one of our clients sent us a hamper of goodies to thank us for some particularly hard work that we did. We divided up the spoils and I got the chocs."

"Thanks for bringing them home."

"Oh, I know that the way to a woman's heart is through a box of chocolates," he told her. He put his arm around her and hugged her to him. Then he kissed her gently on the lips just as Jill walked into the kitchen and made exaggerated sounds of being ill at the sight of her parents' embrace. Which somewhat ruined the romantic moment that Nessa so desperately craved.

There hadn't been time for additional romantic moments. Jill wanted her food, so did Adam, and Nessa knew that she wouldn't have any peace until they'd eaten. After dinner, they all sat down to watch TV.

"Why did Cate pick tomorrow?" asked Adam after she'd told him. "It's bloody awkward, Nessa."

"Tomorrow suited her," said Nessa. "Why is it awkward?"

"I've a few things to do," he said. "I wasn't expecting to be home before eight."

"I never tell you to be home early," said Nessa.

"I know."

"So you can make it tomorrow," she said.

He looked sideways at her but she was gazing at the TV screen.

"Don't tell me that this is one of your sisterly crises," he said. "Remember that time you and Cate got together for a pow-wow about Bree? Because you thought she was doing drugs?"

"We never thought she was doing drugs," said Nessa impatiently. "She was living with someone who was. We were worried about her."

"Don't interfere," warned Adam. "She didn't speak to you for ages last time."

"It's nothing to do with Bree," said Nessa. "Besides, she got over it. And she knew that we were only acting in her best interests."

"Giving anonymous tips to the police wasn't exactly in her best interests," said Adam.

"We didn't!" Nessa turned to him. "We told her that we'd consider it."

"And she told you to sod off as far as I remember."

"Yes, but she left him in the end! Anyway," added Nessa, "I told you. It's nothing to do with Bree. Cate and I are going for a drink together, that's all. It's probably wedding stuff."

Adam grinned. "She's going to quiz you about the length of her veil and things like that, is she?"

"No," said Nessa dryly. "More likely she's going to ask me if it's all worth it."

"Of course it is," said Adam.

"For men," conceded Nessa. "She might want to know if a woman gets anything out of it."

"You got a lot," said Adam.

"I got you," said Nessa.

"Exactly." And although her husband smiled at her and even though she'd decided that her marriage was rock solid after all, Nessa found it very difficult to smile back.

Bree wasn't sure that Michael would consider her new outfit slinky but she rather liked it all the same. She'd taken Cate's words about being comfortable to heart and had discounted four dresses which she'd tried on as being too tight, too low-cut, too short and too scratchy. She knew, too, what Cate meant about her not being able to carry off slinky. There'd been a pale pink slinky creation which she'd imagined would fit the bill perfectly but, as soon as she'd squirmed into it, she knew that she didn't have what it took to carry it off. Slinky required walking in a different way—a kind of gliding motion that Bree couldn't quite master. She knew that she strode across a room instead of walking daintily across it which spoiled the effect of the shimmering fabric. She needed something that could make her look like a person who didn't spend her days up to her neck in oil while still allowing her the freedom to walk like a normal person instead of a model. This left her with a deep purple skirt and matching shoe-string top which could easily be mistaken for a dress. It was something of a compromise but it was a flattering outfit and one that made her look a little more vulnerable than usual. She quite liked how she looked in it even though she felt that the girl who looked back at her from the mirror was miles away from the girl she actually was.

She'd forgotten, of course, that she needed to buy shoes as well. The shoe shops had been another minor nightmare. She knew that she needed proper shoes instead of the trainers or desert boots she favored but she'd been embarrassed by the fact that her feet were a wide fitting and the shoes she'd wanted didn't come in a wide fitting. Eventually she'd found a pair that were reasonably comfortable (even though the heels were definitely too high for her) and that matched her outfit. After buying them she nipped into the Body Shop and treated herself to a new foundation, eyeshadow and lipstick.

And if he doesn't jump on me after this little lot he never will, she decided ruefully as she walked out of the shop laden with carrier bags and made her way back to the flat.

16

♥

Mars in the 1st House

Impulsive, hot-headed but energetic and positive.

Nessa didn't know how she'd find Cate in the crush. The fine weather that had dominated most of the summer had quite suddenly given way to a day when gray clouds had rolled in from the sea and threatened rain. So instead of sitting in beer gardens or spilling out onto the pavement as they'd grown accustomed to, people had thronged indoors into the bars and lounges and Smyth's was crowded. She stood on tiptoe and tried to scan over the heads of the crowd for a sight of her sister.

She jumped in surprise as she felt her phone vibrate in the pocket of her trousers.

"I'm the other side of the bar," said Cate and Nessa looked across the room to where Cate was waving at her. She waved in return and pushed her way through the mass of people, swearing loudly as a girl in platform shoes stood on her toe.

"Not a good choice," mouthed Cate as Nessa reached her. "I can hardly hear myself think."

"D'you want to go somewhere else?" asked Nessa.

Cate nodded and the two of them jostled their way out of the bar again.

"Sorry," said Cate. "I'm clearly getting old. The racket in there was unbelievable."

"Friday night's always like that," said Nessa. "I should've remembered, suggested somewhere else myself."

"Will we just go to the Grand?" suggested Cate. "It'll be quiet enough there. My car's across the road so it'll only take a minute."

Nessa nodded and followed Cate to her car. Her sister drove to the hotel at the other end of the town.

"Much better," said Nessa as they walked inside.

"But worrying," said Cate, "to think that we've abandoned the hip-hop place to be for a bloody hotel bar. I feel like Mum all of a sudden."

"If you want to drink we can go back to the bar," said Nessa. "But if you want to talk . . ."

"To be honest, I'm not sure what I want," confessed Cate. "But let me order a drink anyway. What d'you want?"

"A glass of red wine," said Nessa.

She glanced at Cate in surprise as her sister ordered the red wine for her and a glass of sparkling water for herself.

"On a beauty regime?" she asked. "Detoxing before the big day. Which is when, exactly?"

"It's supposed to be March," said Cate. "Finn's show starts in September and ends in March."

"Good idea," said Nessa. "I bet he's really looking forward to it."

"Yes."

"I can't quite believe that my prospective brother-in-law will be a TV personality." Nessa grinned at Cate. "It must be really weird for you."

"Kind of."

"And I know you said that you didn't expect a media fuss at your wedding but there'll be newspapers at the very least."

"Maybe," said Cate unenthusiastically.

Nessa sipped her wine. "Is there something wrong?" she asked. "Are you really worried that there'll be publicity? Is that what the problem is? Or don't you want to wait until March to get married?"

"Not exactly."

"What then?" Nessa looked curiously at Cate. "Don't tell me you're having second thoughts."

"I—no. I don't think so."

"You don't think so!"

"Oh, Nessa." Cate twisted her hands together. "It's not me and Finn that's the problem. It's—well—you see, if I don't do something about it now I could be having a baby in March."

Nessa stared at Cate without speaking. It was as though she heard the words but couldn't quite grasp their meaning. Yet she knew what Cate was saying. She was pregnant. She was going to have a baby!

"Congratulations!" she cried eventually. "I can see your problem all right, you don't exactly want to walk up the aisle resting your bouquet on your bump! What does Finn think? Is changing the date of the wedding a hassle? Have you booked everything?" She scratched the back of her head. "Or does he want to bring it forward? Rush it? And you're not keen?"

"Nothing like that," said Cate.

"Whatever the problem is, it's not insurmountable," said Nessa. "Except you clearly don't want to have your wedding and the birth of your baby on the same day!"

Cate twisted her hands together again. "I don't want to have the birth of the baby at all," she said blankly.

This time it was much longer before Nessa spoke.

"What are you saying?" Her eyes searched Cate's face.

"I don't want to have this baby."

"You can't mean that."

"Of course I can," said Cate. "I'm pregnant and I don't want to be."

"But—you're getting married," said Nessa. "Maybe you've got pregnant before you meant to but surely that doesn't really matter. You've been living with Finn for years anyway."

"I know," said Cate evenly. "And I love Finn very much. But he doesn't want a child yet and neither do I."

"Is that what he said?" Nessa gulped back some wine.

"I haven't told him yet."

"Cate!"

"Nessa, I can't tell him. He's about to launch himself on a major new path of his career. I can't get him into a state about a baby that I know he doesn't want. Not now."

"Babies aren't like an item on a menu." Nessa's voice was dangerously calm. "You don't just choose what you're having and when you're having it. I should know."

"Oh, God, Nessa—I know that. I know how you feel about kids. I really do. But *you* should know that I feel very differently. And it's not just Finn's career. It's mine too. I had a really shitty first half of this year but things are beginning to turn around and it's all because of some very hard work I put in. This is important to me too. It means that I can live with Finn on an equal footing because we'll both be doing well, not just him. I can't if I'm up the spout."

"Don't talk about it like that," said Nessa furiously. "As though it's a lifestyle choice."

"It *is* a lifestyle choice," Cate told her. "I have to make a choice, don't I? To have children or not to have children. It's my decision to make."

"Sometimes you don't make the decision," said Nessa. "You want them but you can't have them. You don't want them but you get pregnant. Or you get pregnant when you didn't quite expect it. That's the way life works, Cate. You can't plan it all like it was a marketing campaign."

"I know that," said Cate impatiently. "I'm not saying that you can have everything you want. But nobody has to have a baby they don't want."

Nessa stared at her. "Are you saying what I think you're saying?"

"I'm afraid of being pregnant," said Cate. "I thought that maybe if we decided to have kids and if I was totally committed to the idea then I'd be able to do it. Because it'd be like going on a long-haul flight or something. You don't want to, you don't like it, but if it achieves your objectives you put up with it. But from the minute I discovered I was pregnant I was terrified. And I'm still terrified. I don't want another life invading my body and I don't want nine months of having my insides rearranged and feeling sick and not being able to drink and I absolutely, definitely and categorically do *not* want to spend twelve hours panting and pushing while doctors with forceps and scissors and God knows what else are attacking the most vulnerable part of my body."

"You are the most selfish person I've ever met in my life." Nessa stared at her. "I can't believe I'm hearing you say all this."

"Why do I have to be selfish just because I don't want to have a

baby?" demanded Cate. "Surely it's just as selfish to decide that you
do. After all, the child has no say in the matter. It's conceived
whether it likes its parents or not!"

"Don't be so bloody juvenile."

"I'm not. Look, I know you wanted more than one kid, Nessa,
and my heart bleeds for you that you haven't had another. But you
might, one day. At the same time you love Jill. You care about her. If
I had a baby now I wouldn't love it."

"Of course you would," said Nessa. "It would be your baby, Cate.
Part of you. You must love it."

"It's part of me now and I hate it," said Cate baldly.

"I thought I knew you," Nessa said as she looked at Cate. "But I
don't. I'm so far away from knowing you as not to believe it."

"Just because it was right for you doesn't mean it'd be right for
me." Cate's tone was pleading. "I simply can't imagine what it
would be like. I can't imagine living with it."

"So you're saying that you want to get rid of it?" Nessa almost
spat the words at her.

"You make it sound as though I'm a heartless bitch who doesn't
care about anyone."

Nessa raised her eyebrows. "You said it."

"I knew I shouldn't have said anything. I knew you wouldn't
understand." Cate's voice shook.

"I understand that you're not thinking straight. For God's sake,
Catey, it's a baby you're talking about. Not a bloody sports shoe!"
Nessa stared at her.

"It's an unwanted baby," said Cate vehemently. "You just don't
understand how I feel, do you?"

"Of course I don't understand how you feel. I understand that
you might be shocked about being pregnant. I understand that you
might be feeling confused. And a little scared. We're all scared when
we find out. There isn't a woman in the world who isn't scared, Cate.
But don't ask me to understand that you are thinking of getting an
abortion for the simple reason that you're not ready for this baby."

"You don't think that's a good enough reason?" Cate's eyes
brimmed with tears. "You think that feeling that I couldn't possibly
have a child now isn't a decent reason for not having a child now? It's
the best possible reason, Nessa. The absolute best possible reason."

"Nobody is ever ready," spat Nessa. "Nobody expects it to be the way it is. God knows, I wanted Jill. Afterward, I was totally shocked at what the reality of having a baby was like. But I got to grips with it, Cate. Because I loved her."

"Everyone says they're shocked about the reality of having a baby! I'm not stupid!" cried Cate. "I know about it. That's why I don't want to have it. Because I know I couldn't cope with it. Jesus Christ, Nessa, Finn already does ridiculous hours for radio. It'll be even worse when the TV starts. When do you seriously think he'll have a minute for this kid, let alone me? I don't want his child to only know him by seeing him on the telly or hearing him on the radio. And I don't want to have to fit in a school play between a product launch and my monthly sales meetings. We can't have this baby, Nessa. We just can't."

"Listen to yourself," cried Nessa. "You're comparing having a family life with a monthly sales meeting."

"I'm not."

Nessa finished her wine. "You can adapt, Cate," she told her sister. "You *could* adapt. But you can't possibly have an abortion."

"I'm going to." Cate blinked rapidly. "I hoped you'd support me. But I don't care if you don't."

Nessa stood up. "Do what you have to do," she said coolly. "But don't ask me to support you. Because I won't."

Finn flicked the remote control and stopped the video tape as Cate walked into the apartment. But she knew that he'd been watching videos of himself as he rehearsed parts of his show. She found it touching that he didn't want her to see them, that he didn't want her to see any weaknesses in his presentation.

"So, how was Nessa?" he asked as she threw her bag on the floor and sat down in the leather armchair.

"As always," said Cate.

"What did she say about Adam?" He looked at her enquiringly.

Adam! Cate had totally forgotten about Nessa and Adam. Nessa had no doubt expected to be quizzed on Adam's suspected infidelity and instead they'd spent the whole time talking about Cate's pregnancy. All thoughts of Adam and Nessa had been totally banished by Nessa's reaction to her news.

"Nothing much," she told Finn evasively.

"Do you think he's having an affair?" asked Finn.

Cate shrugged. "Wouldn't surprise me. Nessa's a very predictable woman, isn't she? And maybe Adam is fed up with having his home-cooked dinner every night and his freshly pressed boxer shorts laid out for him every morning."

"Cate!" Finn looked amused. "I thought they got on well. Adam likes being looked after, doesn't he? And Nessa likes doing the looking after."

"Only if she thinks the person is worth it," said Cate.

Finn raised an eyebrow. "Have you had a row with her?"

Cate hesitated.

"Oh, Cate, how could you possibly have had a row with her when she's clearly not thinking straight."

"She seemed to be thinking straight enough to me," said Cate.

"I feel sorry for her," said Finn.

"Sorry for her?"

"It means everything to her, doesn't it?" he asked. "If Adam leaves, then what has she?"

"A bloody big house and the kid she's always wanted," said Cate sourly.

"You really did have a row!"

"She's so one-dimensional," said Cate. "She can only see her own point of view."

"Which makes it all the more likely that Adam is having an affair, d'you think?"

"I wouldn't blame him," said Cate.

"You don't really mean that."

"Listening to her tonight I could understand it," Cate told Finn.

"Bloody hell." He grinned at her. "The other day you were ready to murder Adam for cheating on her. Tonight you seem to think it's all her fault."

Cate sighed. "Oh, I suppose if he does leave her I'll rally around."

"Don't fall over yourself doing it," said Finn.

"What's with you?" she asked. "You said that there were two sides to it but now you're taking hers. I'd have thought you'd be up for Adam anyway, for the man's right to have a bit on the side if he felt like it."

"Do you really think I'm like that?" Finn sounded hurt.

"I thought all men were like that."

"Cate, you are in a godawful mood tonight," said Finn. "I don't know whether it's because of Nessa or something else entirely but I've never seen you in such bad form."

"Do I have to be in good form all the time?" she asked. "Am I not allowed a black mood from time to time?"

"Depends on who's causing it," said Finn.

"It's not you." She got up from the armchair. "But I'm not good company. I think I'll go inside for a while. Read a book or something."

"Suit yourself," said Finn easily. He waited until she'd gone into the bedroom before he pressed play on the remote control and watched himself doing the introduction to his show for the twentieth time.

17

♥

Sun in Leo, Moon in Leo

Charismatic and attractive, believing your own publicity.

Nessa didn't go straight home from her drink with Cate but instead walked to the seafront and, ignoring the drizzle, sat on a rock watching the tide ebb and flow. She couldn't believe what her sister had told her. She was caught between rage and disgust at Cate's proposed abortion and jealousy that her sister was pregnant at all. Why is life so fucking unfair, she cried silently. Why don't things happen the way we want them to? Why was the wrong sister pregnant? Why was her marriage under threat? Why, why, why couldn't good things happen?

She sat there for a long time as people walked along the seashore. Couples, of course. And women walking together. It was funny, thought Nessa, how often you saw groups of two or three women walking together but you rarely saw groups of men. She supposed they were all in a bar somewhere, talking about sport. They were right, she decided, not to try to share problems like women did. It didn't always make things better. And, she thought as she finally got up, she hadn't even shared hers with Cate. She'd been too caught up in her sister's revelations to even think about herself and Adam.

She'd come down from the high she'd felt when she decided that Portia Laing had made a mistake about Adam. She was being stupid. The girl hadn't made a mistake. Adam had kissed someone. She had to accept that fact. But, every time she came close to accepting it, another excuse would form in her mind, another reason why Portia's story was incorrect, just to confuse her even more. She was exhausted from the leaps in her emotions—relief and joy every time she thought of a reason that Portia might be wrong, to the deepest despair when she could only believe that the girl was absolutely right.

She walked back to the car and drove home. When she walked into the house she found Adam sitting in front of the TV, a giant size bag of tortilla chips and a bottle of beer beside him.

"Have a good time?" He looked away from the screen.

"Fine," she said. There was that word again, she thought, as she took off her jacket. Fine. And things still weren't fine. Not with Cate and not with her. A month ago they would have been fine. A month ago she would have told Adam all about Cate and her pregnancy and the awfulness of her decision not to have the baby. They would have talked about it together and he would have shared her views but, knowing Adam, would have said something nice and comforting about Cate too. And maybe he would have helped Nessa to get over the anger that still coursed through her at Cate's attitude. But now she simply sat on the sofa beside him and picked up a magazine.

"Jill went to bed ages ago." Adam was still watching the TV, he didn't bother to turn to her.

"Good," said Nessa. She flicked through the pages of the magazine although she'd read it before. It was the issue of *New Woman* that she'd bought on the day when she'd first learned that Adam had been seen shoving his tongue down another woman's throat. She bit the edge of her thumbnail and glanced at him. He was absorbed in the TV program again, some kind of cop drama, she realized. The sort of program he enjoyed. She wasn't really into cop dramas herself but she watched them whenever he was watching them. He assumed she liked them too. She hadn't told him any different.

"Have a chip," he said as the program broke for ads. He pushed the bag toward her.

"No thanks."

"Did you get something to eat with Cate?"

"No," she said.

"I didn't think so. You weren't out as long as I expected."

"We ran out of things to say."

He looked away from the TV and at Nessa. "Did you have a fight or something?"

"Not really." She shrugged. "We disagreed."

"It's a while since you two had a row," he said. "Hope it's not like that last one. You were a bitch to live with while that lasted."

"No I wasn't."

"You were cranky," said Adam. "Just like you are now."

She didn't say anything. She wanted to but she didn't. The program recommenced and Adam turned back to the TV.

What is wrong with me? she asked herself despairingly. I can't bring myself to talk about Cate and I can't ask him the question that's eating away at my insides. I keep making up reasons not to ask him. Surely that's not right? Surely other women don't sit beside their cheating husbands while they watch TV and eat tortilla chips. I should be confronting him and talking about it, not pretending that it hasn't happened.

She bit her thumbnail again. What would it be like when she finally plucked up the courage? She supposed he'd tell her that it was all a mistake. Which was what she wanted him to tell her, wasn't it? She was afraid of him saying anything else. She was terrified at the thought that he might be relieved she knew and that he might suddenly decide that the time had come for them to end the sham that was their marriage and for him to move in with xxx A.

It isn't a sham, she told herself fiercely. It isn't. I love him. He loves me. We both love Jill.

Thinking of Jill brought back her conversation with Cate again. There was a part of her who felt sorry for Cate but Cate was lucky. She had a wonderful, gorgeous, sexy boyfriend who adored her and who had a brilliant job. Cate herself had a good job and plenty of money. So she wasn't destitute and worrying about how to feed an extra mouth. Cate just couldn't see that she was fortunate. Maybe her decision not to have the baby was one made in haste and confusion. Perhaps she'd change her mind. Even though Cate wasn't the changing her mind sort. What would Cate do if she heard that Finn had been seen with his tongue down another woman's throat? Nessa stared unseeingly at the TV screen while she thought about it. Cate wouldn't sit around passively. She'd confront Finn. She'd find the truth. And if the truth was that Finn was seeing another woman, then Cate would leave him. Nessa was absolutely certain about that. She wouldn't live a lie. It wasn't in her nature.

But, Nessa thought, Cate was living a lie now. She hadn't told Finn about the baby and she hadn't told Finn that she was thinking of getting rid of it. Cate had clearly decided to keep that to herself while she worked things out in her own mind. Maybe I'm not so wrong in waiting until I know what I want to do before talking to Adam myself, thought Nessa. Perhaps it's all to the good that I haven't told anyone else yet. Except Bree. She was a little surprised that Bree hadn't been in touch since she'd told her. But Bree was a practical kind of girl, uncomfortable with emotional issues.

Her suggestion of keeping Adam under surveillance had been typical of Bree's approach to life. See a problem, work on it, fix it. Nessa wished it was that simple but she wondered whether there was merit in the idea of having someone follow Adam around for a few days. It seemed such an over-the-top thing to do and yet that way she would surely find out the truth. At least twice a week Adam "worked late." Maybe she needed to know what "working late" actually meant. Should she get one of the detective agencies or should she ask Bree to do it? Her sister was undoubtedly right in thinking that Adam wouldn't even notice her once she was in her biker's gear.

Which was the more sordid? Nessa asked herself as she glanced at Adam. Having a stranger follow him or having her baby sister follow him?

She got up from the sofa. "I'm just going to give Bree a call," she said.

Adam chuckled. "Going to give out to your youngest sister about the middle one?"

"No," she said. "Just going to talk to her."

"This is Bree. Sorry I can't answer the phone. Leave a message and I'll call you back."

Nessa sighed in frustration. She'd almost made up her mind to ask Bree to follow Adam. She'd wanted to ask her before she could change her mind. Now she remembered that Bree was on her hot date tonight. It was, therefore, highly unlikely that she'd be answering her calls at all.

"It's me," she said to Bree's message minder. "Give me a call. I'm sure it'll be late tonight or early tomorrow before you get this. I hope you got a nice slinky dress."

To give the skirt and top a helping hand in the seduction stakes, Bree had spent much more time than usual earlier that evening in getting ready for her date. She took care in applying her foundation cream instead of slapping it on her cheeks like she normally did. She actually used the little sponge applicator that came with her new eyeshadow rather than her finger although she wasn't sure whether or not it made much difference. And she even used Cate's trick of applying her lipstick, blotting it off with a tissue (toilet paper in Bree's case, she'd used all her tissues to wipe the oil from a generator she'd been working on) and then applying it again. The end result, she admitted to herself, was definitely more glamorous than she was used to. It was shocking, really, to see how glamorous she could be when she put her mind to it.

By the time Michael finally rang the doorbell fifteen minutes late, she was as nervous as a kitten. She felt as though this was her first date with him all over again as she hurried down the stairs and just managed to avoid plunging headlong because she caught her heel on the piece of loose red carpet.

"Wow!" His eyes opened wide as she opened the heavy front door. "You look fabulous."

"Thanks." She grinned at him.

"No. I mean it. Really fabulous. And," his eyes twinkled, "you do have legs after all!"

"I nearly broke one of them coming down the stairs," she admitted ruefully. "Caught my heel and only just managed not to end up on my bum."

Michael laughed. "Why ruin my picture of you as a dream girl?"

"Sorry." She laughed too. "I guess I'm not used to being a dream girl."

"You are tonight," he said. "In fact, looking at you now I'm beginning to wonder whether or not we should bother with dinner."

Her eyes widened.

"In that outfit you look good enough to eat," he added. "And I'm not sure that I want to sit opposite you for a couple of hours and not do something about it."

Yes! thought Bree in elation. I've cracked it! If only I'd realized before that all it takes is a skirt and a pair of legs I could've saved myself some anguish.

"However, I promised you dinner and Dad would have a fit if I told him that I abandoned dinner for lust."

"Would you tell him that?" she asked, aghast.

"Nope." Michael grinned. "But he'd find out sooner or later."

"Then we'd better have dinner."

"Ideally we should take your bike." Michael glanced wistfully at it as they walked down the garden path. "I could ride it and you could sit behind me with your hair blowing out in the wind."

"As if." Bree snorted. "Actually what would happen is that my hair would resemble a bird's nest by the time we'd got thirty yards down the road. It's only in the movies that a girl's hair flows out in a golden banner when she's on a bike."

"Oh, don't disillusion me again." Michael made a face at her as he opened the door of the Punto.

"Sorry," she said again as she got into the car. "I guess I'm not great at illusions."

He got in beside her and turned the key in the ignition.

"Running well." She cocked her head and listened to the sound of the engine.

"Like a dream," he told her. He put the car into gear and pulled away.

"Where are we going?" she asked.

"I spent ages thinking about this," he told her. "We're going to a place outside Swords."

"Swords." She looked at him in surprise. "That's a bit out of the way for us, isn't it?"

"I know it's not somewhere that comes to mind immediately," he said. "But friends of Dad opened a restaurant there last year and it's supposed to be really good. He goes there a lot if he's meeting clients from the north side of the city so what's good enough for him is good enough for me."

"What's it called?" asked Bree. "Maybe Cate or Nessa have been there."

"The Old Mill or the Old Stream or something like that." He half-turned to her. "Something old anyway."

She giggled then winced as he cut in front of a car at the traffic lights.

"Relax," he said.

"Sorry." She smiled. "I'm not a great passenger."

None of the Driscoll girls were, she knew. They all preferred driving to being driven and none of them really believed that anyone was a better driver than they were. Except their father, Louis. Bree's earliest memory was of being brought to a motor show where Louis had driven an articulated truck around an obstacle course. It had been a competition and Louis was the only person driving the course who hadn't touched any of the obstacles. He'd won the event because he hadn't had any penalties even though he'd been a couple of seconds slower than one of the other drivers.

"No point getting there if you've written off the truck in the meantime," he'd told Miriam and the girls after he'd accepted the gaudy trophy. She couldn't have been more than three or four at the time, recalled Bree, but she'd remembered his words. She'd kept the trophy too. Louis had given it to her when she passed her driving test.

Once they got out of the city and onto the motorway, she relaxed a little. Michael drove more smoothly and she hit play on the CD deck. She was surprised to find that it was traditional Spanish music.

"I'm picking up the girls from the airport tomorrow," explained Michael. "They're back to school and college soon. I thought I'd play the CD so that they didn't feel too traumatized at being back in Ireland." He laughed. "I know they'd prefer *Top of the Pops* stuff—it's just a silly thing really."

"I think it's nice." Bree smiled at him. "But they shouldn't be too traumatized this year. Not with the weather being so good, despite yesterday's blip."

"I know," said Michael. "It's been a glorious summer, hasn't it?"

"Fabulous," said Bree. "I'm hoping that it stays nice for a little longer. I have to take a week off before the end of October."

"You should have taken it off while the going was good," said Michael.

"I know." Bree made a face. "But we were so busy and," she shrugged, "I like working when we're busy."

"That's terrible." Michael sounded amused. "I thought our generation was supposed to work to live not live to work."

"I don't live to work," said Bree. "I just love doing what I do."

"Didn't you ever want to do anything else? Arsehole!!" he bellowed suddenly at the Ford that moved into the lane in front of them without indicating.

Bree shuddered.

"Honestly," said Michael. "Some people haven't a clue."

"It was a dodgy maneuver," agreed Bree. "And, no, I always wanted to do what I do."

"That must be nice," Michael said. "I've never been sure, to tell you the truth. Part of me thought that I should go into law, like Dad. But it's so much effort!"

"The rewards are good."

"After time," said Michael.

"So why did you choose sales and marketing?" asked Bree. "It's what my sister, Cate, does too."

"I'm good at putting plans together," Michael said. "I can come up with campaigns. But somehow I don't think it's half as much fun as being a mechanic."

"Like lots of men you have an idealized notion of how much fun it is to be up to your armpits in oil," Bree told him, her voice full of laughter.

"Depends on the oil," said Michael suggestively.

She giggled then lapsed into silence.

They arrived at the restaurant fifteen minutes later. Michael made the wheels of the Punto spin on the gravel parking area and Bree made a face at him. She got out of the car and rubbed her arms.

"Cold?" he asked.

She shook her head. The evening air was warm but she was unused to wearing strappy tops that plunged at the neckline and showed rather a lot of her creamy skin.

"Come on then." Michael slipped his arm around her shoulders and led her into the restaurant.

Bree had expected it to be an old building but, despite the weathered granite stonework, she discovered that it was new. It was built to catch the evening sun and had huge windows along the southwest side which gave a view over pretty gardens. Inside, the tables were of opaque glass and set with modern cutlery. One of the proprietors, a petite woman with ash-blond hair and bright blue eyes beamed at Michael.

"I haven't seen you in ages," she said when she'd pecked him on the cheek. "Your dad said you'd grown but he didn't say that you'd grown so much!"

"Give me a break, Carolyn," he said. "I'm with my girlfriend. The last thing she wants to hear are stories about me as a kid."

Bree was pleased that he'd referred to her as his girlfriend. It was, she thought, a major step up from being someone's best friend.

"I'd very much like to hear stories of him as a kid," she told Carolyn. "Maybe you'll tell me some after we've had dinner."

"Do that and I won't pay the bill," he threatened.

Carolyn laughed and led them to a secluded corner table. "I thought about giving you your dad's favorite table," she said. "And then I realized that wouldn't be a very diplomatic thing to do. You're a grown man in your own right now, even though it's hard for me to believe it."

"Thanks, Carolyn," he said.

"I'll get you some menus."

Bree settled in the seat and shielded her eyes from the flaming light of the setting sun. "It's lovely," she said.

"I haven't been here before," Michael admitted. "And when I saw Carolyn I wondered if it was really a good idea. Because she could tell stories of me when I was a baby—suddenly I felt as though I was about ten again."

"She's an old family friend I gather."

Michael nodded. "My mother shared a flat with her when she came to Ireland first," he said. "Not far from where you're living actually. She used to say that it was very convenient for Leeson Street and the nightlife."

"It's hard to imagine your parents having a life before you existed yourself," said Bree. "I can't for one minute picture my mother in a nightclub."

"I know," said Michael. "I find it hard to visualize it myself. But apparently herself and Carolyn were regular fixtures in places like Susey Street and Buck Whaley's and Anabel's back in the seventies and eighties."

"Do all of those places still exist?" asked Bree. "Anabel's does—or at least I think it does. I've been there myself. It's rather creepy to think that I've propped up the same bar that your mother might have done."

"I've propped up that bar too," said Michael. "And I've never thought of it before." He unfolded his napkin and draped it across his lap.

Shit, thought Bree, I might have upset him. I know he was pretty relaxed about his mother the first time he told me but that doesn't mean I can barge in and be tactless. But then I've never been great on tact, I just wade in without thinking a lot of the time.

"So where are your favorite haunts?" He looked up at her again and she breathed a sigh of relief.

"I like being around Camden Street and George's Street," she told him. "I love the juice bars and the alcohol bars and the Oriental shops."

He nodded. "I can see that you would."

"I'm not really a clubbing kind of person though I do go to them."

"Depends on the club," Michael agreed.

"And they only stay hot for a while before somewhere else takes over."

"What else do you like?" he asked. "We haven't really had this conversation before, have we?"

Carolyn arrived with the menus and two glasses of champagne. "On the house," she told Michael. "A mini celebration of your twenty-first birthday even though it's a bit late. Did you have a party?"

"You wouldn't have enjoyed it," he told her. "It was mainly blokes getting sick."

"Oh, Michael!" Both Carolyn and Bree exclaimed in horror together.

"Even Dad was sick at my twenty-first," he said.

He clinked glasses with Bree and they studied the menu together.

"The reality is that I haven't a clue what half of these things are." Michael scratched his chin. "I've always wondered about polenta."

"I'm a burger and chips girl myself," said Bree. "Don't expect me to know much. But I do like the sound of the paella."

He grinned. "You don't have to go down the Spanish route to please me."

"Nothing to do with you," she said. "I lived in Spain for a few months."

"Really?" He looked at her in surprise.

"Yes," she told him. "Villajoyosa."

"I know it," he told her. "Mum was from Valencia. Farther up the coast of course. I've never actually been to Villajoyosa but I know where it is."

"I worked in a garage there," said Bree. "I didn't pick it because of its natural beauty or anything—I was staying in Benidorm and I heard about a job."

"Why did you leave?"

Bree had no intention of telling him about Enrique and his gallery of girlfriends.

"Time to move on," she said. "I went to France after that."

"You like traveling?"

She nodded.

"Will you head off again?"

"Possibly." She smiled. "Unless something makes me stay."

"I was thinking of the States myself," said Michael. "A year or two on the West Coast might be fun."

With or without her, she wondered. Would she go if he asked?

"What would your father say?" she asked.

"He doesn't mind," said Michael. "Once I'm earning a living he's OK with whatever I do."

"And your sisters?" asked Bree. "What about them?"

"They're both girlie girls," said Michael dismissively. "I love them to bits, of course, but they're homebirds at heart. I can't see either of them working abroad."

"Not even in Spain?"

"Not even," said Michael. "Besides, Marta worries too much about Dad to leave him on his own for too long."

Carolyn arrived to take their order just then but they resumed the conversation when she left.

"What does she worry about?" asked Bree.

"That he doesn't have anyone," replied Michael.

"But you said that your other sister was only fourteen," Bree pointed out. "She's hardly likely to be leaving home very soon."

"That he doesn't have anyone his age," explained Michael. "Marta believes that no man can function without a woman to help him."

Bree laughed. "She might be right."

"But I also think that she'd freak out if Dad brought a woman home," Michael said.

"Encroaching on her territory?"

He nodded. "About a year ago Dad was seeing someone. Nice lady, same age as him. Divorced. No kids, so you'd think that'd be a bonus as far as Marta and Manuela were concerned. But he brought her home and Marta didn't like her. So that was that."

"Poor woman," said Bree.

Michael shrugged. "That's the way Marta is. Unfortunately, Mannie is just the same."

"Gosh," said Bree. "Do they vet your girlfriends as well?"

He grinned. "Nope. I don't normally have girlfriends for long enough."

"What's your best run?" asked Bree.

"Best, worst—depends on your point of view," said Michael. "But the longest I've gone out with a girl is three months and the shortest—well, I'd better not say. You'd consider me to be cold and unfeeling."

Bree laughed. "The longest I've gone out with someone is about the same. And the shortest is two minutes."

"Two whole minutes?"

"We made a date. I met him in the pub. He was wearing some godawful aftershave which even drowned out the smell of beer and smoke. I said I was going to the loo and I left."

"You callous bitch." But Michael's eyes held admiration.

"Actually, I felt awful about it. But I made the right decision."

"I'd better not let you out of my sight," said Michael.

"I don't want to be out of your sight," she told him.

The meal was wonderful. They shared mixed salads with peppers, followed by paella and then apricot cheesecake. After that they relaxed in an anteroom off the main dining area where they had coffee.

Bree couldn't remember having a better meal. Or a more sophisticated one. The service had been attentive but unobtrusive, glasses were refilled and empty plates were whisked away before they even noticed.

"I had such a good time," said Bree when she'd drained her cup. "I could just curl up in a ball and sleep."

"That wasn't what I had in mind," Michael told her.

"I guess not." She grinned. "But I can't help it. I'm not used to being looked after so well."

"I'm glad you enjoyed it."

"I did," she told him. "Truly."

"I suppose we'd better get back." He glanced at his watch.

"I suppose so."

"Come on then." He got up from the comfortable armchair and held out his hand.

She took it, enjoying the firmness of his grasp and warmth of his touch. They said goodbye to Carolyn and to her husband, Ken, the chef. Then Michael led Bree outside.

She shivered in the cooler night air and wished once again that she'd brought something to throw over her shoulders. Although this time for warmth rather than decency.

"Hop in," said Michael. "It's not really cold. You'll warm up in the car."

"Thanks."

She yawned and closed her eyes. Maybe he'd divert to the beach on the way home, she thought. He could turn off at the roundabout to Malahide and drive along the estuary where they could . . . She grimaced. Thinking of Malahide had reminded her of Nessa and Adam and the fact that she hadn't talked to her sister today though she'd meant to phone. Nessa might think that she was being terribly unconcerned and unsympathetic. She'd give her a call tomorrow. And reiterate her offer to follow Adam if that was what Nessa wanted. Bree was perfectly prepared to believe that this girl, Portia, had got the wrong end of the stick completely, unlikely as it seemed, but she also knew that Nessa would never be happy until she found out the truth. It must be horrible, she thought, to have doubts about the person you loved. To feel that you couldn't trust them anymore. To believe that everything on which you based your life was a sham.

Poor Nessa. Bree hoped that there was a reasonable explanation, that Adam hadn't—wasn't—cheating on her. If he was . . . she gritted her teeth. If he was, she hoped that Nessa would throw the fucker out and go after him for all she could get. She was surprised at the intensity of her feelings, at how angry she felt on her sister's behalf. She felt the car accelerate and opened her eyes. They were approaching one of the series of roundabouts that bypassed the town of Swords. Traffic was light and Michael had swung out to overtake the car in front.

"Be careful!" Her voice was tense as he closed up on the other car.

"It's fine," he told her, pressing firmly on the accelerator. "Don't worry."

"Sorry," she said. "As I said, I'm not a good passenger."

"I know you told my dad I was a terrible driver but I'm not really."

"It's me," said Bree. "I'm afraid I always think I can do better than whoever is actually driving."

"You're in safe hands, I promise you."

She sat back again as he negotiated the roundabout and continued toward the city. She would have to get rid of her attitude toward other drivers. Particularly men. No boyfriend would take too kindly to being lectured about their ability behind the wheel and Michael was her boyfriend. They'd had a real boyfriend and girlfriend night tonight and she didn't want to ruin it by lecturing him. Besides, he wasn't really a bad driver. He just didn't live up to her exacting standards behind the wheel.

She made herself relax as he turned onto the motorway. Tonight had been great, she thought. And she was glad that she'd bothered to iron her freshly laundered cotton sheets and put them on the bed earlier because she was certain that tonight would be the night when they'd sleep together. It was ages since she'd been to bed with anyone. She was looking forward to feeling Michael's hands on her body, his lips on hers, whispering words of love to her. Or words of lust. She didn't really mind which. Actually, she told herself, she did mind. She wanted them to be words of love. Michael Morrissey was one of the nicest men she'd ever met.

She inhaled sharply as he overtook an articulated truck. She bit back a comment that he'd come up too close behind it and moved out too sharply because she didn't want to annoy him. Or distract him. But she couldn't help looking in her passenger wing mirror and seeing that there was another car coming up fast behind them. Michael noticed it too. He swung toward the inside lane again and Bree had to stop herself from crying out because he'd oversteered and wasn't correcting fast enough.

She couldn't believe that he wasn't correcting fast enough. The car was skidding toward the bank of small trees and shrubs that bordered the motorway and she didn't quite know how Michael was going to get them out of it. She saw the truck pass them by and the red brake lights of other cars in front of them. She couldn't see anyone behind them. She wondered, as the car continued in its skid, how on earth she had the time to notice all of these things.

"Fuck."

She didn't know whether she'd said it or Michael had. But she did know that they were going to crash into the bank and that nothing he could do would stop it. She knew that pressing her own feet to the floor of the car, which she couldn't help herself doing, wasn't going to achieve anything but she pressed harder all the same.

She was still pressing when they hit the first shrub. She wondered then how it was that she had the time to see the driver's airbag deploy and even to see the windscreen shatter but she knew that she saw these things happen. Then she felt the pull of her own seat belt holding her in place while her head jerked forward and the car came to a halt.

18

Moon/Uranus aspects

Tension and emotional strains, changing moods, an overpowering will.

Nessa went to bed early but she hadn't yet fallen asleep by the time Adam joined her. He slid under the covers and automatically put his arm around her.

"Cate's pregnant," she said abruptly.

"What?" Adam had been about to make love to Nessa but, at her words, he propped his head on his hand and looked at her.

"She's pregnant," said Nessa. "That's what she wanted to tell me."

"Oh, Ness." He pulled her closer to him. "I'm so sorry it's her and not you."

She felt the tears sting her eyes. "She doesn't want the baby."

"Doesn't really fit in with her lifestyle, does it?" asked Adam.

"That's what she said."

"She isn't very maternal."

"She's a stupid cow," said Nessa.

Adam cupped her breast in his hand. "Forget about her," he told Nessa. "Don't think about her. Think about us." He leaned over her and kissed her.

She was totally unable to push him away even though his telling her to think of them was making her think of his xxx A woman instead. She rolled onto her back and he entered her quickly. She was disgusted with herself for letting him make love to her when she didn't feel like it and annoyed with herself for not telling him that she wasn't in the mood. She'd never told him that she wasn't in the mood, even on the days when that was true. She wasn't in the mood as often as he was but she liked the intimacy of it and the knowledge that, after ten years together, he still wanted her. So she said nothing.

I need to do something, she told herself as she lay in the darkness afterward. I need to take some kind of positive action. Tomorrow. I'll get to grips with everything tomorrow. I'll phone Bree and get her to play detective, no matter how silly that seems, and I'll find out for once and for all whether or not he's being unfaithful. And if he is I'll . . . I'll . . . she still didn't know what she was going to do if Bree reported back that xxx A was a real woman and that Adam spent his free time sticking his tongue down her throat.

She knew that she was dreaming when she could see Adam's tongue, huge and pink and glistening, as an entity in its own right. And then she woke up.

Bree wasn't sure whether she was unconscious or just dead. She could hear sounds, of people talking, of ambulance sirens, of a busy hospital. And sometimes it seemed to her that she could see things too. A man in a fluorescent yellow jacket. A man in a fluorescent orange jacket. A nurse in a blue tunic.

She wanted to talk to them, to tell them that she was OK. But she couldn't speak and she wasn't sure that she could move either. Once or twice it seemed to her that she was standing beside a bed looking at herself. That was when she thought she might be dead. She'd read lots of news stories in the past about people who'd been pronounced dead floating out of their bodies and watching while a team of doctors and nurses tried to resuscitate them. Only nobody was trying to resuscitate her. They were speeding in and out of the cubicle from time to time, glancing at her and then leaving again.

So, she wondered, am I dead and do they think it's not worth the effort of trying to bring me back? And, if I'm not dead, do they know that? Do they think I'm dead and will they suddenly put me in one of those black sacks that you see on TV and will I be carted down to a mortuary while I'm still alive? She felt herself panic at the thought. She could imagine Nessa and Cate standing by the grave-side watching them lower her into the ground while she was still alive but just not able to speak.

The panic grew inside her. She knew that she had to struggle to let them know that she was all right. She tried to sit up but she couldn't and terror suddenly made her find her voice.

"Help!"

When she spoke she realized that she'd opened her eyes. She blinked a couple of times to focus on the person standing beside her bed who was a tall and beefy doctor. He was, thought Bree, rather attractive. Which made her think that she was dead all over again.

"Hello," he said. "You've woken up."

"I was asleep?"

"Well, unconscious," he told her cheerfully. "But we knew that you were coming out of it."

"Am I alive?" she asked.

He laughed. "Of course you are."

A tear trickled down the side of her face. She was embarrassed at crying when she should be so glad that she was alive.

"You've had a shock, naturally," said the doctor.

And then she remembered why she was here in the first place.

"Michael!" she gasped. "Is Michael OK?"

The doctor scratched the side of his face and looked at her thoughtfully.

"Oh, God!" She struggled to sit up but every muscle in her body protested.

"Take it easy," said the doctor. "Michael will be OK, I promise you. He's just a bit more beaten up than you."

This time the tears cascaded down Bree's face. "I should have driven. He's not as good a driver as me."

"Don't talk about it," said the doctor. "You'll have to give a statement to the police later."

"The police?" Bree looked aghast.

"It was a car crash and they were at the scene," said the doctor. "They'll be here shortly to interview you."

"I don't know what I can tell them," said Bree. "Right now I remember things but all mixed up."

"Don't worry about it yet," said the doctor. "Let me check you out now that you're awake."

"Tell me about Michael," said Bree.

"Let me tell you about yourself first." The doctor took an opthalmiscope from his coat pocket and looked into her eyes. "You're basically fine," he told her. "Bruised, of course. You probably have a headache and you've got a few minor abrasions, including a cut over your eye that we've put a couple of paper stitches in. It shouldn't leave much of a scar. You were pretty lucky. The worst injury from your point of view is that you've torn ligaments in your foot."

"How did I do that?"

"Sympathetic braking." The doctor grinned at her. "You were clearly pressing on a nonexistent brake pedal."

"Yes." Bree nodded. "I remember."

"We're going to X-ray your foot. Both your feet, actually," he said. "Just in case there's anything broken but I don't think so. Walking will be a bit difficult for a couple of days but you'll be good as new eventually."

"Thanks." She smiled wryly. "And what about Michael?"

"He'll be OK too," said the doctor. "But his recovery will take longer. He's broken one or two things. His right leg and his right arm."

Bree shuddered and grasped at the thin blanket that covered her.

"And a couple of ribs," continued the doctor. "His face was more cut up too and his bruising is more severe. He also lost quite a bit of blood."

"Have you told anyone?" she asked.

"We haven't make any phone calls yet," he replied. "If you want, you can do that now. We'll be keeping you in overnight for a bit of observation. Your boyfriend will be here for at least a week."

She started to cry again. She wished she could stop crying because it was bad enough to be here as an accident victim with this doctor being terribly sympathetic while clearly thinking that she was a stupid fool girl who'd been in a car that was driven too fast by a stupid fool bloke and that they were both lucky to be alive.

"My mobile is in my bag." She looked suddenly forlorn. "If my bag survived."

He handed it to her. She realized that her hands were shaking.

"I'm going to get a nurse to bring you a cup of tea," said the doctor. "You'll feel better after a cup of tea."

"Thanks." She sniffed. "I'm sorry. I keep crying and I don't mean to. You've been great."

He smiled at her. "I understand. You can't help crying, it's part of the shock. You'll be OK, I promise."

She managed to control the trembling enough to see that she'd missed a call on her mobile. She didn't care who it was from. She punched in the speed dial for Nessa and waited for her to answer.

It was the ringing of the phone that had woken her. Nessa listened to Bree's trembling voice, then shot out of bed and scrambled into her clothes.

"Whass'matter?" Adam opened his eyes and looked sleepily at her. "Whass'rong?"

"It's Bree," said Nessa. "She's been in an accident."

"What?" Adam focused on her. "What kind of accident?"

"Car crash," said Nessa succinctly.

"My God," said Adam. "Is she hurt?"

"Clearly," snapped Nessa. "She's in hospital."

"Do you want me to go instead of you?" Adam sat up.

Nessa shook her head. "I have to go," she told him. "She says she's OK but she sounded awful. I have to see her."

Adam knew that he wouldn't be able to change Nessa's mind. "Be careful yourself," he warned her. "Don't drive too fast. Don't take risks. You're upset."

"I know." She smiled shakily at him. "But it's me that has to go, Adam. You know that."

"Yes." He got out of bed and put his arm around her. "Let me make you some tea first."

Nessa felt terrible that, while Bree was injured in hospital, the emotion that surged through her now was that Adam really did love her. He'd made love to her earlier and now he was concerned about her and was going to make her tea before she left the house. So he couldn't be having an affair, could he? Men who were having affairs might still make love to their wives but they didn't care about them in the way that Adam cared about her.

When she finally finished dressing and got downstairs, he handed her a mug of tea.

"She'll still be there in the hospital," said Adam. "She won't have gone anywhere. So five minutes for you to get yourself together won't make any difference."

"I feel so responsible," Nessa cried. "She's my sister and Mum is in Galway and I'm in charge of her and she's had an accident!"

"Nessa, she's twenty-five years old," Adam reminded her. "You're not in charge of her. You can't possibly think like that. Now drink the tea, go to the hospital and find out that she's probably fine. If she was well enough to phone you then she can't be that seriously injured."

Nessa smiled at him. "You're a rock," she said.

He put his arm around her again and hugged her. "She'll be fine," he promised.

Nessa sped down the Malahide Road. She kept telling herself that Adam was right, that Bree must be OK because she'd phoned but she was still worried about her. She wished she could think positively instead of thinking terrible things like the possibility that everyone thought Bree was perfectly well but that she'd banged her head and done something that they hadn't spotted and that, by the time she got to the hospital, Bree would be unconscious and they'd all be very concerned.

She drove too fast along the hospital driveway, bouncing over the ramps and shuddering to a halt in the car park.

Accident and emergency was crowded. Nessa had heard that Friday nights were busy times for A&E units but she didn't realize just how busy they could be. There was a steady stream of people presenting themselves, some with gashes and cuts that clearly needed immediate attention, some who simply looked drunk, and some who didn't look as if anything was the matter with them at all but who were sitting on the plastic chairs waiting to see a doctor. She looked around her helplessly and finally saw a clerk behind the desk.

"Bree Driscoll?" she asked the clerk. "A car accident earlier?"

The clerk directed her to a cubicle and Nessa hurried down the corridor. She pushed aside the blue cubicle curtain and saw her sister lying there, eyes closed. She felt a chill rush through her.

"Bree?"

Bree's eyes flickered then opened. "Hi," she said wanly.

"Oh, Bree." Nessa wanted to hug her but was afraid. "I was so worried . . ."

"It's OK," said Bree. "My really nice doctor tells me that the worst injury I have is torn ligaments in my foot. It's agony at the moment but he assures me that the pain will go away and I'll be left with a Technicolor foot very soon. I'll be hobbling for a few days but I'll get over that."

"You have a cut over your eye," said Nessa.

"That's one of my minor abrasions," Bree told her.

"Minor!"

"He says there won't be much of a scar," said Bree.

"What happened?"

Bree told her.

"Was he drunk?" demanded Nessa. "Did you get into the car with a drunk driver?"

"Don't be silly," said Bree tiredly. "He wasn't drunk. He'd had a glass of champagne, that's all. He's just not a very good driver. But he was trying to show off."

"Oh, Bree!"

"He didn't get off as lightly," said Bree. "He's broken his leg and his arm and his ribs and the doctor says his face is cut up too."

"Will he be all right?"

"They say so," said Bree. "I hope so, Nessa." She bit her lip. "I phoned his father. He'll be here soon. And the police are going to question me."

"The police!"

"They had to get the car towed away," said Bree. "It might be a question of dangerous driving."

"Was he driving dangerously?" asked Nessa.

Bree shrugged then winced as the pain hit her again. "Not really," she said. "But, I guess, not very safely either."

"Can you prosecute him?"

"I'm not going to prosecute him," she replied, her tone horrified.

"I'm very glad to hear that." The curtains parted and the sisters looked at Declan Morrissey. He looked grim and determined.

Then Bree started to cry again

19

♥

Mars in the 3rd House

Competitive, often argumentative, a fiery temper.

Because the doctors told her that she'd be able to go home the following morning, Bree gave the key to her flat to Nessa and asked her to bring her some clothes when she came back to pick her up. "Because," she said, "my brand-new slinky outfit is ruined." And she sniffed back the tears that once again threatened. She was really tired of crying now. It wasn't part of her nature to cry. Normally, very few things moved her to tears.

It took ages before Nessa finally left the hospital for the night and Bree was, for a moment at least, alone in her bed. Actually she wasn't sure it was really a bed, she was still in the accident and emergency unit and hadn't been transferred to a ward because they were all full. But it didn't matter to her what she was lying on, she was exhausted and desperately wanted to sleep.

Declan Morrissey had gone to the ward to see Michael again. Nessa had snapped at him when he'd told Bree that he was glad she wasn't thinking of charging Michael with dangerous driving and told him that he was bloody lucky that Bree was alive and in a position to prosecute or not. Foolishly (in Bree's opinion) Declan had wondered whether a fault with the car had contributed to the accident, because that had caused Nessa to fly at him like a banshee and shout at him that if he thought he could pin something on the garage or on Bree, he had another damn think coming and that all lawyers were the same, fucking leeches and blame mongers and that she wished her sister had never met his obviously totally incompetent son. Bree reckoned that Declan had been utterly taken aback by

Nessa's anger because he'd muttered and stuttered in a way which she felt was probably quite unlike him and had said that he wasn't trying to imply anything and he knew that Bree hadn't done something to the car that could possibly have caused an accident and that there was no point in tempers getting heated.

At which point a nurse had poked her head around the curtains and, much to Bree's relief, insisted that both Declan and Nessa should leave because Bree needed some rest.

But almost as soon as Nessa and Declan had disappeared, the Gardai had arrived to question her about the accident. Bree knew that people considered themselves to be getting old when the police looked even younger than them, but she thought it was almost criminal in itself to feel positively ancient when the pretty girl with the carrot curls (who didn't look as if she was old enough to be out of school) had sat down on the bed and asked what had happened.

"It was an accident," Bree repeated over and over again. "He pulled in after overtaking a lorry and the car skidded and nothing he could do would stop it."

"What speed was he doing?" asked the girl.

"I don't know." Bree closed her eyes. "Probably about fifty initially, but he would have accelerated to overtake the lorry. He was slowing down again when the car skidded, I think."

"Had you been drinking?" she asked.

Bree suddenly wished Declan was with her. She didn't know whether or not she should say anything, whether she was obliged to say anything. She didn't know whether or not the guards had already talked to poor Michael who couldn't possibly be feeling all that great at this point and who might say anything simply to be left alone. She felt that way herself.

"We had a meal," she said eventually. "He had a glass of champagne. That's all. I had champagne and wine."

"Do you want to press charges?" asked the guard.

"What kind of charges?"

"Dangerous driving."

"He wasn't dangerous," said Bree. "Really he wasn't. He was just unlucky."

The carrot-haired guard smiled at her. "Life's like that."

"Yeah, well." Bree shrugged and winced as every bone in her body protested. "At least nobody was killed."

The guard nodded. "Thanks for talking to me."

"Sure." Bree was suddenly exhausted. But as the pretty young guard left the cubicle, Nessa came back in. Her face was still grim and determined and Bree wondered, tiredly, what other things she might have said to Declan Morrissey.

The next morning Bree pulled her paper gown around her and hobbled slowly with the aid of her crutches along interminable corridors to see Michael. He was propped up in bed, his face pale against the pillows, an angry gash across his forehead and a couple of less vivid but still shocking cuts across his face. His right eye was bruised and almost closed.

"Hi," she said as she sat down beside him. "How're you feeling?"

"D'you want the truth or what I told Dad?" he asked wanly.

"The truth."

"I feel like shit," he admitted. "My head hurts. My back hurts. My side hurts. My face feels mangled. My leg and my arm are broken. And I nearly killed you too, Bree."

She looked around the ward anxiously. "Don't say that."

"It was my fault," he said. "I told the cops it was my fault."

"I hope your dad doesn't know you told them that," said Bree.

"The guard said that they might prosecute me," said Michael. "Dangerous driving, she said."

"She said that to me too," Bree told him. "But I said that it was an accident."

"It was an accident," Michael said ruefully. "But avoidable."

"Oh, I don't know . . ."

"Of course it was," he said vehemently. "I was messing about because you were in the car with me. I wanted to impress you."

"Michael—"

"I've never met anyone like you before," he said. "You make me feel—you make me feel inadequate."

"I really don't think—"

"You're so good at cars and stuff and I felt that I had to show off."

"I know," said Bree.

"Which was stupid and nearly got us killed."

"But it didn't." Bree smiled weakly at him. "We'll be good as new."

"At least you're not too badly cut, thank God," said Michael. "But I look like I was in some kind of gang fight."

"When all those scars heal you'll look even more attractive," Bree assured him. "Girls like a few scars and stuff."

Michael tried to laugh.

"Of course you never should have listened to your dad and brought me to a flashy restaurant in the first place," said Bree. "We never had these problems when we just had beer and crisps."

"Dad tore strips off me," Michael told her. "After he was reassured that I wasn't going to die or anything he went ballistic about my awful driving with you in the car. He said if I wanted to kill myself that was fine but I wasn't to take vulnerable young girls with me."

"Gosh, he changed his tune," said Bree. "When he called by my little cubbyhole last night he had a row with my sister about the dangerous driving thing."

"Really?"

"It was all silly stuff," said Bree. "Probably because they were both upset." She looked around as a nurse arrived and stood by the bed.

"We have to give Michael a jab," she told Bree. "I don't think it's something you want to hang around for."

"Probably not," agreed Bree. She eased herself to her feet and picked up the crutches. "I'll see you soon," she told Michael. "Take care."

"Don't worry." The nurse grinned at her. "We'll take care of him for you."

"Thanks," said Bree as she made her painful way out of the ward.

She couldn't understand why Nessa hadn't gone to her flat and brought her clothes like she'd asked. Instead her sister had turned up at the hospital with a pair of her own jeans and a bright yellow sweatshirt.

"I look like a kid's toy in this," grumbled Bree as she maneuvered herself along the corridor. Her hands were sore from using the crutches already and she didn't seem to be able to get a rhythm going at all. It looked so simple when you saw other people with them, she thought ruefully, as she narrowly missed a visitor, but they required practice.

She followed Nessa across the car park and sighed with relief when they got to the car. Nessa clucked around her in elder sister mode, making sure that she was sitting comfortably and telling her to fasten her seat belt.

"I *will* fasten it," complained Bree. "Honestly, Nessa, I've injured my foot not my brain. There's no need to talk to me like I was about three years old!"

"I just want to make sure you're OK," said Nessa as she turned the key in the ignition. "I phoned Mum this morning and she was worried about you."

"What did you tell her?" asked Bree.

"That you were fine," replied Nessa.

Bree shot her a grateful look. She didn't want Miriam ringing her up and fussing or, worse still, rushing from Galway to be at her side. Miriam was relatively laidback but Bree couldn't help thinking that a car accident would be cause for dramatics as far as her mother was concerned. She leaned her head against the passenger window and allowed her mind to drift as Nessa eased into the traffic. Michael had turned out to be a weirdo after all, she supposed. Not a full-blown weirdo but weird enough to crash his car and nearly kill her. None of the rest of them had nearly killed her. She winced as the car hit a pothole and a white stab of pain shot through her.

"You all right?" Nessa glanced at her.

"Fine," said Bree. "I'm absolutely fine."

When they got to her flat, Bree was astonished to see Cate's Alfa parked outside.

"You didn't tell me she'd be here too," she said accusingly to Nessa. "I don't need the entire family fussing around me."

"I rang her this morning and she insisted on coming over." Bree was surprised at the coolness in Nessa's tone. "That's why I didn't bring you your clothes. Cate said she'd tidy up for you and get things in order since you were so vehement last night about not staying with me while you recuperate."

"Was I?" asked Bree. "I don't remember."

"You got a bit incoherent at one stage," Nessa said. "After you'd spoken to the police. I asked you to come to my house for a couple of days but you said you couldn't have my broken marriage on your conscience."

"Did I?"

Nessa nodded. "Which, since that boy's father was standing beside us at the time, caused raised eyebrows."

"Oh, God, Ness, I'm sorry!" wailed Bree. "I don't remember that at all."

"It was after I told him that if he tried to stick some kind of lawsuit on you for not fixing his useless son's car properly it'd be the last thing he ever did."

"I remember that bit all right," said Bree ruefully. "I must have tuned out afterward."

"I think I said enough to convince him that he can't mess with the Driscolls," said Nessa grimly.

"I'm sure you did," murmured Bree.

Cate had obviously seen them arrive because she opened the door of the house as they walked up the garden path.

"Jesus Christ, Bree!" She gasped as she looked at her sister. "I thought you'd only sprained your ankle. You look terrible."

"Thanks," said Bree. "So do you." Although, she had to admit, Cate looked as gorgeous and as groomed as ever even in her casual outfit of loose denims and gray sweatshirt.

Cate smiled at her. "Sorry. That sounded bad. I just meant that, well, your poor face!"

"It's not so awful." Bree touched her forehead. "The doctor assures me that this'll heal perfectly. You should see the other guy!"

"Is he OK?" asked Cate.

"Beaten up," said Bree. "But he'll survive." She edged past her sisters and looked at the stairs warily.

"We'll give you a fireman's lift," said Cate who saw Bree's expression.

"Don't be silly."

"We did it before," Cate reminded her. "When you fell off your skates at the bottom of the hill."

Bree grinned. "I was a lot younger and a lot lighter then."

"No bother," said Cate.

"Are you sure you should?" Nessa looked at Cate.

"What?"

"Lifting people," said Nessa. "I don't know if you should be lifting anyone."

"What difference does it make." Cate's voice was brittle.

Bree looked from one to the other in puzzlement. "What's the problem?"

"No problem," said Cate robustly. "Come on, little sister. Let's go."

They carried Bree up the stairs and into the flat where she slid from the chair they'd made with their hands and looked around her in astonishment. The bundle of discarded clothes that normally took up one corner of the room had been tidied away, as had the precarious pile of car manuals and old newspapers that she kept on the table. The mantelpiece over the old fireplace had been tidied too, gone were the nuts, screws, oily rags and other bits and pieces so that, for the first time ever, she could actually see the beautiful black marble.

"I didn't realize you were so domesticated." She turned to Cate. "I thought your place always looked neat because you didn't have anything in it. I didn't realize it was because you spent all day tidying it up."

Cate laughed. "I certainly don't have the clutter that you have," she told Bree. "But I can't stand things being untidy. It offends me."

"You must've had a nightmare when you walked in here then." Bree hugged her. "It looks fabulous, Catey. Thanks. Although," she looked at Cate ruefully, "it probably won't be long before I trash it again."

"Oh, don't trash it." Nessa ran her finger over the rosewood table. "There are some lovely things here."

"First time I've seen them in months," said Bree cheerfully. "The place was a mess when I moved in and I guess I've kept it like that."

"It's actually very nice," said Cate. "Not my thing really, but still nice."

"Can you imagine when these were private houses?" asked Nessa. "No wonder people had maids and servants."

"Just as well I've no chance of affording it as a private house," said Bree. "I can't even keep my two rooms tidy, let alone the rest of it."

"You're just a slob," Nessa agreed. "But, thank God, a slob that's still alive despite the best efforts of that idiot."

"I really don't want to talk about it again now," said Bree.

"Would you like some tea or coffee?" Cate asked.

"I'd love some tea," confessed Bree.

"OK," said Cate. "You sit down and I'll put the kettle on."

She sounded so like their mother at that point that Bree wanted to laugh. It was strange, she thought, how sometimes one or the other of them would show a family characteristic that didn't fit their mental images of each other. Bree never saw Cate as the putting-the-

kettle-on person in the family. That was Nessa. But Nessa, having
been in her bustling, caring mode earlier, seemed to have slipped
into a dream world of her own right now. Worrying about Adam
probably, Bree suddenly realized. Wondering what she should do
about it. And Bree felt guilty that Nessa was here looking after her
when she should be at home sorting out her own life.

"How's Adam?" she asked abruptly.

"What?"

"Adam," repeated Bree. "You and Adam and all that sort of stuff."

Nessa sighed. "I don't know. He was great last night when you
called. And he had to cancel golf this morning to be with Jill so that
I could pick you up. I must have been imagining things, Bree."

"You didn't imagine what you heard, though." Bree wanted to be
sympathetic but equally she didn't want Nessa to pretend everything
was all right if it really wasn't.

"I know. But I've thought about it so many times and I honestly
think that somehow I got the wrong end of the stick. Only thing is,"
she smiled ruefully at Bree, "I'm still not sure what the right end of
the stick is."

Bree laughed. "We'll sort it out," she told Nessa. "Don't worry."

"I'm not worrying."

But Bree noticed that the frown lines on Nessa's forehead didn't
go away.

She frowned herself then, and sniffed the air. "What's that
smell?"

Nessa turned to her. "I don't know. Burning, I think."

"Nothing should be burning," said Bree.

"Oh shit!"

They exchanged glances as Cate's shriek filled the air.

"What's the matter?" Bree hobbled to the tiny kitchen where blue
smoke had begun to fill the tiny area.

"I bought some bread," said Cate. "From the deli down the road.
Part-baked ciabatta. I thought you might like some."

"And for this you have to set my flat on fire?" Bree coughed as she
opened the kitchen window.

"I was preheating your oven," said Cate. "And it started to smoke
of its own accord."

"Oh." Bree bit her lip and held back the laughter as Nessa
crowded into the room.

"God almighty, Cate, what were you thinking of?" she demanded.

"She was heating up some bread," Bree told her. "But what she didn't know was that I use my oven as a storage cupboard. Well, let's face it, I never use it for cooking! So she's just roasted a couple of manuals, a red woolen jumper and two plastic containers full of screws."

"It wasn't my fault," cried Cate. "Nobody uses their oven for storage."

Bree giggled. Even Nessa couldn't help smiling.

"I was trying to be nice!" wailed Cate.

"I'm the nice one," said Nessa. "You're the inconsiderate one. Bree's the flighty one. You can't change that just by buying a loaf of bread."

Bree stared at Nessa in astonishment.

"Forget the bread," said Cate sourly. "There's an ancient packet of fig rolls in her cupboard. They'll have to do instead."

They sat in uneasy silence at the newly visible table with their cups of tea and fig rolls. Bree knew that there was something odd going on between Cate and Nessa but she couldn't figure out what it was. Nessa was continually shooting venomous looks at her sister, who was trying her best to ignore them. Perhaps Cate hadn't wanted to come to the flat today, thought Bree. Maybe she'd had plans for a day of unbridled lust with Finn-So-Cool which had been thrown into disarray after Nessa's phone call. Bree was still surprised at Cate being there anyway because family crises were normally Nessa's speciality and she didn't like other people butting in when she was fussing and organizing and sorting things out. So why had she phoned Cate? And why had Cate come? And, above all, having come, why on earth had she indulged in an orgy of cleaning and tidying herself, the result of which would put even Nessa's best efforts to shame?

Maybe that was it. Bree caught the crumbs of her biscuit before they fell onto the newly polished table. Maybe there was some kind of competitive domestic thing going on between them. Hard though that was to imagine!

"It's strange, isn't it, how different things are now?" Nessa broke the silence.

"Different?" asked Bree.

"To the last time we were all together."

"At my engagement." Cate's voice was brittle now.

"I meant before that. At my house with Mum and Dad," said Nessa. "All of us, in fact. Adam and Finn too."

Bree looked at both of them in turn. "It's not that different," she said.

"Oh, come on!" Nessa glared at her. "Then we were all happy."

"Look, Nessa, I know you're upset and confused about Adam." Bree regarded her sympathetically. "I told you I'd spy on him for you if you liked. Get things sorted in your own mind for once and for all."

"But there's more than that," said Nessa. "We were kind of carefree that night. Me and Adam. Cate and Finn, with his wonderful news about the job even though they hadn't got engaged by then. And you, Bree, happy-go-lucky as always. We did the scratch cards and everything was so much fun. I was convinced that the horoscopes were right myself after Mum won the money. But they gave no sign of the awful things that were going to happen to us all."

"Nessa!" Bree stared at her. "Nothing's changed that much. OK, I was nearly killed but I wasn't. And Cate and Finn got engaged so that's for the better, isn't it? And you'll sort things out with Adam."

"It's not her and Adam she's getting at," said Cate. "It's me."

"You?" A thought struck Bree but it was so monumental that she could hardly believe it had come into her head, let alone say it. Yet she couldn't stop herself. "It's not you he's having an affair with, is it?"

Cate, whose face had been getting grimmer and grimmer with every word that Nessa had uttered, suddenly laughed. She rocked back and forth on the chair until tears streamed down her face. Her laughter was almost uncontrollable. Bree looked at her uncertainly.

"What Cate is talking about is her pregnancy," said Nessa flatly.

"Cate!" Bree's face lit up. "How wonderful for you."

"Not really." Nessa spoke again as Cate wiped the tears from her eyes. "She wants to get rid of it."

Suddenly Cate wasn't laughing anymore and Bree was shocked into silence. She watched while Cate took out her compact and wiped away smudges of mascara from her cheeks.

"So that's what's different," said Nessa. "A couple of months ago everything was exactly in its place. Today I'm a woman whose husband might be having an affair, you've been injured in a horrible road accident and Cate has managed to get both engaged and pregnant and she wants to have an abortion."

"Cate?" Bree turned to her. "Why don't you want the baby?"

"Why do you think?" Cate's voice was steady but her fingers trembled. "It's not the right time for me, Bree. Finn doesn't want a baby. I don't want a baby either. I can't afford to give up my job now, not when things are going really well for me. He'd despise me forever if I did that. And I couldn't stand having a kid while he's doing the TV thing."

"You don't have to give up your job," Bree told her. "Hundreds and thousands of women work and have babies."

"But they don't work the hours I do. And they don't have husbands who get up when most people are going to sleep three times a week."

"Maybe the TV network would like you to be pregnant," suggested Bree. "Then Finn'll be a real modern presenter—wife, baby, twenty-four seven lifestyle."

"I'm not having a baby because the TV network thinks it's a good idea," said Cate. "I don't want a child, Bree. That's the bottom line."

"What about Finn?" asked Bree. "How does he feel about it?"

Cate swallowed before she answered. "He doesn't know yet."

"You haven't told him!" Bree stared at her. "Cate, you have to tell him. He has a right to know."

"He doesn't," said Cate. "And if he knew he'd only get into a panic about it. There's no need for us both to panic."

"Maybe he wouldn't," suggested Bree. "Maybe he'd like a child."

"I think I know my own fiancé better than you," snapped Cate. "He doesn't want a baby and I don't want a baby and that's the end of it."

"Cate—"

"She's too selfish for a child anyway," interjected Nessa. "That's what I said earlier. She's the inconsiderate one."

"Fuck off, Nessa." Cate turned on her. "I told you about it, I wanted your support. I knew it would be difficult and I wouldn't have minded if you said you disagreed with my decision. But I won't have you insult me and upset me and make me feel worse about this than I do already."

"You're feeling bad because you know it's wrong. I'll bring up your baby for you if that's all that's worrying you."

"You are such a patronizing cow, Nessa." Cate's eyes glittered. "What century do you think this is? I certainly won't be having babies to give to other people. I don't want it because I don't want to be pregnant and sick and fat and unhappy and all of those things. And because it'll wreck my life. You just don't understand."

"No, I don't," said Nessa stubbornly. "Think of all the women in the world who can't have children at all, Cate."

"That's such a ridiculous argument!" Cate stood up. "The kind of emotive crap you come out with whenever you're not winning any other way. That's your problem, Nessa Driscoll. You don't think with your head, you get swept along on some touchy feely thing that has nothing to do with real life at all. You were always like that. It's no wonder your husband is having an affair."

"You fucking bitch!" Nessa could barely contain her fury. "You fucking bitch—cow—wagon—" She ran out of insults. "How dare you talk to me like that."

"The same way you dare talk to me the way you do," snapped Cate.

"I haven't insulted you personally," said Nessa.

"Oh, sorry, bitch isn't personal?"

"You were always a bitch."

"Right. Of course. As were you. Queening it over us just because you were older. As if that means anything. Insisting on your room with the view of the sea just because of an accident of birth. Trying to make us do things for you because we were your baby sisters. Huh! Running to Mum and telling tales because you enjoyed it—"

"Cate." Bree's tone was hollow. "That's enough. Stop."

"Yes," said Nessa. "That's more than enough."

"It's enough from you too, Nessa," said Bree. "I can't believe the pair of you. I can't believe what you're saying to each other. It's horrible."

"It's fucking true," said Cate bitterly.

"It doesn't matter. It's not the sort of thing you should be saying."

"You're right." Nessa gathered her things. "So I won't stay here and listen to them. Look, Bree, I asked you last night and I'll ask you again if you want to stay with me until you can get around a bit better."

"Or you could stay with me," said Cate.

"Stop it, both of you!" Bree wanted to sound angry but she couldn't. She was frightened by the hostility between her two older sisters. "I'm staying here. This is where I live. I'll be fine."

"Call me if you need anything," said Nessa.

"Or me."

"I won't need anything. Thank you for coming to the hospital, Nessa. Thank you for cleaning up for me, Cate. I'll probably go to sleep for a while now."

But she knew, as her sisters left the flat, that there wasn't a hope of that.

Actually, she was wrong. She slid between her smooth cotton sheets and felt a pang of regret that they were being wasted on her. Then she closed her eyes and was asleep within seconds. Only she dreamed that she was in Michael's car again. This time they were speeding down a runway, between the bright purple and blue lights that Bree knew were switched on because a plane was coming in to land. She tried to warn Michael, to tell him that they were in big trouble, but he wouldn't listen to her. He pushed his foot to the ground and drove faster and faster while she could see the huge Airbus heading straight for them. She leaned across and yanked at the steering wheel but only succeeded in blowing the horn. Which, for some reason, didn't sound like a horn at all but a bell.

Her eyes snapped open and she realized that it was the bell of the flat, ringing insistently. She groaned and sat up. The bell had stopped but suddenly started again. Bree wished that she lived in a modern apartment like Cate where she could see who was ringing by checking the video monitor and where she could press a button to let them in. But she couldn't do that in the Marlborough Road flat. The bell itself was at least fifty years old.

She made her way to the top of the stairs. She could see the shadow of someone outside the front door. She sat at the top stair and bumped her way down as she had when she was a toddler. Then she hobbled to the door and opened it. The effort had caused beads of sweat to break out on her forehead.

"Oh." She raised her eyebrow at the sight of Declan Morrissey standing before her. He was carrying a small brown paper bag and a bundle of magazines.

"Hello, Bree," he said. "How are you?"

"Is that a lawyer question or a real question?"

He grinned at her. "A real question."

"I'm OK."

"You look a bit shattered."

"That's because someone was crazy enough to ring my doorbell when I live on the first floor and have crocked ankles," she said waspishly.

"I'm sorry," said Declan. "I didn't think of that."

"A common trait among men," she told him.

"Can I come in?"

"Why?"

"I really wanted to see how you were," he said. "I was so worried about Michael that I don't think I expressed how concerned I was about you too."

"You're still concerned that I'll sue Michael," said Bree.

"You said you wouldn't."

"Is it so hard for you guys to take someone's word for something?"

Declan sighed. "Actually, yes. But I did believe you when you said it, Bree."

"So everything's sorted," she said. "You don't need to come around here and pretend to feel concern for me. Honestly."

"I'm not pretending," said Declan. "God knows, Bree, both of you had a lucky escape. And although Michael is certainly more injured than you, I'm horrified to think what happened to you. I truly regret it. And I am, genuinely, concerned."

She looked at him consideringly. He might be telling the truth. He might not. Her experience with lawyers was limited to what she saw on TV and the occasional John Grisham novel. Neither of which gave her a lot of confidence.

"Well, your concern is noted even if it's probably a bit misplaced," she said finally. "I'm not so bad."

"But I made you come all the way downstairs and you can't walk," said Declan. "For that I apologize profoundly."

"You're not in front of a High Court judge now, you know." Bree's eyes twinkled suddenly. "You can talk to me like a normal person."

Declan laughed. "I'm sorry. I can't help it."

"Occupational hazard I suppose," agreed Bree.

"Look, can I help you back upstairs again?" asked Declan. "My conscience is having a hard enough time as it is without thinking of you laboring under your own steam."

"All right," said Bree. "I'll lean on your arm."

Progress was slow. She didn't want him to see how painful walking actually was. And she was feeling tired again.

"This is it." Eventually she pushed open the door of the flat. "Would you like a cup of coffee or anything?"

"Let me make one," said Declan. He stood in the room and Bree was suddenly very grateful that Cate had been around earlier and had turned it into something approximating tidiness. Even though her bed was now rumpled from her nap.

Declan sniffed. "Something burning?" he asked.

"Not now," Bree told him. "My sister was here earlier and did her best to torch the place."

"The girl I met at the hospital? I know she's headstrong but she didn't seem the type to—"

"No," said Bree. "Another one. Not normally the torching type either but she didn't realize that I used my oven as a storage cupboard and she switched it on."

Declan laughed. "How many of you are there?"

"Three," said Bree. "More than enough."

She sat down at the table and looked at the bundle of magazines which he'd left while he made the coffee. There were a number of car ones like *What Car?* and *Auto Mechanic*, and a few women's glossies too.

"I brought them for you." He carried two mugs of coffee into the room as she was scanning an article on touring cars. "I didn't know what you like to read."

"These are great," she said. "Thanks."

"Which do you prefer?" he asked. "The car ones or the girlie ones?"

She grinned. "Depends on my mood."

He put the coffee down in front of her and opened the brown paper bag. "How about these?" He proffered the bag to her and she took out one of the huge chocolate chip cookies inside.

"OK, these definitely help the mood," she told him.

"Good." He smiled.

"Did you bake them yourself?"

He nodded.

"God, but you'd be some woman's dream." Bree sighed. "Rich, attractive, can cook . . ." She blushed as she realized what she was saying but he simply smiled at her again.

"I'm a nightmare according to my children," he said. "Work too hard, perfectionist, living in my own world . . ."

"Michael was supposed to collect your daughters today," remembered Bree.

"I'm picking them up later," he told her. "And dropping in to the hospital with them on the way back."

"Did you tell them?" she asked.

He shook his head. "No need. Better to bring them to see him. I hate phoning anyone with bad news."

She chuckled. "As a lawyer I'd have thought that was another occupational hazard."

"True," he said. "But I don't like it all the same."

She sipped her coffee and ate the cookie. She realized that she was starving. It was a pity, she thought, that Cate hadn't managed to heat up the bread. It would have staved off the hunger pangs. She didn't have any food in the flat. She reached out and took another cookie.

"These are gorgeous," she told Declan.

"So they all tell me." He nodded.

"They're so fresh."

"I did them this morning."

She looked at him quizzically.

"I couldn't sleep," he told her. "I was worried about Michael and about you and baking helps. So I made cookies." He shrugged. "I got into the habit when my wife was sick."

"Michael told me a little about her," said Bree cautiously. "It must have been hard."

"Hard because I realized that I'd spent so much time at work when I could have been with her before she got ill," said Declan. "But it's easy to berate yourself afterward. It didn't seem bad at the time even though we sometimes argued about it."

"And you're still a workaholic now?"

He sighed. "I need it now. It's a reason for going on, isn't it?"

"But you have the children."

"Michael's twenty-one," said Declan. "The girls are in their teens. They have their own lives now."

"So have you," said Bree. "And it doesn't have to be all work and no play." She saw a shadow pass across his face and she bit her lip. "I'm sorry. It's none of my business."

"Monica used to say that to me. I told her there was plenty of time for both. I was wrong. I lost her." He rubbed the bridge of his nose. "And I nearly lost Michael too. It scared me."

She wanted to put her arms around him but she didn't. Instead she looked at him, eyes full of sympathy. "But you didn't lose Michael," she said. "And everything's turned out OK."

"Yes." He smiled at her. "I guess it has."

20

♥

Uranus in Capricorn

A careful thinker with occasional lapses.

They got into a routine the following week. Nessa and Jill called over to Bree in the mornings, bringing food and newspapers while Cate (accompanied once by Finn) dropped over in the evenings. Bree felt that there was a competition going on between Nessa and Cate to see which sister could be the most attentive and the most caring. She thought that it was utterly ridiculous for Cate, who looked pale and miserable, to spend any time at the flat but she insisted on coming anyway. Bree was worried about her sister and wondered whether or not Finn had noticed how awful she looked. But all Finn talked about while he was there was his radio show and his TV show and Bree suddenly realized why Cate was so paranoid about the baby and the effect it would have on their lives. All she talked about the night Finn came over were the radio and TV shows too. When she came on her own, she talked about everything except her pregnancy and Bree didn't have the nerve to bring the subject up again herself.

Nessa's visits were different. Since Jill was with her, Nessa kept up a stream of inconsequential conversation which drove Bree nuts while Jill skipped around the flat looking for things to do and complaining that Bree didn't have any decent videos she could watch.

Bree was lucky, Jill told her on the Thursday following the accident, that the crash had happened when it did, another week and Jill would be back at school, Nessa back at work and—said Jill—there'd be no one to help Bree get around. And then Jill took the crutches and practiced hopping around the overgrown garden behind the flat.

Nessa and Bree sat on the rickety wooden bench in the shade of a cherry blossom tree and watched her.

"It's taking longer than I thought," said Bree. "When I was talking to the doctor he did say that I needed a week before I'd start to feel confident again but it's almost a week now and still hurts a lot. I rang Christy on Monday and told him that I'd be back next week but I don't think so." She sighed. "And I'm getting bloody bored sitting here."

"I'm doing my best to entertain you," said Nessa.

"Sorry." Bree looked at her apologetically. "I know. And I appreciate you coming over every day, I really do. It's just—I'm not a sitting at home kind of person."

"And I am?" asked Nessa.

"Of course not," said Bree impatiently. "You're so damn touchy all the time, Nessa."

"I'm not."

"You are," insisted Bree. "And Cate is as bad."

She watched Nessa carefully as she mentioned their sister's name. She hadn't said anything about Cate since they'd all been together in the flat after she'd come home from hospital.

"I can't talk about Cate," said Nessa. "She's shallow and selfish and she's a fool."

"Maybe she's being foolish," said Bree. "But she's not shallow, Nessa. And she's not selfish."

"Oh, come on!" Nessa looked at her impatiently. "How more selfish could she possibly be? She hasn't taken Finn's feelings into account at all. She's only thinking about herself and her job. Her job! Bree, what sort of girl is she that a job could matter more to her than having a child of her own?"

"I don't think it's just the job," said Bree. "I think it's that Cate is afraid of turning into you."

"Well, thanks very much!" Nessa's fury was barely contained. "I've done my best for both of you. I've looked after you. I've cared about you. Because I'm the eldest and that's what we do! And what's the thanks I get? That Cate doesn't want to be like me! I suppose you don't either. I suppose you're fed up with me and Jill coming here every day just to make sure you're OK."

"Nessa, you jump to conclusions all the time," said Bree impatiently. "All I meant was that Cate has different objectives in life. She's not comfortable with the idea that Finn is the main earner in their house. She doesn't think that he'd respect her if she wasn't as ambitious as him. She was devastated by his new job because she knew that she'd never be able to match up to it. So she starting working harder and harder just to keep up with him. And now she's pregnant and she knows that he doesn't want kids." Bree shrugged. "I'm not saying that I agree with her. I just see where she's coming from."

Nessa plucked at a long blade of grass and twirled it around between her fingers. She was silent as she watched Jill discard Bree's crutches and dance through the garden. Then she tore the grass into little pieces.

"Maybe she's right," she said finally. "But doing what Finn wants—what she thinks Finn wants—isn't necessarily the right thing, is it?"

"She thinks it is," said Bree.

"But if her main reason is because of Finn . . ." Nessa bit her lip. "Oh, Bree, I did loads of things because of Adam and look where I am!"

"Any developments?" Bree was delighted to be able to change the subject.

"I checked detective agencies in the Golden Pages," admitted Nessa. "I even rang one up. They specialized in marital investigations. But I don't want to be a marital investigation, Bree! I want things to be OK."

"You don't think they will be?"

"How do I know?" Nessa sighed and scattered the torn pieces of grass onto the ground. "I haven't had time to think about it this week really."

"Next week," promised Bree. "If I'm back on my feet next week, I'll do it for you. Then you won't have to go to a detective agency."

"It just seems . . ." Nessa plucked at another blade of grass. "It seems like something someone else would do. Not like real life at all. I can't believe I'm even contemplating this."

"You have to know for sure," said Bree. "You can't carry on until you know."

As soon as Nessa and Jill left for the day, Bree rang Michael at the hospital. He was improving every day, he told her. He'd be out by the end of the week. He was looking forward to seeing her again. He missed her. She told him that she missed him too. She wished she was mobile enough to be able to visit him instead of having to sit around the flat all day. She was sick of the sight of the flat.

She spent the rest of the day watching TV and reading the magazines that Declan had brought over. By the time Cate arrived later that evening she was extremely bored. Both Nessa and Cate now had keys to the flat so that they could call in to her without ringing the doorbell and dragging her down the stairs. Cate rapped at the door to the flat and pushed it open.

"Hi." Bree dropped *Bikers Monthly* onto the table.

"How're you doing?" asked Cate.

"Fed up," said Bree. "It's not my thing, doing nothing all day."

"I can imagine." Cate took a six-pack of Miller out of the bag she'd brought with her. "Want a beer?"

"Love one," said Bree.

Cate handed her a beer and reached for the bottle opener on the shelf beside her. She gave it to Bree then took a small bottle of sparkling Ballygowan from the bag.

"Why are you doing that?" asked Bree.

"What?"

"Drinking water?"

Cate shrugged. "I'm driving."

"One beer wouldn't harm you."

"After what happened to you, I'm being careful."

"It never bothered you before."

"Shut up, Bree."

"I could understand the water drinking if it was because of your pregnancy," continued Bree. "That'd make sense. But if you're going to have an abortion it doesn't matter, does it."

"I said shut up."

"Have you told Finn?"

"Bree!" Cate's voice was dangerous. "Leave it alone, will you? You're worse than that bitch Nessa."

"She said what she felt," Bree told her. "Maybe she should've kept quiet. But you really shouldn't hold it against her."

"Listen," said Cate. "She's going to hold this against me forever. Every time she looks at me she's going to think that I'm a murderer. I know she is. She just doesn't understand."

"You should tell Finn." Bree drank some beer, enjoying the feeling of cool liquid on the back of her throat. It had been another hot, sultry day and the flat was airless despite the fact that she'd opened all the windows.

"I know I should tell Finn," said Cate. "But that makes it all much more complicated. It's easier if I do it myself. What he doesn't know won't upset him."

"Would he be upset?"

"Bree, give it a rest, will you?" Cate stood up. "It's bad enough having had to listen to Nessa without you starting at me too."

"I'm not," protested Bree. "I just want you to see all sides of it. I don't want you to do something when you haven't thought it all through."

"You think I haven't spent my whole fucking life thinking about it since I found out?" demanded Cate. "I think of nothing else, Bree. Nothing! So don't tell me I'm not thinking things through. Don't!"

Bree said nothing. She wanted to put her arms around her sister but she was practically stuck in the chair and would've needed Cate to pull her out. Which wouldn't exactly make it a spontaneous hug.

"His show's starting next week, isn't it?" she asked eventually.

Cate nodded.

"Is he nervous?"

She nodded again. "Petrified," she said. "But excited too. It's really, really important to him, Bree. The most important thing ever."

"I understand," said Bree.

"So that's why I'm going to London tomorrow," said Cate. "I'm getting it done on Saturday morning, I'm coming home on Sunday and I'll be ready for his show on Friday and for his new drivetime slot on the radio on Monday too."

"And you're never going to tell him?"

"I couldn't, could I?" She looked at Bree.

"I guess not."

"I'm doing the right thing." Cate looked out of the window and spoke with her back to her sister. "I know I am."

It was after nine o'clock and almost dark when Cate left. Despite the continuing heat of the late summer, the days were getting shorter. Bree wondered whether or not she'd stay in Ireland for the winter. Irish winters were drab and damp and dreary. She wanted to be somewhere light and airy. Maybe she should go to the States. It was a while since she'd been but she liked America. She liked the wide roads and the sense of space and the feeling that you could lose yourself there if that was what you wanted.

Michael had talked about going to the States too. She wondered if he meant it. If they would go together. When you were nearly killed with someone it made the connection stronger; it had to.

Her mobile rang and startled her. She looked around for it, she'd forgotten where she'd left it. The flat was beginning to get messy again despite her best efforts to keep it as tidy as Cate had left it for her.

The phone was under the stack of magazines. There was no caller ID for whoever was ringing her.

"Hello?"

"Hello Bree. It's me. Declan Morrissey. Michael's father."

"I only know one Declan Morrissey," she said.

He laughed. "Sorry. Look, I'm outside your front door at the moment. Can I come in?"

"Is something the matter?" she asked anxiously.

"Of course not," he said. "I just wanted to check on you, that's all."

"Check on me?"

"See how you were doing, that sort of thing."

"I'm doing great," she said.

"That's good," said Declan. "Can I come in anyway? Or are you busy?"

"No." She giggled. "I'm bored out of my mind. I'd love you to come up." She ended the call and eased herself down the stairs.

"Hello," she said as she opened the front door to let him in.

"Hi there." He smiled at her. "Let's have a look at you."

"Not in this light," she told him. "A single bulb in a hallway like this wouldn't do anything for me. Come on up."

She went up the stairs as fast as she could but progress was still slow. He followed her into the flat and put a brown paper bag on the table.

"More cookies?" she looked at him hopefully.

"Muffins," he told her. "And some chocolate fudge."

"Oh my God!" She peered into the bag. "It was almost worth it for this."

He laughed. "I hope not."

"Maybe not quite." She took out a piece of chocolate fudge. "But it's a close run thing."

"Will I make some coffee?" asked Declan.

"Feel free."

She listened as he clattered mugs in the kitchen. She suspected that he was probably doing this because he was still unconvinced that she wouldn't try to take a legal action against Michael but she was perfectly prepared to allow him to try and soften her up with gifts of chocolate fudge.

"So you're recovering?" Declan put a mug of coffee in front of her.

"Oh, yes," she told him. "More slowly than I thought, but getting better every day. I won't be back at work on Monday as I'd hoped but maybe by Wednesday."

"Are you OK for money?" asked Declan. "Is it costing you, being out of work?"

The money question again. She smiled. "I'd be making more if I was working, of course I would, but I'm fine."

"Because Michael told me that you'd only get paid by Social Welfare or something and I don't want to think that you're losing out."

"I'm fine," she repeated.

"I know you said you weren't going to take an action and I trust you but—"

"Declan, please." She looked at him in exasperation. "I'm not doing anything about it. I don't want to. I'm alive. I'm glad to be alive. I'll recover and I'll get back to work. I don't need money because of what's happened. I don't want money because of what's happened. I hate the way people try to bring everything down to money when there are more important things to worry about."

He shook his head. "In ten years' time you might think differently."

"Who cares about how I might think in ten years' time?" she demanded. "Right now, I know what I think. And I definitely don't want to have this discussion again."

"Will you allow me to give you something?" he asked. "Because you have lost out."

"You've given me magazines and chocs and cookies and muffins," she told him. "That's more than enough for any girl."

"Be serious," said Declan.

"I am being serious."

He heaved a sigh. "I want to be fair to you. And to Michael."

"I know," she told him. "And I appreciate that. But I really don't want to have this conversation with you again."

"OK," he said.

"Good." She took a muffin out of the bag. "But don't stop sending the food parcels. I really do love the food parcels!"

"I've never met anyone like you before," said Declan.

She grinned at him. "That's what Michael says too."

"You're so easy-going," said Declan. "I'm either surrounded by fiery women who absolutely love making a drama out of a crisis or battling my fellow barristers and making a drama out of a crisis myself. Nothing seems to bother you."

"What's the point in fussing?" Bree picked a cherry from her muffin. "Losing your cool doesn't change anything." She ate the cherry and looked at him ruefully. "I got pretty fussed about my dinner date with Michael, you know. I even bought a new outfit because I wanted to look different. And see where fussing got me? The outfit was ruined in the crash—I'd have been better off in my leathers."

"Allow me to compensate you for your clothes," said Declan hurriedly. "That's the least I can do."

"Declan! If you try and give me money one more time I will shove these muffins down your throat!" cried Bree. "Please, please, please stop!" To her horror she could feel her eyes filling up with tears. Not again, she thought. She'd imagined she was over the crying by now. She hadn't cried in two days.

"Bree, I'm sorry." Declan looked horrified at the sight of the tears beginning to trickle down her cheeks. "I really am. I didn't mean to upset you."

She shook her head. "You didn't. Honestly. I'm just a bit—you know, shaky or something. Shock and everything, I suppose."

"Here." He took a cotton handkerchief out of his pocket and handed it to her.

"A hanky?" She sniffed and looked at him through her tears. "I didn't think there were such things anymore."

"I still get them from my Spanish in-laws every Christmas," he told her. "They don't know what else to get me. Dry your eyes and blow your nose. It's perfectly clean, Bree. I promise you."

She sniffed again. "I hope so."

She wished he'd go away. He was so kind and so concerned that he made her feel shakier than she already was. She wasn't used to feeling vulnerable in front of men. She was used to showing them that she was as strong as them, as good as them, a match for any of them. Crying into freshly laundered hankies was not the way of the modern woman.

She tried to blow her nose discreetly but it came out like a foghorn. He smiled at her and she shrugged.

"Another cup of coffee?" he asked.

"No thanks."

He looked at his watch. "I'd better get going," he told her. "I'm not entirely popular for coming out tonight. I have a feeling that Marta wanted to be out herself not sitting in looking after her younger sister."

"I know that one." She laughed. "Nessa, that's the oldest—"

"The firebrand," interrupted Declan, "not the torcher."

"Exactly." She smiled. "Nessa would sometimes have to baby-sit me while Mum and Dad went out and she used to go mental over it. From the age of eighteen I think she regarded any night that she wasn't scouring for a potential husband as a night wasted."

"I hope she didn't have to scour for too long," said Declan.

"Oh, she found one all right," Bree told him. "She has a lovely house in Malahide and a gorgeous kid and everything she ever wanted in soft furnishings."

"You sound somewhat cynical."

"They're going through a bad patch at the moment." She frowned as she remembered that she'd apparently said something about it in front of him when she'd been in hospital. But he'd obviously forgotten and she certainly wasn't going to tell him that Adam was suspected of snogging stray women and that Nessa was thinking of employing a detective to find out how true this might be.

"People do," said Declan. "But sometimes that only makes the relationship stronger."

"Did you and Monica ever go through a bad patch?" asked Bree.

He nodded. "Before she was sick. Even when she was sick." He sighed. "I resented her illness. I know that sounds awful—she was the one who was dying and I resented it. Sometimes I wasn't even nice to her which I'm ashamed of now. Because it wasn't what I'd expected. I never thought I'd be spending my thirties looking after a dying woman."

"I'm sorry," said Bree.

"It changed me," Declan told her. "It made me a stronger person and a better person. But I think I would've preferred to be the man I was and still have her with me."

Bree bit her lip. "I think you're great," she told him. "And I love your son."

He smiled at her. "He's very young."

"I know," said Bree.

"Don't expect too much of him," said Declan. "Not yet."

"I won't." Bree leaned back in her chair and closed her eyes.

Declan watched her. The cut on her forehead was beginning to heal but was now surrounded by an enormous bruise. Yet it didn't make her any less attractive. She wasn't, he mused, a pretty girl. But her face had character and determination. Now, though, that determination had given way to a more peaceful look. She snored slightly and he looked at his watch. Nearly eleven. He wondered whether he should wake her and say goodnight but he felt sure that she was exhausted. He sat opposite her for another five minutes. Her breathing was steady and even. He got up and slid his hands beneath her. She yawned but didn't open her eyes. He carried her to the bed and lay her down on it. Then he covered her with the quilt. She rolled onto her side but still didn't waken.

He tiptoed from the flat and pulled the door gently behind him.

21

♥

Moon/Mars aspects

Act first, ask questions afterward.

Cate had never wondered about people at airports before. In the past, she'd collected her boarding pass and strode to the gate, usually only bothering to buy a newspaper or magazine to keep her occupied for the duration of the flight. Even on the couple of occasions when she'd gone to her company's head office in the States instead of the European office in London she hadn't bothered to browse around the Duty Free and buy anything. She never noticed her fellow passengers, seeing them only as obstacles on her way to her seat or people that had to be endured if they sat beside her and struck up a conversation.

But today she found herself looking at them all, wondering why they were on the flight to London, what reason they had to be sitting at Gate A9 waiting for the flight to be called. There were a number of business travelers, easily recognizable because of their suits and their briefcases and the way they took out their mobile phones and anxiously punched at the numbers, clearly unhappy at being away from their office for any length of time. She was dressed like a business traveler too, although for the first time she realized that the waistband on her skirt was uncomfortably tight and that her stomach was beginning to swell very slightly. She was amazed that Finn, who loved to run his fingers up and down the front of her body, didn't seem to have noticed. Or maybe he has, she thought, but he doesn't want to upset me by telling me I'm getting fat.

She'd told him that she was going to the U.K. office on business. She'd told them in the Dublin office that she was going to the U.K. for the weekend. She felt guilty about lying to people but she didn't have a choice.

The girl sitting opposite her was nervously folding and refolding her boarding card. Cate wouldn't have given it a second thought before but today she wondered why the girl was nervous. Fear of flying? Fear of what she was going to? Fear of what she was leaving behind?

She was about twenty, Cate decided, with long straw-colored hair which fell in front of her face. She was dressed in faded blue denim jeans and an equally faded jacket. She wore a ring on every finger, the same kind of ring on each one, thin bands of silver with the ankh sign shaped on the top. Cate was suddenly sure that this girl, too, was going to London for an abortion. That she'd also had to wrestle with the gut-wrenching decision to terminate her pregnancy. That she, too, knew what it was like to be terrified about the whole baby thing.

Every so often the girl looked up and scanned the crowd anxiously. Afraid, thought Cate, that she'll see someone she knows. Someone who'll recognize her and judge her and make her wonder about her decision.

She looked at her watch. Boarding in twenty minutes. She opened her newspaper at the crossword page. Normally she could finish the crossword in five minutes, but today the words meant nothing to her. She colored in the empty squares instead, shading them with her blue Biro, sometimes leaning heavily, sometimes barely touching the page.

"Brian!" The nervous girl opposite her suddenly jumped out of her seat. Her nervousness had disappeared, her face was joyful.

The man, in his early twenties thought Cate, hugged her. "Sorry I'm so late," he said. "You must have been doing your nut. But the traffic was terrible."

"I thought you'd miss it and then we'd miss the connection." She beamed at him. "Can you imagine? Missing our connection to Antigua? Fine start to our holiday that would've been!"

He kissed her and sat down beside her, his arm around her shoulders.

Cate looked at her crossword again and blanked out the final empty box.

The view from her bedroom window was of the back of the hotel. She'd asked for a room near the back of the hotel where it was unlikely that anyone would overlook her. She sat on the edge of the bed and slid her shoes from her feet. She was almost certain that her feet were starting to swell too. Then she went into the bathroom and turned on the taps. A cloud of steam fogged up the mirror. She tipped the hotel bath gel into the water.

So what was she going to do now? she asked herself. What was she going to say? How was she going to explain it to Finn? She had to tell it so that everything made sense. He must never link this weekend to anything else because the most important thing in the whole world was that he must never ever find out that she'd planned to go to London and have an abortion. Not when she hadn't had the nerve to go through with it in the end.

She couldn't believe that she hadn't had the nerve to go through with it. She'd weighed up all the pros and cons, she'd made her choice, she'd rowed with Nessa over it. She'd convinced herself that she was doing the right thing. The only thing. It had been a cool, rational decision based on her lifestyle and Finn's job and her terror of being pregnant. She'd weighed all that up against the things that Nessa had said. And the feeling inside that maybe she *was* being terribly selfish. But still she'd been certain that she was making the right decision. So she'd booked herself into the clinic and she'd bought her ticket and concocted her stories. And then she'd done something that wasn't in the slightest bit cool or rational at all.

They'd called the flight exactly on time. The nervous girl and her boyfriend were first in the queue, ready to board. She'd sat at the gate and waited for everyone else to board first, her overnight bag at her feet. She'd watched the ground staff checking the boarding cards and looking out for stragglers. Three men had come galloping to the gate, huffing and puffing and exclaiming that they'd left their drinks, that they hadn't for a second believed that the flight would go on time. And the girls at the gate had checked the boarding cards again. One of them, effortlessly elegant with fair hair pinned back on her head, had smiled at Cate and asked her if she was leaving on this flight. "Because we have to board you now," she said. "The flight is closing."

Cate had looked at her card and at the stewardess and at the plane sitting on the tarmac outside the window. She got up and walked to the desk.

"Have a nice flight." The stewardess's name tag said that her name was Tanya.

"I'm sorry." Cate held on to the boarding card. "I'm sorry but I can't get on the plane."

"There's nothing to be worried about," Tanya said. "It's really a tremendously safe form of travel."

"I know," said Cate. "I use it all the time."

"We have to board you now," Tanya told her firmly. "You'll delay our slot."

"I'm sorry," repeated Cate. "But I can't get on the plane."

"Why not?"

"Because—I—well, something's come up, you see, and I can't go."

"Have you checked in any luggage?"

"I don't have any luggage on the flight," Cate said. She held up her overnighter. "This is all. You don't have to worry about unloading anything."

"Let me check it out." The girl took Cate's boarding card and looked at it. She tapped at her computer terminal. "You really don't have to be worried about flying," she said again.

"I told you, I'm not worried." Cate was finding it difficult to talk. "I'm really not. But I can't get on this flight because—because, I just can't. That's all." She closed her eyes. She felt sick.

Tanya was talking on her two-way radio now. Cate couldn't hear the words but she felt sure that Tanya was annoyed with her. Causing delays. Causing trouble. She could imagine the other passengers sitting in their seats with their seat belts fastened wondering what was going on. She thought of the girl with the straw-colored hair and her boyfriend worrying, perhaps, about missing their connecting flight to Antigua if this flight was late.

"OK," said Tanya eventually. "It's up to you. You have to make your own decision."

"I know," said Cate. "I already have."

And so now she was sitting in the airport hotel because it was the only place she could think of to go. She could, of course, go home and tell Finn that something had come up and that the London weekend was off after all. He'd accept that even though he'd be angry on her behalf, that she'd had to traipse all the way out to the airport before discovering that something, anything, whatever she could think of, had meant she had to rush back to the office.

But, she thought, as she tested the temperature of the bathwater, she wouldn't be able to go home today and face Finn and not blurt out something about her pregnancy. Then he'd be bound to guess

what she'd been intending to do in the U.K. He wasn't thick. He'd
know that she'd chickened out and she couldn't bear the thought of
his pity or his annoyance or his fury or whatever he'd feel. What will
he feel, she wondered, when I eventually tell him? Will he be so mad
at me that it'll all be over between us? Or have I got him totally
wrong and will he be delighted? She eased herself into the bath. He
won't be delighted? she muttered. I know he won't be delighted.
That's why I was going for the damned abortion in the first place.

She closed her eyes and considered her cover story. The best thing
to do was to stay in the hotel until Sunday when she was due back.
She could then go to the airport with her luggage and Finn would
meet her as they'd planned. She might phone him and tell him that
she'd managed to get an earlier flight. Then they could go home
together and she wouldn't say a single word about being pregnant
until later in the week. She could tell him she was going to the doctor because she hadn't felt well in London. She could say that she
thought she'd picked up a bug or something. And, after she'd been to
the doctor, she'd tell him the news. She'd act surprised and shocked
herself. It wouldn't be hard. She was still surprised and shocked.

And then what? She sighed deeply and moved her feet in the
water to circulate the warmth. He'd be surprised and shocked too.
Knowing Finn, he'd rant and rave at her about their plans. About his
plans. About the fact that they'd both agreed, absolutely agreed, on
no children yet. And she'd cry then, probably. It'd be a kind of relief
to cry in front of him.

Would he blame her because she was the one who'd taken responsibility for their birth control? Would he ask her to have an abortion? When she refused, would he simply tell her it was over because
he didn't want children messing up his life? She exhaled slowly.
Maybe that wouldn't happen. Maybe, despite everything, he'd
understand.

She opened her eyes and drizzled water over her chest. He
wouldn't understand. There was no point in pretending that he
would. But she might be able to make him accept it. She might be
able to persuade him that it wouldn't be the end of the world.
Although it had seemed like the end of the world to her. And it had
taken her a hell of a long time to decide that maybe it wasn't. She
hadn't even decided that, not really. All she'd decided was that she
couldn't go through with the abortion.

She still didn't know why she hadn't gone through with it. But, sitting at the gate and waiting for the flight in her too-tight skirt, she'd suddenly had the feeling that the baby was hers and that she couldn't get rid of it. She hadn't thought like that before. She hadn't wanted to think like that then. Yet she realized, with a growing sense of panic, an abortion wasn't the answer for her, even though the reasoning part of her brain was telling her that it was still the right thing to do. If anything, she felt more weak-willed than ever now. Changing her mind had been an impulsive decision. Maybe even a hormonal decision. Cate had a horrible feeling that her body was taking over her mind and that the clarity of thought on which she once prided herself was getting lost in the weight that she was inexorably gaining day by day. She sighed deeply. She wished she knew her own mind, wished she understood her mixed-up feelings.

Nessa would be pleased. Cate got out of the bath and wrapped a towel around herself. Nessa would think the things she'd said had influenced her. But it wasn't anything to do with Nessa even though it was so utterly unfair that Nessa, who wanted another child, wasn't pregnant and was going through a bad patch in her marriage even if she was trying to pretend that she wasn't. Adam having it off with someone else definitely counted as a bad patch. And poor Nessa was too terrified to confront him about it because, in the end, she was terrified of losing him.

And I'm terrified about confronting Finn, thought Cate as she rubbed body lotion on her arms, because I'm terrified of losing him too.

Although she'd intended to stay in her room for the whole time, she went to the restaurant for something to eat later that evening. She couldn't imagine that she'd meet anyone she knew and being stuck in the room was making her feel claustrophobic. She spent half an hour in front of the mirror doing her face before phoning Finn to say that everything in London was great and that she missed him. Then she went to the restaurant. She'd looked a wreck after she got out of the bath, her eyes red-rimmed, her cheeks pale and her hair limp from the steam. Now she looked good and she felt good. Not like a pregnant woman at all. More like herself again.

The hotel restaurant was almost full which surprised her. But a waiter found her a table on her own and she ordered Caesar salad and pasta. She was, suddenly, very hungry. She wondered whether or not Caesar salad and pasta was nutritious baby-feeding material. She groaned. She didn't want to become a person who thought of her own diet solely in terms of what was good for her baby. So she ordered a half bottle of Pinot Grigio to go with her meal. And I don't care if it gives you a hangover, she muttered in the direction of her stomach, if you're going to live with me you'll have to get used to the idea of hangovers.

"Cate Driscoll!"

She looked up from the magazine she'd been reading while waiting for her food and inhaled sharply. The man in front of her was beaming. She clenched and unclenched her fists under the table.

"Tiernan." She extended her hand to one of Finn's oldest friends who was also in the media. "Nice to see you."

"What are you doing here?" he asked. "Where's Finn?"

"I'm on my way to London," she told him. "Business thing, you know. Finn's working."

"You'll miss the last flight," said Tiernan.

"Mine is a later one than usual," she lied. "Delayed from earlier."

"And you left the terminal and came here for something to eat? Very brave."

"So tell me about you," she said, desperately trying to deflect him away from the unlikelihood of her getting a flight to London this late in the day. "What have you been doing?"

"I was in the U.K. myself," he told her. "Just come back in fact and I'm meeting some people about a radio series. Nothing fancy. Finn's too expensive for us now, I'm afraid."

Cate laughed. "He's busy."

"New show on Friday," said Tiernan. "Bet you can hardly wait."

"We're both very excited," she told him.

"I'll have to call him and wish him well," Tiernan said.

Cate moistened her lips. "I'm sure he'd be delighted to hear from you."

"We must get together for a drink sometime," said Tiernan. "It's ages since we all got together. Moira actually mentioned you the other day."

"How's Moira?" Cate knew that Tiernan had been going out with the makeup artist for at least two years.

"Great," he said. "She's working on that new film they're making in Wexford. You know, the blood and guts one that everyone's so keen on."

"Lots to keep her going there," said Cate.

Tiernan laughed. "A showcase for her, definitely."

Cate glanced at her watch.

"Are you sure you've time for the food?" asked Tiernan as the waiter put her pasta in front of her.

"Just about," said Cate.

"Well, I'd better leave you to it. Have a good trip."

"Yes," she said. "Thanks, Tiernan."

"And we'll get together soon."

"Of course."

She watched him as he left the restaurant. Shit, she thought, as she gulped down some Pinot Grigio. I hope to God he doesn't phone Finn after all.

22

♥

Aquarius January 21st–February 18th
Sensitive one, passionate but wants the head to rule the heart.

Nessa phoned Bree on Sunday morning.

"How're you doing now?" she asked.

"Much better," replied Bree. "My feet are still a little sore but I've got much more movement in them. My minor abrasions must be getting better too 'cos they're itching like mad."

"What are you going to do about work?" asked Nessa.

"I called Christy again. I'm staying out tomorrow and Tuesday and going in on Wednesday to see how I get on." She sighed. "I'm taking out the bike today just to see how I'm doing."

"Be careful on that bike!"

Nessa sounded like their mother, thought Bree. Miriam had been on the phone every day issuing warnings about safe driving and looking after herself.

"Of course I'll be careful. But I can't wait to get out and about again. I'm going out of my mind here, even with people dropping in to amuse me."

"Besides me and Cate?" asked Nessa.

"Listen, if it was just you and Cate I'd be gone demented," Bree told her. "The pair of you would drive even a fit person up the wall."

"Cate's a fool," said Nessa coldly. "And I'm sorry that my company drives you up the wall."

"Oh, you know what I mean!" cried Bree. "I'm walking on eggshells with you both."

"Not on my account," said Nessa. "But I can understand it with her. She's hardly likely to want to talk about it, is she?"

"It's her decision to make," said Bree. "Even if you think it's a mistake."

"You can't call what she's doing a mistake," said Nessa vehemently. "It's much more than that."

"I don't want to talk about this," said Bree. "I really don't."

"OK." Nessa sighed. "I'm sorry. I shouldn't take it out on you anyway when she's the bitch."

"Nessa!"

"All right, all right. Look," she lowered her voice, "Adam's out at the moment and I wanted to ask you—will you do what you said?"

"What?"

"Do what you said. Spy on him for me."

"You really want me to?"

"Yes," said Nessa. "I really want you to."

"OK." Bree moved her ankle experimentally. "I'll start tomorrow if you like. It'll give me something to do. Are you expecting him to do anything odd tomorrow?"

"No." Nessa sounded dispirited all of a sudden. "But I'm never expecting him to do anything odd. He doesn't usually go out on Monday nights, though. But he does on Tuesdays. You could follow him then. Or tomorrow during the day. He's always out at meetings. There might be something in that although I doubt it." She sighed. "Tomorrow and Tuesday. That'll do, Bree. If he hasn't done anything suspicious by then I'll admit that Portia made a mistake and forget about the whole thing."

"Two days isn't a lot to find out anything," Bree told her. "I was thinking more of two weeks."

"Two days is all I'm giving it," said Nessa. "I want to know but if you don't find out in the time then I'll be able to put it behind me."

"But, Nessa—"

"Two days," said Nessa firmly. "Otherwise forget it."

After she put down the phone she looked at her horoscope in the Sunday supplement.

"For some time now changes have been in the air," it said. *"You have been reluctant to make decisions but now know that you must bring some things to their conclusion. Changes are happening in a positive environment. Whatever occurs can lead to superb opportunities in the future."*

It had been the horoscope that had decided it for her. She had been afraid to make decisions but now she'd made one. Bree's findings would bring things to a conclusion one way or another. OK, so two days was a short time frame but that was all she was giving it. And, no matter what Bree found out, she would be ready to make any changes that were necessary so that she would have "superb opportunities in the future." She felt good that she'd given Bree the green light. It felt good to be in control.

Cate phoned Finn from the arrivals area of the airport so that he could hear the bustling sounds in the background.

"I'm home," she told him. "I got an earlier flight."

"Did you?"

"Yes. Things finished up last night so there was no need for me to hang around." She hated lying to him like this. But, she told herself, she'd had practice at keeping things from him these last few weeks. What was another lie among so many?

"And you want me to pick you up?"

"If you like," she told him. "I can get a taxi."

"Would you mind getting the cab?" asked Finn. "I'm a bit tied up here at the moment. I wasn't expecting you yet."

"Oh. Sure." She'd half expected him to say something like this but she'd hoped he'd come to get her. "See you later."

"Yes," said Finn.

She snapped her mobile closed and picked up her bag. The queue at the taxi rank was short and she didn't have to wait long for a cab.

She read the *Sunday Business Post* as they drove to the apartment. She wasn't going to think of talking to Finn about the baby yet. That was for next week, for after his show. This week was going to be an ordinary week. A dull week. Where he came first. How Nessa-like, she thought wryly. Maybe being pregnant has turned me into a Nessa clone. She paid the driver and overtipped him because she was feeling suddenly light-hearted again. She was still terrified, of course she was. She still wasn't sure that she'd done the right thing by not getting on the plane to London. And she still had to sit down and talk to Finn about it all. But she didn't feel as burdened as she had before.

She let herself into the apartment and nearly fell over the suit-case. Her suitcase. The bright red Delsey one that she'd used when she first moved into the apartment with Finn.

"Hello?" she called tentatively. "Finn?"

She'd never seen him looking so angry. His face was set into a grim parody of itself, his eyebrows straight, his lips taut.

"What's the matter?" she asked.

"You bitch!"

She stared at him.

"You lying, cheating bitch!"

"What are you talking about?" she asked.

"Don't insult me," said Finn. "Christ, Cate, I can't believe how stupid I've been. How dense. I always thought this kind of thing happened to the woman, which shows how far along the scale of PC I am! I never thought it would happen to me."

"Finn, I don't know what you're talking about. I really don't."

"How can you lie to me like that?" he demanded. "How?"

She clenched her teeth to stop her jaw from trembling. She didn't know how much he knew. She didn't know exactly what he knew. But he obviously knew something and whatever it was, it wasn't good.

"Tell me how I've lied to you," she said.

"That's pretty easy." He snorted. "I got a phone call from you on Friday. Sometime after six. You told me that everything in London was fine."

She swallowed.

"So how come I get a phone call at eleven o'clock at night from my old friend Tiernan Brennan to tell me that he met you in the airport hotel and that you were on your way to London? When you were already supposed to be there? When you'd told me that you *were* there?"

"I can explain that." My God, she thought, people actually say "I can explain." I always thought it was just dialogue in the movies.

"No you can't," said Finn flatly.

"I can," said Cate.

"Cate, I might be the most awful fool in the world but I'm not foolish enough to listen to some cock-and-bull story about missing flights or late flights or some other nonsense," said Finn. "You can't come up with any explanation that'll mean anything other than you were doing something that you shouldn't have been doing. That you were cheating on me." He made a face. "In the goddamned airport hotel! I mean, Cate, you could've cheated on me in more stylish surroundings."

"I wasn't cheating on you." Cate's heart was beating rapidly. She was going to have to tell him. But she wasn't ready to tell him. She hadn't worked out how to tell him.

"Look, it doesn't matter," Finn told her. "You lied to me. You said you were in London when you were in Dublin. Whether or not you were fucking some guy doesn't really matter. You lied."

"I know," she said. "But I had my reasons."

"I don't want to hear them," said Finn. "I want you to leave. I've packed your stuff. The other case is in the bedroom. I'll get it for you."

"Finn, please!" She caught his arm. "There's something I have to tell you."

"I don't want to hear it."

"It's important, Finn."

"You lied," he repeated. "I've never lied to you. Ever. I don't want to know you anymore, Cate."

"I'm pregnant," she told him.

There is such a thing as the sound of silence, she realized. She could hear the silence around them, feel it. She wasn't going to be the one to break it.

"Say that again."

"I'm pregnant."

"By whom?"

She gasped. In all of her imaginings, all of her playing out of different scenarios, she'd never for one minute considered that Finn wouldn't believe the child was his.

"You're the father," she said jerkily. "Who else?"

"How would I know?" he asked. "You're the one who spends weekends in hotels without me."

"Oh, Finn!" Sooner or later she'd known she'd cry but she wished she could have held out a little longer. "I didn't spend the weekend in a hotel without you."

"Excuse me?"

"Well, yes, I did but—" The tears poured down her face and she couldn't stop them. They plopped onto the side of the red suitcase and onto the floor beneath. She willed Finn to take her in his arms and comfort her but instead he walked away. She followed him into the living area.

"The baby is due in March," she said. "I found out a couple of weeks ago."

"Thanks for telling me."

"Finn, I couldn't tell you!" she cried. "How could I? You had so much on your plate. The TV show, the new radio stuff—everything. You were far too caught up in it. I knew you'd freak out if you thought I was pregnant."

"You should have told me before now," he said coldly. "Although that still depends on whether or not I'm the father."

"Of course you are," she said fiercely. "But I was frightened. I didn't want this baby. I knew you didn't want it either. We talked about it before. So I . . ." her voice faltered, "so I decided to have an abortion."

"What!"

She'd never seen him look so totally shocked before.

"I thought it would be for the best," she said. "After all, I'm so busy in work myself and we have all that stuff with the new HiSpeed shoe going on. Plus you're so caught up in your career—when would we have time for a baby, Finn? When? And I didn't want to bother you with everything so I decided I'd go to London myself."

His expression was still one of shock. "You had an abortion? Of my baby? Without telling me?"

"Well, no, I couldn't go through with it," she said. "But I wasn't going to tell you that I was pregnant until after you'd done the first show because I thought it would distract you."

"You're pregnant and you didn't tell me. You were going to have an abortion without telling me. You pretended to go to London when you were in Dublin. Forgive me, Cate, but I'm not entirely sure what my role in all this is other than an uninformed bystander."

"Look, I wasn't thinking straight. I was upset."

"You were upset!" Finn stared at her. "*You* were upset. What about me?"

"I know I should've told you before now but I just couldn't."

"So you thought it was OK to make this decision by yourself. You lived with me while you knew that you were pregnant with my child and you thought that it was fine for you to decide whether or not it should be born."

"Finn, you sound like Nessa now. She said—"

"Nessa! You told Nessa and you didn't tell me."

"She's my sister. I wanted her advice."

"Oh, come on, Cate. You knew what her advice would be. Have the baby. You didn't want advice. You wanted to share it with someone. But not with me." He shook his head. "So maybe I was right the first time. Maybe it's because it's not mine."

"Finn, it's your baby," she said. "Of course it's your baby."

"How can I be sure of that?" he demanded. "How can I know that every time you said you were in London on business you weren't somewhere else?"

"Because I've never lied to you. I've never been unfaithful to you."

He laughed shortly. "Let's back up on that, shall we? You never lied??"

"This was different," she wailed. "I was in shock, Finn. You can't know what it's like."

"I know what it was like to have a pal ring me up and say he's just seen my girlfriend eating in the restaurant of the airport hotel while I think she's in London," said Finn furiously.

"I've explained," cried Cate. "Surely you understand?"

"No, I don't," said Finn. "I don't understand why you thought it was OK to keep this to yourself. I don't understand why you thought it was OK to make a life and death decision on your own. And I don't understand why you didn't come home when you'd changed your mind about it all."

"I needed some time to think," she said.

"Seems to me that's all you've been doing," he said. "Of course I've had some time to think too, since Tiernan's phone call. And what I'm thinking is that a girl like you can't be trusted. And that once trust has gone from our relationship there's nothing left."

"I know you're mad at me," she told him. "I don't blame you. But I was really confused, Finn. And scared."

"Yes," he said. "I know. I see that. But you didn't come to me."

She pushed her hands through her hair. This was all happening wrong. She'd expected to have to argue about having a baby but that wasn't what he was aruging about at all. He was arguing about trust and confidence in each other and all sorts of things that she hadn't even considered.

"I don't want to marry you, Cate," said Finn.

"But—"

"Right now I can't even bear the sight of you."

"I've done nothing wrong!" she cried. "I've wrestled with the whole abortion issue on my own and made a decision and loads of people would say that I've made the right decision even though having the abortion might be a right decision too, but I've made a good decision and now you're telling me you hate me?"

"I don't hate you," he said. "But I don't think I love you anymore either."

"I'm going to have a baby!" she sobbed. "Your baby."

"I'll support the baby," said Finn. "You're right, Cate. I hate the idea of a baby at this time in my career. But it's happened and I'm prepared to accept responsibility for it. Once a test has been done, of course. Because it's hard for me to be entirely convinced that it's mine. But I'm not prepared to accept that you wouldn't tell me and that you decided to get rid of it without telling me either."

"But I didn't get rid of it!"

"That's really not the point, is it?" asked Finn.

"What is the point?" she demanded. "If I've done what's supposed to be the right thing then what is the point?"

"I'll leave that up to you to work out," he told her. "And I'll carry your cases to the car for you."

23

♥

Scorpio October 24th—November 22nd

Determined and strong-willed, awkward and arrogant.

B ree sat astride the Yamaha R6. She leaned forward and patted the cat's-eye headlights then sat up straight again and looked around in case anyone had seen her. Not everyone would understand how she felt about patting a motorbike. But she'd missed it. A day had never passed before that she hadn't, at some stage, ridden a bike. For a couple of days after the accident she'd wondered whether or not she'd have the strength to ride it again. It might have a lightweight aluminum chassis but it still needed a bit of muscle to keep it upright. And, for those few days, Bree had wondered whether or not she had any muscle left. But she felt strong today. She turned the key and was comforted by the growl of the engine as it sprung into life. She eased her way onto Marlborough Road, testing her ability to control the machine and enjoying the feel of it responding to her. She rode it easily and confidently but didn't take it out of her comfort zone. She wasn't ready to test herself to her limits yet because she knew that, right now, her limits were a lot less than they used to be.

She turned onto the dual carriageway that led to Michael's house. Declan had brought him home yesterday and she'd promised to visit him today. She was looking forward to seeing him again. She hadn't visited him in the hospital because she hadn't wanted to see him propped up in bed and eating himself up with guilt over the whole thing. At home, she thought, things would be different.

She parked the bike in the driveway and rang the bell. She heard scuffling sounds inside the house and then the door was opened by an attractive, dark-haired girl who, Bree assumed, was Michael's eighteen-year-old sister, Marta. Marta was wearing a tight-fitting pair of blue jeans, a plain white T-shirt and flat navy-blue shoes. She was also perfectly made-up. She reminded Bree of Cate.

"Hello," said Bree. "I'm here to see Michael."

Marta looked at her with her dark brown eyes. "Sure," she said. "You're the girlfriend, aren't you? Come on in."

Bree followed her into the living room where Michael sat on the sofa, his leg in plaster stretched out along it.

"Hi, there." Bree kissed him on the cheek. "How're you doing?"

He was still pale, she noticed, and his face was a kaleidoscope of colored bruises.

"How d'you think?" he asked.

She grimaced. "You look a bit better."

He laughed shortly. "I think I'm getting worse."

"Only because of the bruises," she told him. "They'll fade. And I told you, the girls will love the scars."

"And how are you?" asked Michael. "You look great."

"Thanks." She'd gone to a lot of trouble to look great. She'd used the makeup that she'd bought for the night of their date to hide the shadows that were still under her eyes and to add color to her cheeks. "I'm much better. I can ride the bike again, although I won't be going back to the garage until later this week. I'm still a little shaky from time to time. But it was great coming out here."

"You were lucky," said Marta. "The doctor said that Michael could have died."

Bree bit her lip. "I thought we were both dead," she confessed. "I was terrified."

"You shouldn't have encouraged him," said Marta disapprovingly.

"I didn't!" Bree protested. "He said it himself. He was showing off."

Marta didn't look convinced. She plumped up the cushion behind Michael then sat down opposite him again. Bree wished that she'd go away. This wasn't what she'd had in mind for her reunion with Michael. She'd expected to hold him to her and tell him that she loved him and she'd expected him to finally give her the kiss she'd been waiting for. But his sister was sitting there like a chaperone and her presence was severely cramping Bree's style.

"Hello there!" The door opened and Bree was relieved to see Declan even though he would cramp her style too.

"Hi," she said warmly. "Nice to see you again. Sorry about falling asleep on you before."

Declan's glance flickered between Bree and Michael and then he smiled at her. "No problem. You were obviously exhausted. You got here OK? No trouble on the bike?"

She shook her head. "Easier than I thought. But I'll be taking it slow for the next while."

"When did you fall asleep on Dad?" Marta frowned at Bree.

"He called to my flat with some muffins," Bree explained. "After the accident. But I fell asleep and he had to let himself out."

"You never told me that, Dad," said Michael accusingly.

"It wasn't important," said Declan.

"Your dad was trying to bribe me into not charging you with dangerous driving," Bree told him.

"Dad!"

"I wasn't trying to bribe her," said Declan hastily. "Michael, you nearly killed the girl. I was worried."

"She looks OK to me," said Marta.

Bree shifted uncomfortably in the chair.

"Would you like some coffee?" Declan broke the silence that had descended on them.

"Yes please," said Bree.

"I'll make it." Marta stood up. "Sit down, Dad. You've had a hard time lately."

"Thanks." Declan sat in the armchair vacated by his daughter. "Or am I in the way?"

More than in the way, thought Bree. He'd clearly annoyed both Marta and Michael who certainly seemed to be unhappy with him visiting her in her flat to make sure she was OK and not in a litigious frame of mind.

She turned to her boyfriend. "What's on the agenda for next week, Michael?"

"Sitting here," he said. "Watching daytime TV."

"Oh, don't be like that," she said lightly. "I'm sure there are plenty of things to do."

"Like this?" He indicated his arm and his leg. "I don't think so."

She frowned. This was hard work. She'd expected that Michael would be pleased to see her but clearly he wasn't. And he was in a black mood which, she supposed, she should have expected. After all, there had been days when her mood had been pretty black too. And Michael's injuries were much greater than hers.

"How's your sister?" Declan seemed oblivious to the uneasy atmosphere.

"Which one?" asked Bree.

"I was thinking of the firebrand," said Declan. "But the torcher too, I suppose."

Michael looked at them both enquiringly.

"Your father calls my eldest sister the firebrand," Bree told him, "because she attacked him in the hospital. And my other sister nearly set my flat on fire which is why he calls her the torcher."

"He seems to know your family a lot better than I do."

"You were lucky not to meet the firebrand," said Declan. "Injured or not, she'd have attacked you."

"They're great," Bree told Declan. And that's a lie, she suddenly realized. Given that Nessa has just hired me to spy on her husband and Cate is probably recovering from her abortion at the moment. My God, she thought, we're ordinary people. How can these things be happening to ordinary people? Other people's lives just plodded along—why didn't theirs? She blinked as she looked at Declan. He was an ordinary person too but he'd lived through the death of his wife and his son's accident. Awful things did happen to ordinary people. It was just that, for the Driscolls, they all seemed to be happening at once.

"Give Nessa my regards," said Declan. "Maybe one day I'll get to meet the other one."

"You never know." Bree smiled at him but wished he'd go away.

"Coffee." Marta walked into the room carrying a tray. She poured out a cup for Michael, then Declan and finally Bree. "Would you like some cake?" she asked.

"What have you been baking?" Bree asked Declan.

"This is from Spain," said Marta. "From my family."

"Lovely," said Bree hastily. "Thanks."

It was an uncomfortable afternoon. Michael's mood didn't improve even when Marta said that she was going to her room for a while and when Declan eventually left the two of them alone. Michael's answers to her questions were monosyllabic and she felt sure that he'd prefer to be on his own.

"Have I said something?" she asked finally. "Or done something?"

"What are you talking about?"

"To upset you," she told him.

"No," he said. "I'm just tired. It's been a hard time for me. And for my family."

"I know they all got a shock," said Bree. "Everybody did. But you have to move on. It's not as though anyone died, Michael. Things could have been worse."

"I've lived through things being worse. So don't tell me what I have to do now," said Michael tersely.

"OK," said Bree. "I won't. I'm sorry."

He yawned and closed his eyes.

"Will I go?" she asked. "Are you tired?"

"Yes," he told her. "I think I need a bit of sleep."

"I'll be off then," she said. "I'll call you."

"Sure," he said.

Why is it, she thought as she got ready to leave, that the things we look forward to are so often such a disappointment? I had great expectations of today. I thought it would be a romantic reunion. I thought he'd tell me he loved me. I was a bloody fool.

She let herself out of the house and got on the bike. Declan appeared at the doorway before she started it.

"You're leaving?"

"Obviously."

"Everything OK?" he asked.

"Michael's tired," she told him shortly.

"Coming home was hard for him," said Declan. "He's just realized how long it's going to take before he's fully fit again."

Bree nodded. "I understand."

"It's nothing to do with you," Declan assured her. "He likes you a lot."

"Maybe."

"Call out again," said Declan. "He'll be in better form."

"You think so?" Bree looked at him hopefully.

"Absolutely," said Declan. "Oh, and this is for you." He walked to the bike and handed her a brown paper bag. She peeped inside.

"Cookies!"

"To keep your strength up," he told her.

"Thanks, Declan." She put the bag inside her leather jacket.

He laughed. "Nobody would believe that beneath all that gear lies a packet of chocolate chip cookies."

She grinned at him. "But they'd believe that they won't last very long."

•   •   •

She opened her eyes wide in surprise as she saw Cate's car parked outside the flat. Surely her sister wasn't calling around to see how she was, not when she'd just gone through a trauma of her own. She eased the bike behind the car and got off. Getting off was still difficult, she was afraid to put her full weight on one foot.

Cate's head was resting against the driver's window. Bree tapped it gently and Cate jumped in fright. She pressed the button and the electric window slid open.

"What are you doing here?" asked Bree. "Are you all right?"

But she knew that Cate couldn't possibly be all right. Her face was blotched and mascara tracks ran down her cheeks. Her eyes were red. Her lips without lipstick. She didn't look like Cate.

"I will be," croaked Cate.

"What the hell happened?" Bree asked anxiously. "Did they botch the operation, Cate? Did something go wrong?"

Cate moistened her lips and shook her head.

"What then?"

"Finn threw me out."

Bree opened the car door. Cate stumbled as she got out and blinked in the evening sun.

"What do you mean he threw you out?" demanded Bree. "Why did he throw you out? What happened?"

"Can I come in?" asked Cate. "I don't want to talk about it here."

"God, yes, of course. Sorry."

Cate went around to the back of the car and opened the boot. She took out the red Delsey suitcase and a smaller cabin bag.

Bree watched in disbelief as she carried them up the steps to the house.

"So, tell me," she ordered when they were inside the flat. "Tell me why you're here, Cate. Did Finn freak out about the abortion? Is that it? He didn't really throw you out did he? Couldn't you stay with him anymore?"

Cate told her. Even as she said the words she couldn't quite believe what had happened. She couldn't believe that Finn had been so angry with her. She couldn't believe that he didn't understand. She couldn't believe that, somehow, she'd managed to throw it all away.

"I'll get somewhere else," said Cate shakily. "I won't stay here for long. I just need some time to get my head together."

"Take as much time as you like," said Bree, while secretly wondering how long it would take before she and Cate would kill each other. And how they were going to manage the sleeping arrangements. Cate seemed to have forgotten that she only had one double bed.

"I mean, I did the right thing," said Cate. "Everyone will say that I did the right thing but he threw me out anyway."

"Don't worry about it right now," said Bree.

"And Nessa—I thought of going to Nessa but she has her own problems and anyway she'd be so moralistic and everything . . ."

"Don't worry about Nessa either," said Bree.

"You're really kind." Cate pushed some papers out of the way and laid her head on the rosewood table. "You're a good baby sister."

"Thanks," said Bree. She took off her leather jacket and took out the brown paper bag. "Would you like a slightly squashed chocolate chip cookie?"

Cate shook her head. Bree went into the kitchen and put on the kettle. She washed the cups which had accumulated in the sink in the last couple of days and dropped tea bags into two of them. She'd become a tea junkie lately, consuming it by the gallon. She was sure it was as bad for her as coffee in large quantities but she'd found it helped her to relax. And she'd needed to be relaxed when she was stuck in the flat unable to move.

"He's not worth crying over," she said as she brought the mugs of steaming tea and set them on the table and saw Cate's shoulders shake. "Come on, Catey, have some tea. You'll feel better."

"Why do people always say that?" Cate raised her head. "You don't feel better."

"Have some anyway," coaxed Bree.

Cate pulled the yellow mug toward her and sipped the tea.

"D'you want me to torture him for you?"

They exchanged small smiles. Bree had been a tormentor in her youth, managing to annoy and irritate and sometimes scare her older sisters by threatening to torture them. Her methods varied but were always effective. Like the time she'd hacked off Nessa's fringe while she was asleep because Nessa had reneged on a promise to bring her to the cinema, or the day she'd put a matchbox full of spiders in Cate's bed because Cate had accused her of being a scaredy cat over something trivial.

"I just feel such a fool!" Cate sniffed. "I knew already, you see."

"Knew what?" asked Bree.

"That he didn't really love me anymore."

"How can you say that?" asked her sister. "You were engaged, Cate!"

"But *I* asked *him*," said Cate. "I shouldn't have asked him. It was stupid. I knew his career was more important than anything but I was afraid of losing him and I asked him to marry me only he never really wanted to."

"That's nonsense!" cried Bree. "If he didn't want to marry you then he wouldn't have said yes."

"But it was good PR," said Cate. "Even you and Nessa thought it was good PR."

"Cate, you've got to remember that you've hurt him," said Bree after a moment's silence. "You didn't tell him something very important. You lied to him. That doesn't mean he didn't love you."

"I don't want to talk about it anymore," said Cate abruptly. "I'll just unpack my stuff if you don't mind."

"Sure." Bree didn't know what to say. She was so accustomed to seeing Cate in control of everything that this new, unhappy version of her sister was someone she couldn't quite relate to yet. She watched as Cate hung her clothes in the tiny wardrobe and wondered again how long it would actually take her to find somewhere else to live. She was welcome to be here, of course she was, but they were simply too different to get on for any length of time. Bree knew that the soft brown suit that Cate was sliding onto a hanger was expensive—it shouted Brown Thomas designer boutiques at her. Bree's clothes were practical and oil-stained. She dreaded to think of how Cate would react to an oil slick on her Karen Millen.

"Would you like to go to the pub?" asked Bree. "We could have a couple of drinks, take your mind off it."

"I can't drink," said Cate baldly. "I'm pregnant."

"Oh, shit." Bree buried her head in her hands. "I'm sorry. That was so stupid!"

"You go," said Cate. "I'd like to be alone for a while."

"Sure?"

"Sure."

"OK." Bree picked up a bag and slung it over her back. She couldn't quite believe that she was going for a drink when she really didn't want to simply so that her sister could have some time alone in her flat. "Make yourself at home. The big bathroom is on the next floor if you want a soak but I wouldn't honestly recommend it, six people share that bath and four of them are blokes. I'm never quite convinced . . ." She shrugged. "You could sit in the back garden for a while. It's a bit on the overgrown side but it's restful."

"I know," said Cate. "I've been here almost every day for the past week!"

"Sorry. I'm losing it. I know you have." Bree looked at her anxiously. "You'll be all right here on your own, won't you?"

"Of course I'll be all right," said Cate impatiently. "I'm not suicidal or anything, Bree."

"Sure. Well, yes, fine." Bree smiled doubtfully. "Have a sleep, maybe."

"Maybe," said Cate.

"I'll be back later."

"Whatever."

"See you."

"Goodbye, Bree," said Cate.

The garden was a complete mess. Cate pushed her way through knotgrass and ground elder to the weather-beaten bench near the back wall. She sat down gingerly, afraid of splinters, then drew her legs up onto the bench and rested her chin on her knees. She closed her eyes and remembered the row.

The soft breeze rippled through the cherry blossom and eucalyptus trees and she shivered in the evening air. She felt stunned by the way her life had suddenly been turned upside down. She hadn't even got to grips with actually being pregnant. She couldn't quite believe that she was now sharing a rundown flat with her younger sister instead of a designer apartment with her successful boyfriend. And she hated the fact that Finn was probably delighted that she'd left, free from her at last.

Is this it? she wondered as she opened her eyes again and looked around her. Is this what I'm left with after three years? Crying in the garden of a shabby house in the middle of Donnybrook and not knowing where I go from here?

24

♥

Capricorn December 22nd–January 20th

Treasures the past, creates opportunities for the future.

Bree woke up when she heard the sound of the shower the following morning. She peered at the alarm clock beside the bed and shuddered to think that it was only six o'clock. Did Cate get up this early every morning, she wondered. Or was this early morning stuff just because they'd spent the most restless night ever? Bree had forgotten that Cate made little sighing noises in her sleep which drove her crazy. Cate had forgotten that Bree snored if she lay on her back. Every time one of them rolled over in the bed, the other woke up. It wasn't altogether surprising, Bree conceded, that Cate was awake but she considered it to be almost criminal that she was up.

She heard Cate get out of the shower and walk back into the room.

"Good morning," said Bree.

"Did I wake you?"

"No, I'm always awake in the middle of the night."

"Sorry," said Cate. "I don't want to be late for work."

"Late!" squeaked Bree. "What time do you start, for heaven's sake?"

"Whenever we like, more or less," Cate told her as she rummaged in her case for her hairdryer. "But I'm nearly always in by eight at the latest."

Bree groaned. "I do some early morning shifts at the garage but I don't get up hours beforehand."

Cate shrugged and plugged in the dryer. "I like being in early. I get more done that way."

Bree pushed the duvet out of her way and got up. There was no point in lying in bed while Cate was making such a racket with the hairdryer and she supposed that it would be a good idea if she got up and ready for her day's work as an undercover agent for Nessa too. But, she thought, Nessa and Adam and Jill would still be asleep by the time she was ready for her spying mission.

When Bree emerged from the shower, Cate had finished drying her hair and was putting on her makeup. Bree watched in fascination as her sister applied moisturizer, eye cream, foundation, eye shadow, concealer, blusher, mascara, lip cream, lipstick and lipstick fixer.

"No wonder you have to get up so early," she told Cate. "Don't tell me you go through all that every morning."

"I have to look good," said Cate. "It's part of my job."

"I thought you were the sales director," said Bree. "Surely the sales director doesn't have to slather her face in all that muck every day."

"It's not muck." Cate put her jars and tubes back in her vanity case. "It's necessary."

"Why?"

"Because I deal with lots of important people," said Cate. "I feel better when I look my best."

"You know, you look perfectly presentable without all that stuff," Bree told her. "You don't need to wear it."

"I do," said Cate. "Especially today. I looked a total wreck when I got up."

"Maybe today," conceded Bree. "But not always, Cate. You're the good-looking sister."

"According to Nessa I'm the selfish, inconsiderate sister," said Cate bitterly. "And now I'm also the unmarried, pregnant, without-a-boyfriend, sister."

"You're not selfish and inconsiderate," said Bree. "You *are* good-looking. You'll find someone else, Cate."

"Yeah, right." Cate tried to smile but it came out as a grimace. "Me and the baby that I thought I didn't want."

"We'll talk about it again later," said Bree. "Have a good day at work."

"Thanks." Cate reached out and hugged her. "Thanks for everything."

After Cate had gone, Bree phoned Nessa.

"Why are you calling so early?" asked Nessa. "Adam hasn't gone to work yet."

"I thought you might like me to follow him to work," said Bree.

"He's hardly likely to—" Nessa broke off as Jill, wearing her school uniform for the first day back since the holidays, strolled into the kitchen. "This evening's more likely," she said.

"I thought you said he didn't go out on Monday evenings," Bree protested. "Anyway, I thought I should do the evenings for the rest of this week despite what we said before. There's no point in doing two days, particularly if he doesn't go out on one of them!"

"I said just today and tomorrow," Nessa said shortly.

"But that's silly."

"Not half as silly as this whole damn idea," hissed Nessa. "I wish I hadn't said yes to it now."

"All right, all right." Bree sighed. "Where exactly does he work?"

"Merrion Square," said Nessa softly. "Time Concepts. I can't remember the number but the front door is green."

"I'll find it," said Bree.

"You're sure you're OK?" asked Nessa anxiously. "Only I don't want you falling off your bike or anything."

"I'm fine," said Bree. "I went to see Michael yesterday."

"How is he?"

"A little under the weather," Bree told her. "But his dad gave me some chocolate chip cookies."

"I don't like his father," said Nessa. "Arrogant sod. Just because he's a flipping lawyer."

Bree laughed. "He's quite nice really."

"Don't trust him," warned Nessa. "You never know with those legal types."

"For heaven's sake, don't be so paranoid!"

"You hear about it all the time," said Nessa. "People think that something's over and done with and the next thing they know there's a summons on their doormat."

"You've been watching too much TV," said Bree.

"All I'm saying is that he could still try and make out that there was something wrong with the car," said Nessa.

"He's not like that," Bree said. "He's honorable, Nessa. Really he is."

"We'll see."

"I'd better go." Bree really wanted to tell Nessa about Cate but she thought Cate would prefer to talk to Nessa herself. Eventually. It was hard, though, to keep the news to herself. She was beginning to feel very burdened by her sisters' traumas.

"OK," said Nessa. "I don't know whether I should be saying good luck or not."

"Neither do I," said Bree.

"Call me later," said Nessa as Adam walked into the kitchen.

"Who's ringing so early?" he asked.

"Bree," said Nessa.

"What's wrong with her now?"

"Nothing."

"I thought she was going back to work this week."

"Wednesday," said Nessa.

"Good," said Adam. "At least it'll mean you have some time to yourself again."

"I'm back to work today," she said. "It doesn't really."

"You miss it during the summer, don't you?"

"Sometimes," said Nessa.

Adam looked at his watch. "I'd better be off myself." He pecked her on the cheek and, quite suddenly, she put her arms around him and pulled him close to her.

"Nessa!" He looked at her in amusement.

"I love you," she said.

"I know," said Adam, then kissed her on the lips.

Bree parked her bike opposite Adam's offices close to a van belonging to some workers who were just about to dig a hole in the road. If he looked out of the window he'd think she was one of the hundreds of motorcycle couriers that covered the city. He'd never guess that the person in the black leather jacket and matching black trousers was his sister-in-law.

She took out her mobile phone and called his number. According to his personal assistant he was at a meeting. In-house, she said, in reply to Bree's question. He wouldn't be free until lunchtime.

Bree chained her bike and walked into the park opposite the Georgian office building. Although the temperature had dropped noticeably today, the sky was still blue and it was good to be outdoors. She looked at her watch. It was just after eleven. She'd return to her surveillance at twelve. It was unlikely that Adam would leave the building before then. It was unlikely, she admitted to herself, that he'd leave the building at all. This whole thing was really rather stupid. It sounded good in theory, like some of the mad games they'd played as children, but in practice it was silly. Adam probably wasn't having an affair at all. Chances were the whole thing was a once-off stupid mistake. He could have kissed another woman, Bree conceded, but it wasn't in his best interests to be having a full-blown affair and Adam was always someone who looked after his best interests. Besides, she thought, he does love Nessa. I'm sure he does. And he's mad about Jill.

She sat down on one of the park benches and took out the cryptic crossword book that Cate had given her the previous week to help her to pass the time. Cate loved cryptic crosswords and had implied that Bree would probably find these ones a bit on the easy side, but she was still struggling to complete one. Nevertheless she was getting the hang of it. It would be a real triumph, she decided, if she managed to finish this one while she was waiting for Adam.

It was slow work though. She'd just elatedly filled in the answer to "Xse" (and how apt it was, she decided) when she glanced at her watch and realized that it was after twelve. She panicked momentarily at the thought that she might have already missed Adam and hurried toward her bike. In reality, she thought, he's probably still at his meeting. She'd watched hundreds of detective movies in the past and she knew that stakeouts were usually long, boring and fruitless. Unless the leading man was involved, in which case they were tense (or, as the crossword would say, Xse!) affairs that ended in violence and special effects. She rather hoped that this one wouldn't end in violence and special effects. She put on her helmet just as the green door of the office building opened and Adam walked out. She started up her bike while he stood at the top of the steps and then she thought that she'd feel particularly silly if he was just nipping around the corner to pick up a sandwich.

But he walked slowly down the steps, stood at the side of the pavement and looked up and down the road. Bree watched him. He didn't seem to be in a hurry, didn't seem to have anything specific on his mind. She revved the bike. A bright yellow Audi stopped in front of him. He opened the passenger door and got in. Shit, thought Bree, maybe this is it! Maybe this is his secret lover. And then she shook her head. He'd hardly meet her here, in full view of everyone. He was probably being picked up for a meeting or something. But she followed them anyway, the yellow car easy to spot as it headed out of the city and toward Ballsbridge. They drove along the Rock Road toward Booterstown. Then the car turned into the car park of Gleeson's pub. Bree followed. She wasn't sure how she was going to keep Adam under surveillance in a pub.

He got out of the car, his red-gold hair glinting in the early afternoon sun. The driver got out too and Bree winced. It was a woman. The sort, she wondered, that Adam might be having an affair with? She watched as the woman said something to Adam which made him laugh. Then he put his arm lightly across her shoulder and ushered her into the pub.

Still nothing conclusive. The gesture had been friendly. Proprietorial, perhaps, but not passionate. Bree sat on her bike and chewed at her bottom lip. She didn't know what to do now. She knew that the pub was big and sprawling but she couldn't imagine how she could walk through it without Adam seeing her. And what would be the best time to walk through and catch him engaged in a bit of extra-martial kissing anyway? Nessa should've got a detective agency, she thought gloomily. A detective would be able to go in with a hidden camera and do some surreptitious photography. All she could do was sit in the car park and get bored. She yawned, took off her helmet and slid her earphones into her ears. Then she settled back and waited. Her stomach rumbled. She thought of Declan Morrissey's chocolate chip cookies and wished she'd had the presence of mind to bring them with her.

She was starving by the time Adam and the unknown woman emerged. He was laughing (again, thought Bree; is the woman some sort of comedienne?) as he followed his companion down the steps. She wasn't unlike Nessa, Bree thought. Taller, perhaps. About the same age. But definitely took much more care about her appearance. This woman looked as Nessa might if she spent as much time and money on herself as Cate did.

It didn't have to mean anything. A man could walk out of a pub with an attractive woman and it didn't mean he was having an affair with her! It could still be—and at that point Bree groaned because the woman turned to Adam and kissed him. Not an air kiss. Not a businesslike kiss on the cheek. She kissed him the way Bree had wanted to kiss Michael Morrissey. She kissed him the way someone who's in the throes of lust and passion kisses their lover. She kissed him like she'd kissed him before.

Shit, thought Bree. Shit, shit, shit.

She followed them back to Adam's office. She watched him get out of the car and the Audi drive away. Then, suddenly remembering her role, she followed it up Merrion Street, into Ely Place and around St. Stephen's Green. The car then turned up Camden Street and finally into a car park outside a small office block off the main street. The driver reversed into a marked space and gently nudged an awkward pillar at the back of the space. Bree sighed. If Adam was getting it together with this woman it wasn't because she was a better driver than Nessa. She watched the woman get out of the car, lock it and walk into the office block.

Bree got out and looked at the brass plate on the wall. It listed four companies. On the second floor was A. Boyd & Associates. She chewed her lip again. It looked as though she'd found bloody xxx A. She somehow wished she hadn't.

She rode slowly back toward Merrion Square. She'd have to tell Nessa. She hadn't expected to have to tell Nessa anything yet. She realized, as she stopped outside a newsagents and bought herself a club baguette and a can of Coke, that she hadn't expected to have to tell Nessa anything at all.

She'd convinced herself that Adam had committed a minor indiscretion, made a stupid mistake; overseen by someone else as stupid mistakes so often are. And she'd offered to follow him because she wanted to help Nessa but not because she thought she'd be the one to break it to her sister that Portia had been telling the truth. Bree sighed deeply. Despite the fact that she hadn't been kissed herself recently she recognized a passionate clinch when she saw one.

Why? she wondered furiously. Why was he playing away like this? What was the point? She finished her roll, drained the Coke and put the refuse into a bin. There was no reason to hang around here for the rest of the afternoon, she decided. Adam wasn't going anywhere and, if he was, she really didn't want to know where it was anyway. She'd seen enough.

She turned the bike around and headed toward Donnybrook. She rode past the flat and out to Michael's house. She needed to see him. She needed to know that there were nice blokes out there. Blokes who didn't pretend.

Marta opened the door. Bree's heart sank as she smiled at Michael's younger sister but the girl seemed in much better humor than the day before and she led Bree into the living room. Michael was in an armchair, watching the TV.

"Hi." Bree wanted to hug him and to kiss him but she was afraid of hurting him.

"Hello," said Michael. "I wasn't expecting you."

"I'm not back in work till Wednesday," she told him. "And I wanted to see how you were."

"Not much different." He hit the mute button and the clatter of gunfire from the movie he'd been watching was silenced.

"Marta looking after you?" she asked.

"She was at college this morning," said Michael. "I was on my own."

"I would've called out if I'd known," said Bree. She wondered whether she was telling the truth or not. If he'd phoned her and asked her to see him would she have abandoned her surveillance of Adam? Probably, she admitted to herself. And then maybe I wouldn't have found out about his damned affair and Nessa could've gone on living in blissful ignorance.

"I wanted some time to myself," Michael told her. "I've been surrounded by people fussing over me for the past couple of weeks. It's driving me nuts."

"I suppose they're concerned," said Bree. "Like me."

"I'll be fine," he said. "I know I've been a bit down about everything but it's such a pain not to be able to get about by myself. And every so often it hits me that I nearly died."

"No you didn't," said Bree robustly. "You were badly injured but you never nearly died."

"Another yard and we would've plowed into a lamppost," said Michael. "I'm pretty certain that would've killed us."

"But we didn't," said Bree.

"It was still a near-death experience."

She shrugged. She didn't want to think about it anymore. It was over. There was nothing to be gained by reminding herself how lucky they'd been.

"And it was my fault," said Michael.

"We've been through all this," she told him. "Forget it. It could've been awful. It wasn't. We'll both be OK. There's nothing to beat yourself up about."

"One of the many things Dad said to me afterward was that I was immature," said Michael. "And, of course, he's right. I was trying to impress you, Bree. Because you're so good with speed yourself."

"You didn't need to impress me with that," said Bree. "There are plenty more impressive things about you."

He grinned. "So I'm told."

She was relieved to see some of his old spark reappear. A gloomy, introspective Michael was not what she wanted right now.

"The thing is," he went on. "I like you a lot, Bree. I really do."

"I like you too," she said swiftly.

"And you're an extraordinary girl."

She looked at him warily. She'd heard this sort of thing before. A sentence which contained the words "wonderful girl" "brilliant girl" or "extraordinary girl" usually had a "but" tagged on.

"But I don't think I'm the right person for you. And I don't think you're the right person for me either," he finished.

She said nothing. What was it about her, she wondered bleakly, that made them all give up on her like this? They all liked her at the start, they all thought she was great fun to be with, some of them even took her to bed. But. But. But. She bit her lip. She'd felt so hopeful about Michael. She liked him. She thought he liked her too. Yet it seemed that sitting on the sofa all day unable to move had suddenly changed his mind.

"I'm sure there's someone else for you," said Michael. "Someone who's less likely to kill you when they take you for dinner."

"It was an accident," she said dully.

"I know," said Michael. "But I feel that you're the kind of girl that I'd have an accident with again. Because I'd always be trying to do stupid things to impress you."

"Why?" she asked. "I already said I didn't need to be impressed, Michael. I love you the way you are, honestly."

"I just think it's best," he told her. "And you don't love me, Bree. You hardly even know me."

She struggled not to cry. She reckoned that she'd done more crying since the accident than she'd done in her whole life before. So she wasn't going to cry now even though she knew that tears weren't far away. But she wasn't going to let him see them. If he thought she was tough and cool and impressive then that was the way she was going to be now.

"That's a pity," she said eventually. "I thought we got on well. Especially at dinner."

"We did," he said. "I'm sorry, Bree. It's just . . ."

She shrugged. "No problem."

"I bet you have loads of blokes trying to ask you out."

If only, she thought, bleakly. But she smiled at him. "I should never have worn a slinky dress," she said as cheerfully as she could. "I knew it'd all go wrong as soon as you saw my legs."

25

♥

Moon in Leo

Confident, pushy, a desire to impress.

Her mobile phone rang just as she arrived home. She sat on the bed and answered it.

"Hi," said Nessa. "I wondered how it was going? Adam phoned me just now to say he'd be home by six this evening and he's not going out so there's no need for you to be on watch tonight."

Bree struggled to find the right words and then stalled for time. "He might go out," she said lamely. "Even though he says not."

"I doubt it." Nessa sounded incredibly cheerful which made Bree feel even worse. "He told me that he's knackered, he's been in meetings all day plus he had a working lunch so he just wants to put his feet up tonight."

The lying bastard, thought Bree furiously.

"He did have a working lunch," she said after a moment. "In Gleeson's pub."

"Oh, well," said Nessa lightly. "I suppose a working lunch can be in a pub as well as anywhere else. Typical bloke."

Was she thick, wondered Bree. Did she deliberately delude herself? And was she being particularly stupid simply because she knew he had been followed?

"His working lunch was with a woman." Bree felt that she was being unnecessarily brutal but she couldn't keep the facts from her sister.

"But it *was* a working lunch?" asked Nessa, the hope coming through her voice.

"Oh, Nessa," Bree said miserably, "it might have been. I wasn't there for the working part of it. Just the part where she kissed him."

Nessa gripped the receiver tightly. She'd been expecting this, she knew she had. She'd tried to prepare herself for it. But expecting it and hearing it were two completely different things.

"Are you all right, Ness?" asked Bree anxiously. "I didn't really want to tell you this over the phone."

"She kissed him or he kissed her?" demanded Nessa.

"It was mutual kissing," said Bree. "She started it but he—"

"Did he stick his tongue down her throat?"

"You know, Ness, that's just a turn of phrase," said Bree. "I don't think you should dwell on the tongue business."

"They kissed in a public place?"

"Obviously," said Bree. "I saw them. It was the pub car park."

"He never kissed me in the car park of a pub," said Nessa.

"I don't think that means much," said Bree.

"It does," said Nessa. "He always told me that he hates people making spectacles of themselves in public places. Were they making a spectacle of themselves?"

"They were kissing," Bree reminded her. "If kissing is a spectacle then, I suppose, yes."

"The fucking bastard!"

Bree had never heard so much venom in her sister's voice before.

"Look, Ness, maybe I should come over?"

"Are you out of your mind?" Nessa asked her. "Do you really want to be here when I murder him?"

"Oh, come on, Ness—"

"He's lied to me and humiliated me," said Nessa. "You don't think that means I can't kill the fucker?"

"Nessa, maybe—"

"Maybe nothing," snapped Nessa. "He's cheated on me, Bree. I don't suppose you know what that feels like with your free-as-a-bird lifestyle but I gave years of my life to that man and he's reduced them to nothing. Nothing! What was the point of it all?"

"I'm not saying he's blameless," said Bree. "Of course not. God knows, Nessa, I'm totally on your side. You were the one trying to make excuses for him and I disagreed with you. All I'm saying is that you should approach it gently."

"Gently with a mallet," said Nessa.

"Are you going to tell him I followed him?" asked Bree.

"I don't know whether I'll give him the chance to talk at all."

"Maybe I should come over," Bree said again. "Give you some moral support."

"No." Suddenly Nessa was deflated, her anger gone. "No. Don't. Leave it with me, Bree. I'll decide what to say and when to say it."

"I'm sorry," said Bree. "I really am."

"Who was she?" asked Nessa.

"I'm not sure," said Bree. "I followed her to an office building and there was a plate on it that said A. Boyd & Associates. I'm kind of assuming she might be your triple x lady."

Nessa felt a lump in her throat. There was a real triple x lady. She'd always known there was. She just hated to believe it.

"Thanks for doing it for me," she told Bree. "I'm glad it was you who told me."

"I wish it hadn't been me who found out," said Bree. "I know I told you that you had to face up to things but, bloody hell, Nessa, I didn't want it to be true either."

"I know," said Nessa.

"Will you call me?" asked Bree.

"Sure," said Nessa.

"You'll be all right?"

"Fine."

"Certain?"

"Certain."

"OK then," said Bree.

"I forgot to ask how you're feeling." Nessa tried to sound caring.

"Nessa, I'm great. Not a bother."

"Good," she said.

"Phone me," said Bree.

"I will."

Nessa replaced the receiver and looked at herself in the wall mirror. The gray eyes that stared back at her were suspiciously bright but she blinked away the tears. She didn't want to cry. She didn't want to admit that there was something to cry about. She wanted to be angry. At Adam for kissing the triple x woman. At the triple x woman for trying to rob her husband. And at herself for not doing something about it sooner. But what could she have done? She blinked furiously again. What sort of person could she have become to stop him finding another woman to kiss? She'd always thought that she was the right person for Adam. The woman he wanted to be with. He'd broken up with his previous girlfriend because of her. Now did he want to leave her to be with someone else? Or was there still something she could do about it? Should do about it?

She covered her eyes with her hands.

She's staying with him for the money and the house. That was what Portia had said. Something like it anyway. And she'd been furious that the girl would think like that. But was it true? she wondered. Had her love for Adam been taken over by her love for her Malahide house and satisfaction that he was generous with his money if not with his time? Did she have her priorities all wrong? Was it, after all, her own fault?

She turned from the mirror and walked into the living room. There was a photo of them on a shelf. Adam, herself and Jill. She'd wanted to believe that they were a secure unit. That she'd managed to keep it together when so many other people had failed. But she hadn't. Her husband was having a bit on the side just as millions of other men had done before him. And would do after him. Despite everything she'd done to make him happy it wasn't enough. And now their future as a family was threatened. How would Jill feel if she left Adam? Or if Adam left them for his damned floozy? Was that part of his plan? Could she stop him if he did? Remind him that, even if he didn't love her anymore there was still Jill to consider. She swallowed. She could stop him seeing Jill. She could make sure that if he left them he'd suffer by not being able to see his daughter. She rubbed the bridge of her nose, disgusted with herself for thinking those kinds of thoughts. Jill wasn't a prize. She was a person. No matter what happened she had to make sure that Jill came out of it all right. Oh God, she thought miserably. I don't want to have to deal with this. I don't want it to be true. But I want to know why. Why he needed to have someone else.

Was it her looks, she wondered? She wasn't as attractive as she'd been ten years ago but she hadn't let herself go that much. Sure, she'd put on a bit of weight but who the hell hadn't? She asked him about it sometimes and he always told her that he loved her the way she was. She believed him. Besides, Adam wasn't so shallow as to go by looks alone. He'd said that when he married her. He'd told her that he was lucky because she was pretty and smart and interesting to know. And because she didn't make a fuss about things. That was true. Sometimes she felt fussed and pressurized inside but she never let him know about it. No matter what domestic crises might arise she dealt with them so that he didn't have to worry. They had their areas of responsibility. He worked outside the home. She did her mornings at Dr. Hogan's and she ran the house. Like it was a business. She looked after everything. She paid the bills, she did the shopping, she made sure that appliances were serviced. And she cooked and cleaned and did all the things that she thought she was supposed to do. As well as sleeping with him. She bit her lip. Surely it wasn't the sex? She thought he enjoyed sleeping with her. She never lay on her back and looked at the crack in the ceiling and wondered about the things she had to do the next day. (Paula had done that—she'd admitted that her sex life with John hadn't exactly set the world alight and that, sometimes, she'd gone through a checklist of things for the kids while he was making love to her. It was hard, Paula had said, to stay interested all the time.) But Nessa knew that she'd always responded to Adam, even in the last few weeks when she'd harbored the awful suspicions about him. She'd put them to the back of her mind, decided that they couldn't be true even though she must have known that they were.

How could I deceive myself like this, she wondered. Why did I?

Jill clattered down the stairs and into the room. She was still wearing her school uniform. Gray skirt, white blouse, blue cardigan and socks around her ankles. Was it a rule, Nessa wondered, that kids had to have their socks around their ankles? They were new socks. She'd bought them during the summer. They shouldn't be around her ankles yet.

"Why haven't you changed?"

"I was doing my homework." Jill's voice was laden with injured innocence.

"You're supposed to get changed when you come home," said Nessa. "And I thought you hated that uniform so I can't understand why you're still wearing it. Besides, you've been finished with your homework for ages."

"You're very narky," Jill informed her. "I was watching TV in my room."

Adam had bought the TV for Jill for Christmas. He'd laughed and joked about how it was far from TVs in the bedroom he was reared and how he was probably ruining his daughter's life but everyone's kids had TVs and so Jill should have one too. Nessa had been doubtful but had acquiesced. Do I do that all the time, she asked herself. Do I compromise for him because I'm afraid to do anything else? What the hell has happened to me?

"Are you all right, Mum?" asked Jill. "You look kind of funny."

"Funny ha-ha or funny peculiar?" asked Nessa.

"Funny peculiar," said Jill definitely.

"I must be getting old," said Nessa.

"Prob'ly." Jill grinned at her. "I'm eight. That's pretty old. So you're actually ancient, aren't you?"

"I guess I am," said Nessa. "I feel as though I'm a hundred."

Jill went into the kitchen to get a drink of juice. Nessa opened *The Year Ahead for Cancerians*. She'd already read the piece at least fifty times. *"You feel imprisoned by unfair circumstances and you've been trying to ignore certain personal issues. Tackle these and you'll bring about the changes you long for."*

She closed the book again and waited for Adam to come home.

Cate left the office at six o'clock. She got into her car and switched on the ignition trying to keep her mind on the fact that they had just, gloriously, received another massive order for the new sports shoe and that this month was going to be their best ever. Everyone in the company was talking about the great turnaround and how well things were going. The atmosphere all day had been one of jubilation and excitement. Ian Hewitt had called her into his office to congratulate her on her hard work.

Why couldn't all this have happened two months ago, she asked herself as she eased into the traffic. Why couldn't it have happened at a time when I would have been delighted by it? Now, although she was pleased about the order and the fact that the sales graph was looking healthier than it had for months, she couldn't generate any real enthusiasm for it. Somehow it didn't seem to matter anymore.

She sat at the traffic lights and stared, unseeingly, at the snake of cars in front of her. It's all gone wrong, she thought miserably. We were meant to be a good couple. A successful couple. A modern, new millennium type of couple. Now he's successful and on his own—not that he will be for long. And I'm just another unmarried, pregnant woman. Why didn't I just go ahead with the damned abortion, she thought furiously, instead of getting all fuzzy and emotional about it? I'm not the sort of woman who lets her heart rule her head. I'm strong and decisive and businesslike. So why the hell couldn't I have been strong and decisive when I needed to be?

The lights changed and she put the car into gear. She switched on the radio as she moved away.

". . . so this is Finn Coolidge thanking you for your company and looking forward to having you with me again tomorrow."

His voice filled the car. She tightened her grip on the steering wheel. She'd forgotten that today was the first day of the new drive-time radio show. As the music for the end of the program began to play (bright and cheerful, great drivetime sound), she visualized him slipping off his earphones and leaning back in his chair, satisfied and relieved that everything had gone OK.

The next set of lights went red. She blinked and then blinked again as she realized that she was on Amiens Street. She was driving home, but toward the apartment, not toward Bree's flat. She groaned. She'd been on automatic pilot, she realized, driving without consciously being aware of what she was doing. She frowned as she tried to plot a route back to Donnybrook. She'd have to go all the way to East Wall and turn down toward the quays again. That'd take ages in traffic that was still heavy. She looked around her. There was no right turn at this set of lights but if she nipped across quickly she could get to the quays in half the time.

I can't believe, she thought as she slipped the Alfa into gear, that I was so stupid as to come this way. The lights changed and she yanked the wheel to the right, cutting in front of the traffic coming toward the city. She could hear the blaring horns of angry drivers as she turned. Then she groaned again. She hadn't spotted the traffic cop astride his motorbike before she'd pulled her illegal maneuver. She pressed the button and her electric window slid down.

"You know that there's no right turn at that junction?" The guard peered into her car.

She nodded. "I'm sorry. I was in a hurry."

"You wouldn't believe how many people say that," he told her. "This your vehicle?"

She nodded again.

"May I see your driving license?"

She wasn't sure that she had it with her. She rummaged in her bag while the guard walked around the car, checking it, Cate presumed, for any defect that he could also pull her up over. She felt queasy. They'd only fine her for this, she hoped. Not take away her license or anything like that. She needed her license. A lot of her time was spent out and about meeting various clients. She couldn't be without her car.

I thought things were bad earlier, she muttered to herself as she continued to search her bag, I didn't actually think they could get any worse.

Suddenly, her feeling of queasiness intensified. She realized that she wasn't just feeling queasy, she was feeling sick. Very sick. In fact, she thought as she flung open the car door and jumped out, she was going to be sick.

She threw up beside the front wheel. The guard looked at her with both astonishment and concern.

"Are you all right?" He put his notebook into his pocket and came closer to her.

She nodded gingerly and pushed her hair out of her eyes.

He was looking at her suspiciously. Cate realized, with a mixture of amusement and horror, that he thought she'd been drinking. He was probably going to breathalyze her!

"I'm pregnant." She sighed. "I'm sorry. I couldn't help it."

Was she imagining it or did he look more sympathetic? As well as slightly uncomfortable.

"It's still early in my pregnancy," she told him. "I know I'm supposed to be sick in the mornings but I seem to feel sick at all sorts of odd times during the day."

He definitely looked more sympathetic.

"Being pregnant doesn't give you the right to make illegal turns," he said sternly.

"I know," said Cate. "It's just—I usually drive home this way. Only tonight I'm staying somewhere else. I forgot."

He pursed his lips.

"I'm a safe driver," said Cate. "Honestly."

"What you did certainly wasn't safe," he told her.

"I know."

His eyes searched her face and then he sighed. "Oh, go on," he told her. "Only no more mad right-hand turns."

She beamed at him. "Thank you. Thank you very much."

"I hope you have a lovely baby," he said. "And that the sickness wears off soon."

"I hope so too," she agreed.

She felt much better as she got into the car and drove off. Getting sick like that had been humiliating but ultimately useful. Men were nervous about pregnant women, she realized. Despite society trying to make them at ease with the experience, they remained unsure of the whole biological thing. As she was herself. But for one brief moment she'd felt as though she and the baby were acting together to get her out of her predicament. Which she knew was silly. She had said that she was pregnant, though. Just like that. As though she had a perfect right to be pregnant. As though it was OK. As though it was a normal occurrence in her life. Maybe, she thought, she was getting used to the idea. She actually wasn't sure whether or not she wanted to be used to the idea.

She arrived at Bree's flat half an hour later. Bree was sitting by the window, the crossword book in her hand. She looked up as Cate entered the room.

"Hi there," she said. "Her distant object isn't worth very much."

"What?" Cate went into the kitchen and filled a glass with water. Throwing up had been a good way to get out of her encounter with the police but it had left a vile taste in her mouth.

"The crossword," called Bree.

"Penny farthing." Cate came back into the room sipping the water.

"Huh?"

"Not worth very much," said Cate. "Penny. Plus it's a girl's name. And a distant object is a far thing. Penny farthing. Simple."

"I'll never truly get to grips with this crossword," Bree grumbled. "Some of it is utterly twisted."

"Most of it is utterly twisted," admitted Cate. "That's why I like it." She finished the glass of water. "I had an incident on the way home," she said and recounted her experience with the guard.

"I'm surprised he didn't issue a summons," said Bree. "They're on performance-related pay you know. All the same, puking was a clever ploy."

"I couldn't help it," said Cate. "One minute I was fine, next—I couldn't stop myself." She shuddered. "That's the thing about being pregnant, Bree. You can't stop it. It just goes on and on and you know how it's all going to end—painfully and horribly and—"

"It won't be that bad," said Bree.

"I wish I could be so sure of that." Cate sighed. "I know that Nessa probably enjoyed every pang of labor but it's not high on my list of great ways to spend an afternoon."

Bree grinned and then looked serious again. "I followed Adam today," she told Cate.

"And?"

"He met someone."

"Oh, Bree!" Cate bit her lip. "Poor Nessa. Have you told her yet?"

"Of course. I couldn't keep it from her. You know, she only wanted me to check him out today and tomorrow. If I hadn't found out anything she was perfectly prepared to pretend that everything was all right."

"I can understand that, amazing though it may seem," said Cate.

"I don't see how she could go on living a lie!" Bree sounded indignant.

"You'd be surprised." Cate shrugged. "Has she confronted Adam yet, I wonder?"

"She sounded murderous on the phone," said Bree. "I don't think he's in for a very comfortable evening."

Nessa wished she felt murderous but she simply felt inadequate. She'd spent the entire day trying to figure out what had happened to her and where it might have gone wrong. OK, she told herself, so she looked after the house and did all the stuff Adam expected her to do but had she changed too much over the last ten years? Had she turned from fun-loving Nessa to floor-sweeping Nessa? Maybe putting on some weight had been a big turn-off for him no matter what he said. Despite the fact that she lectured Cate about being too thin, she secretly envied her sister's fat-free figure. But though she'd often thought about going on a diet herself, she never quite managed to get around to it. It was too difficult when she had to cook for Adam and for Jill and so she was secretly relieved whenever Adam told her that her bum didn't look big in anything, even when she knew he was probably lying. Her bookshelf was full of ways to lose twenty pounds and still eat the things that you liked but none of them worked because they required a discipline that she knew she didn't possess. Anyway, she never really started any of them. They were always for tomorrow. But, she thought sadly as she sucked in her stomach and stood up straighter, maybe tomorrow was too late.

Adam phoned later in the afternoon to say that he had yet another meeting and it was scheduled for half-five so he wouldn't make it home by six after all. But he'd be home by seven for sure. She didn't pick up the phone and he left the message on the machine. He ended it by saying that he'd had lunch so not to bother making anything for dinner. She gritted her teeth at that and deleted the message.

When Adam finally came home—at nearly half-past seven—she was worn out with practicing what she was going to say to him. And as soon as she saw him she forgot it all anyway.

He poked his head around the living-room door, told her that he was going to make some coffee, and asked her where Jill was. She'd sent Jill out to play with Nicolette and Dorothy. They were at Dorothy's house right now, probably driving poor menopausal Darina Richardson around the bend.

"Sure you don't want any coffee?" asked Adam as he walked into the living room with a mug in his hand.

She shook her head.

"What a day!" He sighed theatrically. "We lost electricity this morning. Apparently some telephone company managed to cut the wrong wires or something when they were digging up the road—pity they didn't cut their own wires because the noise was shocking. It was so hard to think! And we had loads of meetings so everyone was trying to keep their wits about them but finding it incredibly difficult."

"So difficult you went out to lunch?" asked Nessa.

"You couldn't blame me," said Adam cheerfully. "Besides, I was working."

"Good lunch, was it?" she asked.

"It was great to get out of that hellhole," he told her.

He wasn't in the slightest bit fazed by her questions. Nessa felt the surge of hope run through her again. But Bree had seen him, she reminded herself, seen him kissing a woman. In a public car park. She had to keep that in mind.

"Who did you go to lunch with?" she asked.

He looked at her warily. "What d'you mean?"

"I mean, who did you go to lunch with?" she repeated. "It's not a difficult question, Adam."

"No," he said. "It's the way you asked it."

"How did I ask it?"

"Accusingly," he told her. "As though I shouldn't have been at lunch."

"I've no problems with you going to lunch," she said. "It's the kissing in the car park afterward I have difficulty with."

He drained his cup and put it on the coffee table. "Kissing in the car park?"

"Don't bother to tell me you didn't kiss someone in the car park." She kept her voice under control with difficulty. "And don't bother to pretend that it was the first time either."

"You're talking about Annika, I presume," said Adam calmly.

Annika! xxx A Annika. Wish you were here Annika. Nessa swallowed the lump in her throat.

"This Annika?" she said carefully as she handed him the postcard.

He took it from her and turned it over. He read the message on the back and turned it over again. Then he smiled slowly.

"Is this a case of adding two and two together and getting four hundred?" he asked. "Which is what happens when you burrow around in people's private papers."

"It fell out of a book," she said flatly.

"Which book?" asked Adam.

"I don't remember."

"Not any of the books you read," he told her. "Not a historical romance book. Not one of those doctor nurse things that you like either."

"I read other books too," she said. "Don't patronize me, Adam."

He sighed. "Annika Boyd is one of our best clients," he told Nessa. "She's a charming woman but very effusive. I can't help it if she kisses me."

"But you can help kissing her back!" cried Nessa.

"It's not important," said Adam. "I meet Annika quite regularly, I'm her account manager so I don't have any choice. She's a very tactile kind of woman. Enjoys kissing and hugging, that sort of thing."

"You're seriously telling me that you were hugging and kissing this woman in Gleeson's car park because that's the kind of woman she is?" demanded Nessa. "You hate kissing in public, Adam. You don't even like holding hands in public! At least, not with me. So don't give me that crap."

"You're being silly," said Adam. "Who saw me with Annika anyway?"

Nessa said nothing.

"OK, have it your way," said Adam. "Decide that someone who saw something completely innocent is right while I'm telling you a pack of lies."

"It wasn't just Gleeson's," she said tightly. "It was somewhere else too. You had your tongue stuck down her throat."

"Nessa, this is ridiculous." Adam stood up. "I've told you what happened and you can believe me or not."

"I want to believe you!" she cried. "Of course I do. But—but you've been seen with this woman more than once and she sends you cards from her holidays . . ."

"Nessa, loads of people send me cards. Loads of people send you cards. It doesn't mean that we're having affairs with them. Because I presume that's what you're accusing me of, isn't it?"

"I don't understand why you need to see her for lunch and kiss her," said Nessa mutinously.

"Because she's a client," Adam said. "I've told you. She's a touchy feely kind of client but she pays the company good money and I'm not going to tell her to sod off just because my wife is jealous of an innocent kiss."

"I can't see how it's innocent if you're sticking your tongue down her throat."

"I didn't stick my tongue down her throat!" cried Adam. "I just kissed the damned woman."

Nessa blinked. She wanted to believe him. He sounded so sincere. But it was his job to sound sincere, wasn't it?

"If you loved me you wouldn't kiss another woman," she said stubbornly.

"For God's sake, Nessa! I told you. It was perfectly innocent."

"We have a good life, don't we?" she asked. "There's no need for you to kiss other women."

"You're blowing this up out of all proportion."

"In a car park." Nessa's eyes glistened with tears. "Why did you kiss her in a car park?"

"This is a futile conversation," said Adam tersely. "It doesn't matter what I say, you're prepared to believe the worst."

"I need to know," said Nessa. "I need to know why you betrayed me."

"I didn't bloody betray you," snapped Adam. "For God's sake, Nessa, you sound like a particularly corny episode of *EastEnders* or something."

"You're my husband!" she cried. "And you kissed someone else."

"I'm not staying here to listen to this rubbish." Adam took his keys from his pocket.

"Where are you going?" she asked.

"I don't know," he said furiously. "To find some woman and stick my tongue down her throat, I suppose."

He stormed out of the house and banged the front door behind him. Nessa picked up the xxx A postcard from where it had fallen on the floor. She turned it over and over in her hands as she heard the sound of the car starting up. She rushed to the window, expecting to see him reverse into the gate. But he didn't. He pulled out into the road and drove away.

26

♥

Moon in the 7th House

Subject to mood swings, seeks close emotional ties.

Things hadn't gone the way she'd expected. He hadn't denied kissing Annika but he'd made her feel small and silly for asking him about it. As though she was a paranoid woman with nothing better to do other than to wrongly accuse him of having an affair.

Maybe he was right. Maybe she was blowing things up out of all proportion. She moistened her lips. What was she supposed to do now? Forget about it? Carry on as normal? But she didn't know what normal was meant to be. And how could she carry on if she suspected him of telling her lies?

Could he be telling the truth? she wondered. Was it possible that it was as innocent as he'd asserted? After all, he'd been so supportive about Bree's accident, he'd been there whenever she needed him—surely that wasn't the behavior of a man who was having an affair. Nessa wasn't entirely certain what the behavior of a man having an affair should be but she didn't think that being loving and caring toward his wife was part of it. Surely he'd be distant with her, not wanting to be with her? And Nessa knew the sort of woman he claimed Annika to be. The kind who hugged you and kissed you even when you didn't want them to. But Portia had described a very different kind of kiss. And so, reluctantly, had Bree.

She needed to talk to Bree face to face. To get some idea of how her sister had assessed the situation. To get a feel for whether or not Adam was a lying shit or simply misunderstood.

She picked up the phone and called Ruth Butler, a sixteen-year-old who lived at the top of the road and sometimes baby-sat for them. Ruth agreed to stay with Jill until Nessa got home. Jill, who'd come in just as Nessa was saying goodbye to Ruth, wanted to know what was going on.

"Dad's gone out," said Nessa. "And I have to drop over to Bree's for a little while. So Ruth will look after you."

"Why didn't you and Dad go out together?" asked Jill.

"Because he had something to do and I have something different to do," Nessa told her.

"You never go out together," remarked Jill. "Lots of people go out together but you don't."

Oh God, thought Nessa, she's right. We don't. Not anymore. She couldn't remember the last time they'd gone for a meal or to the movies or even to the pub. The magazines warned against not going out together. Against getting into a rut. Taking each other for granted. That was where all the trouble started. How was it, she asked herself, that the fabric of her marriage had started to sag but she hadn't even noticed?

Ruth arrived with a video starring Colin Firth and loaded it into the machine. Jill sat on the sofa beside her.

"Bed when Ruth says," warned Nessa while her daughter looked at her pityingly and turned back to the TV screen.

Nessa got into the Ka and drove across the city. It seemed to her that her mind was unable to focus on either Adam's guilt or his innocence for very long. As soon as she thought he was telling the truth a hundred little doubts came into her mind. Whenever she decided he was lying, a hundred different doubts challenged that. She'd thought that challenging him would result in a black-and-white solution. But it had made things worse.

And she didn't want to think about where he might have gone tonight. Back to the office? To the pub? Or straight into the arms of Annika, the triple x lady.

She pulled up outside Bree's flat and frowned. What was Cate doing here, she wondered, as she got out of the car. The last person on earth she wanted to see right now was Cate.

Although she still possessed a key, she pressed the bell and waited for Bree to come downstairs. Her sister looked at her in surprise.

"What are you doing here?" she asked.

"That's pretty welcoming," said Nessa.

"I'm sorry," said Bree. "I just wasn't expecting—"

"Not while you have Cate here anyway," interrupted Nessa. "But she'll go now that I've arrived, I presume."

"Not quite," muttered Bree as they went upstairs.

Cate looked equally surprised when she saw Nessa but she smiled sympathetically at her.

"I'm sorry about Adam," she said.

"What?" Nessa looked from her to Bree. "What have you been telling her about me?" she demanded. "Everything about my life? Stuff that was private between the two of us? And now you're muckraking and telling lies? With this person? The girl who was quite happy to get rid of her own child?"

"Nessa, for heaven's sake!" Bree's eyes glittered. "As usual you're jumping to insane conclusions."

"Oh, really?" asked Nessa skeptically. "So why's she sympathizing with me?"

"You're such a cow, Nessa," said Cate. "Always convinced you're in the right about everything."

"At least I haven't had an abortion."

"Nessa!" Bree was furious. "If you can't keep a civil tongue in your head then leave. You're in my place and I won't have you carrying on like this."

Nessa looked at her in astonishment. She'd never heard Bree sound so forceful before.

"OK," she said. "But I wanted to talk to you and I really don't want to do it in front of her."

"Well, you'll have to," said Bree shortly. "Because she isn't leaving."

"Why?" asked Nessa. "Surely the luscious Finn-So-Cool will be wondering where she is."

"You really are a bitch, Ness, did you know that?" Cate got up from the chair she was sitting on. "If you want to talk to Bree that badly, I'll go."

"Sit down!" snapped Bree. "Nobody's going anywhere!"

Cate and Nessa both stared at their younger sister. Her cheeks were pink and her eyes flashed anger.

"I can't believe that the two of you are behaving like this," she continued. "Simply because you have different views on things. Nessa, you can certainly believe that abortion is wrong but you don't have any right to be a vicious bitch to Cate because of it. You know, she made her choices for her own reasons and you don't know, you just *do not* know, all of those reasons. You can't get inside someone's head, Nessa and you can't expect everyone to believe the same things as you."

"But—"

"Shut up," said Bree fiercely. "Just shut up! Over the last couple of weeks I've listened to both of you giving your side of things until I'm blue in the face. OK, Cate made a decision and you thought it was wrong. Fine. But there's no need to treat her as though she was dirt because of it."

"Thank you, Bree," said Cate. "Of course, as it turns out—"

"Hang on for a minute," said Bree. "You have to remember something too, Cate Driscoll. You might not think much of Nessa's choices either. You have a thing about being an independent woman and earning your own keep and doing your own thing and living a kind of designer life. And so you're perfectly prepared to look down on Nessa because she did the thing that you so desperately didn't want to do. Get married, have a kid and put your family first. There's nothing wrong with that either, you know."

"I know," said Cate. "But—"

"Despite all of this, things have changed somewhat," continued Bree. "So you can both share your stories with each other and I'll just sit back here and listen but only if you behave like grown-ups."

"I don't really have a story to share," said Nessa tightly.

"I do," said Cate. She looked at Nessa and took a deep breath. "I'm living here for the time being."

"What?"

"Finn and I have split up."

"Cate!" Nessa's eyes widened. "Because he found out you were pregnant? Because of the abortion?"

Cate tried to look nonchalant. "As it turns out I changed my mind about the abortion thing too."

"Cate!"

"But Finn found out that I'd considered it and he threw me out."

"He . . . Why?"

Cate told her and Nessa looked at her sister in amazement. "What a bastard," she said when Cate had finished. "Doesn't he understand how hard it was for you?"

"You didn't understand, why should he?" asked Cate.

"I did understand," said Nessa. "Only—I didn't think your reasons were good enough."

"Neither did he," said Cate wanly. "So I did the only thing I could do when he'd already packed my bags—came here."

"Oh, Catey!" Nessa threw her arms around her sister. "I'm so, so sorry."

Cate disentangled herself from Nessa's grip. "So am I," she said. "And I'm also still pregnant. And still not sure whether or not I'm doing the right thing."

"I think you are," said Nessa. "But that's my point of view, isn't it?"

"I still love him," said Cate bleakly. "At first I couldn't understand why he'd freaked out but now I do. I didn't tell him, Nessa. I should've told him."

"Maybe he would've freaked out differently if you'd told him," said Nessa.

"Maybe."

Nessa looked at her. "I suppose saying sorry for being a bitch to you isn't enough."

"It's OK."

Nessa shook her head. "No it's not. I said horrible things to you. I thought I was right." She swallowed. "I still think I'm right in what I believe but—but I was wrong about you, Cate. You're not shallow and selfish. And you were doing what you thought was right."

Cate shrugged.

"I was angry," said Nessa. "And jealous."

"It doesn't matter," said Cate.

"Of course it matters," Nessa told her.

"Yes," said Cate after a pause. "It does matter, Nessa. You said things and you meant them and part of you was right but part of you wasn't."

"I know," said Nessa. "I don't expect you to forgive and forget straightaway, Cate. I probably wouldn't myself. But I am truly sorry."

Cate rubbed the bridge of her nose. "Just because I don't sob and cry and wear my heart on my sleeve doesn't mean I don't feel things as much as you, Nessa. And it doesn't mean I haven't agonized over my choices."

"I know," said Nessa. "I made things harder for you because I let my own feelings get in the way. I suppose I've carved out a niche for myself as being the emotional Driscoll and I kind of forget that you and Bree can get emotional too."

"Probably," said Cate.

"Can we get over it?" asked Nessa.

"Don't we always?" Cate smiled faintly. "Didn't I get over the time you pinched my new, expensive extra-lengthening mascara and lost it?"

"It's not quite the same thing," said Nessa.

"I know," said Cate. "But, yes, we'll get over it."

Nessa smiled shakily at her. "Thanks."

Bree looked from Cate to Nessa and sighed with relief.

"Anyway, you've plenty to pick over in my life now, haven't you?" Nessa told Cate who raised an eyebrow inquiringly.

"Bree's told you about Adam," Nessa said. "At least, I assumed so from what you said when I arrived."

"Sort of," Cate told her. "I didn't quiz her about it or anything.

She just told me that she'd followed him for you and saw him with someone else."

"Kissing someone else." Nessa's tone was harsh.

"I wish I hadn't," said Bree miserably.

"I confronted him about it tonight," said Nessa. "That's why I'm here, Bree. Because he told me that, yes, he'd been in the pub with her. He said she's a good client. He says she's the touchy feely sort. And that he had no choice but to kiss her."

Bree looked at Nessa warily. "It seemed a bit different to me."

"How?" asked Nessa.

"Well—oh, bloody hell, Nessa, I hate having to say this—he didn't exactly look as though he was trying to fend her off."

"But could he have been?" asked Nessa.

"I've just said that it didn't look like it."

"He said—"

"What about you?" demanded Bree. "I thought you were going to murder him. You talked about mallets earlier. Why didn't you give him what for?"

"I was angry at first but it wore off," Nessa said. "If he'd walked in the door straightaway then maybe I would've killed him. But all afternoon I kept thinking of all the good things we have and how much he loves Jill and—and . . ." Her voice trailed off. She twisted her wedding ring on her finger then looked up at Bree and Cate. "I thought maybe if he was—well, you know, I thought it might be my fault because I'm not glamorous enough for him anymore."

"For heaven's sake, Nessa!" Bree sounded exasperated.

"When he came home and I asked him about it he didn't turn a hair," continued Nessa. "He didn't even look guilty. He said that it was all perfectly innocent. Then he drove off in a huff."

"Why?" asked Cate.

"Because I kept asking him about her. And he got annoyed with me."

"Where did he go?" Bree looked inquiringly at her sister.

"How do I know?" demanded Nessa. Then she looked miserably at both her sisters. "Maybe he's gone to her."

Bree sighed deeply. "Anyone want a beer?" she asked.

"I'm dying for a beer," said Cate. "But, you know . . ."

"Have you been to a doctor yet?" asked Nessa fussily.

Cate shook her head.

"You'll have to see someone soon," said Nessa.

"I know." Cate sighed. "But I didn't have time today. I was up to my ears. And as far as I was concerned, last week I wasn't expecting to still be pregnant by today so there was no need for me to be going to any doctor."

"Dr. Hogan is good," said Nessa. "I could book you in for tomorrow."

"Nessa, I don't want to go to Dr. Hogan," said Cate firmly. "I have a doctor of my own. I'll go to her when I'm ready."

"Sure. Yes. Of course," said Nessa hastily

"What are we going to do about Adam?" asked Bree.

"What can we do?" Nessa looked at her doubtfully.

"I can get you proof," Bree told her. "I can tail him again and get you proof."

"That would mean that I don't believe him," said Nessa.

"Do you believe him?" asked Cate.

"I want to believe him."

"It's entirely up to you," said Bree. "What difference would knowing mean? Will you leave him if he's having an affair?"

Nessa tugged at her fingernail. She'd asked herself the same question over and over again. When Bree had told her about the kiss her first instinct was to pack her bags and walk out there and then. But when she thought about it a bit more, she wasn't sure that it was what she wanted after all. She still loved him. She couldn't just walk out on something that had been so precious to her for the past ten years, that had been the whole cornerstone of her existence. She knew that things hadn't always been perfect. But they'd been pretty good.

She shivered suddenly. Was that all an illusion? Had they ever been good?

"I suppose so," she said finally.

"Let me follow him again, Nessa," said Bree. "Let me see if I can catch him with this woman."

"I don't want you confronting him yourself!" Nessa looked horrified.

"I won't. But I didn't get to see them in the pub. If I follow him in the evenings . . ."

"Maybe he'll stay home now that I've brought it out into the open," said Nessa. "Maybe that's all it needed."

"So if he has seen someone but it's all over now, will you stay with him?" asked Cate.

"I—oh, I don't know!" cried Nessa miserably. "Would you go back to Finn tomorrow if he asked you?"

Cate grimaced. "I don't know that either."

"We are such bad examples for you, Bree." Nessa shook her head. "Don't let us influence your relationship with Michael."

"Actually . . ." Bree paused for a moment then shrugged. "That's over too."

"What!" Both sisters looked at her in surprise.

"I thought you two were getting along really well," said Nessa. "I thought the accident had brought you closer together."

"So did I," said Bree glumly.

"But when?" asked Cate.

"Today."

"Oh, Bree." Cate stared at her. "Why didn't you say something earlier?"

Bree shrugged. "I'm used to it. I'm bloody hopeless with boyfriends, always have been, always will be. I just haven't got what it takes."

"Nonsense," said Cate spiritedly. "Of course you have."

"We've been through the mill, haven't we?" Nessa sighed. "Who ever would have thought it?"

"You," said Bree sparkily. "You're the one with the damned horoscopes. You were the one who nearly had me believing in them that night at your house when Mum won on the scratch cards."

"I'm throwing out my horoscope book," said Nessa. "Even today it lectured me about tackling personal issues. So I thought things would be resolved with Adam. But they're not. I might have simply made things worse."

"You'll have scared the shit out of him if nothing else." Bree grinned.

"D'you think so?" Nessa looked hopeful.

"Nessa, even if he's as pure as the driven snow he'll be feeling a touch tense about being caught kissing someone in public."

"Adam doesn't get tense," said Nessa. "He's laid back."

"Laid back or not, he'll be worrying that you're about to throw him out and take him for everything he's got," Cate told her.

"I can't throw him out if he hasn't done anything," said Nessa doubtfully.

Bree and Cate exchanged glances.

Nessa looked at her watch. "I'd better go," she said.

"OK," said Bree. "Drive carefully."

"I will." She looked at Cate. "Mind yourself," she said.

"Sure."

"I'll give you a shout tomorrow, Bree."

Bree nodded. Then Nessa picked up her bag and left the flat.

27

♥

Moon in Aquarius

Desires physical and intellectual freedom,
sometimes critical or stubborn.

Her mind was in a whirl as she drove home. She'd come over to Bree's full of her own worries and had been plunged into her sisters' worries too. Why had all this happened to them? It wasn't fair. Cate had made a brave decision and Finn had done a terrible thing to her. Bree had nearly been killed but her well-off ex-boyfriend didn't seem to care. And she—she sighed as she turned down Pearse Street—she didn't know what to expect when she got home.

Maybe by now Adam had left her. The thought made her shiver. Maybe he really was having an affair with this Annika person and maybe her challenging him was the catalyst he needed to move out of their home. Perhaps by the time she got there she'd discover that he'd already moved out. She rammed the gear lever into fifth. It was her marriage! Even if he was having an affair she should fight for it. People got over affairs, didn't they? Sometimes marriages were even stronger afterward.

Adam's Alfa was in the driveway. She felt a wave of relief wash over her. She got out of her car and unlocked the hall door.

He was sitting in the living room watching *Newsnight*.

"Hi." He looked up as she walked in.

"Hello," she said warily.

"How's Bree?"

"Much better."

"Back at work yet?"

Nessa shook her head. "Wednesday."

"She was bloody lucky," said Adam.

"Yes." Nessa dropped her bag on the armchair. "Where were you?"

"Smyth's," he said. "One drink. Then I came home."

"Right," said Nessa.

"I paid Ruth."

"Good."

"Jill told me where you were."

"Wasn't she in bed?"

He nodded. "But not asleep."

She wondered when he would say something, when he would explain it to her properly. They'd done the accusation and denial bit, but she wanted something more than that. She wanted him to tell her that she was the most important person in the world to him and that there was absolutely nothing whatsoever going on between himself and triple x Annika or, if there was, that it hadn't really meant anything and it was all over now anyway. Then she wanted him to put his arms around her and hold her to him and make everything OK again.

"Would you like a cup of tea?" he asked.

"I'll make it," she said.

"No, I will."

She sat down while he went into the kitchen. She tried to get her own thoughts into some kind of order so that she could speak to him coherently. But she was finding it difficult to concentrate. She watched the images on the TV—a politician had just been accused of taking bribes to have a factory located in his constituency and reporters were harassing him to make a comment. What's new, she thought, dispiritedly. The same things happen over and over again in life, don't they? People cheat on other people. No matter what way they do it.

Adam walked in carrying a tray.

"Here you are," he said.

"Thanks."

She sipped the tea. He sat beside her and watched the news. This was almost normal, she thought. Like hundreds of nights that they'd spent together—although those nights she'd usually made the tea. He must be going to say something else, though. He couldn't pretend that the last conversation they'd had wasn't her accusing him of having an affair and him walking out on her. He couldn't go on behaving as though nothing had happened.

"About this Annika thing," she said eventually as she put her cup on the coffee table in front of her.

He looked at her.

"I just need to be sure," she said.

"I've told you everything," said Adam. "I don't know what information you've got but it's wrong. I kissed her, yes. But it was only a kiss. She's not important to me, Nessa, other than as a client. She's a damned important client."

"Jill said that we never go out together." Nessa picked up her cup and then put it back on the coffee table again. "And I thought about it. She's right."

"When do we have time?" demanded Adam.

"Maybe we should make time," said Nessa.

"But it's being at home with you that I like so much," Adam said. "All the comforts. Able to relax."

"We should socialize a bit more, though. We're in a rut."

Adam shrugged. "I do so much already," he said. "All this corporate stuff. I like coming home to my family. I like chilling out with you and Jill."

"But *I* don't do much," said Nessa. "I don't have any corporate things."

"You used to come to some of them," Adam pointed out. "You said they were boring."

"They were," admitted Nessa. "But perhaps I should make more of an effort."

"You're very welcome to come to any of the functions," said Adam. "Just let me know."

"OK," she said.

"So we don't need to talk about this again," said Adam.

Nessa shook her head. "I guess not."

She got up and brought her cup into the kitchen. She rinsed it under the tap and put it on the drainer. Then she walked back into the living room.

"Do you love me?" she asked.

He looked up at her. "That's a stupid question."

"Why?"

"If I didn't love you d'you seriously think I'd be here right now? When half the women in Ireland are obviously trying to get me into bed with them?"

She smiled wanly at him.

"Do you?" she asked again.

"Nessa—"

"Am I too fat or too old or too unattractive for you?"

"Now you're being really silly," said Adam. "You're the loveliest woman I know, Nessa. And you're just perfect."

Their lovemaking was fierce that night. He pulled her to him the moment she got into bed beside him and he held her so tightly that she could hardly breathe. As she lay beneath him, the pent-up emotions of the day surged through her and she raked his back with her fingernails until he gasped that she was really, really hurting him— and then he grinned at her and told her that it was rather good. He flipped her over until she was on top of him and he told her to work at it. She slid along him, touching him, flexing her muscles, being more energetic and inventive than ever before. Then he shuddered and pulled her to him again and she told herself that he must love her because he'd said so, over and over again. And, she realized, it had been a long time since he'd said it like that. It had been a long time since they'd made love like that.

He always fell asleep quickly afterward. She put her arm around him. He sighed contentedly in his sleep. She closed her eyes. She wished she could fall asleep too. But sleep eluded her. Every time she felt herself drifting into unconsciousness she'd suddenly wake up again. She'd think about what he'd told her and what Bree had told her and she wished that she'd never suggested to Bree that she follow him. It had been a stupid thing to do. She wondered whether both of them were telling the truth, just seeing things from a different perspective. Bree had been looking for guilt and she thought she'd found it. Adam had kissed a woman but he thought it was perfectly reasonable in the business context. So he didn't feel guilty at all. Both of them could be right from their point of view.

But she was the one who couldn't sleep.

She was relieved when the alarm went off and it was time to get up. She got out of the bed, woke Adam and Jill, then went downstairs to start breakfast. Adam was in surprisingly good form for the morning and Jill managed to get through breakfast without spilling anything on her school uniform. They left the house on time and she arrived at Dr. Hogan's with five minutes to spare.

Everything will be all right, she told herself as she opened the appointments book and looked at the list of patients. We made love last night and it was bloody brilliant. Everything will be just fine from now on.

Cate had morning sickness. Bree heard her rush out of the bed and into the bathroom. She burrowed down beneath the covers to muffle the sounds of her sister's discomfort. She felt bad about wishing that Cate had somewhere else to go but the idea of this happening every morning for the next few weeks was horrifying. She fell asleep again thinking about how horrifying it was.

The sound of the door closing woke her. She pushed the sheet from her face and sat up. It was only seven o'clock. She couldn't believe that Cate was still going in to work at the crack of dawn. Cate had told her that the staff had flexible working hours. Bree didn't think that seven in the morning until nearly seven at night was very flexible. But Cate had said that it was all about getting the work done and being there and, above all, being seen to be there. She especially wanted to impress her hardworking nature on their minds now, Cate told Bree, because she'd need some goodwill when she went on maternity leave. And she flushed when she said maternity leave as though embarrassed by the whole idea.

Bree threw back the duvet and looked at her legs. The bruises were fading and the pain in her foot had almost gone. She ached in the evenings but was fine during the day. She yawned and walked slowly to the bedroom window.

The road outside was the same as always. A row of redbrick houses opposite. Three blue cars parked in one of the graveled gardens. Her bike parked outside her own door. The bin from the house next door on its side again. A selection of people hurrying down the road on their way to work. As early as Cate, poor things. It was getting monotonous, Bree thought. Stifling even. Maybe it was time for her to consider moving on again. If she moved, Cate could stay in the flat, although she conceded that Cate would probably have hysterics at the idea. Because it wasn't Cate's sort of flat, cool and modern and uncluttered like the apartment in Clontarf. Nor was it really suitable for a mother and child. Bree suddenly wondered what Miriam would say when she found out that her middle daughter was pregnant. She'd be delighted, Bree supposed, until she learned about Finn.

She made herself a cup of strong, sweet tea. Definitely time to move on, she thought. Let Nessa and Cate work out their own problems. She'd never got involved with them before and she was beginning to wish she hadn't got involved this time either. She could go to California where the sun always shone and the sky was always blue and where she'd easily get some work. And where she could meet some tanned and healthy man (definitely not a weirdo, though that might be difficult in California) with whom she could have a carefree relationship and put the messiness of the Michael Morrissey episode behind her.

She sighed deeply. He'd always been too good to be true and, of course, they'd never even got around to a decent kiss! But she'd miss him. She'd miss being part of a couple again. Of course she'd miss Declan Morrissey too, she thought, as she reached into the biscuit barrel and realized it was empty. He was a nice man who was easy to talk to. It was a pity that Michael hadn't been as easy to talk to as Declan. Or, somehow, as understanding.

She had a shower, got dressed and debated whether or not to ring Nessa. The original plan had been for her to tail Adam today but, having spotted him with his so-called client the day before, there didn't seem much point. Perhaps she'd hang around outside his office all the same. After all, if he met the same woman for a second day in a row even Nessa would have to think seriously about the truth of what he was telling her. She was so bloody gullible, thought Bree. Or maybe it was just that she wanted to believe him.

It was a hazy day, not warm but not exactly cold either. Less amenable to sitting in the park, she thought, as she secured her bike. Yesterday there'd been a number of people strolling through it or sitting on the benches reading newspapers or books. Today she was on her own. She'd decided against struggling with another crossword and had brought one of her car mechanics books instead. She was engrossed in the chapter about pistons when her mobile phone rang.

"It's me," said Nessa.

"How are you?" asked Bree. "I wanted to ring earlier and then I thought I should leave you alone."

"I'm fine," said Nessa. "So is Adam."

"What's new?"

"He went for a drink last night after we'd had our row but he was home before me. He'd paid the babysitter and checked on Jill. He made me a cup of tea."

Big deal, thought Bree. "Did you talk to him?"

"Of course," said Nessa. "What d'you take me for? He explained it all again and we agreed that it was in the past."

"Nessa—"

"I thought about it all night," said Nessa. "I love him. He loves me. He loves Jill. He has no reason to jeopardize all that for the sake of one little kiss."

"Are you sure you're not . . ." Bree fumbled for the words.

"Fooling myself?" supplied Nessa. "I don't think so."

"Did you sleep with him last night?" asked Bree.

"What?!"

"Did he make love to you?"

"That's none of your business, Bree," said Nessa. "Absolutely none of your business!"

"I had a boyfriend who made love to me every time I asked him about other women," said Bree. "It shut me up for a while. Then I realized it was only an excuse."

"You might not believe his explanation, Bree, but I do," said Nessa coolly. "And whether or not my husband and I made love last night has nothing to do with it."

"Why don't you wait until tomorrow before you decide to hang up your mallet for good," suggested Bree. "Let me follow him for you today."

"There's absolutely no need for that," said Nessa sharply. "I don't want you to follow him."

"But—"

"You're not following him now, are you?" she demanded.

"It's mid-morning," said Bree disingenuously. "I'm sure he's in his office."

"Don't follow him," said Nessa again.

"OK, OK," Bree sighed. "Have it your way."

"It's up to Adam and me to work things out," said Nessa. "I don't need you messing it up any more."

"Thanks," said Bree.

"Sorry." Nessa sounded abashed. "I didn't mean—"

"It doesn't matter," Bree told her. "This surveillance business is a pain in the neck anyway."

"Maybe we can get together at the weekend," suggested Nessa. "Yourself, myself and Cate. Go out for a meal again, something like that."

"Maybe," said Bree unenthusiastically.

"I have to go," Nessa said. "Surgery is busy. I'll talk to you again."

"Right," said Bree. She slipped her mobile back into the pocket of her jacket. She thought Nessa was being foolish but it was her right to be as foolish as she liked. And maybe it was just as well to leave things as they were. People might look for perfection in relationships but perfection didn't happen, as she knew only too well. So if Nessa and Adam were happy, if Nessa could live with the idea that he might be engaging in a little bit of offside, what was the point in rocking the boat?

She glanced at her watch. It was nearly lunchtime. She'd wait for just a little longer to see whether or not he was being picked up outside the office again. It was highly unlikely, she felt, that he'd be seeing his touchy-feely client two days in a row. So if she turned up again Bree would know that he was a liar and a cheat and she'd make Nessa take her head out of the sand and face up to it. And she didn't care whether or not Nessa lost her cool at her for disobeying her.

By one o'clock, to her secret relief, there was no sign of Adam. But as she revved up her bike the Alfa drove past. She recognized it immediately as Adam's just as she recognized his profile in the driver's seat. He hadn't seen her. The car stopped at the traffic lights and she came up behind it. She wasn't going to follow him. He was in his own car, he hadn't been picked up by anyone. But he was going in her direction, toward Donnybrook, so she didn't have any choice but to tuck in behind him.

She didn't turn onto Marlborough Road. She meant to but she didn't. She wanted to see where he was going. She didn't have to tell Nessa but she needed to know.

He drove past the turn for Michael's house and out toward Stillorgan. Then he turned left toward the coast.

Perhaps he was going to Gleeson's by a different route, thought Bree, as she kept a safe distance behind him. But he suddenly indicated to the right and turned into a small development of town houses and apartments. Bree cut the engine and stopped opposite. She could see him parking, brushing the car against an escallonia bush in the process. He got out and walked toward the entrance to the apartments. He rang the bell, the door to the lobby opened and he went inside.

It was midday. Bree sat indecisively astride her bike and wondered what to do next. She really wasn't sure what Adam actually did for a living so it was entirely possible, she supposed, that calling to people's homes was part of it. It could be that whoever he was calling on worked from home. Lots of people did nowadays. But she couldn't help thinking that she was making excuses for him. Just as Nessa did.

She felt conspicuous on her bike in the middle of a residential area. She took off her helmet and shook her hair. There was a small corner shop at the end of the road. She walked to it and bought a roll and a Fanta. Then she sat on the small wall outside the shop, took out her book and waited. She wasn't sure how long she should wait. She wanted to see Adam coming out of the apartment again. As if, she thought wryly, she'd be able to tell what he'd been doing by his demeanor as he left. But it might give her some clue. She'd completely forgotten that she wasn't meant to be following him. She felt that it was important to be here.

Half an hour later she went back to the bike. She hadn't seen his car leave the complex so she knew he was still there. And to be fair to him, she thought guiltily, he probably was there on business. It was just her nasty, suspicious mind making her think differently. She put on her helmet, uncertain as to what she should do next.

Then she saw him. On the balcony of the top floor apartment. He was leaning over the rail and looking into the flowered garden beneath. She stepped behind a sycamore tree so that she could see and not be seen. As she watched him, a woman came and stood on the balcony beside him.

It wasn't the woman from the car park. This woman was dark-haired. She was wearing a bright red T-shirt and loose black jeans. She leaned toward Adam and he turned to her. He kissed her.

Bree was quite, quite certain about that. The woman hadn't

kissed Adam. He'd kissed her. And he was kissing her now. Bree realized that she was holding her breath as she watched him kiss her. She was still holding it when the woman wrapped her arms around Adam's neck. She didn't breathe while they continued kissing as they stumbled back into the apartment.

She was shaking. She stared up at the empty balcony where her brother-in-law had been kissing a woman who wasn't his wife. The second woman who wasn't his wife that she'd seen him kiss in as many days.

Her breathing was ragged and uneven as she started up the bike and made her way back home.

28

♥

Sun in Capricorn, Moon in Libra

Charismatic, successful, but believes that dreams don't come true.

"You have to tell her."

Cate and Bree were sitting in the flat later that evening surrounded by the debris of the Indian takeaway that Cate had brought home. The air was heavy with the aroma of cumin and coriander.

"I can't," said Bree. "I told her that I wouldn't follow him."

"But you can't keep it from her," Cate protested. "I'd want to know if my husband was banging some other woman. The lying shit!"

Bree squirmed uncomfortably. "The second other woman," she said. "I can't believe it, Catey, I just can't! He always seemed so nice."

"That's where they all get us." Cate's voice was brittle. "They pretend to be nice but they're not really."

"He probably could've explained away the first one, it was just a kiss even though it was a damn sight more than a peck on the cheek. But this . . ." Bree shuddered. "Oh, Cate, why is he messing around like this? Why?"

"Who knows?" she said tautly. "Most of them don't bloody need an excuse, do they?"

"I thought he was into the whole home and family thing just like Nessa," said Bree. "The barbecues in the back garden. DIY in the house. All that sort of stuff."

"She must have guessed before now," Cate said. "She can't be as blind as all that! How many women do you think there are?"

Bree looked horrified. "More than two?"

"Why not?" Cate shrugged. "You've followed him for two days and seen two different women. Why shouldn't he have one for every day of the week?"

"Oh, Cate, he couldn't!"

"I'm not saying that he has, just that it's a possibility."

"When would he have time to work?" asked Bree. "If he had all these women?"

"Nessa complains that he's forever working," said Cate. "Maybe the days he nips out for some lunchtime nookie he works late in the evenings."

"I thought that the days he worked late were the days he might be seeing women," said Bree.

"Could be either. Or both."

They looked at each other in silence. Eventually Bree got up and scraped the remains of the beef byriani into the bin.

"Do you want some coffee?" she asked Cate.

Cate shook her head. "I'll stick with water."

Bree made herself a mug of coffee and sat down beside Cate again.

"If it was me, I'd want to know," she said.

"Me too," Cate agreed. "Why don't you follow him again tomorrow?"

"I'm at work tomorrow," said Bree. "I can't follow him when I'm meant to be servicing cars. And I'm desperate to get back to work, Cate. I've been going crazy here."

"I understand." Cate nodded. "And, just so's you don't think I'm planning to stay here indefinitely, I'll be looking at some apartments myself tomorrow night."

"Don't feel as though—"

"Bree, this flat is for one person. It's your space. And your bed too," added Cate. "I'm in the way here, I know that."

Bree shrugged.

"Besides," said Cate, "you know that I need to be somewhere pure and minimalist!"

"I was thinking of leaving this place myself," said Bree abruptly.

Cate looked at her in surprise.

"I thought maybe I'd go to the States for a while," Bree told her. "I'm getting restless here. It might be time for me to move on."

"Why do you feel like that?" asked Cate. "What's wrong with settling down?"

"Like Nessa?" demanded Bree.

"I see your point."

"Settling down is all a con," Bree told her. "People who get married and have kids and everything just want everyone else to do it too because they resent their lost freedom."

"Oh, Bree, that's not true."

"You said yourself that you resented your baby."

Cate sighed. "I know."

"Do you still?"

"I—don't know. Well, yes, of course, I resent what's happened now! And I resent the fact that my whole life is going to change. But I'm looking on it as a challenge."

Bree smiled at her. "Typical you, Cate. If you can't change it, you want to overcome it. I haven't got to that point about kids yet though."

"I didn't think I'd got to it either," said Cate.

"Have you heard from Finn at all?" asked Bree.

Cate shook her head. "I blew it with Finn," she said. "Funny thing, Bree, I always thought I'd blow it with Finn one day. He's so ambitious and I was constantly struggling to keep up."

"He's as much of a shit as Adam," said Bree.

"And what about your bloke?" asked Cate. "What about Michael?"

"As much of a shit as both of them," she replied. "Although I wanted it to work with him. I really did."

The following evening Cate signed a six-month lease on a tiny one-bedroom apartment near Christchurch. The rent was horrifying but it included a car parking space which was essential for her. She stood in the living room while the letting agent told her how popular these apartments were because they were so close to the city and how difficult it was to get a short lease these days and how he had about fifty other people lined up to view it. So she wrote a check for the first month's rent and he told her she could move in the following week.

She'd wanted the short lease because, as far as she was concerned, this was a temporary arrangement. By the time the six months had run out she hoped to have found somewhere more suitable for herself and the baby although it was hard, right now, to know what that might be.

After signing the lease she opened the living-room window and stared out at the jumble of buildings opposite her while the letting agent packed away the paperwork. This was an interesting part of the city, she told herself. Everyone said that there was a great sense of community here. And it wasn't far to the office either.

But she ached inside for Finn's apartment with its spectacular view of the bay. And she wished that things had turned out differently.

At the Donnybrook flat, Bree was exhausted from her first day at work since the crash. But it was great to be back. She'd missed the banter and the easy way everyone got on with each other. She'd even missed Christy Burke's ascerbic tongue and his lectures on good workmanship and best practice. At eleven o'clock he'd called them all up to the monkey room and produced a luscious and sticky cake which said "Welcome Back Bree" and he made a little speech about how relieved they were that she hadn't been killed. She was utterly dumbfounded by the gesture, it brought an unexpected lump to her throat which she only managed to hide by making a joke about how she'd been hoping they'd get the job of repairing Michael Morrissey's Punto.

They'd ate the cake and drank cups of tea together and Bree had felt part of a family with them. It was a most unexpected emotion.

"We were quite worried about you," Dave told her when they went back to the workshop.

"I was always going to be fine," said Bree. "I'm a tough cookie, you know."

"I know that." Dave grinned. "I was here the day you walked into the hydraulic lift and nearly cracked your skull open."

"There you go." She giggled. "Not a bother on me."

"And the boyfriend?"

She grimaced. "Ex."

"Oh, Bree, you didn't dump him because he nearly killed you, did you? That's totally unfair!"

"I didn't dump him at all," she said. "He gave me the push, the shit."

"I'm sorry." Dave's voice softened. "I wouldn't have said anything if—"

"It never would've worked," she interrupted him. "He was a useless driver and he didn't know one end of a camshaft from the other."

Dave hugged her. "That's my girl," he said and left her to check out a strange, whining noise in a bright red Cinquecento.

Anyway, thought Bree, as she stretched out on her bed, it had been good to get back to work again and the tiredness she was feeling now was very different to the lethargy that had threatened to engulf her the previous week. It was good, too, to be on her own in the flat for a while. Cate had rung to say that she'd signed the lease on the place in Christchurch but that she was going to have something to eat in town and come home later. Bree knew that this was because Cate was uncomfortable at having landed on her so unexpectedly and, because she was enjoying the solitude, she didn't try to change Cate's mind.

I'd rather have my trauma than Cate or Nessa's, she mused. After all, physical scars heal. Emotional ones are different. She didn't want to think about the emotional scars that Michael Morrissey had left. It was strange, she thought, how quickly she'd decided that he was different. And how easily she'd fallen for him. She didn't normally fall for men so suddenly. She usually had to find out that they were weird before she fell for them and before she realized, almost at the same time, that she'd made another terrible mistake.

So, she thought. What about the States? Of course her secret dreams of going with Michael were out of the question now. But if she was going to go she should go soon. Certainly before Christmas so that she could be in California when the dark and damp days of the winter hit Ireland.

There was no need to hang around for much longer. If she stayed in Ireland—and especially in Donnybrook—there was always the possibility of bumping into Michael again. Or, worse, bumping into his father who might call into the garage one day, particularly since he was friendly with Christy Burke. She really didn't want to see him again either, it would be humiliating. The girl that wasn't good enough for his son. She yawned. She'd check out the States next week. Definitely.

The doorbell rang and startled her. She sat up and glanced at the mantelpiece to see if Cate had accidentally left her keys there. But she hadn't. Bree sighed. She didn't feel like talking to anyone tonight. She just wanted to chill out on her own.

The bell rang again and she swung her legs off the bed. She went downstairs and opened the door.

"Oh." She looked at Declan Morrissey in surprise.

"Hello there," he said.

They looked at each other for a couple of seconds then she shrugged. "Did you want to come in?"

"Thanks," said Declan.

He followed her upstairs to the flat. She made a face as she opened the door. Despite Cate's obsession with tidying things away, it had never been designed for two people and Bree was conscious of the fact that there were clothes everywhere, a couple of unwashed mugs on the table and a pile of new magazines on the floor.

"Here you go." She hastily removed a mountain of underwear from one of the chairs and motioned for Declan to sit down.

"Have you been shopping?" he asked.

"Shopping?"

"There seems to be a lot more stuff here than usual."

"My sister is staying with me for a couple of days," Bree explained. "The torcher."

"Oh." Declan looked uncomfortable. "Where is she now?"

"Signing the lease on another apartment," said Bree.

"You're going to move?"

Bree shook her head. "Not me, just Cate. Her being here was only a temporary arrangement."

The silence between them was unusually awkward.

"I brought you some more muffins." Declan handed her the paper bag he'd been clutching.

"Thanks," said Bree. "But I'm back at work now. I'm able to fend for myself in the food department again."

"Take them anyway," said Declan.

"I never turn away food." Her eyes twinkled at him. "Even when I can fend for myself."

He laughed. "How is work going for you?"

"Today was my first day back. I'm tired but happy."

"You like your job, don't you?"

She nodded.

"I'm sorry about you and Michael."

She was glad he'd finally said something. She'd been wondering if he even knew.

"Oh, well, these things happen."

"He told me that he liked you a lot but that you were too much of an idol to him."

"For heaven's sake!" She looked annoyed. "Idols are pop stars, not bloody mechanics."

"I know what he meant," said Declan. "Michael's always been fascinated by cars and boats and planes. He hasn't a clue, really, but he loves the idea of engines and speed. I think he couldn't believe it when he met you. Mind you, he didn't intend to nearly kill you."

"It's a creepy feeling knowing that someone looks up to you for ridiculous reasons," said Bree sharply. "All I wanted was a boyfriend."

"He's very young," said Declan. "He'll grow up eventually."

"He's not much younger than me," protested Bree. "And I thought he was grown up already."

"He's a bloke." Declan grinned at her. "All our lives women tell us how bloody immature we are. How could you possibly expect him to be grown up?"

Bree smiled too. "You've got a point."

"Better that it happened now," said Declan. "He's not exactly a one-woman man. He had at least twenty girlfriends last year. I spend hours on the phone placating women who are desperate to talk to him."

"Really?"

Declan nodded. "They send him cards and flowers and . . ." He sighed. "One poor girl sent him a giant teddy bear with a ribbon around its neck."

"Thank God I never got that far!"

"I can't see you doing that somehow," said Declan.

"No," admitted Bree. "I'd be more likely to send him a spanner. But he's so charismatic, you know? He asked me to buy a slinky dress for our ill-fated date and I did. For him! I've never done that before."

"I'm sorry I never got to see you in it," said Declan.

Bree looked at him in surprise. "Why would you want to?"

Declan rubbed at his temples. Then he got up and walked to the window where he looked out onto the street below.

"Are you all right?" asked Bree eventually.

"Of course." He turned to face her again. "It's just that—I thought . . ." He shook his head. "I'm really sorry, Bree, I've done something very stupid."

"What?"

"I came here and I shouldn't have."

She looked at him inquiringly.

"When Michael told me that he'd split up with you—he told me after you'd gone—I couldn't believe it."

"I don't know why," said Bree. "From what you've told me it seems a miracle that we actually went out as often as we did!"

"I told him he was a fool to let you go."

"Declan, you know that's terribly nice of you. But—"

"And he knew why. He said it to me. It's because I like you myself."

Bree's eyes, as big and as gray as Nessa's, widened. "Like me?" she said.

"You know what I mean," said Declan.

"I certainly think I know what you mean but I'm not sure that you want to tell me what you mean."

"I'm attracted to you," he said. "God, that sounds so corny and so old fashioned and so . . . so . . ."

"Yes, it does." Bree was shocked. She hadn't expected anything like this. This was Michael's father, for heaven's sake! He was old enough to be *her* father! He didn't look as old as her father, of course, and he was undeniably attractive, but all the same . . .

"When Michael told me that he'd broken up with you I was delighted." Declan interrupted her thought. "Obviously I didn't want to look delighted but he could see it. He laughed at me, said he'd known it from the way I reacted after the accident."

"What!"

"He said that it was quite clear that I cared for you more than he did."

Bree looked at him in horror. "Is that why he broke it off with me?" she demanded. "Because he thought that *you* fancied me? Is that why he was so annoyed?"

"A little," confessed Declan.

"Oh, bloody hell!" Bree looked at him in disgust. "The one bloke I really cared about and he breaks it off because his father fancies me!"

Declan rubbed his forehead. "Not entirely," he said. "Honestly, Bree. He—he said that you were too strong for him and too self-sufficient for him and that you didn't need him. I told him he was talking rubbish, that you were sweet and not half as self-sufficient as you appeared and that all he had to do was to treat you right and then he said that he didn't think he'd ever be able to treat you as anything other than a cool mechanic but that it was patently obvious I was looking for a chance to have a go."

"And did he say all this before or after he dumped me?" demanded Bree furiously.

"After," said Declan. "I didn't influence him, Bree. I really didn't. You don't have to believe me of course but . . ."

Bree ran her fingers through her hair so that it stood up in spikes. "Declan—"

"I know that I'm twenty years older than you," said Declan. "I know that you're probably looking at me as some sad old git who's lost his marbles. But I haven't been able to get you out of my head."

"I can't deal with this right now," said Bree. "I'm sorry."

"That's OK," said Declan. "I just had to let you know." He twined his fingers together. "I appreciate that I'm probably being totally unfair on you. I know that people would say that I should just leave you to do your own thing. But I—I just couldn't help myself. I had to come here."

"You shouldn't have come here," said Bree.

"I know," said Declan. "I told myself to walk away without ringing the bell but I couldn't help it."

Bree bit her lip. "I liked you," she said. "I thought you'd be a great father-in-law."

"I'm sorry," said Declan. "I guess I'm no better than Michael really."

"I—you know, I really *fancied* Michael," said Bree despairingly. "I wanted to be with him. I wanted to go to bed with him." She watched as Declan's face flushed.

"I'd better go." He patted his jacket pocket to locate his car keys. "I guess that better men than me wouldn't have come. I used the muffins as an excuse. That's rather sad, isn't it?"

Bree grinned lopsidedly. "I'll still eat them."

"I didn't mean to make you uncomfortable," said Declan. "I kept telling myself that coming here would be a mistake but then I argued that not telling you would be an even bigger mistake." He sighed. "I'm forty-five years old, Bree. I've been married. And I'm still no better at this sort of thing than I was when I was twenty-five. I guess men never grow up."

"Guess not," she said shortly.

"If you ever . . ." Declan didn't finish the sentence.

"Goodbye, Declan," said Bree.

"Right," said Declan. He opened the door of the flat. "Thanks for not laughing at me."

"Thanks for the muffins," said Bree as he left.

29

♥

Sun in Aquarius, Moon in Aries

Fast and furious, makes things happen.

Nessa took a chicken out of the fridge and put it on the worktop ready to be seasoned. She was doing roast chicken, sweet peas, potatoes and gravy for dinner. It was one of Adam's favorite meals. It didn't matter to her though. She was on a diet, determined to lose a stone in weight. So far she'd lost three pounds. It wasn't difficult. She wasn't hungry.

It had been an uneasy week. Adam had been home early every night since their confrontation about Annika and that bothered her even more than his previous lateness would have done. It felt as though he were changing things simply to prove to her that he was telling the truth but she didn't really want him to change anything. All she wanted was to live their lives the way they always had. And to know that he wasn't having an affair with anyone. They hadn't made love again either, although that wasn't entirely unusual. But it worried her all the same. When she'd asked him, jokingly, the other night why he hadn't touched her, he'd said it was because he was waiting for the scars on his back to heal.

It might be different next week, she thought, as she switched on the oven. By then maybe we'll stop being extra polite to each other and get back to normal. Whatever normal really is.

She sprinkled herbs onto the chicken breast and sighed deeply. How was it that even though she believed him, she couldn't get the picture of him kissing this woman out of her mind? Nor could she quite get Bree's misgivings out of her mind either. But Bree didn't know Adam. Bree was looking at things the wrong way around.

All the same, she thought, as she slid the oiled and seasoned chicken into the oven, maybe she should talk to Bree again. She hadn't spoken to her sister since their conversation on Tuesday morning when she'd told her not to follow Adam anymore. She'd half expected Bree to call at some point during the week but of course Bree had gone back to work and perhaps she'd been both too busy and too tired to call. I'll phone her later, Nessa decided, maybe both her and Cate would like to come over for something to eat next week. She'd have to talk to Cate about her eating habits. Now that she was pregnant she couldn't get away with nibbling on a celery stick and pushing food around her plate. She'd have to take more care of herself. Especially since she didn't have anyone to look after her. That bastard Finn! He could've been more understanding.

Thinking of Finn suddenly reminded Nessa of his TV show. Tonight was his big night, she remembered. Finn Coolidge, the voice of a nation. She wondered whether he'd do any programs on unmarried mothers. If he did, she'd ring up the station and complain.

The TV show started at nine o'clock. Bree hadn't said anything to Cate about it, unsure as to whether or not her sister would want to watch. But Cate said that she did—if half of the country was watching him, she'd watch him too.

"Have you told them in work yet?" asked Bree.

Cate shrugged. "Nobody even noticed that I wasn't wearing my engagement ring until yesterday," she said. "Then Glenda spotted it and so I told her that we'd changed our minds. She was afraid to ask for details and I didn't give her any."

"I bet that put the cat among the pigeons all the same," said Bree.

"Oh, the news is all over the company by now," agreed Cate. "People give me strange but sympathetic looks every time I walk by. Although Ian Hewitt hasn't said anything to me yet."

"And have you told them about the baby?"

Cate squirmed in her seat. "No. I was going to but I just couldn't."

"Well, if the news about your engagement went around like wildfire I can only guess what the news about your pregnancy will do!"

"I've done it all the wrong way around, haven't I?" asked Cate wryly. "I've messed it up so much."

"Listen, Catey, none of us get it right all the time," Bree told her. "Not even you."

The intro music to the show silenced them and Cate watched the screen while fragmented images of Finn filled the screen. Her heart thudded in her chest. It hardly seemed believable that this was the same Finn who'd clattered around the apartment every morning. The Finn who'd once held her in his arms and told her that he loved her. The Finn who'd packed her bags and told her to leave.

Then the show started and Finn strode into the studio to prolonged applause from the audience. He was right about the TV adding pounds, she thought, he looked a little heavier than usual although impeccably dressed in an olive green suit and casual top. Striking a chord, Cate decided, between being serious and fun. The clothes were all new. She'd never seen those shoes before either. Just as well she'd moved out. There wouldn't be room for both of their stuff in the wardrobe.

He was welcoming the audience now, setting out his objectives for the show, telling them that he wanted it to be a blend of issues that would interest people, provoke them, maybe change their minds about things. Not wild and wacky, he told them apologetically. He was far too old for wild and wacky. The audience laughed. With him, Cate realized. He had them now and they wanted him to succeed.

His first guest was a classical singer who'd battled with alcoholism. She was a pretty, chestnut-haired girl with an extraordinary voice who didn't look old enough to have graduated beyond fizzy lemonade. But, according to Finn, she used to knock back a bottle of vodka a day.

"Oh and more," she agreed when he asked her about it. "I didn't see anything wrong with it at the time."

He presented her case sympathetically but without the patronizing tone that so many other hosts adopted when they talked to anyone who'd had problems with addiction. He talked to her as though they were chatting informally together, as though neither the audience nor the viewers at home even existed. And it seemed to everyone watching that Finn and the singer were simply good friends exchanging stories.

Afterward she sang for them and as the camera panned the audience when she finished, their appreciation and support for her was quite clear.

"Christ, she's good," said Bree. "And he's turned her into an icon!"

Cate's smile wobbled but she nodded her agreement.

Another section of the program had Finn out and about interviewing people about their jobs. For this edition he'd visited a community project in Christchurch. Cate's heart lurched to think that he'd been interviewing people in the area where she would soon live. Maybe he'd been there on Monday night when she'd signed the lease. She nibbled at her fingernail and broke it. Once again, Finn's technique was chatty and interested and people responded easily to him.

The show was going to be a success. The camera loved Finn and he loved the camera. He wasn't going to fail. Cate wondered, as she watched, whether there'd been even a small part of her that hoped he might fail but she didn't think so. She wanted him to do well. She wanted his dream to come true.

"Bloody good," said Bree when the final credits rolled. "You might not want to think it, Catey, but he's a natural."

"I know," she said. "I always knew. And I'm glad for him."

"You could blackmail him," said Bree thoughtfully. "You know, say that you'll go to the tabloids with your story of his love child."

"Don't be silly," said Cate. "You know I wouldn't."

"I know," said Bree. "But you have the power, Cate, to totally scupper his career."

Cate looked at her sister thoughtfully. "I suppose I do."

"And nobody would blame you."

"They would," she said. "After all, he only has to say that I was thinking about an abortion and half of Ireland would have me demonized as a murdering bitch."

"Half of Ireland doesn't know you like I do," said Bree. "You're actually a softie at heart."

Cate grinned wryly. "You think so?"

Bree's mobile phone rang and she picked it up.

"It's me," said Nessa.

"I know it's you," said Bree. "Your name comes up every time you ring."

"Right. Sorry."

Bree waited for Nessa to say what she had to say. She didn't feel comfortable talking to her sister while she was hiding the knowledge that Adam was a lying, cheating bastard from her. She'd thought about ringing her every day but hadn't been able to pluck up the courage to tell her. And to admit that she'd followed Adam despite Nessa's very strict instructions not to do so.

"Did you watch Finn's show?" asked Nessa.

"Yes," replied Bree.

"He was good, wasn't he?"

"Very."

"Did Cate watch it?"

"Yes, she did."

"What did she think?"

"That he was good too."

"Does she still love him?" asked Nessa.

"I don't know," said Bree.

"Adam thinks he's a fool," said Nessa.

"Adam does?" Bree's voice was a squeak. "You told Adam about Cate and Finn?"

"Well, sure," Nessa said. "How could I not? He says that Cate was as good a catch for Finn as he was for her. And that the baby could only enhance Finn's career."

"He would," said Bree shortly.

"He's right, though, isn't he? They loved Finn tonight. They'd love him even more if he was married with a kid."

"And still more if they discovered that he'd thrown out his fiancée because she was pregnant?" Bree raised her eyebrow at Cate who was listening to the conversation.

"I didn't think of that," said Nessa. "Actually, it's strange that nothing about their break-up has appeared in the papers. You'd imagine it'd be all over them by now."

"Somebody will start digging the dirt soon," agreed Bree.

"I'll just say no comment if they ask me anything," said Nessa.

"Don't be so bloody silly, Ness, nobody's going to be asking you anything!"

"If they do," repeated Nessa.

"Did you want to talk to Cate?" asked Bree.

"Is she there?"

"Of course she's here."

Bree handed her phone to Cate who told Nessa that, yes, Finn had been great and no, she hadn't been to the doctor yet, and yes, he was a right swine and no, she didn't hate him. And no way was she talking to anyone in the tabloids about their break-up. Fortunately, she told Nessa, most of the articles about Finn had been pre-publicity for the show so she wasn't expecting too many of them afterward.

"You haven't told her about Adam?" Cate looked questioningly at Bree as she finally ended the call from Nessa.

Bree shook her head. "I haven't had the nerve," she said.

"I'll tell her," said Cate firmly. "She needs to get a grip on reality."

"Never her strongest point," Bree agreed.

Cate's mobile rang and shuddered across the table as it vibrated. She caught it just before it fell onto the floor. She looked at the caller ID and took a deep breath before she answered.

"Hi Mum," she said. "Yes, he was good wasn't he? Look, before you say anything else, there's something I have to tell you."

Miriam listened while Cate told her about her pregnancy and told her simply that she'd split up with Finn.

"But why?" Miriam was stunned. "I thought you and Finn loved each other. Surely a child should bring you closer together not drive you apart."

"There were reasons," said Cate abruptly. "He wasn't ready."

"And are you?" Miriam could hear the tension in Cate's voice. "It was never your priority, was it?"

"No," said Cate. "But I've got used to the idea."

"What are you going to do?" Miriam kept her tone as practical as she could. She didn't want Cate to hear how shocked she was that her middle daughter's life had suddenly unraveled at the seams. She didn't want Cate to worry about her reaction, although she knew that Cate had probably worried about it a lot. She knew that no girl, not even a successful, career girl like Cate, ever wants to have to tell her mother that she's pregnant and that the father of the child isn't going to be in the picture.

"I'm staying with Bree for a while," said Cate.

"Bree!" This time Miriam couldn't keep the shock out of her voice.

"For the moment," Cate repeated. "I'm getting a place of my own. And I'll be fine."

"Would you like to come here for a few days?" asked Miriam. "Get away from it all?"

In some ways, thought Cate, it would be lovely to go to Galway and simply chill out. But she wasn't ready for her mother's more probing questions yet. She knew that if she went to Galway she'd end up spilling her guts to Miriam about almost having the abortion and that being part of Finn's reasons for throwing her out and she definitely wasn't ready to tell Miriam that.

"Maybe in a while," said Cate. "Right now I just want to get my head around things."

"He'll provide for the baby of course?"

"I'm sure he'll be more than generous." Cate absolutely couldn't tell Miriam that Finn had doubts that he was the father.

"Cate, you know I love you," said Miriam. "I want to be there and put my arms around you and tell you not to worry. Everything will be OK."

"I know," whispered Cate.

"I wish it hadn't happened," said Miriam. "But these things do. And I like the idea of another grandchild."

"Thanks, Mum." Cate's voice trembled. "I'm sorry I let you down."

"You haven't let me down," said Miriam firmly. "Promise you'll visit us, Catey."

"I promise," said Cate.

"Look after yourself," Miriam said. "Eat decent food."

"I'll try," said Cate.

She ended the call and put the phone back on the table. Bree looked at her inquiringly.

"Mum's being really good about it." Cate sniffed. "I dreaded telling her because I thought she'd take it badly but she's doing her best to sound supportive."

"That's because she is supportive," said Bree firmly. "Just like Nessa and I are supportive. Look at it this way," she added cheerfully. "In sixteen years time when the kid comes home with a pierced belly button or something much worse and you're ready to flip your lid, you can remember today and how understanding Mum was!"

"A pierced belly button will be the least of my problems as a mother." Cate sighed deeply.

"Not at all!" Nessa hugged her. "You'll be a wonderful mum. You really will."

"If only I believed you," said Cate.

Bree had just finished a delivery check on a Brava the following Monday when Christy stopped beside her.

"You haven't forgotten that you're supposed to take a week off before the end of September, have you?"

She looked at him, startled. "I thought it was October."

"No," said Christy. "September."

"But I've only just come back from sick leave," Bree told him. "I can hardly head off again."

"You have a statutory entitlement to your holidays," said Christy. "You've got to take them."

"Oh."

"So let me know as soon as possible, will you? I want to make sure we have adequate cover."

Bree nodded as she ticked off the checklist. She hadn't even thought about holidays this year. The last thing she wanted right now was time off, it had been bad enough being out of work because of her injuries. She could go away for a week, she supposed, although her finances were in a somewhat precarious state. But maybe getting away would be good for her. Or she could use the time to do a bit of investigation regarding the States. She thought she could get a job easily enough but she wasn't sure whether or not she could actually get a green card. She scratched her head with her Biro. Maybe a week's holiday would be a better bet. She could recharge her batteries—despite her enforced layoff she felt unusually tired all the time. And she was finding it difficult to concentrate. That might be because of Declan Morrissey. She leaned hard on the pad as she signed her name and moved to another car.

Sometimes she thought that she'd imagined his visit to her flat and his stumbling declaration of—well, what, exactly? Interest? And sometimes, when she closed her eyes and remembered, it was as though he was right beside her. She'd liked him so much as Michael's father. Maybe if he hadn't been Michael's father then things could have been different. If he hadn't been twenty odd years older than her, things could have been different too. And there was the question of the protective daughters to think about. Bree didn't think that Marta was overly fond of her—and that was with Marta knowing her as Michael's girlfriend. She'd surely freak out completely at the idea of Bree getting involved with Declan. But, she reminded herself, there was no chance of her getting involved with Declan anyway. Even if there hadn't been the issue of Michael, he was a man with too much damned baggage. He was a widower with three kids, one of whom she'd nearly kissed. She couldn't seriously consider a relationship with him. It simply wasn't practical. And he really was too old for her. She wasn't ready to go out with someone nearly twice her age. He was older than Adam Riley, for God's sake!

Leaving Ireland would help. Leaving was how she'd dealt with things in the past and was why the States was so appealing now. Leaving would mean that she wouldn't have to worry about Declan or Michael. Or Cate. Leaving would mean that she wouldn't have to tell Nessa about Adam's second woman. But leaving would also mean that she wouldn't be around to help support Cate through her lone pregnancy. Or at least to provide a buffer between Cate and Nessa who would probably try to interfere in everything to do with Cate and the baby and drive poor Cate around the bend. Nor would she be able to be there for Nessa when she eventually accepted that Adam Riley was a lying, cheating bastard. Because one day Nessa would realize that. It was only a matter of time.

She didn't have to make a decision on the States yet of course. She could take her week's holiday and leave Crosbie's afterward if she wanted to, although she didn't like the idea of grabbing her time off and leaving them in the lurch when they'd been so good to her.

Perhaps Nessa would like to come on holidays with her. The

thought suddenly struck Bree as she finished another inspection. Maybe they could go away together for a week. It'd give Nessa some time to get her head in order about Adam (and maybe give Bree the opportunity to tell her that he was a lying shit anyway) and it'd give her some time to think about what she wanted to do too. She opened the door of yet another Fiat Bravo and sniffed the new-car smell appreciatively as she slid inside. What if Cate came on holiday too? The three of them could go somewhere nice together and chill out for a week. They'd never done that before. Admittedly it wasn't something that she imagined she'd enjoy before but why not? They'd all been through a lot over the past couple of months and some time together in a different environment might be a good idea. They could get a cheap flight to Spain or Portugal and spend a pleasant week lying on the beach doing nothing in particular. It'd be good for all of them. She smiled as she remembered a place in Spain that she might be able to rent for a week.

She liked the idea. She wondered if her sisters would too.

30

♥

Aries—Fire; Cancer—Water; Sagittarius—Fire.

Three weeks later Nessa, Cate and Bree arrived at Alicante airport. Once they'd collected their baggage they went to the car hire desk to pick up the keys of the car that Bree had already reserved. Nessa looked at her watch and worried that Adam wouldn't get Jill to school on time, that something would go wrong with the arrangements for collecting her later (although she knew she could trust Jean Slater who'd volunteered for pick-up duty), that neither Adam nor Jill would eat properly while she was away.

Adam had been shocked when she told him about the holiday.

"You and your sisters!" He couldn't keep the incredulity out of his voice. "Together? For a week?"

"It was Bree's idea," explained Nessa. "She wants to get away and, of course, Cate could do with a break and . . ." her voice faltered, "so could I."

Adam didn't comment on Nessa's desire for a break but he did ask her how she proposed that Jill would be looked after.

"I thought you'd do it," she said. "You're her father."

"Be realistic, Nessa. It's not as though I can take the whole week off myself," said Adam tersely.

"Why not?" asked Nessa. "We didn't go on a family holiday this summer. You must have loads of time off to take."

"We're very busy." Adam's tone was patient.

"If I can get someone to pick her up from school and look after her till you get home then it shouldn't be a problem, should it?" Nessa was surprised at how forceful she was being.

"I suppose not," conceded Adam. "And if something comes up in the evening I can always get Ruth to babysit."

"But nothing will come up in the evening," said Nessa firmly. "Come on, Adam. It's only a week."

He sighed. "Oh, I suppose I'll cope."

"I know you will," said Nessa.

It had been Adam who dropped them all to the airport. Nessa had felt extremely guilty as she waved goodbye to her husband and to Jill who was holding his hand and calling after her to bring back a nice present. It wasn't fair going off and leaving them, she thought, as she followed Cate and Bree to the departure gate. It wasn't as though they had any experience in fending for themselves. And maybe it wasn't a good idea to leave Adam on his own. He hadn't had the opportunity to meet women and stick his tongue down their throats over the past couple of weeks but her being away could change that. Yet she desperately wanted to be away. She wanted some time to be herself, not just Adam's wife and not just Jill's mother. So she put her fears and her guilt to one side and told Bree to count her in.

She'd felt guilty again during the flight although her horoscope in one of the collection of magazines that she'd bought at the airport had urged her to "broaden her horizons" and put "personal concerns ahead of other obligations." She'd smiled wryly as she read it and remembered that she'd made a resolution not to look at them anymore. But she couldn't help herself. She read hers and then Cate's and Bree's. They were all upbeat and positive. Even Adam's was cheerful, she noted. It was telling him that he could find time to mix family responsibilities and fun. Not this week, she thought, as she slid the magazine back into her bag. This week it would be nothing but responsibilities for Adam Riley!

"OK, girls!" Bree turned from the desk with the keys to the car in her hand. "Let's go."

They'd arrived early in the morning and the sky was a pale, hazy white with a smattering of gray clouds moving rapidly eastward. During the flight the captain had advised passengers of a weather front moving across Spain but the sisters were hoping that they'd managed to avoid it and that the week ahead of them would be one of clear blue skies with nothing more taxing to do than lie on the beach and observe the local talent.

"Where's it parked?" asked Cate as they dragged their cases across the road to the car park.

"On the upper level." Bree consulted the diagram in front of her and strode onward.

"Are you sure you're right?" asked Nessa when they'd reached the spot where Bree had told them the car would be and found it empty.

"Of course," she said irritably. "It says here it's—oh, sorry! I was looking at the wrong number. It's over there."

They pulled their suitcases across the car park to where the dark green Mondeo was parked. Bree unlocked it and they heaved their cases into the boot.

"Who's going to drive?" asked Cate.

"Me," said Nessa.

"You?" Bree looked at her in surprise. "I'll drive."

"Why?"

"Because I booked it, didn't I?"

"But that doesn't mean you should drive. You're still injured."

"Oh, for heaven's sake, Nessa, I'm fine now."

"All the same—"

"Also, I'm used to driving here. I lived here, remember?"

"I know, I know. But that was ages ago. I just thought—"

"It really doesn't matter who drives," said Cate impatiently. "I will if you two are going to argue about it."

"I'll drive," said Bree firmly. "You can drive tomorrow, Nessa. And you can drive the day after, Cate."

Cate giggled. "You sound like a schoolteacher."

"I feel like one." But Bree chuckled. "Now get into the car and let's have no more nonsense!"

They were all laughing as she reversed out of the space and drove carefully out of the car park and onto the main road. Nessa consulted the map.

"You have to turn onto the motorway," she told Bree.

"I know what I'm doing," her sister replied.

"Why are we going toward Alicante?" demanded Cate. "I thought you said this place was south of it, Bree?"

"It is," said Bree patiently. "Trust me."

"Oh, look!" cried Nessa. "Cartagena. That's the direction, isn't it? Turn now, Bree. Now!"

"I know. I know." Bree accelerated and passed a tour bus as she left the motorway and turned south.

"It's a nice idea, booking a place of our own and not having to worry about being with a gang on a tour bus," said Cate. "Is the owner a good friend of yours, Bree?"

"Nope." Bree shook her head. "I just knew her from the time I was here before so when I rang and asked about her place she said no problem. I haven't been in it before but it sounds lovely. It's a renovated farmhouse so it has all we need."

"Except being close to the beach," grumbled Nessa. "I still think it would've been better to do a package and get an apartment on the beach."

"You're so lazy!" cried Bree. "And this way you get to see more of the countryside."

"It's only a couple of miles inland," said Cate. "That's nothing, Nessa. We can drive to the beach."

Bree flicked on the window wipers as a few spots of rain began to fall. Cate peered out of the window anxiously. "There's a dirty great black cloud heading for us," she told Bree. "I suppose it's the weather front they were talking about. I hope it passes by."

The rain grew heavier and heavier until it was drumming the roof and lashing against the windscreen. Bree slowed down and switched on her headlights.

"It did this when I was here before," she told her sisters. "Kind of tropical really. It belted down rain for half an hour then the sun came out and everything was fine."

She drove carefully along the increasingly greasy road. She hoped that the rain would ease off soon; it was difficult driving in these conditions and she didn't want to miss her turn. A huge truck rumbled past, sending up a wave of rainwater which almost engulfed the car.

"Moron!" yelled Cate whose hand gesture, rather fortunately, was unseen by the truck driver.

Bree had the wipers on at full speed but they were making very little difference to visibility. She shifted uncomfortably in the driver's seat and glanced at the milometer.

"Watch out for a small church coming up soon," she told Nessa and Cate. "We turn at the church."

A minute later both of them had spotted it and Bree turned off the main road and headed inland.

"Three kilometers up this road," she said. "We pass a funny shaped tree and it's in to the right. It's signposted as Villa Naranja. After the orange trees, I guess," she added as she nodded at the orange and lemon trees which grew either side of the road.

"I bet it's lovely when it's not raining," said Cate. "This isn't much of a road, is it, Bree?"

"It's a minor road," said Bree. "I suppose they don't get a lot of traffic on it."

A crash of thunder startled all of them.

"Bloody hell," said Nessa. "This is obviously the middle of your tropical thunderstorm."

"It sounds like it's closing in," agreed Cate.

"Keep your eyes out for the villa, will you?" pleaded Bree. "It should be soon."

After six kilometers she stopped.

"What's the matter?" asked Nessa.

"We should have seen it before now," Bree said. "Dolores told me that it was exactly three kilometers from the turnoff. I've gone twice that far."

"Maybe it's a Spanish kilometer," suggested Nessa. "Like an Irish mile."

"Dolores wouldn't say exactly if it wasn't exact," said Bree. "We missed it."

"How could we miss it?" demanded Cate. "I was looking for a signpost."

"Maybe it's not exactly a signpost," said Bree. "Maybe it's just a small sign."

"Do you want to turn back?" asked Nessa.

"Well, there's no point in going any further. We'll end up in the damned mountains."

"OK," said Nessa. "Let's go back. We'll watch out for anything that looks like a farmhouse."

"It's a *small* farmhouse," Bree told her. "Not what you might be thinking of."

"You told us about it at home," said Nessa. "Renovated. Three bedrooms, living room, bathroom, kitchen, verandah. Can't be that small."

Bree looked cautiously around her as she turned the car. The road was narrow and twisting and she didn't really want an oncoming vehicle to smash into them. But the road was deserted.

She drove back slowly.

"It's not that ramshackle old place there, is it?" Nessa sounded worried as she pointed to an off-white building slightly back from the road with a collection of fallen roof tiles in the garden. "Your friend wouldn't totally mislead you, Bree, would she?"

"I don't think so," said Bree. "It belongs to her family. It's their holiday home. They'd hardly stay in it if it was falling to bits."

"I still don't see anything remotely resembling a farmhouse," said Cate. "But there have been a couple of really narrow roads that might end up with a building at the end of them. Any likelihood it's one of them?"

"I suppose so." Bree rubbed the back of her neck. She was tired from the flight, tired from driving and anxious that they seemed to be lost.

"There! There!" Nessa exclaimed suddenly.

Bree slammed on the brakes and the car skidded gently to the side of the road.

"God, Bree, be careful!" gasped Cate. "We nearly ended up in the ditch."

"Sorry." Bree flexed her ankle which had hurt when she stamped on the brake. "Where were you pointing at, Ness?"

"Back up a bit," directed Nessa. "See. The sign. Villa Naranja. Two kilometers."

"Two kilometers!" cried Cate. "It's in the arsehole of nowhere!"

"I told you we should have gone with a package holiday," said Nessa. "Come on, Bree. Off you go again."

The road that they were on was probably a dirt track during the summer. But now, with the heavy rain continuing to pound down, the sandy soil was soft and sticky. Bree felt the tires skid a couple of times and hoped that her sisters wouldn't notice. The track twisted and turned and then, quite suddenly, opened out in front of a small, whitewashed building with a terracotta roof and a tiled verandah at the front. A ceramic sign on the wall said La Villa Naranja.

"It looks all right." Cate sounded relieved. "Those flowers are pretty."

The verandah was crammed with pots of brightly colored flowers, jostling for position along the edge.

"Great." Bree sighed with relief and massaged the back of her neck again.

"We should probably just sprint for the house and come back for our bags when the rain eases off," suggested Cate.

"You mean tomorrow?" asked Nessa tartly.

"It'll ease off," said Bree confidently. "It always does."

"Come on," said Cate. "Let's go."

"Bree got out of the car first. "Be careful," she warned them, "the ground is really soggy and slippy."

"Ugh!" cried Nessa as she followed Bree and slid in the mud. "My shoes are going to be ruined! And they're my most comfortable pair."

Cate stepped tentatively onto the muddy ground. "Oh shit!" she yelled. "This is really awful."

"Don't worry about it now," said Bree. "Let's just get in out of the rain."

She slammed the driver's door closed and hurried toward the farmhouse, followed by Nessa.

"Wait! Wait!" Cate stepped around the car and tried to follow them. But she suddenly found herself sinking into the mud. "I'm going to fall!" she cried.

Bree and Nessa, who'd both reached the verandah and were squeezing rain out of their hair, turned to look at her. Bree covered her mouth with her hand and Nessa bit down very hard on her lip. Cate was ankle deep in mud, her new white designer trainers completely covered. Her pale lilac trousers were spattered with the sandy-red clay and her hair was plastered to her head.

"Oh shit." Bree's shoulders shook with laughter.

"She's pregnant," said Nessa urgently although she was close to laughter herself. "She might damage herself or the baby if she falls."

"Bloody hell," said Bree. "Let's rescue her."

"I'm taking my shoes off first." Nessa slipped out of her soft leather shoes which were already coated in mud and walked gingerly toward her sister. "Are you all right?" she asked.

"How could I be all right?" demanded Cate. "I'm up to my neck in this shit! I'm wet. I'm cold. And I can't move!"

"Give me your hand," said Nessa.

Cate reached out and took Nessa's outstretched hand. Bree grabbed her other hand and both of them tugged. Cate's feet came out of the ground with a squelching noise that had both Nessa and Bree shaking with laughter again.

"It's not funny!" cried Cate.

"I know." Bree tried to keep a straight face. "But you looked so—so—un-Cate like."

"You'd look bloody awful too if you'd got stuck like that," said Cate angrily. "Honestly, Bree, why didn't you park a bit closer?"

"Because there's a massive great puddle just ahead," said Bree. "I didn't want you to step out into a puddle."

"But it was OK to step out into a quagmire?" demanded Cate. "My new trainers! They're totally destroyed."

"Come on, Catey, you probably got them for free." Bree grinned at her.

"I did not!" snapped Cate.

"They'll be all right once they dry out," said Nessa comfortingly.

"No they won't," said Cate. "You can't even see the uppers for the mud."

"It'll brush off," promised Bree. "Honestly it will."

"Huh." Cate wasn't convinced but she followed her sisters into the farmhouse. "We can't walk anywhere," she said. "Our feet are filthy."

Nessa took some tissues out of her bag and they dried off as best they could. Then they looked around them at the farmhouse and heaved a collective sigh of relief. All of them had been worried that it wouldn't live up to expectations but the small living room was comfortably furnished in traditional Spanish style. The yellow sofa was covered in bright and cheerful multicolored cushions while a selection of modern prints hung on the walls.

"Not bad," said Bree.

The three bedrooms were decorated in the same traditional style, each with a different vivid and lively color scheme. The enormous bathroom was tiled from floor to ceiling and the kitchen had everything they could possibly want.

"Thank God for that," said Nessa as she flopped onto the sofa. "I had a horrible feeling that we'd been sold a pup!"

"Dolores isn't like that," Bree told her. "I said it would be OK and it is."

"I know, I know," said Nessa. "It's lovely, Bree. Honest. And it'll be great once the rain stops."

"If the rain stops," said Cate grimly.

"It'll stop." Bree glared at her sister.

"Of course it will," said Nessa brightly.

"Maybe the thing to do would be to turn on the immersion heater so that we could all have showers," suggested Cate. "That'll freshen us up. And I'll make some coffee."

"Good idea," said Nessa. "Where's the immersion, Bree?"

Bree shrugged. "In a cupboard somewhere, I guess."

They found it in the small utility room and Nessa flicked the switch.

"Shouldn't that little light come on?" she asked Bree.

"I'd have thought so." Bree peered over her shoulder.

"Hey, Bree, you need to turn on the power at the mains," called Cate. "I've plugged in the kettle but nothing's happening."

Bree padded into the hallway and looked for the mains. Her feet were cold now from the soaking they'd received while they were pulling Cate out of the mud and from the chill of the tiles beneath her. She located the panel and looked at it.

"The power *is* on," she informed Cate. "Are you sure there's nothing happening?"

Cate hit the light switch. "*Nada*," she said.

Bree looked at the fuses. They were all fine. The board was on. There should be power. She turned it off, then on again. "Try it now," she called.

"Still nothing," said Cate.

"Flippin' heck," said Nessa. "Don't tell me we've been cut off."

"Maybe the rain has caused some problems with the electricity," said Bree. "That happens sometimes."

They stood in the kitchen and looked out of the window. By now the rain was so heavy that they could barely see the car.

"You might be right," said Cate and then shrieked as a sudden flash of lightning lit up the sky.

"Oh my God!" cried Nessa. "That was almost on top of us."

"That means it'll be gone soon," said Bree comfortingly. "Then the electricity will probably come back and everything will dry out."

"You're sounding very optimistic," said Cate.

"Don't worry, Cate. Things'll be fine," said Bree.

"I'd really love a cup of coffee," said Cate plaintively. "I haven't had coffee since that muck on the flight."

"That's a good thing," said Nessa. "Now that you're pregnant you should cut down on the coffee anyway."

"Don't tell me we're going to have a whole week of you telling me what I should and shouldn't be doing because I'm pregnant," said Cate.

"No." Nessa shook her head. "I'm just saying that you'd be better off having herbal tea or something."

"I drink herbal tea quite a lot," Cate informed her. "But right now I'd love a cup of coffee. Strong black coffee."

"There's loads of cafés near the beach," said Bree. "You could get coffee at any of them."

"If you think I'm stepping outside in this . . ."

Another flash of lightning ripped through the sky and lit up the room. It was followed by a crash of thunder so loud that the cups on the sideboard rattled.

"Jesus," breathed Nessa. "That's definitely on top of us."

"Why don't we go to bed for a while," suggested Bree. "We could get a bit of rest and wait for the rain to ease off. Then, if the electricity hasn't come back, we could go out and get something to eat and drink."

"I'm starving now," said Cate. "And I couldn't possibly sleep with that racket going on."

"Have a Mars bar if you're hungry." Nessa took one from her bag.

"Ugh, Nessa, they're crowded with calories," said Cate.

"Make up your bloody mind then," cried Nessa. "If you're hungry, eat it. If not, I will."

"Is this our only food?" asked Bree anxiously.

"I have two more Mars bars," said Nessa. "And three apples."

"I didn't bring any food," said Bree. "I thought we'd go shopping when we got here."

"I have a jar of coffee," said Cate. "That's all."

They looked at each other.

"I'll eat the Mars bar," said Cate. "And I'll do what Bree says and go to bed. It can't rain all day and I am tired. Maybe I'll drop off in spite of the thunder."

"Right," said Bree. "See you later."

They disappeared into the bedrooms and lay down. The rain continued to beat against the roof. And the lightning continued to split the sky above them.

More than an hour later Nessa got up and went into the living room. She looked out of the window at the ever increasing puddle outside the villa. At this point it resembled a small lake. But the rain had eased off a little. Instead of pelting down in an unremitting sheet as it had earlier, it was now falling in a gentle hiss. A soft day, as they'd call it at home, she thought and hoped that it was the beginning of the end of the storm.

She tried the lights but the electricity was obviously still off. She hoped it would come back before the end of the day, she desperately needed a shower and she was simply gasping for a hot drink of some description. She looked at her shoes which she'd left just inside the door. They were soaked through although the earth clinging to them had started to dry out.

Only I could come on holiday, she thought, and be sitting in an ice-cold renovated farmhouse with nothing to eat or drink. Adam would laugh at her when she told him. Whenever they'd gone away as a family he was the one who took charge of everything. And he was good at it. She'd never had a holiday disaster with Adam. No matter where they went, he was prepared. When they went to hot climates he brought anti-mosquito sprays and face spritzers and all sorts of things that she wouldn't even bother with. Last year they'd gone to Scotland. It had rained in Scotland, despite the fact that they'd traveled in August, but he'd been prepared for that too and had brought wet weather clothes and boots so that they coped with the conditions better than anyone else there. Having decided against a holiday during the summer this year they'd gone to France for a week at Easter instead. The weather had been mild without the blazing heat that Nessa liked but which Adam really didn't. They'd had a good time in France, she remembered, as she curled up on the sofa and pulled the cushions around her. She'd enjoyed every minute of it.

Had Adam? she wondered. Had he simply pretended to enjoy it but instead been pining for triple x Annika, the client who was touchy feely and to whom he had to be touchy feely back? She leaned her head against a cushion. Somehow it was easier to believe in him having an affair with Annika when she was here, a couple of thousand miles away. When she was home, seeing him every day, she didn't think him capable of having an affair. From a distance, it was easier to imagine.

She shook her head. It wasn't something she wanted to imagine. After her periods of equal rage and despair she'd tried to put the whole episode out of her head. She'd made her choice. She'd chosen to believe Adam and work at her marriage and this holiday was meant to be a kind of closure for her so that she could come home and start again with him. So that she could banish those thoughts forever.

"Hi." Cate walked into the living room. "How're you?"

"I couldn't sleep," said Nessa. "The thunder was so loud and the rain so heavy that I kept thinking the roof was going to cave in. When it eased off I couldn't get used to the quiet either!"

Cate laughed. "I did sleep for a while and then I woke up with a jump and didn't know where I was."

Nessa smiled sympathetically.

"It's cold, isn't it?" Cate sat down on the sofa beside her and covered her feet with spare cushions.

"I have socks in my suitcase," said Nessa. "I was thinking of going out to get them but it's still a mudbath out there."

"Has it stopped yet?" Cate peered at the window.

Nessa shook her head. "Eased off, that's all."

"What are we going to do about food? I'm absolutely ravenous."

"I've no idea," said Nessa. "I assume there's a supermarket of some sort nearby."

"There's nothing nearby," said Cate acidly. "We're in the middle of an orange field."

Nessa giggled. "Orange grove."

"That sounds warm and romantic," said Cate. "I'm neither."

"Hello." Bree walked into the room, her hair tousled, her eyes still sleepy. "I heard you guys yakking. What's up?"

"The rain has eased off, there's a lake outside the front door and we're dying of starvation," Nessa informed her. "And we're still without electricity."

"Oh, God." Bree groaned. "What d'you want to do?"

"Don't ask me," said Nessa. "You're the one who lived here."

"Not here," said Bree. "I was about fifty miles up the coast."

"You mean you haven't a clue what's nearby?"

"Vaguely," said Bree. "I met Dolores on the beach last time I was here."

"Why don't you ring her?" asked Cate suddenly. "Maybe she'll be able to tell us about the shops and the electricity."

"God, but you're smart!" Nessa looked at her in mock admiration.

Bree grinned and took out her phone. Then she groaned.

"No signal," she informed them.

"This is officially the holiday from hell," said Nessa.

"We need to find a shop," said Cate. "If I don't get some food soon I'll collapse."

"That doesn't sound a bit like you, Catey," said Bree. "I'd have thought you'd be happy to be on an enforced diet."

Cate sighed. "Normally, yes. But in the last two weeks I've been eating for seven. I suppose it's probably a good thing to cut back but whenever I do I just get incredibly cranky and light-headed."

"I think there's a hypermarket farther down the main road," Bree said. "We could go there."

"But we need something to eat now," said Nessa. "There's no point in buying food if we can't actually cook anything."

"I'm sure there'll be a cafeteria attached to it," said Bree. "There nearly always is here."

"Lead me to it!" cried Cate.

"I'll drive this time," said Nessa. "You must be knackered, Bree."

"I don't mind," said Bree.

"Oh, let her drive," said Cate. "She's been aching to have a go ever since we got here."

"Actually no," said Nessa. "I hate driving in the rain. But I'm happy to inform you that it has now stopped and there's even a scrap of blue appearing in the top corner of the window."

"Yes!" Bree rushed over and looked out. "Although scrap is the operative word, Ness. Still, better than nothing. I told you it'd stop."

"After half an hour you said."

"I lied." Bree shrugged.

They piled into the car again and Nessa began to turn it cautiously.

"Back up a bit," suggested Bree.

Nessa shot her a dark look and slid the car into reverse. At least it had completely stopped raining now, she thought, with relief. She edged backward and then put the car into first again. The tires whirred. The car didn't move.

"Oh shit!" She revved the car some more.

"Don't! Don't!" cried Bree. "You'll dig it in deeper!"

They got out of the car. The tires had sunk into the soft, wet soil and the three sisters knew that there was no way it was coming out again in a hurry.

"Oh—my—God," said Cate slowly. "You've practically buried it, Nessa."

"It wasn't my fault," said Nessa quickly. "Bree told me to reverse."

"Reverse, I said. Not speed backward into the puddle!"

"I didn't speed backward into the puddle," said Nessa. "You know I didn't."

"I never should've let you drive."

"You would've done better, would you?"

"I couldn't have done any worse."

"Nessa, Bree, shut up." Cate snapped. "There's no point arguing about it. We need to get the damned car out of the damned mud before it goes down any farther."

Bree knelt down and looked at the tires. "It's really stuck," she said. "We'll never get it out."

"We need to put something under the tires," said Cate. "Give them a bit of grip."

"Like what?" Nessa looked around helplessly.

Cate shrugged. "Cardboard would be best."

"Right." Nessa nodded. "I'll just shred the cardboard box I brought with me, shall I? What fucking cardboard?" Her voice rose to a shriek. "We don't have any cardboard, you idiot."

"Don't call me an idiot," cried Cate. "I'm not the one who sank the car."

They stared at each other in tense silence. Then Nessa's mouth began to twitch. Suddenly she began to laugh. Cate and Bree watched her, smiles playing on their lips. Her laughter was infectious. They began to laugh too.

"It's surreal." Nessa wiped her eyes. "Here we are in the middle of the countryside with no electricity, no food and a car practically buried in the mud. And we thought it would be warm and sunny and we'd be getting away from it all." She laughed again. "I didn't realize that we were somehow bringing it all with us."

Cate grinned at her. "The Driscoll family personal black cloud?"

"But the cloud has gone," said Bree. "It's actually quite sunny now."

"So what are you suggesting?" asked Nessa. "That we wait for the ground to dry out and then drive?"

"There's no way this'll be dry until tomorrow," said Bree. "Look at it, for heaven's sake!"

"I can't last until tomorrow without something to eat," said Cate. "I'll faint with hunger before then."

"I never thought I'd hear those words," murmured Nessa. She stood back from the car, her hands on her hips. She could feel the warmth of the sun on her back now and she wriggled with pleasure.

"There might be some planks of wood or waste behind the house," said Bree. "Something we could use, at least."

"Let's look." Cate led them around the back where they searched for anything that might work. The topsoil was beginning to dry out, and steam rose in a gentle spiral from a cloth which hung over a makeshift washing line.

Eventually Nessa gave a cry of delight and held aloft a brown cardboard box which she'd found in the tiny outhouse. "Believe it or not!" she yelled. "The very thing."

"Peachy," said Bree.

They brought the box to the front of the villa and tore wide pieces from it which they placed under the wheels of the car.

"OK," said Bree. "Best thing would be for Cate to get behind the wheel and you and I can give it a push, Nessa. What d'you think?"

Nessa and Cate both nodded. Cate got into the driver's seat, making expressions of disgust as yet more mud fell from her shoes and ended up in the footwell.

"Are you ready?" called Bree.

"Absolutely." Cate started the car and revved it loudly. Bree and Nessa positioned themselves behind it and began to push.

"Now," shouted Bree as she felt the car move a little.

Cate let out the clutch and the Mondeo leaped forward. She kept it going and stopped a yard farther down the driveway where the ground was solid. Then she turned back to look for Bree and Nessa.

"It's just not our day," she said as she got out of the car. Her two sisters were on all fours in the mud, having been unable to stay upright when the car had moved.

"You OK?" she asked.

They looked up at her. Their faces were splattered with mud and their clothes were utterly ruined.

"Couldn't be better," said Nessa and dissolved into fits of laughter once again.

31

♥

Virgo August 24th–September 22nd
Shy, self-critical, easily hurt.

Every so often, and completely out of the blue, Nessa would start to laugh again. And each time she did, both Cate and Bree joined in, unable to help themselves. They laughed at the supermarket checkout (where the assistant looked curiously at their mud-streaked clothes and ratty hair), they laughed back at the villa (where the electricity had been restored and where Nessa discovered that the cooker was, actually, gas and so they could've heated up water in a saucepan for a hot drink any time if any of them had had their wits about them) and they laughed again that night as they sat in a small seafront restaurant and drank coffee having stuffed themselves with food earlier.

Three days into their holiday, as she stretched out her beach towel on the pale golden sand, Nessa chuckled again. Cate looked at her inquiringly.

"It's just the memory of your face when you saw us," said Nessa. "Total shock."

"You looked indescribable," said Cate.

"As you did when you were stuck in the mud," Bree reminded her.

"It's one of those things that's going to haunt me," Cate said. "This holiday has already acquired the status of a legend."

"It's been fun though," said Nessa. "I haven't laughed so much in ages."

"Neither have I," admitted Cate. She rubbed cream onto her legs and replaced the cap on the tube. She was turning a pale golden brown and she felt healthy for the first time in weeks. She lay back on her towel and looked at the swell of her stomach through her stretchy Lycra swimsuit. She looked pregnant in the swimsuit, she thought, although both Nessa and Bree had told her that she just looked like a normal person. But she knew she didn't.

Before she'd got pregnant, when she went to the gym, she used to stride confidently to the swimming pool, certain that her body was almost perfect under the unforgiving tightness of her swimsuit. She used to look at other people as they wandered around the pool area and quietly congratulate herself on the fact that she had no bulges where bulges shouldn't be. But she wouldn't be able to do that anymore. Soon her stomach would be completely out of control and she didn't know whether—despite her plans for a very strict diet and workout regimen—she'd ever get it back again. She wondered whether or not people would look at her in the future and see the tone and perfection she'd always strived so hard to achieve and maintain with her body. Or whether they'd simply see a sagging stomach and drooping boobs.

Unlike the girl who was lying a few yards away from them, her stomach taut as a drum and her long legs elegantly stretched out in front of her. Hers was the figure of a person who would never dream of spoiling it by anything as traumatic as childbirth. It was the figure of someone who took looking good very seriously indeed. But it was also the figure of someone who hadn't had any qualms about the surgeon's knife. A pair of rounded breasts proudly displayed like two inverted suction cups were a tribute to his skills. By rights (children or no children) breasts of that magnitude should have flopped either side of her chest but these were upright and firm with flopping never a likelihood. They probably looked great underneath a T-shirt, Cate mused, but they looked bloody silly perched on her body like that now. They detracted from the overall perfection rather than enhancing it. Maybe real perfection, natural perfection, wasn't an option after all. For anyone.

She shifted her gaze from the enhanced body and looked farther along the beach to where a family had just arrived and were staking out a plot. There were four of them—a good-looking father (a *very* good-looking father, she amended as he peeled off his T-shirt), a pretty, slightly plump mother, a small child and a baby. The parents were arguing happily about where to put the parasol while the mother was making sure that the older of the two children wore a sun hat. The baby—a girl, Cate guessed, because of her pink cotton top—was sitting on a towel waving a bright yellow plastic spade in the air. Cate wondered how old she was. One? Two? She had absolutely no idea where kids were concerned. None whatsoever. She was going to be a hopeless mother, she knew she was. She wouldn't be able to pick up her child as confidently as the Spanish mother. She wouldn't be able to hold it casually in one arm while helping someone to do something else at the same time. She'd panic if it squirmed like the little girl was squirming. The father said something to the mother and she laughed. Then he kissed her.

Cate bit her lip. That was the way it was supposed to be. Happy families. Like the books told you and the movies told you and the TV documentaries told you it could be. Like it had been for her and for Bree and for Nessa. Miriam had done all right. How was it that her daughters hadn't?

Cate had fulfilled her promise to Miriam and had gone to Galway the previous weekend. Miriam had hugged her tightly and told her that she loved her and had then proceeded to try to build her up, as she put it, by placing mountains of food in front of her at every available opportunity. Cate, in her new permanently hungry state, had eaten it all. Louis had told her gruffly that he wished things hadn't turned out like this but that he knew that Cate was a wonderful daughter and would be a wonderful mother. Cate was grateful to her parents for not judging her and grateful that Miriam didn't question her too much about her split with Finn. She knew that her mother desperately wanted to know everything and she knew that she'd tell her one day. But not just yet.

She lay down and closed her eyes, not wanting to watch the Spanish family anymore. She wanted to forget them, forget everything and sleep. She used to enjoy sleeping under the sun but it was years since she'd gone on a holiday like this. Finn didn't like sun holidays, he was too impatient to sit on a beach for more than half an hour and too curious about what was going on around him to allow himself to fall asleep. So, although he liked warm places, he liked plenty of activity to keep him occupied too. Cate had been happy to go along with his interests because she also enjoyed being busy. Their holiday to the Caribbean had been a scuba holiday where they'd spent every day diving in the warm, blue tropical waters; in Mexico they'd explored the ruined Aztec cities; in Egypt they'd spent their time visiting the temples and the pyramids. She couldn't remember ever taking her towel to the beach and falling asleep with Finn. But it hadn't mattered. They'd been together.

She wondered what he was doing now. Preparing for his evening radio show, she supposed. Looking through the news of the day and deciding what stories to concentrate on. Talking to his researchers and his producer. Doing what he'd always wanted to do.

She slid her hand gently across her stomach. He was doing those things while she was doing something she'd never thought she'd do. She swallowed hard. A tear rolled from her closed eye and plopped gently onto the towel.

I should have told him, she thought. I should have shared it with him and asked him what he wanted me to do. It wasn't really my decision to make. Not without talking to him first. I might have had the best of reasons but I still should've told him.

Even so, his reaction had been horrible. He could have listened to her, given her the time to explain. He should have understood. It wasn't all her fault. He could have cut her a little slack. He was a fucking talk show host, for God's sake! He was supposed to have empathy and understanding. He was supposed to be sensitive and caring. Why could he be sensitive and caring about other people but not about her? Why was it easier to show understanding toward perfect strangers than people you were supposed to love?

Bree was watching the family too. She'd whistled under her breath when the father had taken off his white T-shirt and revealed a six-pack body and she'd given him eight out of ten. She'd had to deduct two marks because of his married state. Otherwise, she thought, as she watched him kiss his wife, he was the kind of bloke she'd always gone for—dark, rugged, very attractive. Like Michael, in some ways, only more masculine than Michael. Michael had been almost too chiseled in his good looks; this guy's face was less symmetrical, more hardened. They were a good family unit. He was, Bree reckoned, in his late twenties, early thirties. She was about the same. They had shared experiences together. They'd grown up with the same music, the same books, the same movies. He'd never turn to her when one of those TV retrospectives were showing and say, "Gosh, I remember when that song was in the charts," or mutter that he recalled platform shoes the first time around or make her feel like a kid because he'd left school before she was even born. But that's what it would be like with Declan Morrissey.

She wished she could stop thinking about him. She couldn't understand why she wasn't able to forget about him and put everything to do with him out of her mind completely. But the night in her flat seemed to be etched in her brain and she wasn't able to erase it. She hadn't told anyone else about it, nor had she tried to contact him again. She truly wished that he hadn't made her suddenly start to think of him as a man with whom she might actually be able to have a relationship. Part of the reason they got on so well was because she hadn't thought of him like that at all. She hadn't been extra nice to him or extra flirty or extra anything that she normally thought she should be with men whom she regarded as potential boyfriend material. She'd just been ordinary and herself and she'd seen him in the same way as she saw the guys she worked with at the garage. He wasn't a man that she could contemplate getting involved with. Really he wasn't. It might be fun for a time but it'd never work out. And she didn't want to get involved with Declan if it wasn't going to work.

Although why not? she asked herself, as she picked at the sky-blue varnish that Cate had insisted on putting on her toenails the previous night. She'd gone out with loads of blokes in the past when she'd known it wasn't going to work, just to have some fun. And, mostly, it had been fun. So why shouldn't she have a bit of fun with Declan if that was what she wanted? She knew the answer to that already. Because he was too bloody old and because he was her ex-boyfriend's father. She tore at another piece of varnish. She was losing it completely if she could even contemplate the idea of a relationship with her ex-boyfriend's father. Not to mention the added complication of his two protective daughters.

She glanced around her. Cate was stretched out on her towel, eyes closed. Nessa had wandered down to the water's edge and was letting the sea wash over her toes. Oh hell, thought Bree, as she lay down on her towel too. I'm just not going to think about it anymore. I haven't got the mental strength to think about it anymore.

Nessa walked back up the beach to where Cate and Bree were now both lying with closed eyes. She sat on her red and white striped towel and buried her toes in the warm sand. The mother of the two Spanish children had bought them ice creams. The older girl (about three, Nessa guessed) was licking hers delicately, turning the cone around and around so that she caught all of the colored candy sprinkles on her tongue. The baby (eighteen months, she thought) was mashing hers into her mouth so that her whole face was covered in ice cream and sprinkles. Nessa bit her lip. She was an adorable little baby, with her tuft of almost black hair, her dark, dark eyes and her little gold bangle (also covered in melting ice cream) on her arm. Nessa ached. Would it have been different, she wondered, if there'd been another child? Would Adam stick his tongue down other women's throats if he had a brood of kids at home?

She sighed and leaned her head against her knees. She wished she knew what she wanted from her life now. What she wanted from Adam. What was going to happen to them in the future. She wished that there really was a way to predict it. She hated not knowing. She really did.

They left the beach at half past six and drove back to the villa. The huge puddle outside the house had been dried by the sun of the last few days and now resembled a parched and cracked desert gulch. Instead of spraying mud in all directions when the car stopped, it now sent up a cloud of dust. The sisters took their gear out of the boot and went inside.

They'd decided on a night in tonight and had bought meat and vegetables and Spanish tortillas at the supermarket as well as some bottles of wine. Nessa sat on the verandah and sipped a glass of Faustino while Bree had a shower and Cate pottered around the villa. Nessa took her mobile out of her bag, got up and stood in the middle of the garden to get a decent signal. She'd called home every evening about this time and Adam had always answered, asking her if she was enjoying herself, telling her that everything was going well and reminding her that he'd pick her up at the airport on Sunday. Then she'd talk to Jill who'd chatter about her day at school, recount the row she'd had with Dorothy, ask her if she was having fun with Bree and Cate and then tell her that she missed her.

Nessa missed Jill too. But it was nice to have some time to herself.

"Hi, this is the Riley family. We can't take your call right now but leave your name and we'll ring you back."

Jill had recorded the message (had insisted on recording the message) at the beginning of the summer. Nessa frowned and wondered why they were out.

"It's me," she said to the recording. "Checking in as usual. Are you there?" But nobody picked up the phone to answer her. She could feel her heart beat faster as she tried to think of where they might be. They knew she phoned every evening. They wouldn't have gone out, would they? She held on for a little longer, reminding herself that Adam could have been late getting home, that a few moments delay in the office could have had him stuck in traffic and fuming.

She ended the call and dialed Adam's mobile number instead. But all she got was his recorded message too.

"Hi," she said lightly. "Where are you? I rang home and got the machine. Give me a shout."

Nothing awful would have happened, she told herself as she put the phone on the table in front of her. They might have forgotten to switch off the machine at home and be watching TV and not heard it ring. She didn't always have to assume the worst.

But Adam hadn't rung even by the time Cate and Bree had finished their showers and had joined her on the verandah.

"Don't be silly," said Cate when Nessa told her that nobody was home. "Adam might have brought her to the movies or something to keep her amused. He's never had to look after her for a whole week on his own before. He's probably running out of conversation!"

Nessa hadn't thought of it like that before. She conceded that Cate could have a point and then went in to have her shower.

Bree poured herself a glass of wine from the open bottle and looked at Cate inquiringly.

"Yes please," said Cate. "While the earth mother is out of eye-shot! I can't enjoy a glass of wine when she's looking at me disapprovingly and I'm gasping for something other than fizzy water."

Bree grinned and filled Cate's glass.

"I know that I shouldn't." Cate sipped the wine appreciatively and put the glass back on the table. "But an occasional glass can't do any harm."

"If it keeps you calm it's probably doing you some good," said Bree. "Though it's been very handy having you on the dry in the evenings, Catey. Means we haven't had to worry about a designated driver."

Cate snorted. "Totally unfair! Here I am on my first girls on tour holiday in years and I end up being behind the wheel the whole time."

"It's been fun so far, hasn't it?" asked Bree. "I was afraid we'd fight all the time but we haven't."

"When we got over the first day without killing each other it was downhill all the way," said Cate.

Bree laughed. The two of them sat in companionable silence, their feet propped up on the whitewashed balustrade in front of them, as they watched the sun slide behind the purple-tipped mountains.

"Has he rung back yet?" Nessa walked out onto the verandah wrapped in a bath towel.

"No," said Bree. "But there's no need to get into a state about it, Nessa."

"It's getting late," Nessa said. "It's eight o'clock."

"Only seven at home," Cate reminded her. "Why do you fuss so much, Nessa?"

"I worry about them."

"I bet you anything he'll ring soon," said Bree.

"Oh, OK." Nessa went back inside to get dressed. Bree and Cate exchanged looks.

"Where d'you think he is?" asked Cate.

"Clearly he's gone out and left Jill with someone," replied Bree.

"Gone out with one of his floozies?"

Bree giggled then looked serious again. "Probably."

"Oh, Bree—we have to tell her," said Cate. "We can't keep it a secret."

"I know that we should," said Bree. "But she's having such a good time. And she says that she believes him about the Annika woman."

"That's because she doesn't know about the other one."

"I know," said Bree again. "It's just that telling her will be such a nightmare."

"And if we don't?"

Bree sighed. "I wish I knew what the best thing to do was. I really do."

Nessa reappeared a moment later, dressed in jeans and a T-shirt. "I'm going to start cooking dinner," she said. "Call me if he phones."

Cate and Bree nodded.

"He'd better phone soon or she'll have a heart attack," said Cate.

"He'd better phone soon or *I'll* have a heart attack," muttered Bree.

It was twenty minutes later before Nessa's mobile rang. She was out to the verandah and down the garden before either Cate or Bree could call her.

"Hello," she said.

"Hi, Mum!" Jill's voice was clear and pleased. "Are you having a good time?"

"Of course I am," said Nessa. "How are you? Where were you earlier when I rang?"

"I was in Nicolette's," said Jill. "And then when I got home me and Ruth couldn't find your phone number."

"Where's Dad?" asked Nessa.

"He had to go out," said Jill. "He told me to tell you. A 'zecutive meeting."

"Oh," said Nessa.

"But Ruth will be here until he comes home," Jill informed her.

"Can I talk to Ruth?" asked Nessa.

"Sure."

"Hello, Mrs. Riley," said Ruth. "Are you having a great holiday?"

"Yes thanks, Ruth," said Nessa. "Where's Adam tonight?"

"I don't know," said Ruth. "He rang me last night and asked if I could babysit Jill. He said he'd be working late."

"I see," said Nessa.

"So I picked her up from Mrs. Slater's."

"Great," said Nessa. "Thanks very much."

"It's OK," Ruth told her. "I'm saving up for a new pair of leather trousers. Mr. Riley's paying me double tonight. 'Cos I had to collect Jill and let myself in and everything."

"Right," said Nessa. "Have you picked out the trousers yet?"

Ruth laughed. "I saw them in the Omni Centre in Santry. They're really great."

"Can I have another word with Jill?"

She heard the phone being passed over again.

"Do what Ruth tells you," she said. "Go to bed when you're told. You have school in the morning."

"I know," said Jill. "Dad's so narky about getting everything ready in the mornings! But he puts out the breakfast stuff the night before."

"Does he?"

"Yes," said Jill. "He says that one good thing about you being away is that he has to have breakfast every morning to put in the time until I go to school. He says it's a healthy option for him."

"Fair enough," said Nessa.

"I love you," said Jill.

"I love you too."

"See you soon. Take care."

"G'night," said Jill and hung up.

Nessa walked slowly back to the verandah and put the phone on the table.

"Everything OK?" asked Cate.

"Yes. Fine."

"Sure?" asked Bree.

"Adam had to work late," said Nessa. "He arranged for the babysitter to pick up Jill from her friend's house and bring her home."

"At least he arranged something," said Cate.

"Jill says he had to go to an executive meeting."

"I hate meetings," said Cate feelingly. "Especially after-hours ones."

Nessa looked at both of her sisters. "Do you think he's at a meeting?" she asked. "Or do you think he's—you know?"

"Maybe we're not the best people to answer that," said Bree uncomfortably.

"Why?" asked Nessa. "You followed him for me, Bree. And I

bet you've talked about it between yourselves. So what d'you think?"

"Would you like a glass of wine?" Cate lifted the bottle.

"D'you think I need one?"

"Actually, maybe." Cate filled Nessa's glass and glanced at Bree.

"I know you told me not to," said Bree cautiously. "But I followed Adam again."

32

♥

Mercury in Sagittarius

Sometimes unrealistic but grasps situations quickly.

As soon as Bree had finished telling her about Adam and the woman in the apartment, Nessa got up from the table and, without a word, walked into her room, closing the door firmly behind her. Bree stood up to follow but Cate stopped her.

"Leave her," she said.

"But the state of mind she's in," protested Bree. "She needs someone with her."

"What d'you think she's going to do?" asked Cate.

Bree shrugged. "Nothing, I suppose. Only—oh, Cate, I wish I hadn't followed him. I wish I'd done what she said."

"It wouldn't have made things any better," said Cate. "He'd still be cheating on her."

"But she wouldn't know!" cried Bree. "She'd be able to rationalize it all like she's done before."

"She'd have found out eventually," Cate assured her. "It's not your fault, Bree."

"I know," said Bree miserably. "But I feel as though it is."

It was five minutes later before Cate remembered that Nessa had been cooking dinner and she rushed into the kitchen to turn off the grill. The peppered steaks were charred. *Why do I always end up in the kitchen when there's a food disaster happening?* she asked herself. She slid the blackened meat onto a plate and looked at it doubt-fully. It only reinforces everyone's opinion of me as a hopeless home-maker.

"I'd eat it." Bree poked her head around the doorway. "But it's probably not very tasty."

"Even your cast-iron stomach might have trouble with boot-leather steaks," agreed Cate. "I think I'll pop some of the microwave popcorn instead."

"Good idea," said Bree. "And we could have the tortilla chips. We bought salsa dips to go with them, didn't we?"

Cate nodded and indicated the steaks. "What'll I do with these?"

"Put them in the fridge," said Bree. "God knows, Nessa might be able to turn them into something edible although I can't imagine what." She opened the fridge door and took out a bottle of beer. "Want one?"

"I wish." Cate sighed. "But whatever about having a glass of wine in my current condition, mixing wine and beer would be a night-mare."

"Poor old Catey." Bree put her arm around her sister and hugged her. "Never mind, when the infant is finally born you can go on a binge."

"By that stage a bottle of beer probably *will* be a binge," said Cate gloomily. She put the popcorn into the microwave and switched it on. After a couple of seconds the kernels began to pop gently and she took a couple of brightly colored ceramic bowls out of the cup-board. She emptied the large bag of tortilla chips into one of them and brought it outside. By the time she returned the popcorn was ready and Bree was emptying it into the other bowl.

"Maybe I should go in and see her now," suggested Bree.

Cate shook her head. "Give her a little more time."

"Would it've been better if I'd told her sooner?" asked Bree. "Some people would have done, Cate. Some sisters wouldn't have been able to keep things like that secret."

"We're not the kind of family who blurts everything out to each other." Cate shrugged. "We're different. We do our own thing."

"I know." Bree sighed. "These last few months we've got caught up in each other's lives and it's kind of strange."

"Is that why you're thinking of heading off to the States again?" Cate took a bottle of mineral water out of the fridge and followed Bree back out to the verandah.

"Not really." Bree sat down, propped her feet on Nessa's empty chair and idly scratched at a mosquito bite on her calf. "I'm not good at staying in one place."

"Why?" asked Cate.

Bree shrugged.

"Not that it matters," Cate added. "Lots of people like traveling. I just wonder do any of them settle down eventually."

"It's the settling bit that I don't like," said Bree. "Settling sounds so—so middle-aged!"

"Sometimes it's nice," said Cate. "To feel that you have a place of your own that'll always be a place of your own."

Bree nodded slowly. "I can see that. I've even felt it occasionally. But the feeling usually passes." She picked up a handful of popcorn. "Did you feel like that about your place in Clontarf?"

"Finn's place in Clontarf," Cate amended. "Yes. I did. It was a comforting place to be."

"And now you have to start all over again," said Bree.

"If we'd split up and there wasn't a baby . . ." Cate sighed. "I could've done things differently then. Maybe I could've gone to the States too. But this changes everything, Bree. I have to settle now."

"Why did you change your mind about the baby?" asked Bree. "You were so determined that you didn't want it."

Cate broke a tortilla chip in half. "I don't know," she said. "I *was* determined. Of course I didn't want the baby, Bree, and I was sure I was doing the right thing." She gazed out over the garden. "But when I was sitting in the airport waiting to go I suddenly felt that this was my chance to have a child. It had happened! And it seemed like the wrong choice to get rid of it even though I knew it would be a disaster. Not as much of a disaster as it turned out, of course," she added savagely as she dunked one of the halves into the salsa dip.

"No," said Bree sympathetically. "But it must have been so difficult for you."

"You know, what's difficult is that I believe in the woman's right to choose," said Cate. "And then when it came down to it I went all soppy and couldn't go through with it."

"Oh, Cate!" Bree made a face at her. "You believe in a woman's right to choose and you made a choice. A different choice to the one you thought you were going to make, but still your choice."

Cate smiled wryly. "I guess so. It's just—well, I feel for all those girls who made the other choice. Because it's hard, you know. Your whole body is a mess and your mind is a mess and everybody judges you."

"I think you did the right thing," said Bree. "No matter what you did I'd still think you did the right thing."

"Thanks," said Cate. "But I've ended up without Finn."

"Oh, sod Finn!" cried Bree. "If he doesn't understand then he's not worth it."

"I wish I could think like that." Cate sighed. "I haven't managed to get around to it yet."

"You will," said Bree robustly. "You and Nessa both. You'll realize that no man is worth agonizing over."

"End of the day, maybe you did learn from Nessa and me," Cate told her. "At least you've kept your heart intact even though you and Michael broke up too."

Bree said nothing. She drained her San Miguel and went into the kitchen for another. She stood in the narrow hallway and listened for sounds from Nessa's bedroom but she couldn't hear anything.

"Did mentioning Michael annoy you?" asked Cate when Bree returned. "Only you got out of that chair like a scalded cat when I said his name."

Bree shook her head. "Of course it didn't annoy me. I liked Michael a lot but if it wasn't going to work, well, better sooner than later."

"Maybe you'll fuck it up too, one day," said Cate. "You'll meet someone different and he'll tug at your heartstrings and no matter how sensible you want to be about him you'll end up doing something stupid like moving in with him instead of marrying him."

"Don't be silly," said Bree mildly. "Marrying Adam didn't do Nessa much good."

"Marrying anyone doesn't do any woman much good." Cate poured herself more fizzy water.

"We're getting very cynical," said Bree. "Maybe there are men worth marrying out there."

"I was going to marry Finn." A tear slid down Cate's cheek. "I loved Finn. I still love Finn."

"Oh, Cate." Bree bit her lip.

She watched as her sister covered her eyes with her hands and allowed the tears to trickle through her fingers. She wanted to say something but there was nothing she could say. She wanted to do something but there was nothing she could do. Why, she asked, why are men so bloody difficult? Why do they make us cry even when they don't know they're doing it? Why does it matter so much?

She thought of Michael, half terrified that she'd cry too now. But she didn't. He was a nice guy, a gorgeous guy, but somehow she thought she'd rather been in love with the idea of being in love with Michael rather than the man himself. She'd wanted to love someone as attractive as him. She always wanted to love the attractive ones. She didn't miss him as much as she'd expected. How could she when most of her relationship with him had been a dream relationship—dreaming about going out with him, kissing him, making love to him . . . but never actually getting around to it.

She missed Declan more.

She shivered as she thought of Declan again. She didn't miss him. She missed the muffins, that was all.

The sound of a door slamming shut brought her back to the present. Then she heard a car engine start. She frowned, then got up and walked along the verandah just as the green car shot by.

"Jesus!" she jumped back in fright.

"What's going on?" cried Cate.

"It's Nessa." Bree peered through the dusk after the car. "For a second I thought someone might be robbing the car but I'm sure Nessa's driving."

"What the hell is she doing?" demanded Cate. "Where's she off to?"

"I don't know, do I?" snapped Bree. "Maybe it wasn't her. Maybe I'm imagining it. Let me check." She hurried into the villa and knocked on the door to Nessa's room. There was no answer so she pushed it open and looked inside. Everything appeared the same to her but it was hard to be sure because Nessa was so neat and tidy that there was never anything lying around her room anyway. She opened the wardrobe door and frowned. Nessa's sundresses and jeans were still on their hangers, her blue and white fleece was on the shelf and her shoes were arranged neatly on the wardrobe floor.

"Well?" Cate stood in the open doorway.

"Her stuff is still here," said Bree. "So she can't have gone far." She opened the drawer to the beside locker. A blue toilet bag was on the shelf. Then she looked under the bed. Nessa's green suitcase was still underneath it.

"If she's left everything then she'll be back," said Cate. "She probably just wanted to be on her own for a while, Bree."

"She should have said something," said Bree furiously. "You don't just walk out on people."

"She's upset."

"I know she's bloody upset." Bree's tone was scathing. "All the more reason for her not to act like an idiot."

"Maybe she's gone to the beach," said Cate. "You know, for an evening stroll or something. While she gets her head together."

"She still should have said something," muttered Bree. "Besides, she's had a few drinks. She shouldn't be driving."

"She's had a bottle of San Miguel, that's all," Cate told her. "She'll be fine."

"If she's gone off in a temper . . ." Bree looked anxiously at Cate. "Well, you know how it is, Cate. She could be careless, do something stupid."

"Like what?" asked Cate.

"Crash the car," said Bree. "She might forget what side of the road she should be driving on or go the wrong way around a roundabout."

"Bree, she's a sensible woman." Cate steered her sister out of Nessa's room and back onto the verandah. "She just needs some time to herself. That's fine. She's had a shock."

"I know," said Bree. "I know I'm overreacting. It's just that I was the one who followed Adam again when she told me not to. I feel responsible."

Cate shook her head. "It's not your fault, Bree. She had to find out sooner or later. And she's the one who's responsible for her own actions, not you."

"Well it isn't very responsible to go haring off without saying anything," said Bree stubbornly.

Cate sat down at the patio table. "There's nothing we can do until she comes home," she told Bree. "You can argue with her later. Come on, have a beer yourself."

"Oh, OK." Bree sighed as she took a bottle from Cate. "But I don't like it when people act out of character. And it's not like Nessa to run off by herself."

"We've just told her that her husband is shagging at least two women," said Cate. "I think she has a good enough excuse."

"I suppose you're right." Bree picked at the label on the bottle. "But I don't like it all the same."

33

♥

Pluto in Cancer
Usually emotionally strong and intuitive.

The N332 was busy. Nessa blinked as the headlights of the oncoming cars dazzled her and she rubbed at her cheeks to wipe away the falling tears.

How could he do this to me? she whispered. Why did he do this to me? Her foot pressed down on the accelerator as she thought of Adam. Betraying me with two women. Or more. Just because Bree had only found out about two didn't mean that there weren't others. Hundreds of them! Thousands of them! Maybe he was like rock stars who slept with a different woman every night. Perhaps that was how Adam got his kicks. She didn't know. How would she? She didn't know him at all.

She flicked the indicator and overtook a Seat Toledo which was hogging the road in front. The driver banged the horn furiously. Nessa didn't care. She overtook another car and then another. The road snaked along the coast, through the salt marshes and past the little seaside towns until it widened again and she saw signs for the airport.

She could go home, she thought. She could get a flight now and go home. She could be back in Malahide in a few hours and she could put her key in the door and confront him. She swallowed. Confront him with another woman, perhaps. For all she knew he could have his other women in the house now, while she was away. Maybe he'd sneak them in while Jill was asleep in bed and sneak them out again before she knew about them. Or maybe he hadn't come home at all tonight. Maybe he was spending the night with xxx Annika or with the new Monkstown lady. Or with any of them.

Fucking whores, she thought, as she sped through the tunnel which led to the motorway. Didn't they know that he was a happily married man with a lovely, precious daughter? Didn't they care? Those women were helping to ruin their lives and it meant nothing to them. But why should it? She wiped away the tears again. Why should they know anything or care about anything? What did he tell them, after all?

She missed the turn for the airport. It didn't matter. She wasn't going to go home unexpectedly. She probably wouldn't have got a flight anyway. She didn't want to go home. She didn't want to see him. Not now. Not ever. She didn't want to look at him and know that he clearly found her undesirable. Or lacking.

What had she done wrong? What had made him look for other women? What had changed it all? He'd loved her when he married her. She knew that. He'd broken up with his other girlfriend because of her and he'd told her that it was the easiest thing he'd ever done. Because he loved her and wanted to be with her forever.

Lying bastard! She accelerated again and overtook a tour bus, two motorcyclists and a Mercedes. Lying fucking cheating bastard! She rubbed at her cheeks, this time with the sleeve of her top. They were sore from the salt of her tears. So, she thought, when people talked about feeling hurt they actually meant it. She was hurting inside like she'd never hurt before and now she was hurting outside too. And he'd done it, he'd hurt her like this. The man that she loved, the man she'd do anything for, the man she'd built her life around.

She's staying with him for the money and the house. Portia's words, coming back to her once again, made her hands jerk on the steering wheel. The Focus veered to the left and the driver of the Mercedes— which had been pursuing her ever since she'd overtaken him and who was trying to get past her again—flashed his headlights angrily at her. "Oh fuck off," she yelled through the open window. You're probably a fucking man. So fuck right off, lying, cheating, bastard!

She finally allowed the Mercedes to pass her out and then flashed her headlights equally angrily at him. Did Portia know her better than she knew herself? "No," she said out loud. She didn't. She'd wondered about it before and she'd already decided that Portia was wrong. She wasn't with Adam for the house. She wasn't with Adam for the money. She was with Adam because she loved him. And because she thought he loved her.

But if he didn't . . . She gulped. If he didn't love her, if instead he loved his triple x lady and his other lady, well then why was she with him? For the money and the house after all? For the so-called lifestyle? Was that really it? She swallowed the lump in her throat. He didn't love those other women. He couldn't possibly love them. He loved her and he loved Jill and that was the way it was. Anything else—anything else was a mistake. It had to be a mistake. She couldn't have spent her whole life living a lie.

She glanced at a road sign and saw that she was now on the motorway which ultimately led to Valencia. It was miles away. I could drive to there, she thought. I could drive all night and stay there and never come home. I could be like Shirley Valentine and get a job in a seafront café and find romance with a local man who'd care for me and say nice things about me. And find someone else too, she thought, as she remembered the movie. A seafront café wasn't the answer. There was no damn answer.

A string of lights across the motorway made her slam on the brakes suddenly, her heart pounding. She'd come to a tollbooth. She took the ticket that told her where she'd joined the motorway and glanced at it. The various exits were marked on it but she didn't care about the exits. She didn't care about anything.

She pressed down on the accelerator again and the car leaped forward. Unlike in Ireland, this motorway wasn't jammed with almost bumper-to-bumper traffic. It was wide and empty and a joy to drive on. She found herself slipping into a trance as the miles slid past. She wasn't thinking anymore. She wasn't feeling anymore. She was simply existing, inside the car, outside herself.

The motorway cut through the mountains, twisting through deep gorges and climbing around the contours of the surrounding countryside. Nessa kept her foot near the floor, unconcerned at her speed, not needing to worry about oncoming traffic. She wondered what she'd do when she got to Valencia. Find an all-night bar, maybe. Drink herself stupid. It would be nice to drink herself stupid. She occasionally drank enough to have a bit of a hangover but she never drank enough to collapse in a heap on the floor. Not now anyway, because she was a wife and a mother and she couldn't afford to collapse in a heap on the floor. When she was younger she used to. Not regularly but sometimes. And she'd do silly things like try to dance on tables or sing rebel songs or smoke big fat cigars just for the heck of it. She used to do lots of silly things. But she didn't anymore. Maybe that was why Adam didn't love her. Maybe he wanted someone silly. Maybe xxx Annika was silly. Maybe the Monkstown lady was silly. Maybe they made him laugh. But he laughed at home, didn't he? He didn't need her to be silly to laugh at home.

A shrill sound echoed around the car and caused Nessa to stamp on the brakes again in fright. The Mondeo skidded along the road and she had to fight to keep it on line. God, she thought, as she pulled into the hazard lane, I could've been killed. And it frightened her to think that, right now, she really wouldn't have cared. The shrill sound had come from her mobile phone which was in the bag she'd thrown onto the backseat when she rushed from the villa. She switched on her hazard lights and pulled the bag to her. Maybe it was Adam. Maybe he'd come home and spoken to Jill and maybe he'd decided to ring her and tell her that, yes, he'd been working late and he was utterly exhausted. And she could ask him about his other women and find out about them and if he told her that it was all true and that they really did exist and that he loved them—if he told her that then she could take the car and point it toward the ravine because really and truly she didn't think she had the strength to carry on anymore.

The phone stopped ringing. She didn't know who'd called because the Spanish phone network couldn't pick up the phone number. So maybe it had been Adam. But maybe it hadn't. Probably it hadn't. Adam didn't give a toss about her. He was too busy with his other women.

She opened the car door. She knew that opening the car door on a motorway was a silly thing to do but she didn't care. It was time for her to be silly, wasn't it? She stood beside the Mondeo and wondered why it had all gone wrong for her. Why she felt so uncertain when once she'd been so sure of everything. Why things hadn't worked out like she'd always believed they would. She looked at the phone, willing it to ring again, willing it to be Adam. But it remained obstinately silent.

"Oh, fuck you," she cried out loud. "I hate you! I really and truly hate you!" She raised her arm and then threw the phone as hard as she could across the motorway and toward the ravine. In the few moments while it was soaring through the air it began to ring again. Then it crunched onto the black asphalt and was silent.

Nessa stared at it for a moment but, as she was about to run along the motorway and pick it up, a huge, white articulated truck rumbled around the bend and drove over it, crushing it completely.

Nessa got back into the Mondeo and sat in the driver's seat. Her hands were shaking. The tears were falling again. She leaned her head against the steering wheel and wished that she'd been the one that had been run over.

Bree looked at Cate and shook her head.

"She's not answering," she said. "Oh, Catey, I just don't like to think of her all on her own, in a state, and driving in a country that she doesn't know."

"That's funny coming from you," said Cate.

"What?"

"You're the one who always goes on the run whenever you get into a state. Now you're getting your knickers in a knot because Nessa's doing exactly the same thing."

"I do not go on the run!" cried Bree.

"Yes you do," Cate said. "France, Spain, England—"

"I'm not in a state every time I move," snapped Bree. "I do it for the excitement."

"Or because you've broken up with someone and you can't bear to be around them," said Cate. "You can't bear the thought of seeing them again, knowing that it's over between you."

"Oh, shut up." Bree looked at her in disgust. "You don't know what you're talking about. I break up with blokes when I find out that they're weirdos. You're the one who went to England because you couldn't face up to telling your boyfriend that you were up the spout."

"Thank you for that caringly bitchy comment," said Cate coldly.

"Well, honestly, Cate, you said you loved him. If you loved him you could've told him."

"I explained," said Cate tightly. "I told you why I couldn't say anything."

"Bullshit," said Bree. "You couldn't face being pregnant and you couldn't face him and then, in the end, you couldn't even face having an abortion!"

"How can you say all that? I thought you understood—you said you understood . . ." She put her hand to her temple. "You don't see it at all, do you? You've never loved anyone because you never go out with the kind of blokes you could fall in love with. In case they wanted something more than you could give them. That's why you pick weirdos. And you don't understand what it's like to love someone and lose them."

"Of course I do," said Bree flatly. "I lost Michael, didn't I?"

They sat side by side on the verandah without saying anything. Cate pulled at pieces of popcorn and threw them into the garden without eating them. Bree chewed at the fingernail on her little finger until it was short and jagged.

"I'm sorry," she said to Cate eventually.

"Forget it."

"We're always apologizing to each other, aren't we?" said Bree. "Do the three of us deliberately say things to hurt each other?"

"I've never deliberately said anything to hurt you or Nessa," said Cate.

"You called Michael a toy boy."

"For God's sake." Cate glanced at her. "You described him as a toy boy to me one night. You were the one who said he was young but sexy."

"He's only four years younger than me," said Bree. "Not so much a toy boy."

"Clearly his mental age was younger still," Cate said. "Showing off like he did. Nearly killing you. Scaring the life out of us."

Bree sighed deeply. "How did you know you were in love with Finn?" she asked. "How did you decide that he was the one?"

"I just did." Cate got up, leaned against the balustrade and stared unseeingly at the tubs of potted plants. "We met and I went back to his apartment and I was with him and everything seemed just perfect." She looked up at Bree and smiled faintly. "I wasn't totally stupid. I hardly knew him, after all. I'd been 'in love' before. Then I moved in with him and—oh, I don't know, Bree—it was different to anyone else. We didn't need to go out all the time. We didn't need to hop into bed all the time. We enjoyed each other's company even when we weren't being lovers."

"I've never been friends with any of my boyfriends," said Bree. "I'm with them for the excitement not the friendship."

"But you have lots of male friends," Cate told her. "You work in a bloody garage, don't you? The ideal stomping ground."

"That's different," said Bree dismissively. "I don't see any of my colleagues as potential boyfriends. Even Dave, who's nice and who asked me out . . ." She shook her head. "It should be different, shouldn't it? Loving someone and liking them."

"I think you have to like someone before you can love them," said Cate. "I liked Finn when I first met him. Then I fancied him. Then I loved him."

"I like Michael's father," said Bree abruptly.

"What?" Cate looked at her questioningly.

"Michael's father," said Bree. "His name's Declan. I like him."

"Yes, well, I didn't mean you have to go out with every man you like," said Cate dismissively.

"He likes me too."

"And?"

"He called around to the flat a few times while I was laid up," said Bree. "He brought cookies and muffins."

"I know." Cate nodded her head. "You told me before. You said he was checking up to see if you were all right because he was terrified you'd sue Michael. You said the muffins were a ploy to soften you up."

"He called around when you were signing the lease on your apartment," Bree said. "I didn't tell you about that."

"And?"

"And he told me that—that he liked me."

"Liked you?" Cate's finely arched eyebrows almost disappeared into her hairline.

"He wanted to go out with me."

"Oh, come on, Bree!" Cate stared at her. "He's a married man with three kids! And he must be in his fifties!"

"He's forty-five," said Bree. "He's a widower. His wife died of cancer."

Cate swallowed. "Well, of course, I'm sorry for him—it must have been terrible," she said. "But you can't possibly be thinking of going out with him. That's sick."

"Why?"

"Because—because—oh, look, it just is! The man's clearly a perv. Who in their right mind would even consider going out with his son's girlfriend? Ugh, Bree, don't tell me he was fancying you while you were seeing Michael. That is absolutely gross!"

"That's what I thought at first," said Bree. "I kind of said as much to him. And I told him to leave." She chewed at the remains of her fingernail again. "But I can't stop thinking about him."

"Probably in horror," said Cate.

Bree shook her head. "No, Catey, I really like him. I find him attractive, though I never really considered it when I was going out with Michael. But Declan's a good-looking man. And when I'm talking to him I feel like I'm talking to an old friend."

"I wish I hadn't said anything about having to be friends," muttered Cate. "I've clearly set you off on the wrong track altogether."

"I don't know," said Bree. "I've been wondering these last couple of days whether or not I should do anything about it."

"Oh, Bree." Cate sighed. "I don't know if you should or not but whatever problems you've had with toy boys and strange blokes that you end up leaving the country over, don't you think you're going to have even worse ones with a forty-five-year-old widower who happens to be the father of a bloke you went out with?" She shrugged. "I mean, wouldn't you be better off waiting for Mr. Right?"

"Mr. Right?" Bree's tone was sardonic.

"Mr. Nearer-Your-Own-Age, Same-Interests—you know what I mean!" cried Cate.

"I know what you mean," said Bree. "I'm just not so sure that that's the Mr. Right I'm looking for."

"I'd be surprised if Declan was," said Cate.

"So would I," Bree agreed. "But nobody else has been either."

Nessa was still shaking as she took the next exit off the motorway, too terrified to stay on it anymore. She fumbled in her bag for the toll and handed it to the girl in the booth. She was conscious that her eyes were red and puffy and that her cheeks were probably red and puffy too. But the girl simply took the money and waved her through. Nessa didn't take any notice of where she was driving. She followed the road aimlessly until suddenly she was at the outskirts of a town. There were signs for the town center and the sea. She followed the signs for the sea.

Five minutes later she parked in front of a picture-postcard bay. Despite the darkness she could make out the silhouette of high cliffs around a crescent shaped beach, which was lined by colored lights and a row of bars and restaurants. Very few of the restaurants were still open and, although there were some people in the bars, it all seemed very quiet. She got out of the car and shivered as a cool breeze wafted in from the sea. She pulled her light cotton top more tightly around her.

She walked to the water's edge and took off her shoes. Although the water was cold it was refreshing. She sat down on the damp sand and allowed it to lap at her feet. Occasional bursts of laughter floated from the bars. It seemed strange to hear laughter. It was hard to believe that other people were happy. I don't want to live like this, she thought miserably. I don't want to live a lie with him. She leaned her head on her knees as she realized that she was already living a lie. That she'd been living a lie without knowing it. And that, to keep her family together, she'd have to keep doing it.

"It's one o'clock in the morning," said Bree. "Where the hell can she be?"

"One of the bars in town?" suggested Cate. "She might have gone for a walk, then decided to have something to eat."

"Cate, she's distraught!" cried Bree. "She'd hardly go for something to eat if she was distraught."

"Maybe it's worn off by now." Cate dipped a tortilla chip in chilli salsa. "We were too upset to eat earlier but hunger kicked in and we had those cheese and crackers a while ago. Perhaps it's the same with her."

"Nessa's devastated, not just upset," said Bree. "It's not going to 'wear off' after a drive in the car, for God's sake! I knew we shouldn't have left her on her own."

Cate sighed. "OK, I'm a bit worried about her myself, Bree. But there's nothing we can do at the moment."

"We can look for her," said Bree.

"How?" Carey asked. "She took the damned car."

Bree took out her phone and pressed Nessa's number. "I wish she'd turn the bloody thing on," she said as she got Nessa's message minder which told Bree that Nessa was on holiday and to leave a message.

"Maybe she doesn't want to talk to anyone," said Cate.

"Fine," said Bree. "But she still could've told us that she was going off to commune with nature. Surely she'd know that we'd worry."

"Nothing's happened to her," said Cate. "She's not stupid, Bree."

"Sometimes I wonder," retorted Bree. "I'd like to think that I'd know before anyone else if my husband was bonking a selection box of other women."

"She may not be stupid but she blocks out things she doesn't want to know about," said Cate. "Remember when we were kids and she wouldn't ever watch a film with a sad ending?"

Bree sighed. "She's having to face up to things with a bang now I suppose."

"Which is why she needs a bit of time and space," said Cate. "If she came back now we'd be asking her if she was all right and fussing over her and everything. Maybe she doesn't want that yet."

"If she came back now I'd hit her over the head." Bree rubbed her forehead. "Oh, Cate, if something's happened to her . . ."

"Nothing has happened to her," said Cate firmly. She put her arms around her sister and pulled her close. "Nothing has happened to her, she's perfectly all right and she'll be back eventually. Then you can hit her over the head if you want."

"Thanks." Bree's voice was muffled. "I'll tell her you said that."

"Fine by me," said Cate. "I'll hit her over the head too."

The sea was ink-black and warmer than she'd expected once she got used to it. She floated out of her depth and looked up at the sky, crammed with thousands upon thousands of stars. You never really got to see stars in the sky at home anymore, she thought regretfully. The lights of the city meant that all but the brightest were difficult to see. She remembered, as a child, Louis pointing out different constellations to her and telling her that she was made out of the same stuff that was in the stars and the planets. She'd felt close to them then, almost part of them, and later, when she was older and when she started reading horoscopes, she told herself that she was made of star stuff and that was why they might influence her life. But in the end they simply told her that things were hard to figure out and they'd never even hinted that Adam was cheating on her. She closed her eyes and blocked out the stars.

It was peaceful here. She felt almost content, bobbing up and down with the waves, listening to the sound of the waves breaking on the shore. She could drift here forever. Nobody would miss her if she didn't come back. Who would care? Not Adam, clearly. He had plenty of other fish to fry. He'd probably be relieved that he didn't have to spend his days concocting lies to tell her. Jill would miss her, of course. Terribly at first. But only temporarily. Jill was her own person already. She would grow up and make her own decisions and live her own life. In the end, everyone had to make their own decisions. Everyone was on their own. As she was now. She could lie here and allow the water to eventually take her out to sea and, in the end, what difference would it make to anyone? And she wouldn't have to face the humiliation of going home and confronting Adam about his girlfriends. She desperately didn't want to have to confront Adam about his girlfriends. She wanted to sleep. That was all. Just sleep.

"I can't stand this much longer." Bree paced anxiously around the verandah and peered out at the road. "She wouldn't have stayed out this late without contacting us. Her phone is switched off. There's something wrong."

Cate chewed at her bottom lip. She thought that there must be something wrong too but she didn't want to make Bree any more worried than she already was. She'd never realized that Bree got so anxious about things before.

"Even if something has happened to her, there's very little we can do," she said eventually.

"Christ, Cate, how can you say that?" Bree stared at her. "Maybe she got as far as the end of the road and plowed into the palm tree. Maybe she's lying concussed a mere ten-minute walk away! She could be bleeding to death—and if only we'd looked for her sooner we'd have saved her life."

"You're getting hysterical," said Cate. "But maybe we should at least walk along the road. She might have just pulled over to the side and fallen asleep."

"At least we'll be doing something." Bree slung her bag over her shoulder.

"I hope we're doing the right something," said Cate.

The narrow country road was dark and deserted.

"It doesn't feel like there's been a crash," Cate told Bree.

"How would you know?"

Cate shrugged. "I suppose I thought we'd smell petrol or something."

"Get real," said Bree.

Cate turned toward her and stumbled over a small rock in the middle of the road. She yelped.

"Are you OK?" asked Bree. "Have you twisted anything?"

"I'm fine," said Cate. "Sorry about that."

"Watch where you're going," advised Bree. "I really don't want to have to carry you back to the villa with a broken ankle."

They walked in silence, the only sounds coming from the crickets.

"It's actually quite lovely, isn't it?" said Cate eventually. "The middle of nowhere, perfect peace, the sky full of stars."

"Just as well," said Bree. "At least the moon and stars are giving us a bit of light. Otherwise this'd be a complete nightmare."

"It's not so bad. Oh!" Suddenly Cate doubled over and clutched her stomach.

"Cate!" Bree looked at her with concern. "Are you all right?"

"Pain," said Cate through gritted teeth. She sank to her knees at the side of the road. "Hang on a minute."

Bree's heart was racing. She could see that Cate was in agony and she didn't want to question her but she was terribly afraid that she'd injured herself seriously when she tripped over the rock. Only she couldn't have, thought Bree. She'd stumbled, that was all.

"Cate?" she said tentatively.

"I'll be all right," gasped Cate. "I—oh, shit." She doubled over again.

"Cate, it's not the baby is it?" Bree's voice was horrified. "Please tell me you're not going into labor at the side of the road."

"The baby isn't due till March," said Cate. "If it's the baby, then I'm losing it."

"Oh, Cate, no."

"I hope not." Cate bit her lower lip and then suddenly relaxed as the pain subsided. "It's OK," she said. "It's easing off."

"If you lose the baby then I really will kill Nessa." Tears were streaming down Bree's face.

"Bree, please, it's all right. I'm sorry," said Cate. "I'm not losing the baby. Honestly I'm not." She looked at her sister ruefully. "I think it was just heartburn. I shouldn't have dipped those tortilla chips in the chilli sauce."

Bree wiped her eyes. "Are you sure?"

Cate nodded. "I've been getting it lately. But this was the worst ever."

"You scared the living daylights out of me," said Bree shakily. "Between you and Nessa I'll be lucky not to have a heart attack before the night's out."

"I'm sorry," said Cate again. "It's just such an awful pain."

"Let's get back." Bree looked up and down the road. "There's no sign of Nessa. She must have done what you said, gone into town. Maybe she's had a few drinks. Doesn't want to drive back."

"Absolutely," said Cate. "And she could've booked herself into the hotel near the beach."

"Do you really think so?" asked Bree.

"Remember when you were sixteen?" Cate did her best to smile. "And you had that speed limit sign tattooed on your arm? You and Mum had a monumental row over it."

"Yes," said Bree.

"You stalked out of the house and you didn't come home until two in the morning," said Cate. "We were all terrified then. But you were OK. Nessa'll be OK too. But if she hasn't come back by the morning we'll contact the police."

"All right," said Bree.

"She'll be back," said Cate with a confidence she didn't quite feel. "Once she gets over the shock, she'll be back."

She was remembering. Good times with Adam, times when he'd loved her. Times when she'd felt secure in his arms. Times when she hadn't doubted him or doubted her reasons for being with him. It was nice to remember those times, to know that they'd existed. But, she thought now, maybe they'd only existed in her imagination. Maybe even then he'd been seeing other women. Seeing other women! It was such a coy way of saying what he was really doing. Fucking other women. That's what it was, after all. She hated to think about it. She didn't want to think about it, wasn't going to think about it anymore.

"Hola!" The yell was urgent. Part of her knew that it was directed at her but she didn't want to acknowledge it. She kept her eyes resolutely closed.

"Hola! Señora!" She could hear splashing now and she sighed. Somebody obviously thought that she was in trouble out here on the water but she wasn't. She was fine. She was tired. She wished they'd leave her alone.

The splashing was closer now and she could hear a stream of words in Spanish. She opened her eyes and a wave of water splashed over her. She spluttered and righted herself. A man was swimming toward her, closing in on her. She shook the water from her face and her eyes widened. She'd drifted farther out to sea than she'd thought. Much farther. The lights of the bars and restaurants lit up the shore, but they were indistinguishable from each other. She took a deep breath and swallowed some water. She began to cough.

The man drew level with her and caught hold of her. He spoke to her again in Spanish and, when she said nothing, spoke in English. "Are you all right? I will bring you back. Please relax."

She felt his arm around her and she struggled to free herself. She slid under the water and he grabbed her, then slapped her on the face. In the back of her mind she knew that this was what people were supposed to do when they were saving hysterical people from drowning but she wasn't hysterical and she wasn't drowning. She struggled again and he slapped her again. Then he began to tow her back to shore.

There was a small group of people standing on the beach beside her bundle of clothes. As soon as she stumbled out of the water, supported by the Spanish man, they all began to speak. A woman handed her a pink woolen shawl which Nessa, conscious of her nakedness and now also shivering with the cold, wrapped around herself.

"I'm all right," she said in English. "I wasn't drowning. I was perfectly safe."

"You were too far out." The man who rescued her looked at her accusingly. "It is not safe to swim on your own this late at night."

"I would have been fine." Nessa's teeth chattered as she realized that maybe she wouldn't have been fine.

"Why did you do this?" he asked. "This was a silly thing to do."

"Because I felt like it," said Nessa. "I felt like being silly."

"Where are you staying?" A dark-haired woman of her own age broke into the conversation.

"Staying?" Nessa looked at her in confusion.

"In the town? Are you staying in an apartment? Or a hotel?"

"I'm not staying here," said Nessa. "I drove from somewhere else. Past Alicante."

The woman looked at the man and spoke to him in rapid Spanish.

"Perhaps you should stay in a hotel tonight," he suggested. "It is late and it might not be a good idea for you to drive."

Nessa laughed. "You think I'm mad, don't you? You think I tried to top myself in the sea and you think I've been drinking."

He frowned. "I do not understand what you are saying. But I think it would be a good idea for you to get warm and have some rest before you go anywhere else." He put his arm around her. "You might have been safe but it was a dangerous thing to do all the same."

Maybe he was her seafront café lover! The thought came to her suddenly and she looked at him more closely. He was a better looking version of Tom Conti. Tall. Tanned. Not handsome, exactly, but attractive. She could stay with him and work in his café and make love to him on a boat and everything would be all right.

The dark-haired woman spoke to him again. He nodded a few times and then turned back to Nessa.

"My wife thinks you should register in our hotel," he said. "We will escort you there. It's not far. You need to rest."

So much for her Shirley Valentine fantasies, thought Nessa wryly.

The man's wife picked up Nessa's clothes and handed them to her. Nessa hurriedly slipped into her cropped trousers and cotton top and handed the shawl back to the woman. Then, accompanied by the other people in the group, they walked up the beach and to the road toward a curved building which Nessa had noticed earlier.

One of the group pushed open the glass door which led to a gleaming modern reception area. Nessa followed them to the desk. The man spoke quickly to the receptionist who nodded and pushed a registration card toward Nessa. She filled it in and, surprised that it was still in her bag, handed her passport to the receptionist who, in turn, handed her a key.

The man and his wife accompanied Nessa up the white marble stairway and along the deep blue carpeted hall to her room on the third floor. He opened the door for her.

"You will be all right?" he asked.

"Sure," she said. "I was always all right."

He smiled at her. "Better to be safe, no?"

"Better to be safe. Thank you."

"You are welcome," he said.

"Goodnight," said his wife.

"Goodnight." Nessa closed the door and walked into the room. She opened the window to the balcony and stepped outside. Once again she could see the crescent beach and the sea which broke gently on the shore. It was beautiful, she thought. Really beautiful. It wouldn't have been such a bad place to end it all. She pushed her damp hair back from her forehead. She wouldn't have died there. She'd have been able to swim back to shore. She'd just wanted peace and quiet and that was what she'd found. It wasn't her fault if other people had got the wrong end of the stick.

But now she was on her own and it was peaceful and quiet here too. She'd wanted to be on her own from the moment that Bree and Cate had sat beside her and told her about Adam. They'd looked at her, eyes full of concern, and she hadn't been able to take their unhappiness and their pity. She didn't want to be pitied by them. She was their older sister. She was the one that had got everything right. Only she hadn't. She'd got everything wrong. Completely.

34

♥

Moon/Pluto aspects

Changeable, prone to emotional outbursts.

It was nearly ten o'clock the following morning when she woke. A warm breeze was blowing through the open balcony door. She sat up abruptly as the events of the previous night rushed back into her head. But the sequence was jumbled, it took her a few minutes to sort them out. She rubbed her eyes and massaged the back of her neck. She felt as though she had the biggest hangover in the world. She'd taken some paracetamol before she'd finally crawled into bed last night but a pounding headache was rooted behind her right eye. She rotated her neck the way she'd learned at the stress management classes that Dr. Hogan gave. Then she got out of bed and went into the bathroom. She took another couple of tablets then pulled back the shower curtain and got into the shower. She closed her eyes and let the water run through her hair and over her body. Then, for the first time in her life, she actually used the miniature shampoo and soaps that had been left for the use of the guests. By the time she got out of the shower and wrapped herself in an oversized white towel, her headache had abated and she was feeling much better.

It was at that point that she remembered Bree and Cate and the fact that she hadn't said anything to them in her frenzied dash from the villa. Although she was certain that they'd realize she needed to be on her own, she was equally certain that they'd want to hear from her. She went back into the bedroom and picked up her bag. Then she remembered that her mobile phone was lying in its component parts on the motorway and without it she didn't have a clue as to Bree's mobile number.

She sat on the edge of the bed and rested her head in her hands. She'd never bothered to memorize mobile phone numbers. What was the point when they were in her own phone's address book? But now it seemed incredibly stupid not to have learned them. She felt daft sitting here, knowing only that the first three numbers were the 086 code and not having the faintest idea what came next. Of course, she could ring Adam. Not being totally senseless, she conceded, she'd also written them down in her address book which was on the shelf beside their bed at home. Adam could tell her the phone number and then she could ring Bree and apologize and say not to worry, she'd be back soon. With the car, she then realized. In abandoning them last night she'd left them 5 kilometers from the nearest shop without transport. And Cate was pregnant. Nessa sighed deeply and decided that she was, after all, an incredibly stupid, incredibly selfish, incredibly unlovable woman. Couldn't she do anything right anymore?

She couldn't ring Adam. She just couldn't. She couldn't talk to him as though her heart wasn't smashed into as many pieces as her mobile phone and she couldn't pretend that she didn't know about the other women. In fact she knew that if she heard his voice right now she'd simply burst into more uncontrollable tears. She tried to concentrate but her thoughts were incoherent bubbles floating in her head which she just couldn't seem to pin down. It was only when she was on the absolute brink of despair that she realized that her mother would have the phone numbers. And she knew Miriam's home number off by heart.

She picked up the phone beside the bed, dialed nine for an outside line, and waited while it made the connection.

"Hello?" Miriam sounded breathless.

"Hi, Mum," said Nessa.

"Hello darling, how's the holiday going?" asked Miriam. "The weather's lovely here too, you know, I was having breakfast in the garden. Had to run when I heard the phone ring."

"We're having a great time," Nessa lied. "What I was wondering was, do you have Bree's mobile number?" She winced as she realized how insane the question sounded.

"Bree's number?" asked Miriam. "Why do you need Bree's number? Don't tell me you've had a row, Nessa, and she stormed off."

"No," said Nessa. "I came away for a day and I've lost my phone and I need to ring her."

"You?" Miriam sounded astonished. "On your own?"

"Yes."

"Are you OK, Nessa?" asked Miriam. "Only you're not the one who usually disappears on her own. Bree I can understand. Even Cate, although maybe not in her current circumstances. But not you."

"Why not me?" demanded Nessa.

"Because you like people around you," said Miriam. "You like your friends and your family and you've never been a solitary person."

"Well I'm a solitary person today," said Nessa shortly.

"Are you sure there wasn't a row?"

"I told you, no," said Nessa. "I just wanted some time on my own, that's all."

"The sun must be having a strange effect on you if that's the case," Miriam told her.

"Please, Mum." Nessa's fragile temperament was beginning to fray. "Can I have the phone number?"

She waited while her mother got it and then read it out to her.

"Thanks," she said when she'd written it down.

"Nessa?"

"Yes?"

"Cheer up."

"What?"

"You sound a bit down," said Miriam. "No matter what it is, whether you've had a row with them or whether it's something else, life's too precious to be miserable."

"I'm not miserable." Did she always lie so much to her mother? Nessa wondered.

"Well, you sound it," said Miriam. "And I'm asking you to think about why and think about what you can do to make things better."

"It might not be up to me," said Nessa. "Maybe there's nothing I can do. Perhaps I was born under a miserable star."

"It's always up to you," Miriam told her. "There's nothing you can do about the shit life throws at you, but you can choose to be happy or sad."

Nessa said nothing.

"Still there?" asked Miriam.

"Just chosing to be quiet at the moment," Nessa said briskly.

Miriam laughed. "There you go! Back to your old self again." Her voice softened. "Take care, Nessa. Enjoy the rest of your holiday."

"I will," said Nessa.

She replaced the receiver and looked at the notepad beside her. Bree's number didn't even look familiar—one thing she was going to do right away was to learn people's mobile numbers by heart instead of depending on technology to do it for her. In fact, she thought, as she began to dial, she wasn't going to depend on anything or anyone else in the future. She was going to depend on herself.

Bree and Cate were sitting in the living room. They'd decided to wait until eleven o'clock and if they hadn't heard from Nessa by then they were going to contact the police. Bree kept looking at her watch, wondering why it was that time was inching forward so slowly. Cate listened for the sound of a car on the country road.

When the phone finally rang, they both jumped in fright. Bree grabbed it and pressed the green button.

"Hi," said Nessa. "It's me."

"Well, bloody hell, Nessa, thanks very much for calling." Bree felt a wave of relief and anger wash over her and her voice rose as she talked. "We've been demented with worry about you. Where are you? What the fuck were you thinking of disappearing like that without telling us? Do you realize what the shock almost did to Cate? Do you?"

"I'm sorry," said Nessa. "I really am. I needed some space."

"We all need space," snapped Bree. "Most of us are a bit more considerate about the way we get it. Cate and I didn't sleep a wink last night!"

"I didn't mean to worry you," said Nessa.

"Didn't you?" demanded Bree. "What did you think taking off like that would do? Make us jump for joy?"

"I was upset," said Nessa.

"I know you were upset," said Bree. "Now we're all upset."

"Bree, I'm sorry," said Nessa. "I really am. It was just—it all got too much for me, you know? The idea that he—I couldn't stay there. I needed to get away."

"And where are you now?"

"Up the coast," Nessa told her. "I don't know exactly where."

"Great," said Bree. "So what's your plan now?"

"I don't have one yet," said Nessa.

Cate reached out and took the phone from Bree.

"Hi," she said. "Are you all right?"

"Yes," replied Nessa. "I'm fine."

"You scared us," said Cate.

"I know. I didn't mean to."

"It's the first time you've ever done anything like that," Cate told her. "If it had been Bree we wouldn't have panicked so much."

"Am I so bloody predictable that when I do something a little bit different everyone panics?" asked Nessa bitterly.

"Of course not," said Cate. "But you've got to admit that when anyone disappears without a word people tend to panic."

"I didn't mean to." Nessa was tired. "I just wanted to think."

"And have you?" asked Cate.

"Nothing sensible," answered Nessa. "It seems like I'm in a mud-bath or something right now. I can't seem to function."

"Take some time," said Cate gently. "Don't rush back. Stay wherever you are if you need to."

"I have to get back," said Nessa. "I have the car and you're pregnant and stuck in the middle of nowhere."

"It doesn't matter," Cate told her. "We're fine."

"Oh, Cate." Nessa's voice broke. "I could have taken it if he'd been having an affair. It's almost obligatory that husbands have affairs these days isn't it? But doing what he's doing? It makes me feel so—so insignificant."

"You're not insignificant," said Cate. "You're a decent woman and a good mother and don't you dare think anything else."

"Thanks," said Nessa wryly.

"You do whatever you need to today," said Cate. "We'll see you when we see you."

"OK," said Nessa. "Thanks, Cate."

"You're welcome," said Cate, and ended the call.

Bree stared at her. "You didn't give her much of a hard time," she said accusingly. "After what she did to us."

"Come on, Bree," said Cate. "She's having a hard time already. And she feels guilty about haring off and not saying anything. What's the point in making her feel worse?"

Bree sighed. "I suppose you're right," she said. "But I never realized before what a nice person you are, Catey."

"Well, thank you!" Cate grinned at her. "It's good to be appreciated. And you can show your appreciation by peeling some fruit. I haven't eaten anything since those damned tortilla chips last night and now me and my baby are both starving!"

Nessa was starving too. She realized that it was ages since she'd eaten and that suddenly she was very hungry indeed and she wanted some breakfast.

She wondered, as she got dressed in her crumpled top and trousers, exactly how expensive her night in this hotel would be. She doubted very much that breakfast would be included in the price. Then she laughed dryly because it didn't really matter since Adam paid all the credit card bills. So she clipped her hair back from her face and went downstairs to see what she could find to eat.

The dining room was bright and airy, with glass doors opening onto a canopied terrace which, in turn, led onto beautifully maintained gardens. Beyond the gardens, the sun danced on the azure blue water of the sea. Nessa had never had breakfast in such elegant surroundings before.

She sat down at a table and ordered coffee. The waitress gestured to her to help herself to the expansive buffet which was laid out at the far end of the room. Soon Nessa was piling her plate with ham, cheese, tomatoes, cold tortilla and freshly baked bread. She also helped herself to some fruit and yogurt. As she sat back at her table, the man who had plucked her out of the sea and his wife, plus two adorable twin sons, walked into the dining room. At first she wasn't certain that it was him, then he smiled at her and came over to the table.

"How are you feeling?" he asked.

"My face is sore where you slapped me," she told him.

"I am sorry. I thought you might drown both of us."

"I'm sorry too," she said. "I didn't mean to swim out so far and I didn't mean to nearly drown."

"And it is all right?" he asked. "What you were upset about?"

She smiled at him. "It will be. Thank you."

He smiled in return. "My wife was worried about you. She wanted to check on you earlier but I thought you might be sleeping."

"I had a wonderful sleep," she said, although she'd really only dropped off as the eastern sky had started to lighten. "But thank your wife for her concern." She glanced at the woman and smiled at her. "Your children are beautiful," she told him.

"Yes," he said. "They are the most important people in our lives. I think once you have children nothing else is so important."

"Yes," she said.

"You have children?"

"A daughter," she told him. "And you are right. She's the most important person in my life."

He smiled at her again. Then he told her to enjoy her breakfast and went back to his family.

After breakfast she went back to her room and combed her hair with the complimentary comb. She rubbed complimentary body cream on her face and blew her nose in a complimentary tissue. Then she went to reception to check out. The receptionist was different to the one who'd been there the previous night. She nodded briefly at Nessa as she handed her the credit card slip to sign—Nessa was pleased to see that her one night's stay had been delightfully expensive and that breakfast had been extra. She walked down the steps of the hotel and toward her car. But she diverted to the beach once again and stood there, looking out to sea, wondering if she would have drowned. Then she shook her head. She wouldn't. She was a survivor. Survivors didn't give in that easily.

She walked along the seafront and into a shop where she used her credit card to buy a new set of wispy underwear. She also bought a multicolored sarong, a shocking pink swimsuit and a beach towel. She withdrew some cash on her card and then bought sunscreen, a pair of inexpensive sunglasses and half a dozen English magazines in the shop next door. She went back to the beach and stretched her towel on the sand. She changed into the swimsuit, smeared herself with sunscreen and opened the magazines on the horoscope pages.

"Seize opportunities that come your way. Changes of plans might seem alarming but will bring positive experiences. A new relationship will be very influential in your future. Avoid entering into legal arguments. Believe in yourself. A change of career might mean a move."

She read through each one. She wanted someone to tell her what she should do, she wanted a clear-cut answer in her horoscope. But she knew that she wouldn't find one. Horoscopes were never clear-cut. Except, perhaps, that one telling her not to get into a legal argument. Did that mean she should stay with Adam? Because if she broke up their marriage there would definitely be a legal argument. More than one, she guessed. And yet they told her to believe in herself, that change could be positive, that there were opportunities coming her way. If she stayed with Adam and lived the way she'd been living for the last ten years, would she even recognize an opportunity when she saw it?

When she'd been younger and faced with difficult decisions she'd always made a list of the pros and cons. She made a mental list now. On the pro side she put the fact that they had a good marriage. (Well, she told herself, if she didn't rock the boat it was good, wasn't it?) She had a nice house. (Portia would be pleased to know that she did think it was important.) She didn't lack for anything. (At least, not materially.) And Jill was happy. Jill's happiness was very, very important. On the con side she looked at the fact that her husband was being unfaithful with at least two women. That she would never be able to trust him again. That she didn't know if she'd ever be able to sleep with him again. That she didn't love him anymore.

As she realized that she didn't love Adam anymore she stopped making a list. She thought about him for a moment and felt the rage and hurt of betrayal. But she didn't feel love. She knew that the love they'd had was gone. And that it was never going to come back.

Bree and Cate were both on the verandah when she arrived back at the villa that evening. She got out of the car and looked sheepishly at them.

"Hi," she said.

"Hello, Nessa." Bree looked at her angrily for a moment then rushed forward and hugged her. "Never, ever do that again!" she said. "You frightened me to death."

"I'm really sorry." Nessa looked over her head at Cate. "Honestly I am."

"It's OK," said Cate. "We had a very relaxing day sitting in the sun and listening to Bree's rock and roll CD selection."

"Glad I wasn't here for that," said Nessa shakily.

"Are you OK?" Bree released her. "What do you do last night? What happened?"

Nessa had already decided not to say anything about her late-night swim and rescue. She was afraid that Cate and Bree would misunderstand. So she simply told them that she'd driven for a couple of hours and eventually booked herself into a hotel for the night.

"Actually I thought you might have found a bloke," said Cate. "Had a fling with him for revenge."

"Give me a break." Nessa's laugh was stronger though still shaky. "The coast is swarming with thin, long-limbed sex bombs. I don't think that I'm top of anyone's list for a fling."

"So you just spent the night on your own?" asked Bree.

Nessa nodded. "Did a bit of thinking, you know."

"And?" Cate looked at her inquiringly.

"Did you come to a decision about Adam?" asked Bree.

"I'm not sure," said Nessa.

"You don't have to make any decisions," said Cate. "Not now anyway. Wait till you go home. Talk to him."

"Talk to him?" Nessa looked bitter. "I don't want to talk to him, Cate. He'll lie to me like he always has."

"So do you want to talk about it with us now?" asked Cate. "Or do you want to forget him for the rest of the holiday?"

Nessa pulled up a chair and poured herself a glass of water from the bottle on the table.

"I know I have to face up to it," she said. "But my head's been spinning around in circles. If I leave him—or throw him out—whatever, then we'll probably have to sell the house and Jill and I are on our own, and no matter what people say, it isn't easy being a single mother. That's assuming he doesn't try to fight for custody of Jill, of course."

Bree looked at her skeptically. "Him? Fight for Jill? I doubt it."

"You don't know him," said Nessa. "He does love her."

"Not enough to be with her every night while you're away," said Cate.

"I know, I know!" cried Nessa. "And I'm not trying to get at you when I say it's difficult for a single mother either, Cate. But I don't have to be. I can stay with Adam until Jill's older. I could pretend it never happened."

"You couldn't, could you?" Cate looked horrified.

"I know it seems strange to you," said Nessa. "But wives have been doing that for years! You trade off between what you have and what you'd end up with. Portia told her friend that I was only staying with him for the lifestyle and I was so angry when I heard her say that because I thought I was staying with him because I loved him. But the alternative is so hard. Especially for Jill. If I tell her that I don't love her father anymore, will she think that one day I might not love her either?"

"Oh, Nessa, no, she'd never think that," cried Bree. "She knows how much you love her."

"I know that I don't love him," said Nessa. "It's weird. I was sitting on the beach and I thought of him and I suddenly knew that no matter what he does, it won't hurt me because I don't care about him. I don't respect him. If I stay with him, it'll be on my terms."

"It's still a lot to ask," said Cate.

Nessa shrugged. "It's a lot to give up too."

"Does the house and being married really mean that much to you?" asked Bree.

"It used to," said Nessa. "Now all I'm thinking about is what's good for Jill."

"You being miserable with him wouldn't be good for her," said Cate.

"It's such a big step," said Nessa. "When you read about it and see it on the movies and everything, it seems so simple. You find out your husband's having an affair and you blow your stack. One minute you're married, next you're divorced. Then, amazingly, you find inner strength, lose seven pounds, start up a business and become rich beyond your wildest dreams. But life doesn't work out like that, does it?"

"It'd be nice if it did." Cate sighed. "But in my case the man I love threw me out of the house and has seen nothing but improvement in his life ever since, while I moved into my sister's flat and woke her up at the crack of dawn every day for a week with morning sickness."

"At least your life is simpler, Bree," said Nessa. "OK, so your boyfriend nearly wrote you off but at least you managed to keep your heart intact, even though the rest of you was a bit bruised."

"Nothing to do with men is simple," said Bree bitterly.

"It depends on what yardstick you use to measure it, I suppose," agreed Nessa.

Bree and Cate exchanged glances.

"What?" Nessa stared at them. "What's going on that I don't know about?"

Cate smiled faintly. "Just because you were off having a crisis doesn't mean we sat here and didn't explore other issues."

"What on earth are you talking about?" asked Nessa. "Did Michael ring you last night, Bree? Is that it?"

"Don't be silly," said Bree uncomfortably.

"You're in the right ballpark," Cate told her.

"What then?" asked Nessa again. "Oh, God, Bree, you're not pregnant too, are you?"

"No!" Bree looked horrified. "I never even got to sleep with Michael."

"Just as well," said Cate. "Given your current state of mind."

"So why are you two exchanging knowing looks?"

"Only that our baby sister is thinking of embarking on a relationship with Michael's father," said Cate.

Nessa stared at Bree who flushed under her gaze. "You're joking," she said. "The lawyer? Declan? The man who wanted to sue you?"

"He didn't want to sue me," said Bree impatiently. "And I'm not thinking of embarking on a relationship with him."

"So what's all the fuss about?" demanded Nessa.

"He said—I was talking to him a while ago and he—"

"He asked her out," supplied Cate.

"No!"

"He didn't ask me out," said Bree. "He just told me that he was, you know, kind of interested in me but he didn't say anything before because of Michael."

Nessa's gray eyes were wide with amazement. "And you're thinking of it seriously?" she said. "The man's old enough to be your father, Bree. Are you mad?"

"I like him." Bree looked at her defiantly.

"I think it's sick myself," said Cate. "And I told her so last night. But she seems to want to take it a step further."

"But Bree, didn't you say he had three children?" asked Nessa. "And how can you possibly go out with him when you snogged his son? That's seriously weird."

"I never snogged his son," said Bree flatly. "We never quite got around to it."

"Huh?" Cate looked astonished. "I can accept that you didn't go to bed with him but don't tell me you went out with him dozens of times and you never even kissed him?"

"Not dozens of times," said Bree. "Not that often actually. And, no, I never kissed him."

"And you think that helps?" asked Nessa.

"I don't bloody know!" snapped Bree. "I haven't decided yet."

"We're a right trio aren't we?" Nessa looked at both her sisters. "Me teetering on the brink of divorce. Cate pregnant and on her own. Bree considering hopping into bed with an aging Lothario."

"He is not an aging Lothario," said Bree furiously. "I wish to God I'd never said anything."

"I'm sorry," said Nessa. "I was trying to lighten the mood."

"Don't," said Bree.

They sat in silence.

Then suddenly Nessa began to laugh. Bree and Cate looked at her in surprise.

"I'm just remembering," she told them. "Cate's face when she got stuck in the mud. You and me after we pushed the car out."

Bree and Cate began to smile too.

"I know that the holiday hasn't exactly been what we planned," said Nessa. "And I'm really sorry for my part in scaring the life out of you. But it's been good to have you around."

"We're family," said Cate. "We're supposed to stick together."

"Even in the mud," added Bree.

"Especially when things are muddy," agreed Nessa.

35

♥

Saturn in Leo
Determined, organized, often arrogant.

Adam was at the airport to greet them. Nessa saw him straight-away, looking casually handsome while Jill tugged at his hand. Nessa rushed over to her and picked her up. She held her close, breathing in her familiar scent, realizing how much she'd missed her.

"Do I get one of those too?" asked Adam.

Nessa put Jill down and kissed him on the cheek.

"Did you have a good time?" he asked the sisters.

"Absolutely," said Cate.

"I'll help with your bags." Adam made to pick up her case.

"It's OK, Adam," said Bree quickly. "Cate and I will get a taxi. She's coming to my place before going to her apartment."

"I don't mind dropping you there," said Adam.

"It's a bit of a squash," Bree told him. "And it'll be much quicker for us in a taxi."

"Sure?"

"Yes," said Cate. "Thanks anyway, Adam." She turned to Nessa and hugged her. "Take care. Give me a call tonight."

"Will do." Nessa hugged her back.

"Mind yourself," said Bree. "Call if you need anything."

"Thanks," said Nessa. "See you soon."

They walked out of the terminal together, then Cate and Bree hopped into a taxi while Adam, Nessa and Jill went to the car park.

"I missed you," Jill told Nessa. "Did you bring me home a present?"

"How did I raise such a mercenary daughter?" Nessa asked. "Don't you care about anything except a present?"

Jill smiled at her.

"When we get home," said Nessa.

"It was a quiet enough week while you were away," said Adam. "I was busy, of course, but nothing new there. Your mum rang this morning, asked for you to phone when you get home. She wants to hear more about your holiday—she said you were doing a lot of thinking. I put her right and told her you were doing a lot of drinking!" He laughed.

"Not enough," Nessa told him. "But I enjoyed being away with Cate and Bree. We might go again sometime."

"It'll be a bit different next time," said Adam. "If Cate has excess baggage."

"Adam!" Nessa sounded furious. "A child isn't excess baggage!"

"Cate doesn't have a child," said Jill.

Nessa said nothing.

"Is she going to have one?" asked Jill.

"Yes," said Nessa eventually.

"Great! It takes ages, though, doesn't it? Mrs. Slater says it's months of hell."

"Does she?" Nessa turned to look at her daughter in the backseat.

Jill nodded. "Mr. Slater says it's the wages of sin."

Nessa laughed. Adam grinned. Jill looked pleased with herself.

There were fresh flowers in the Waterford glass crystal vase. Nessa turned to Adam.

"Where did they come from?"

He looked pained. "I got them today. To welcome you home."

"Why?"

"Because we missed you. Didn't we, Jill?"

"We kept having to have takeaways," Jill told her. "Because Dad's actually quite useless in the kitchen."

"Are you?" asked Nessa.

"I suppose I'd manage," he said. "If I absolutely had to. But we did well on Burger King and pizza deliveries."

"Oh, God, Adam, you didn't feed her exclusively on fast food, did you?"

"Not exclusively," said Adam. "I bought a couple of ready-meals from the supermarket and we had those too."

"I'm glad you're back, though," confided Jill. "I like Burger King but not all the time."

"It's good to be missed," said Nessa.

"Oh, you were definitely missed," Adam assured her. "Definitely."

She curled up on the sofa and switched on the TV. Jill was asleep in bed, thrilled with the new jeans and the Lara Croft–logoed PVC bag that Nessa had brought home for her.

Adam walked into the room and sat down beside her.

"So what was it like?" he asked.

"What d'you mean?"

"You and your sisters. Did you fight all the time?"

"Why should we fight?" asked Nessa.

"Because there always seems to be two of you against the other one," said Adam. "You know, you and Cate fussing about Bree, Bree and you pissed off with Cate and Finn over their extravagant lifestyle—that sort of thing."

"Bree and Cate feeling sorry for me because I'm the older, married sister," said Nessa. "Whose husband is having it off with a few other women."

"Sorry?" Adam looked at her.

"You heard me. And you lied to me." There was a part of her that didn't want to have this conversation now. A part of her that never wanted to have this conversation. But they needed to have it. And she couldn't pretend anymore.

"What?" Adam looked uncomfortable.

"You said that the Annika woman was a touchy feely kind of woman and she was your client and that you didn't go around sticking your tongue down people's throats." She spoke quickly. "But you lied."

"I certainly did not," said Adam. "That's exactly the sort of woman she is."

"And what about the other woman?" asked Nessa.

"Other woman?"

"Oh, come on Adam, stop pretending. The one in the apartment block near Monkstown."

Adam stared at her in silence. She looked back at him, her gray eyes clear and steady.

"What the fuck is this all about?" he asked finally. "What are you getting at, Nessa?"

"How many women are there?" she asked. "How many touchy feely women who kiss you but you don't kiss back?"

"There aren't loads of touchy feely women," he said.

"So the other ones are the ones *you* kiss?"

"Nessa—"

"I want to know," she said. "I want to know exactly about this Annika person and I want to know about the woman in Monkstown and I want to know about any others too."

"There aren't any others," he said.

"But there's Annika and the Monkstown lady."

"Regan," he said eventually.

"What?"

"Regan," said Adam again. "That's her name."

Nessa felt a cold ball form in the pit of her stomach. If she'd held the faintest hope that there had been some terrible misunderstanding, it had now evaporated.

"So we have Annika and Regan and nobody else." Her voice shook.

Adam clenched his jaw. "That's right."

"And your relationship with them is . . . ?"

"Nessa, you've got to understand that I love you," said Adam tautly. "I always have and I always will. And I love Jill too. I'd die if I didn't have you and Jill. You're the most important people in my life. It's simply . . ." he sighed. "I like women. You know that. I get on better with women than with men. I enjoy their company. I enjoy their conversation. It's so different from work stuff and domestic stuff and the kind of things that can get you down. I need a break from that."

"You need a break from me and Jill so you go to Annika and Regan."

"It's just sex," said Adam. "It's nothing to do with love."

She could hardly breathe. She'd imagined this moment ever since Cate and Bree had told her about his second woman but she hadn't imagined how she'd feel when he told her it was true. And now he'd just admitted that he had sex with other women because he liked it.

He hadn't even tried to deny it. He was looking at her defiantly, waiting for her to argue with him. But she couldn't speak. She didn't know what to say. He was a stranger to her. The man she'd married, the Adam she'd loved and cared about and made love to with such enjoyment herself, had been replaced by someone who thought that having multiple affairs was a normal sort of thing to do. She felt as though she'd mistakenly walked onto the set of Jerry Springer.

How could it have happened, she wondered.

"You know I had lots of girlfriends before you," said Adam. "But when I met you, I knew you were the only one for me. I don't want to be married to anyone else, Nessa. I love you."

"But you have sex with other women?" She could barely speak the words. She'd thought that he was having affairs with other women but this seemed worse, somehow. She was trying to get her head around the fact that he thought that he was being perfectly reasonable. And if that was how he thought, then there was a huge part of him that she just didn't understand at all. Affairs at least had emotions attached. He was simply talking about sex.

"It's a no strings thing," said Adam. "It doesn't affect how I feel about you."

"Well it sure as hell affects how I feel about you!" She was suddenly angry.

"I understand how you feel right now," said Adam. "I wouldn't have had you find out for anything, Nessa. I know that you probably hate me at this point. But I love you. I love our marriage. I love our daughter. I don't want to ruin what we have."

"And what exactly have we?" asked Nessa.

"We have a marriage that works," said Adam. "We get on well together. We enjoy each other's company. We love our daughter. We have a nice home in a nice neighborhood and we have all the things we want. You look after me. I look after you. We're a partnership, Nessa, and that's so much more important than anything else."

She stared at him. He was saying the kind of thing that she'd said to herself over and over when she thought of him being unfaithful to her. And when she'd said it to herself it almost sounded reasonable. But listening to him say it, it sounded sad.

"So when you're making love to me, what are you thinking?" asked Nessa.

"Sorry?"

"Are you thinking that you'd rather be with one of your women for sex?" she asked. "Are they better at it than me?"

"No."

"So why don't you just make love to me more often?"

"Nessa, you don't want to make love every time we go to bed. Some nights you fall asleep before your head hits the pillow."

"So does yours," she said.

"That's different."

"This is all a load of shit," she said. "You like the excitement of being with them, don't you? The variety?"

"I won't deny that," said Adam. "You know I like different experiences and I do like different women. But I only *love* one woman. And that's you. How can I make you believe that?"

"And if I said that I'd leave you?"

"I don't want you to leave me," said Adam. "You've got to understand, Nessa. Sex and love are completely different things."

"I know that they can be," she said. "I also know that they can be the same."

"I make love to you and I have sex with them."

"You're having sex with all of us," she said. "You could be picking up all sorts of disgusting diseases."

He shook his head. "No. I'm careful."

She thought she was going to be sick.

"I know it seems terrible to you, I understand that, Nessa. I feel terrible myself right now. But you've really got to see that it isn't an emotional thing with Annika and Regan. They know that. I know that. It's fun, that's all."

"Fun?" She stared at him. "You're ruining my life and you think it's fun?"

"Nessa, think about it properly. You know that men aren't meant to be monogamous—think of all those damned magazines you read about how faithless we are. Loads of men have mistresses. Think of politicians. Think of royalty. Think of anyone you like! It doesn't mean that they don't love their wives."

"That's crap," said Nessa.

"President Mitterrand," said Adam triumphantly. "Both his mistress and his wife were at his funeral. There can be room for both."

"You're saying to me that you want to stay married to me and stay seeing other women too. Are you mad, Adam?"

"You make it sound clinical when you put it like that."

"Don't you remember *Fatal Attraction?*" she demanded.

"Ah, but Jill doesn't have a rabbit." He smiled cautiously at her.

"Adam, I don't know you at all." Whatever reasoning she'd thought he'd use, whatever excuses she thought he'd make, they weren't the ones he was using now.

"I'm the same person you married," said Adam. "And, if it makes you feel better I'll stop seeing Annika and Regan."

"But there'll be others."

"No," said Adam. He put his arm around her and she flinched. "If it upsets you that much, then there won't be anyone else. I love you too much to throw it all away. Honestly."

"And you expect me to believe that?"

"I promise you," he said firmly. "I really do, Nessa. My marriage is the most important thing in my life. The rest—it's exciting, sure, I admit that. But it's not everything to me."

"How many?" she asked. "Since we were married."

"I don't know." He grimaced. "Not that many, honestly. I didn't keep count. But you didn't know and it didn't bother you. So the only thing that worries you now is being aware of it. If you hadn't found out—" He looked at her questioningly. "How did you find out?"

"By accident."

"Both times?"

She shook her head. "Bree followed you to Monkstown."

"The little bitch."

"I asked her to."

"Why?"

"Because I knew. And when I asked you about Annika I knew you were lying."

He sighed. "I nearly told you. But I couldn't."

"Because you knew that I'd hate you for it."

He shook his head. "I didn't want to hurt you. I love you. And I don't want you to hate me."

"Why?" she asked.

"Why what?"

"Why do you love me?"

"Because you're pretty. You're a good mother. You're a good wife. I like living with you."

"It doesn't sound much."

"It's a lot," said Adam. "One of the guys in the office left his wife and moved in with another girl. Only it didn't work out. Being involved and being married are very, very different."

"But she was good at sex."

"That doesn't last," said Adam. "The other stuff is more important in the long run."

"Yet you were perfectly prepared to jeopardize our marriage for the sex."

"I didn't think I was jeopardizing it," he said. "I was careful. And it wasn't as though I didn't treat you well at home. I always did."

She remembered how well he treated her. How good he'd been the night of Bree's accident. How he'd made her tea and had cancelled his golf and hadn't made a fuss because he knew how upset she was. He was a good husband. He was a good lover.

And he was a fucking liar.

"I can't live with you anymore, Adam," she said.

"Don't be stupid ," he told her. "Look, I know this isn't easy. I'm sorry. I really am. I didn't ever want you to know. But it's not the worst thing in the world. We can get through it. We're perfect for each other."

"I was such an idiot," she cried. "I wanted to believe that! I really did. I lived all my life trying to keep things perfect. But it was all a sham, Adam. It was never real."

"It was real enough to me," he said.

"How could it be?" she asked. "When you needed other people?"

"I'm sorry," he said again. "You know I love you, Nessa. You know I do."

"But I don't love you," she told him. "I did once, but I don't now."

"I suppose those bitches put you up to this," he said angrily.

"What?"

"Your sisters. This sudden 'all girls together' holiday. You probably spent the whole time plotting and scheming and talking about me."

Nessa shook her head. "They didn't tell me until halfway through. Until the night you left Jill to be collected by the babysitter while you were at an executive meeting."

He said nothing.

"Which one of them?" asked Nessa.

He raised an eyebrow.

"Which?" she said more fiercely.

"Annika," he told her.

"You are such a shit."

"Look, Nessa—"

"It's over, Adam." She got up from the chair.

"Where will you go?" he asked.

"I'm not going anywhere." She looked at him the same way as she looked at Jill whenever the little girl had driven her to the end of her patience. "Why should I? I haven't done anything wrong. You're the one who's going, Adam. I've made up my mind. I'm throwing you out."

36

♥

Mars in Cancer

An emotional commitment to see things through.

It was definitely easier in the movies, thought Nessa, as she sat on the edge of the bed. In the movies you could throw someone out of the house and they'd go. But Adam had simply looked at her and told her that he wasn't leaving the family home without some kind of court order. He said that he loved her and he loved his daughter and that everyone knew it. She'd gritted her teeth and told him that he could hardly call it a family home when he spent most of his time out of it having affairs with other women. And that, no matter what he said, he couldn't possibly love her if he was having affairs with other women. To which he'd retorted that they weren't affairs and that he'd apologized for hurting her and that he was perfectly prepared to change so why wasn't she?

They'd never raised their voices to each other in the past. They'd disagreed but they'd never shouted. But this time she yelled at him that he was a sick bastard and that she'd clearly been out of her mind when she married him.

Eventually he'd stormed into the spare bedroom and had closed the door firmly behind him. And she was left sitting on the bed in the bedroom that they'd once shared and wondering why it was that everyone else's marital break-ups seemed to be so simple compared to hers.

John Trelfall had moved out as soon as Paula had played his girl-friend's message to him on the phone. He might have denied the affair at first but he'd buckled afterward and he'd moved into an apartment a couple of miles away. But Adam didn't seem to have any intention of moving into an apartment a few miles away, Adam had drawn lines in the sand and Nessa knew that it wasn't going to be easy to move him.

She got up and looked out of the bedroom window. She felt nothing for him now. Nothing at all. She didn't feel hurt anymore. Or betrayed. Or sad that their marriage was over. She simply felt incredibly angry that she might be forced to stay in the same house as him when all she wanted to do now was to get on with her life. It would be wonderful if getting on with it did result in losing weight and becoming incredibly successful, but right now it just meant coping. Yet she knew she could cope.

She didn't want to stay with someone who could lie to her and cheat her and feel justified in doing so. She didn't want that kind of marriage to be a role model for Jill. She didn't quite know how she was going to tell Jill that she didn't love Adam anymore but she did know that she'd be able to do it. And that, whatever it took to keep Jill from feeling as though it were partly her fault, she'd manage to do that too. She'd keep it together for Jill. And for herself. She didn't need Adam. She wished that things had turned out differently but she didn't need him for the lifestyle and for the family and for any-thing else because, if she didn't love him, none of those things were worth anything anyway.

Cate got into bed and pulled the duvet around her shoulders. She squeezed her eyes tightly shut to block out the fizzy yellow light from the streetlamps outside the apartment building. She needed to buy curtains for the window—the previous occupant had obviously decided that nobody would be able to see in to the building and hadn't bothered. But the light was too bright, it was keeping her awake and, when she finally did fall asleep, the early morning sun woke her again anyway so that she was tired before she even got out of bed. All the same, would there be any point in buying curtains for a place where she didn't intend to stay for very long? she wondered. Wouldn't she need all her spare cash for baby clothes and baby-minders and buggies and all of the paraphernalia that went with babies rather than blowing it on a pair of curtains?

I'm losing it, she thought, as she turned over in the bed. It's only curtains! I can afford to buy curtains. Besides, if I don't, I'll never get any sleep. She pulled the duvet higher and willed herself to empty her mind.

It was the first night in a week that she hadn't been able to sleep. At the villa she'd dropped off almost as soon as she'd climbed into bed and her sleep had been (if not quite as long as Nessa's and Bree's drink-induced comas) deep and satisfying. While they'd been in Spain she'd been able to put things to the back of her mind and not think about them or worry about them or constantly wonder what she should have done differently. But here she couldn't help worrying about how she was going to cope and what things would be like in March when she had the baby and what would've happened if she'd simply gone ahead and had the abortion like she'd planned.

If she'd gone through with it she'd never have met Tiernan Brennan in the airport hotel and he would never have phoned Finn and told him, and her whole web of lies wouldn't have come collapsing down on top of her. And she'd be in Clontarf right now, listening to Finn's steady breathing and feeling the warmth of his body beside hers and everything would be exactly the way she'd always wanted.

Her hand slid over the gentle hill of her stomach. And she wouldn't be pregnant. "I'm sorry," she whispered softly into the darkness of the room. "I'm sorry for what I nearly did to you and I'm sorry about the life that you might end up living with me anyway. I'm sorry that you've been landed with such a hopeless fuck-up of a future mother when really you should have had it all. I'll try and make it up to you but I know I never will."

She closed her eyes and, quite suddenly, slept.

When Bree woke up the following morning she was shocked to realize that it was only seven o'clock but that she felt totally alert. She got out of bed and had a shower. The face that looked back at her from the mirror was softly tanned and her blue-gray eyes looked brighter than usual. She pulled her hair back into a curly ponytail and secured it with a black bobble. Then she dressed in a black T-shirt and her most comfortable pair of jeans.

She whistled as she put on the kettle for a cup of coffee. While she waited for it to boil she straightened the bedclothes on the bed, folded the jumper she'd been wearing last night and hung her trousers, which had been draped over the back of a chair, in the wardrobe. She closed the wardrobe door and then stopped in surprise as she looked around the flat.

It was neat and tidy and she'd just kept it that way. Perhaps, she thought, as she spooned coffee into a mug and then poured steaming hot water over it, perhaps living with both Nessa and Cate has rubbed off on me. Maybe I'm going to turn into a domesticated kind of girl after all! She grimaced. She didn't want to be domesticated but after Cate had moved out she'd tidied up again. And she'd been pretty neat on their Spanish holiday too. Surely she couldn't have changed in such a short space of time.

She sat on the windowsill and sipped her coffee. Domesticated certainly wasn't on her agenda but she could see how life could be improved by just being a little bit tidier. She hated the idea of turning into a tidy person but maybe it was something that you couldn't do anything about. Maybe Cate and Nessa were tidy simply because they were older than her.

She shook her head and drained her mug. They'd always been tidy. Their bad influence had obviously just rubbed off on her a bit. She looked at her watch. She wasn't due in until nine this morning but it wouldn't do any harm to be a little bit early. She got up and went into the tiny kitchen. She rinsed the mug and put it on the draining board.

A few weeks earlier she wouldn't have rinsed it. She'd have left it there, along with a pile of other mugs and cups, until she was forced to wash it because she'd run out. She sighed deeply. Her sister's influence had been much deeper than she'd thought. It was going to take a lot to change back again.

Cate walked into her office and sat down at her desk. She switched on her computer and while it was whirring into life she looked at the pile of white phone message notes that Glenda had left for her.

Most of them were from sales reps and stores. One was from a market research company. And one was from Finn. She felt her stomach turn over at the sight of his name on the flimsy piece of paper in front of her. She blinked as she looked at the stark message in Glenda's neat printing—day: Wednesday, time: 10:15 A.M., caller: Finn Coolidge, message: none.

Why had he phoned? Why had he phoned her at the office instead of on her mobile? She could have spoken to him if he'd called on her mobile. And then she remembered that Bree and Nessa hadn't let her switch on her mobile while they'd been on holiday. If Finn had called he would've simply got her message minder. But he could have left a message, couldn't he? If it was important.

She clicked on the training shoe icon on her computer to see a breakdown of last week's sales. It's probably not important, she told herself as the spreadsheet opened. It's probably something stupid like wanting to give me some of the things out of the apartment that I left behind. Or to tell me that he has no intention of paying maintenance for the baby.

She looked down at her stomach. She was starting to feel solidarity with this baby. As though the two of them were taking on the world together. Even though she knew that was silly.

"I want to talk to you." Adam strode into the kitchen and put his briefcase on the table. In the few days since Nessa had confronted him they'd barely spoken. He'd slept in the spare room and got up early every morning so that he'd already left the house before she came downstairs. A complete change of behavior, she noticed, from all the mornings when she'd had to call him again and again to make sure he got up at all.

Nessa turned from the sink where she'd been peeling potatoes. "Sure."

"I spoke to a solicitor today," he said. "He agrees that I shouldn't leave the family home."

Nessa swallowed.

"But I can't stay here, can I?" He looked at her angrily. "You've ruined that for me."

"For God's sake, Adam!" She put down the potato peeler. "You ruined it for yourself."

"I told you I was prepared to give it a chance," he snapped. "But you—you can't be bothered to try. You're acting like some tragedy queen, freezing me out, making life intolerable."

"Oh, get real." She picked up the peeler again and viciously dug an eye out of a potato.

"I'm going to move out for a few weeks despite his advice," said Adam. "I can't live like this. It'll give you time to come to your senses anyway, to see what life is like without me. But I'll still pay the mortgage, it's still a family home and I'm very definitely not leaving you."

Nessa shrugged.

"If you think for one minute that you can throw me out and hang on to everything I've worked for, you have another think coming," said Adam.

"You slept with other women." Nessa picked up another potato.

"I told you it was nothing," said Adam angrily.

"How can you say that?" demanded Nessa. "How can you stand here and tell me that disregarding our marriage vows was nothing?"

"Don't be so bloody sanctimonious," retorted Adam. "You were never a Holy Joe, Nessa. Don't start now just because it suits you."

"I keep thinking that I'm in a bad dream and that I'll wake up," Nessa told him. "But I'm not. I'm married to someone who seems to think that being married means that there'll always be someone to cook his meals and wash his underpants and run his home. I can't believe that in the twenty-first century there are actually blokes who believe that!"

"Doing those things never bothered you before," snapped Adam.

"No. Not when they were for someone who was supposed to love me," said Nessa. "But for someone who's shagging half of Dublin, it's an entirely different matter."

"Your language is disgraceful," said Adam.

"Your behavior is disgraceful," said Nessa.

"Why can't you see the difference?" Adam looked at her pleadingly. "Love and—"

"Don't start all that crap again," Nessa interrupted him. "Love and lust may, in your book, be different. But there's such a thing as respect too. You didn't show any to me and I sure as hell don't have any for you anymore."

"I always respected you!"

"Oh, please!" Nessa laughed shortly. "You fooled me. That's completely different."

"I'm going to pack some things," said Adam. "But not everything. Because I'll be back, Nessa. You may be going through some silly feminist shit thing right now but you know you'll come to your senses."

"I just have come to my senses," retorted Nessa. "I seem to have been without them for the last ten years!"

"Nessa, please." Adam's voice was suddenly conciliatory. "Listen to us. We don't fight like this. We work things out. We can work this out too, honestly we can. Just tell me that you'll think it over for a while."

She dropped the potato into the sink. "OK," she said eventually. "I'll think it over."

Jill watched him as he packed. "How long do you have to go away for?" she asked.

"A little while," said Adam. "I have to go to work."

"But you do go to work," she objected. "Every morning."

"It's different this time," said Adam grimly.

"Why?"

"It just is. I have to live somewhere else for work. But I'll think about you all the time." He turned to his daughter. "No matter what anyone says I love you very much."

"I know that," said Jill. "Mum told me too."

"Did she?" asked Adam.

Jill nodded. 'She says that both of you love me very much."

"There you go." Adam smiled brightly at her. "You're obviously a very important person if we both love you so much."

"I still don't want you to have to live somewhere else," Jill said.

"I'll phone you every day," said Adam.

"OK." But Jill's voice was full of doubt.

"I promise," said Adam.

"Every day?"

"Every day," he assured her.

The last thing Nessa wanted to do was to have to tell Miriam. She felt that her mother had gone through enough with Cate's pregnancy and Bree's accident and she also felt, that as the eldest, she should be the one for whom everything was going right. Miriam had always gone on at her about being a good example to her sisters when she was younger. Nessa had taken her role as a good example very seriously. She didn't phone Miriam until Jill was in bed and then she spent ages talking about inconsequential things.

"What's happened?" asked Miriam eventually.

"What d'you mean?"

'For heaven's sake, Nessa, I know there's something the matter. You've been rambling for the best part of fifteen minutes. There's something you want to tell me, isn't there?"

Nessa sighed. "Adam's gone," she said baldly.

"Gone?"

"He—oh, Mum, he was having—there were other women." To her horror, Nessa began to sob convulsively.

"I'll come to Dublin," said Miriam firmly.

It would be nice to have Miriam fussing over her, thought Nessa. But she didn't want to be fussed over yet. She couldn't face being fussed over. She took a deep breath and got her sobbing under control.

"I'd love you to come," she said. "But not just yet. I need to be on my own for a while."

"Is he gone for good? Are you going to get a divorce?"

"I haven't thought as far as divorce yet," said Nessa tiredly. "He wants me to think things over. But I have been thinking things over. I don't want him back."

"I knew there was something wrong when you phoned me from Spain," said Miriam. "I should've done something."

"Don't be silly, there was nothing you could do." Nessa sniffed. "But, you know, I'm OK on my own, Mum. I can cope on my own." She clutched the receiver more tightly. "I never realized that before. I thought Adam was the cornerstone of my existence, I never would've believed that I could even live without him. But I can. I know I can."

"I liked him," said Miriam. "But he was always a bit too sure of his charm for his own good."

"He was very charming," agreed Nessa. "Oh, Mum, in loads of ways he was a great husband. But when you don't trust someone . . . it doesn't mean anything if you don't trust them, does it?"

"'No," said Miriam.

"I'm really sorry." Nessa felt her eyes sting with tears again.

"Sorry?"

"For messing it up. For getting it wrong. For becoming your separated daughter. And now Jill will be brought up in a single parent family."

"You've nothing to be sorry about," said Miriam vehemently. "Nothing. You're a great daughter and you were a great wife and you're a great mother. Jill is lucky to have you. So don't start apologizing, Nessa." Cate was the same. I can't have been much of a mother if you both think you need to say sorry for how your lives have turned out."

"That's not true," said Nessa. "You were great. But you got it so right and we got it so wrong."

Miriam sighed. "Your Dad and I worked hard at our marriage," she said. "Sometimes things were wonderful, sometimes they were lousy. But I'll tell you now, Nessa, if he'd ever betrayed me with another woman I would've thrown him out there and then. It's not your fault that Adam has done what he's done so don't blame yourself. And don't feel as though you've let me down. You would've let me down if you'd done nothing about it."

"Really?" asked Nessa.

"Absolutely," said Miriam. "I want my girls to be strong. And they are."

"But we've all managed to have disastrous relationships," said Nessa.

"Not disastrous," said Miriam. "You and Cate did find love. And maybe it all went pear shaped but at least you know what it's like. I do believe in the cliché that it's better to have loved and lost. Really it is. I'm hoping that one day Bree will find someone to love too."

Nessa was silent. She didn't think that Miriam was ready to hear that Bree had fallen for a forty-five-year-old widower with three children. There was only so much she could expect her mother to take at any one time.

"I'll see you soon," she said eventually. "Perhaps Jill and I could come to Galway for a few days rather than you having to drag yourself up here."

"That'd be lovely," said Miriam.

"Thanks," said Nessa.

"For what?"

"For understanding"

"Take care of yourself," Miriam said. "Take care of Jill. And call me every day."

"I will," said Nessa. "Goodnight, Mum."

"Goodnight," said Miriam.

She replaced the receiver and looked at Louis who was sitting in the armchair opposite pretending to read the newspaper. Her heart swelled with love for him and gratitude that they'd been lucky enough to have had a long and happy marriage. Louis had never looked at another woman in all their time together. Well, she conceded, he might have looked once or twice but he'd never done anything more than that. And there'd been that awful time when he'd lost almost all their savings on some sure-fire invest-ment which had opened a rift between them and which had taken a lot of time to heal. But it had healed. And they'd grown stronger as a result.

"Problems?" he folded the paper and peered at her over his reading glasses.

"Nessa," she told him. "Adam and Nessa. I always thought she'd go to pieces if anything went wrong between them. Not that I thought anything would go wrong. But now that it has, she seems to have found a strength I never knew she had."

"All our girls are strong," said Louis. "They get it from you. Now tell me what's happened. I was never as confident about Adam and Nessa as you. I always felt that a bloke who couldn't park a car with-out scraping it wasn't worth a toss anyhow."

I seem to spend my whole life on the phone, thought Nessa, as she dialed Bree's number. She was relieved that she'd told Miriam what had happened but it had been very difficult. Talking to her youngest sister would be easier.

"He's gone," she said, as Bree answered the phone.

"What?"

"Adam. He's gone."

"Nessa!" Bree shrieked. "You've done it. You've thrown him out."

"Well, not exactly." Nessa related her conversation with Adam. "So he's insisting that this is a temporary move to give himself time to think and for me to come to my senses and he's adamant that whatever happens I won't be left with the house. And the only reason he went at all was because I agreed to think things over."

"Oh, Nessa." Bree groaned. "Here I was thinking you'd made a decisive stand and that you'd got rid of him but you haven't, not really."

"I have," said Nessa surprising herself with the firmness of her tone. "If I hadn't told him I'd think about it there would've been another row and he'd have stayed camped in the spare room. So it was just to shut him up. It may have taken me some time, Bree. But I've made my choice and there's no going back. I don't want to go back now anyway."

"Well done," said Bree admiringly. "You sound so certain now."

"Making the decision was easier than I thought," said Nessa. "It's all of the shit that happens afterward that's going to be difficult." Her tone changed. "I need to get a solicitor, Bree. And I need to find out about the whole family law thing and where I stand."

"Don't you have one already?" asked Bree.

"Of course," said Nessa. "But Adam has always dealt with him and he's probably acting for Adam now. So I need someone else."

"Get someone good," Bree told her. "Someone who'll really fight for you."

"I thought Declan Morrissey might be able to help," said Nessa casually.

Bree was silent for a moment. "Declan's a barrister," she said eventually. "I'm not terribly clued in on the whole hierarchy but he goes to court and pleads cases. I think solicitors do the donkey work first."

"Oh," said Nessa.

"But he might know a good one," Bree said. "Because you'll want one who specializes in family law, won't you? Rather than someone whose expertise is getting you off with a slap on the wrist when you've committed a major art robbery or something."

Nessa laughed. "Is that Declan Morrissey's speciality? Does he look after the Dublin underworld?"

"I don't know," said Bree. "I don't know what he does really."

"If you don't want to phone him then don't," said Nessa. "I just thought it might be an area he dealt with. It's not a problem."

"But if I do want to phone him it gives me an excuse," said Bree. "I know."

"Nessa, please don't tell me that you threw your husband out simply to give me an excuse to ring my only friend who knows anything about the law," begged Bree.

"I might be good to you in an older-sister sort of way," Nessa said, "but not that good, Bree, honestly!" Her voice softened. "Do you want to phone him?"

Bree sighed. "I wish I knew." And then, more forcefully, she said that no, she didn't want to phone him.

"Why?" asked Nessa.

"Like I said before, there's no future in it. I wasn't thinking about him like that until he said what he said. And it just doesn't make sense."

"Who says it has to?"

"I can't believe you're encouraging me!" cried Bree.

"I'm not," said Nessa. "I'm simply saying that maybe you and he—well, maybe it's worth a try."

"Nessa, I hardly know the man," Bree protested. "I've gone out with his son, for God's sake! And you and Cate both agreed that the idea of me and Declan was kind of gross."

"I admit that I was a bit shocked because of his age," said Nessa. "But if he's the right one for you, Bree . . . even if there's a chance . . ."

"I'd have thought that with your experience you'd be warning me off for life," said Bree.

"I can't help myself." Nessa sighed. "It's my nature, I suppose. I want everyone to be happy and everyone to have someone and I just have a good feeling about you and Declan."

"You hated him when you first met him," Bree pointed out.

"That's because I thought he wasn't being nice to you," said Nessa. "But a man who brings you chocolate chip cookies when you've got a sore leg—well, Bree, he sounds like a man in a million to me!"

"I don't know yet," said Bree. "But I will call him for you, Nessa. And that's the only reason I'll call him. To find you a good solicitor. Because I want to make sure that you get everything you're entitled to from that bastard Adam Riley."

"Thank you," said Nessa sweetly.

"It's the only reason," said Bree again.

Nessa grinned as she put down the phone. She was about to

embark on probably messy and definitely bitter divorce proceedings. She knew that life was going to be bloody difficult for the next few months. But she was making the decisions. She was in charge of things now. And, despite the fact that she knew that tears would never be far away, she hadn't felt as confident in years.

37

♥

Moon in 1st House

A natural instinct to care for others.

B ree finished work at half past three on Friday. She'd come in very early that morning to do an urgent job on a company car which was needed before nine o'clock. By the time that most of the others had arrived, she'd finished the repairs and had started on the service list.

At a quarter past three Christy told her to go home.

"Why?" she asked. "There's a few more still to do."

"The others can finish them," he said. "You've been here for hours. It's Friday, Bree. Go home, wash your hair and do whatever it is you young, free and single girls do on Friday nights."

"Actually I'm going to my sister's apartment tonight," said Bree. "The three of us plus my niece are getting together for a girls' night in."

"What does that entail?" asked Christy. "Sitting around talking about how much you hate men, sticking pins into Action Man dolls, that sort of thing?"

Bree laughed. "No. We're going to watch videos and wish we knew men like the handsome, soulful, caring, Hollywood heroes."

"Is that what girls do on nights in?"

"Absolutely," said Bree.

"Then you should definitely go out instead," said Christy. "It sounds a bloody boring way of spending Friday night to me. Besides, you've just been away with your sisters. I'd've thought you'd had enough of them by now."

"I almost have," said Bree. "But there's a little bit to go yet, I guess."

"One day you'll find yourself a nice bloke," Christy told her. "And you won't have to stay at home with the girls."

"Girls are easier to get on with," Bree said.

"I never found it like that," Christy told her. "Not until I met my wife anyway."

"God love her," said Bree.

"You never got back together with young Michael Morrissey after the accident, did you?" Christy's tone was casual.

"Is that what this conversation is all about?" she asked. "You know I didn't get back with Michael. He was a nice guy but a bit of a speed freak when it came down to it."

"I haven't seen Declan in a while," said Christy. "Nice man."

She'd been thinking about Declan because of her promise to Nessa to get the name of a family law solicitor from him. It was ten days since she'd told Nessa she'd ring him but although it was a ready-made excuse to call she hadn't had the nerve to pick up the phone. And now she was feeling pressurized because she didn't want to mess up Nessa's life by not getting her the very best solicitor she could, even though Nessa had said that if Declan couldn't recommend anyone she'd use the same firm as her friend Paula had used.

"Go on," said Christy. "Get home with yourself, Mizz Driscoll. Even if you are spending the night in you'll probably want to soak the grime off first."

She looked down at her hands. Despite the latex gloves she wore they were still streaked with oil and dust.

"OK," she said. "See you Monday."

"Have a good weekend," said Christy.

She walked out of the garage and got onto her bike, adjusting her helmet as she sat astride it, feeling suddenly tired. Christy was right. She should go home and have a shower (there was no way she'd dream of using the shared bathroom at the flat, much as the idea of soaking in a bath appealed) and she should make a bit of an effort to look nice tonight even if it was just a girls' night in.

When Cate invited them to her new apartment for the evening, neither Bree nor Nessa felt that they could refuse. They were both worried about Cate who seemed to be holding herself as tightly as a coiled spring since they'd come back from Spain and who looked thinner than ever despite the bump of her pregnancy. She'd told Nessa that Finn had called while she was away but that he hadn't left a message nor called again. She didn't know whether or not she should call him. Part of her wanted to but another part of her just couldn't face it. Nessa, Cate and Bree talked about it for ages and finally decided that if he'd called once he'd call back. He was probably trying to get her into a state by not calling back straightaway, they decided. Cate should be cool and aloof. Unavailable, Nessa and Bree told her. Getting on with her life. She'd agreed with them eventually but Bree hated to think of Cate worrying about Finn's reasons for getting in touch. Now that a few days had elapsed she was beginning to think that maybe they'd given Cate the wrong advice. Maybe she should just have picked up the damn phone to him and discovered what he wanted.

Bree sighed. Men were so complicated. Or at the very least, they complicated things. Women were so much more straightforward. And then she smiled to herself because the blokes in the garage were always complaining about how complicated women actually were and how they just didn't understand them.

She revved up the bike and went down the road, her mind still racing. But even if women were as complicated as men, it was always men who made them cry. Men had made her cry in the past. Both Finn and Adam had caused Cate and Nessa to sob their hearts out. She wondered was there a woman in the world who hadn't been reduced to tears by the actions of some bloke somewhere.

She thought about Michael Morrissey. He hadn't made her cry, of course, even when he told her it was over. If they hadn't been in the car accident, would things have turned out any differently between them? Would he have been her ideal man after all? Would their relationship have developed any further? And in that case would Declan have ever said anything to her? What would it have been like, she wondered, to go to that house on a regular basis not knowing that Declan was attracted to her while all the time she was in love with his son?

Or not, of course. Because she was fooling herself to think that she'd ever really been in love with Michael. Love had to be more than thinking that someone looked sexy. Love had to be more than being good in bed—not that she'd even got that far with Michael anyway. But if the accident hadn't happened then he mightn't have broken it off with her and she might have gone to bed with him and maybe they would have fallen in love eventually. Then Declan wouldn't have had the opportunity of saying anything and she wouldn't be biking down this road with her mind in a complete whirl. Bloody hell, she thought angrily. Why did he have to say something? Why did he make me think that he and I were in any way a viable proposition?

Going out with Declan wouldn't be like going out with anyone else. Not like Gerry or Enrique or Fabien. Not like Terry the legionnaire or Marcus the snake charmer either. Or even like the speed freak that was Declan's son. The bottom line was that Declan wasn't a weirdo. But, she told herself savagely, he was a man, wasn't he? He was already making her life more complicated than she wanted. And one day he'd do something to mess it all up and she'd be like Nessa and like Cate, miserable because of a man.

She slowed down and pulled to the side of the road. Her hands were shaking. This was totally ridiculous. She was getting herself into a knot about nothing. Declan Morrissey didn't matter to her. There was no chance of a relationship with him. It wasn't practical. She frowned as she removed her helmet and rubbed her hair. Of course she liked him, she'd always liked him, but it was hard to think of him as anything other than her ex-boyfriend's father.

But if she hadn't known Michael, if she'd simply met Declan . . . she shook her head. She still wouldn't have considered Declan to be relationship material. She wouldn't even have noticed him in a crowded room. The only reason she was thinking about it at all was because he'd told her that he liked her. And how serious was he about that anyway? He'd met her at a traumatic time, worried about Michael, concerned about her, and maybe just missing his wife. There were lots of reasons why he might have said something to her and regretted it since. Still his words were etched in her mind, niggling at her, confusing her. She'd dismissed him when he'd come to the flat but hadn't been able to forget him ever since. She was usually reasonably good at forgetting men—once the weirdos were out of her life she normally accepted their weirdness and congratulated herself on her lucky escape.

So why should she feel different this time? And about someone who was so much older than her, who'd lived such a different life and had lived so much of it already. If he wasn't older, if he didn't have a family, if she hadn't nearly kissed his only son, then would she think it was OK? Bree wondered. She laughed at herself. All those things made Declan who he was, without them he wouldn't be the same person and she mightn't even like him very much.

Because, she told herself, she did like him. He was very difficult not to like if only because of his knack with cookies and muffins.

She sighed and replaced her helmet. Then she revved up the bike and moved into the afternoon traffic again.

She hadn't meant to go to the High Court but she couldn't help herself. She wanted to see the type of place where Declan worked, to get a sense of the kind of person he was. It was unlikely, she thought, as she found a place to park her bike, that he'd be in court on a Friday afternoon.

She walked up the steps, conscious of a certain sense of occasion. She'd never been here before but she'd seen the building as a backdrop to many news stories where reporters spoke breathlessly of cases hanging in the balance and where cameramen zoomed in on both the victor and the vanquished with equal interest.

A number of people stood in the domed, circular hall which lead to the different courtrooms. They talked in hushed tones which nevertheless echoed like whispers in a church. Occasionally, and incongruously, a peal of laughter cut through the otherwise serious atmosphere.

The door to court number three opened and a girl rushed out, her face streaked with tears. Two women followed her and caught up with her at the entrance to the building. They put their arms around her and whispered to her.

Bree bit her lip. There were all sorts of things going on here, people's lives being judged and decided on, truth and lies being told and justice being apportioned—only probably not all of the time. She remembered her father once commenting that the law and justice were poles apart. She wondered how Declan felt about it.

Another flurry from a different corner of the hall caught her eye. This time three barristers strode toward the exit, gowns flapping, wigs perched ridiculously on their heads. Bree couldn't help smiling. Did Declan wear a wig? She couldn't imagine him with a patch of white curls on top of his thick, graying hair.

Suddenly she felt uncomfortable being here. And out of place— she realized that some people were looking at her curiously, wondering no doubt why a girl in black leather biking gear was standing in the court, looking around aimlessly. She didn't want to simply walk out again, thinking that this might look odd. She caught sight of a sign for the Ladies and walked toward it purposefully. She walked down the stone steps and pushed open the door. She leaned against the tiled wall and closed her eyes.

The court was different to anywhere else she'd ever been in her life. There was a sense of solemnity and occasion which even the white wigs couldn't lighten. To work here, to listen to the traumas and the crimes and the grievances that were brought before the court, you would want to have some sense of purpose. A sense of purpose that she could never have herself.

She opened her eyes again. She'd been right to come, it had put Declan and everything to do with Declan into perspective. He was a grown up who lived and worked in a grown-up world. She was a car mechanic who liked having fun. Their lives and their dreams were poles apart and it was pointless to think it could ever be any different. He probably saw her as a young thing to amuse himself with, intrigued by her, just as Michael was because she did what was perceived to be a man's job and she did it well. But she didn't want to intrigue anyone. She just wanted to love someone. And to be loved in return.

She washed her hands (still grimy despite having scrubbed them before she left the garage) and ran lightly up the stairs again. She hurried into the hall and collided with a group of chattering barristers.

"Sorry!" she gasped as one of them fumbled with a file and almost dropped it. He grunted in annoyance. Then one of the group looked at her in surprise.

"Bree?"

Declan Morrissey *was* wearing a wig. And it looked as vaguely silly as she'd imagined it might.

"Hi, Declan." She looked at him uneasily.

"What on earth are you doing here?" He pulled her to one side and then looked at his colleagues. "I'll catch up with you later, Raphael," he said to one of them, who nodded and looked at Bree with undisguised curiosity.

"Well?" Declan asked her.

"I—I didn't think you'd be here," she said. "I wanted to see what it was like."

"What it was like?" he asked.

"The court. Where you worked. What you did."

"Why?" he asked.

She shrugged as carelessly as she could. "I wanted to know about it."

Declan looked at her in silence.

"What did you want to know?" he asked eventually.

She smiled faintly. "I've no idea. I just thought it would be interesting."

"And is it?"

"Probably," she said. "To be honest I just got overawed when I walked in the door."

"Did you want to see a case being heard?"

She shook her head. "I just wanted to see somewhere different."

"Right."

They stood silently beside each other while another eddy of robed barristers brushed by them.

"I suppose people will think I'm a client," said Bree.

"Probably," Declan agreed.

"Do you do criminal cases?" she asked.

"Yes," he said.

"So I could be a criminal?"

"Or not." He smiled at her. "You don't have the look of someone who's lived a life of crime."

She smiled faintly. "I suppose that's something to be pleased about." She looked around her again. "I should get going," she said.

"I have an office nearby," said Declan. "Would you like to have a cup of coffee with me there?"

Bree said nothing at first then nodded.

She'd expected Declan to bring her to an old and crumbling building where the walls would be festooned with portraits of dead judges. But he led her out of the court area and across the street to a modern building with blond wood furnishings and highly polished tiled floors. She followed him up a flight of stairs and into a small suite of offices.

A girl working at a computer looked up as he entered.

"Four phone calls from Bernard Fallon," she said. "One from Mrs. McAllister and one from Gerry Rhodes."

"Fine, Sally, thanks," said Declan.

He pushed open the door to another office and beckoned Bree inside.

She probably thinks I'm some kind of criminal too, thought Bree, as she caught the other girl's mildly curious glance. I hope she thinks I'm a jet-setting jewel thief or infamous forger, not a murderess or a petty smash-and-grab merchant.

Declan went over to a coffeepot in the corner of the room.

"Maybe I should make some fresh," he said. "I'm sure this has been brewing for hours."

"It doesn't matter," said Bree. "I probably don't want coffee after all."

"Neither do I," said Declan.

They shared brief smiles.

There was a small sofa alongside the wall. Declan gestured Bree to sit down.

"This is really weird," she said. "I feel as though I've stepped out of my life and into something else completely."

"So do I." Declan sat down beside her. "I've never been totally stunned in court before, but I sure was today when I saw you."

They were silent. Bree could hear the sound of her own breathing.

"My sister needs a solicitor," she said suddenly. "Her marriage has broken up."

"Oh." Declan looked at her. "So that's why you came really?"

Bree cleared her throat. "I told her I'd check with you."

"Which sister?" asked Declan.

"Nessa," said Bree. "The firebrand."

"I'm sorry to hear that."

Bree recognized the professional tone of his voice.

"Family law isn't my area," Declan told her. "But I do know of a couple of firms who—"

"She needs the best," Bree interrupted him. "That shit has been playing away with at least two other women."

Declan raised an eyebrow.

"She didn't have a clue," said Bree. "She believed him when he said he loved her."

Declan nodded. "I'll check for you," he said. "I'll recommend somebody good."

"Thanks."

They sat in silence for a moment. Then Declan stood up. "If there isn't anything else?"

Bree didn't look at him. She stared across the room at the abstract picture on the wall. "I keep thinking about you," she said abruptly. "What you said to me."

Declan sat down again. "I'm sorry about that," he told her. "It wasn't very fair of me, I knew that I'd taken you by surprise."

"Tactics." She smiled shakily at him. "That's probably what you do all the time."

He laughed. "Not deliberately in your case," he assured her. "At least, I don't think it was deliberate."

"You said those things but you didn't try to get in touch with me again."

"I was embarrassed," he confessed. "I thought that I'd rather horrified you in the first place. And I did leave the ball in your court, so to speak."

"Surprised me." Bree felt herself relax a little. "Not horrified."

"Afterward I thought of how ridiculous it was. Me with three almost grown-up children. You so much younger and with a totally different kind of life. I was supposed to be a kind of friend to you and I know that's how you thought of me. I shouldn't have said anything." He grinned ruefully. "I'm probably going through a mid-life crisis or something."

"I go through some kind of life crisis every few months," said Bree. "I wouldn't worry about it too much." She reached out and removed the wig from his head. She turned it over in her hands.

"I forget about it," Declan told her. "When they were younger the kids used to rob it for dressing up."

"You only have one wig?" she asked.

"No, but that's—" he broke off and looked at her uncomfortably. She raised her eyebrows in silent query.

"Monica bought that one for me," he said.

"Oh." She put it on the small table in front of them.

"That's what'd it be like, isn't it?" asked Declan. "You say something or do something and I'd tell you that Monica didn't say things like that or do things like that."

"You think so?"

"I don't know!" He looked at her despairingly. "I haven't done this sort of thing since she died. I haven't tried, Bree. I haven't wanted to."

"I've gone out with a good few men," she told him. "Sometimes they've done things that have reminded me of previous boyfriends. Sometimes they've done things that have reminded me of boyfriends I wished I hadn't split up with." She smiled slightly. "It's not the same but it can't be helped."

"You're very sensible for someone who's only twenty-five," said Declan.

She laughed. "I'm not at all sensible, really," she told him. "My sisters think I'm the flighty, slightly mad one. I'm sensible about cars and bikes, that's all."

"I really like you," said Declan. "You—you intrigued me straightaway. As my son and your ex-boyfriend pointed out to me already."

"The ex-boyfriend being your son is a definite complication," said Bree. "As are your overprotective daughters."

"It's too much, isn't it?" Declan picked up his wig and put it down again.

"It would be very, very difficult," said Bree.

"Because of the girls or because of Michael?"

She laughed shortly. "It's hard to know which is worse."

"You never got to kiss Michael," said Declan.

"Nope." She looked steadily at Declan. "I wanted to, though. I really did."

"Would you want to now?" he asked.

She shook her head. "That time has gone." She smiled wryly. "I never really figured out why we didn't."

"I'm glad you didn't," said Declan. "I really don't think I could kiss you myself if you had."

"Are we going to kiss each other?" asked Bree.

"What do you think?" Declan's brown eyes met hers again.

"Perhaps I shouldn't let another kissing opportunity pass me by," she said.

His lips were soft but his kiss was confident. She put her arms around him and pulled him closer to her. He tasted, very slightly, of coffee and his aftershave was musk.

When he let her go she ran her tongue across her bottom lip. He looked at her anxiously.

"How often do barristers kiss people in their offices or chambers or whatever it is you like to call them?" she asked.

"I really don't know," said Declan. "I'm not sure how often barristers actually want to kiss people in their offices."

"Do you want to do it again?" she asked.

"Oh yes." He smiled at her and this time held her even closer. And she was very glad it was Declan she was kissing.

Cate was wearing a tracksuit. It was one that her company distributed, plain gray with an embossed logo and its sales for the past month had been well above target. Cate knew why—it was tremendously comfortable as well as being stylish and the subdued logo of the manufacturer had become the fashion statement of the autumn.

She glanced at her watch before picking up her brush and sweeping her hair into a ponytail. She slicked some tinted lip balm on her lips and sprayed Escada Sport behind her ears and on her wrists. She didn't bother with any more makeup. She knew that a few months ago she would have spent ages on getting her face exactly right—even for a night in with her sisters—although that in itself would have been an unlikely event. But in the time since they'd come back from Spain, she'd used her makeup more sparingly than ever before and never bothered retouching it in the evenings.

Ian Hewitt, her boss, said that he liked her more natural look. "It wasn't that you looked unnatural before," he told her frankly, "it was just that you looked too perfect to be true sometimes. And I think that the clients like the softer appearance."

She didn't look perfect now, she thought, with her ever more discernible bump making the tracksuit more of a necessity than a choice. She had a healthy glow courtesy of her holiday tan, although her face was thin and, despite the extra weight of her pregnancy, she knew that she wasn't eating enough again. Since coming home she'd felt too tense to eat properly.

She went into the living room and plopped onto the sofa. Nessa, Jill and Bree would be here shortly. Nessa was bringing a collection of videos. Upbeat ones, she said, so that they could have a good laugh if they got low.

Bree and Cate had suggested that neither of them were feeling especially low and Nessa had agreed that she wasn't either right now because since Adam had moved out she was feeling incredibly good about things but upbeat videos would be a good lift all the same.

Undemanding, Nessa had said, and despite feeling good about Adam's departure, she could only cope with undemanding at the moment.

Cate thought that Nessa might have a point. She didn't feel like watching anything very taxing either and, even if she wasn't feeling low, she was terribly uneasy. Her mind was still occupied with either thoughts of the baby or thoughts of the company's sales graphs. The sales graphs were great but she was still terrified about giving birth. She thought about it every single day and every single time she could feel her heart race with fear. But she was coping with it. Sort of. Whenever she thought about it now she allowed herself to feel the fear for a couple of minutes and then she resolutely put the thoughts to the back of her mind again. She knew that she'd never be able to think of this as a joyous experience like Nessa did but she hoped that she'd manage to get through it.

The buzzer sounded and she got up.

"We're here!" cried Jill as she waved at the monitor. "Open up, Cate!"

She released the entrance door and then stood at the apartment door to wait for them.

Jill was first up the stairs carrying a huge bouquet of flowers.

"They're for your new apartment," she told Cate.

"Thank you." Cate took them from her.

"I'm sorry that you and Finn don't love each other anymore," said Jill.

"So am I," said Cate.

"It's a bit of a mess, isn't it?" said Jill. "Like Mum and Dad."

"Oh?" Cate looked at Jill then at Nessa who rubbed the back of her neck and shrugged.

"Did Mum tell you that they're probably going to get a divorce?" Cate nodded.

"It's not my fault," said Jill. "It's not anybody's fault. They don't really love each other anymore."

"I know." Cate wanted to cry at the practical tone in Jill's voice.

"I told Mum I'd prefer if they did live together but she says they can't. Dad says he'll come home but Mum says that if he does that we'll have to leave. They've got other people talking about it for them. To make an arrangement."

"It's hard to live with someone when you don't love them any-more," said Cate.

"They both love me." This time Jill was unable to keep a trace of anxiety out of her voice. "Dad said so and Mum said so."

"And it's true," said Nessa forcefully. "We love you most of all."

"I still wish you loved each other," said Jill. "I don't like it the way it is now. I want us to be together like we were before."

"I'm sorry it can't be," said Nessa. "But sometimes you stop loving someone. Or you can like them a lot—I like your dad a lot—but you have to live in different houses."

"But your Mum will never stop loving you," Cate reassured Jill. "It'd be impossible to stop loving you."

"She says I drive her to despair sometimes," said Jill.

"You probably do." Cate smiled at her. "But she still loves you."

"And so does your dad," said Nessa.

Jill sighed deeply. "I hate people not loving each other."

Cate swallowed hard. "So do I, honey," she said. "So do I." She looked at them both brightly. "What'll you have to drink?" she asked.

"White wine for me," said Nessa.

"Juice," said Jill.

"Any special juice?"

"What d'you have?"

"Orange, passion fruit or cranberry," said Cate.

"Orange," said Jill.

"Please," added Nessa automatically.

"Please," said Jill.

Cate got the drinks and was just sitting down again when the buzzer sounded.

"I'll get it!" cried Jill. She pressed the intercom button.

"It's me," said Bree.

"I know," said Jill. "Come on in."

A minute later Bree bounded into the room. Her face was flushed and her eyes sparkled. Both Nessa and Cate looked at her in surprise.

"Are you on happy pills or something?" asked Nessa. "I've never seen you look so cheerful."

"No." But Bree couldn't keep the smile off her face.

"What then?" Cate's tone was suspicious.

But at that moment Jill pressed the remote control for the TV and the theme tune to Finn's show started.

Bree and Nessa exchanged looks of horror as Cate stared at the screen. The images of Finn came one after the other and Jill looked around at her. "It's Finn's show," she said. "D'you want to watch it even though you don't love him anymore?"

He called me, thought Cate. He called me but he didn't call back.

"Leave it on until I get Bree a drink." Her voice croaked. "What'll you have, Bree?"

"Beer," said Bree.

"Beer is disgusting." Jill was still watching the TV.

"When have you drunk beer?" demanded Nessa.

"When you were on holidays," said Jill. "Dad shared some with me. He said it would educate my palate."

Nessa sighed

Jill turned up the volume as Finn strode across the studio.

"This evening we're going to be talking about perceptions," said Finn. "How people see us, how we see ourselves, preconceived notions about each other. I'll be talking to an interesting array of guests, all of whom have suffered from the ideas that others have had of them."

"Put on a video now," she told Jill. "I don't want to see any more of him."

"I think I left them in the car." Jill looked around.

"For heaven's sake, Jill, it was your job to look after them!" Nessa looked at her crossly.

"There's one already in the machine," said Cate hastily. "Play that until you find the other one."

She put a bowl of nachos on the coffee table, along with a tube of Pringles and a couple of dips.

"Oh, great, it's *Friends*," said Jill as she sat on the floor with her juice and grabbed a handful of Pringles while still watching the TV. "That's much better than the ones we brought. I like Joey the best. He wants to be an actor. I want to be an actress when I grow up."

"Do you?" asked Nessa in surprise. "I thought you wanted to be an astronaut."

"Not anymore," said Jill. "People are always nice to actresses. They give them clothes and everything."

Nessa grinned and looked at Bree. "Sorry, sis," she said. "She used to be like you but now she's turning into Cate."

Bree smiled. And then grinned. And then she giggled.

"Bree Driscoll, what on earth is the matter with you?" demanded Nessa. "You were beaming like a Cheshire cat when you came in and you're still at it."

Bree felt as though her whole body was fizzing with excitement. Yet she wanted to savor the moment, not to blurt things out in one go.

"Bree?" Cate looked at her curiously. "What's happened?" Then her eyes widened. "Have you seen Declan? Is that it?"

Bree nodded. "I kissed him," she said. "I really did."

"Yuch!" cried Jill. "Kissing boys is yuch."

"Hardly a boy," said Nessa.

"Are you getting at me?" demanded Bree.

Nessa shook her head. "Of course not. So, come on, tell us— what happened?"

Bree told them, even including the part where Declan's secretary, Sally, had walked into the room while his arms were still around her. She'd looked at them in shock and walked out again, closing the door firmly behind her and leaving Declan looking at Bree with an expression of amused guilt.

"And it was then I realized that he's a real person," she told Cate and Nessa. "Not some older man figure and not someone I want to depend on, but someone I really like and someone who has feelings of his own."

"So what next?" asked Nessa.

"I don't know," said Bree. "We're going out tomorrow night." Her eyes sparkled. "Maybe it'll be a complete disaster. Maybe not. But it's worth a try."

"I've never seen you like this before," said Cate.

"I've never felt like this before," admitted Bree. "Oh, girls, I know that things can all go horribly wrong. I know there's no guarantees. But I really, really think—"

"Are you madly in love?" Jill interrupted her.

"Maybe I am," said Bree. She sounded pleased and surprised at the same time. "Maybe I am."

The episode of the sitcom ended and another one began.

Cate groaned. "I've seen this about a hundred times."

"I'll go and get the other videos," said Nessa. "I think they're still on the backseat."

She got up and went out of the apartment. When she came back,

Jill was leaning against Cate's legs and her eyes were closed. Nessa realized that Jill was asleep. She told Cate that maybe she should bring Jill home and forget about the videos until some other time.

"Don't go yet," said Cate. "Put her in the bedroom. It seems a shame to wake her. We can watch TV for a while anyway."

Nessa nodded. Jill hadn't been sleeping well since Adam's departure and she desperately wanted the little girl to have some rest. She carried her into the bedroom and laid her down on the bed. Jill slept on. Nessa watched her for a few moments.

She hoped that she'd done the right thing. There had been a part of her that, despite everything, had thought that maybe she should stay with Adam because of Jill. But she knew that she couldn't. She knew that the relationship had broken down too much. She'd never really thought that it would happen. She never thought she'd be strong enough to ask him to leave. She couldn't have stayed married to him because of Jill. She could have stayed with him and been unhappy if there hadn't been other women. But staying with him for the wrong reason was worse than telling him to go.

She closed the bedroom door and walked back into the living room. Cate was looking for the remote control to turn off the video.

"Jill had it," said Nessa. "It might be under the sofa. It's where most things Jill touches end up." She groped beneath the furniture and her fingers found it. "Told you," she said triumphantly as she pointed it at the TV and hit stop. Then she wished she hadn't. Because Finn's show was still on.

"Leave it," said Cate tightly. "Don't turn it off."

Bree and Nessa looked at her. Her face was rigid as she looked at the screen. Finn was talking to the audience, wrapping up the show.

"And so people are not always what they seem," he told them. "But we make sweeping generalizations. And, of course, we live our lives always wanting something more than we have, whether it's fame or money or critical acclaim. When we get it, it isn't always what we expected." He turned to face a different camera and spoke again. The move had been unexpected. The cameraman had to pan in on him rapidly. "I want to share something with you," he told the audience. "The same way as my guests tonight shared things with you. I always wanted to be what I am now. I wanted to work on TV. I wanted people to listen to me. But because I was so obsessed with that idea, some of the people I loved most thought it was more important to me than anything else. And maybe, for a time, it was. But it's not. And I want all of those people to know that. Especially Cate."

Nessa and Bree both gasped. Cate's eyes were still fixed on the screen. She said nothing.

Finn smiled at the audience. "I messed up with my girlfriend because I was a prat," he told them. "I blamed her for things going wrong when it was just as much my fault."

There was a murmur from the audience.

Finn shrugged. "I doubt very much that she's watching this program tonight. Poor girl had to put up with me practicing for months, she's heard it all already."

There was laughter in the studio.

"I thought for a while about saying this on TV. I don't want people to think I'm some kind of self-serving egoist. I didn't tell my producer I was going to do this which is why you see people at the edges of the studio looking very worried and why the autocue man is having hysterics at the moment."

There was more laughter in the studio. A smile flickered across Cate's lips.

Finn wiped his brow with the back of his hand. "This is difficult, you know. When I was talking to Misty,"—he gestured to one of his guests, a well-known soap star—"and she was telling us about her trouble in finding a bloke who didn't think of her as her actual character, I suddenly realized how lucky I'd been. And how stupid. And I know that hijacking the airwaves to tell someone that you love them is totally crass and very unsophisticated but, well,"—he wiped his brow again,—"Cate, I love you."

He smiled his quirky smile and looked at the audience again. "If she doesn't come back to me, I'll take it on the chin. If she does, you'll know next week. Thanks for being with me tonight. And thanks for watching."

"Cate!" Nessa jumped up. "Cate, he loves you. He said it on national television."

Cate said nothing. She clenched and unclenched her fists.

"Oh, Cate, do you believe he's actually done that?" asked Bree. "He's told the whole country that he loves you. Isn't that just fantastic?"

"Maybe." Her face was expressionless.

"Only maybe?" Bree looked surprised. "Cate, the man bared his soul in front of the whole country tonight."

"Great ratings," said Cate.

Nessa put her arm around Cate's shoulders. "I don't think he did it for the ratings," she said. "He looked—well, genuine."

"He always looks genuine," said Cate. "That's part of his charm."

"He must have meant it," said Bree. "Oh, Cate, you can't think that it's all a con!"

Cate smiled a little. "You've gone from being the most cynical girl on earth to the most love-struck person I know," she told Bree. "All because of Declan Morrissey I suppose."

"Cate, I'm not love-struck," said Nessa. "And if anyone knows anything about being cynical or lying bastard blokes trying to fool you, I'm your woman! I allowed Adam to lie to me and I allowed myself to believe him. But Finn didn't look as though he was lying. He looked as though he meant it."

"It's a brilliant career move," said Cate. "If I go back to him, everyone will think he's Mr. Sensitive. And if I don't, they'll think I'm Miss Callous Bitch."

"They won't," said Bree. "If you go back to him they'll be happy for you. And if you don't, they'll know that he must be a right shit that you didn't fall for his routine tonight and his career will go down the toilet!"

Cate laughed suddenly. "Maybe."

Her mobile phone rang and she looked at it warily.

"Let me," said Nessa who picked it up and answered it.

"Actually, yes, we did see it," she said and then mouthed the word "Mum" at her sisters. "Wel,l I know, it does put a different complexion on things. We're talking about it now."

She was silent and then passed the phone over to her sister.

"I don't know what I'll do," said Cate having listened to Miriam for a while. "But I'm not going to do anything rash."

She spoke to her mother for a little longer then ended the call.

"He did sound genuine, didn't he?" Her voice was faintly hopeful.

"Absolutely," said Bree and Nessa in unison. "Absolutely."

38

♥

Sun in Sagittarius, Moon in Gemini
Looking for a long and stable relationship through trial and error.

Normally Finn had a drink with the guests and the production team after the show. It was his wind-down time when he came off the high that a successful show gave him and when he felt the adrenaline buzz start to fade. But he didn't stay this time. He popped his head around the door of the hospitality room, wished everyone goodnight, and walked to the exit.

"Finn!" The producer waved at him.

He turned around. "Hi, Carol."

"Finn, don't you ever do that to me again."

"I'm sorry."

"This show isn't your personal confession box," she said.

"I know."

She looked at him sympathetically. "It'll probably do the ratings no harm."

"I didn't do it for the ratings," he said. "I wasn't going to do it at all. But I suddenly thought that maybe a big gesture would make her believe that I really care about her."

"Oh, Finn." Carol shook her head and her long earrings jangled. "Girls don't want big gestures. That's a male myth. We want someone to be there when we're down and someone to share things with when we're up. We can do without the flowers and the chocolates and everything else once we know that we have someone to depend on."

"Is it really that simple?" asked Finn.

"Of course it is." Carol smiled at him. "You're supposed to be the voice of the nation. Surely you know that already?"

"I wish." Finn sighed. "I thought I knew everything I needed to know. I prided myself on being a sensitive sort of bloke. But when it came down to it, I wasn't."

"She'll forgive you," said Carol. "We mightn't need the big gesture but it sure as hell takes some beating."

"She didn't return my phone call," said Finn. "It was the only thing I could think of."

"Maybe she'll phone you tonight," said Carol.

"Maybe," said Finn, although his tone was doubtful.

It was nearly midnight by the time he got back to the apartment. He opened the door and let himself in. As always, since Cate's departure, he was struck by how empty it seemed. Cate had been a neat and tidy person but he missed the scent of her perfume or seeing her jacket on the rail when he came home. He missed the curve of her body beside his in the bed at night and the way she closed her eyes tightly shut in the morning to stay asleep when he got up. He sighed and thought that he hadn't always been very considerate in the mornings because he knew that he always woke her even though she never said anything.

He flopped down on the leather couch and draped his legs over the armrest. The big gesture had been inconsiderate too, he realized now, putting her under pressure and no doubt making her feel uncomfortable. He hadn't meant to do that but he'd acted without thinking. Selfishly, he thought. Putting his feelings before hers again. After all, he'd been the one to ask her to leave. Why should she suddenly decide that she'd want to come back?

Maybe she was happier without him. She'd reconciled herself to the idea of her pregnancy and he knew how much she'd feared it; there was no reason for her not to reconcile herself to being a single parent either. She was such a capable person she could easily build a life for herself and for the baby without him. She was already doing that, wasn't she? He didn't even know where she lived anymore. How was it, he wondered bleakly, that everything had once been so right and now it was so wrong?

At first he thought he'd imagined the sound of the buzzer. He'd closed his eyes and was trying to empty his mind of any thoughts. And noise of the buzzer had seemed to come from miles away. Then he heard it again. And he shot out of the couch and pressed the intercom.

"It's me," said Cate.

"Come up." He wiped his hands on the seat of his trousers.

She looked different, he thought, as he led her into the apartment but she didn't look pregnant because the gray tracksuit was loose and he couldn't see any discernible bump. Her hair was clipped back from her face in a style he hadn't seen before. She wore no eye shadow and only a smear of lip gloss. She looked beautiful, he thought, and she still wore the same perfume.

"Would you like something to drink?" he asked. "Wine, water?"

"Water would be nice." She walked over to the couch and sat down. The lights of the coast road gleamed their familiar orange through the apartment window.

"Here you are." He handed her a long glass filled with sparkling water.

"Thanks."

He sat in the armchair opposite her. "I guess you saw the show."

"Only the beginning and the end actually," she said. She sipped her water. "I watched *Friends* during the middle."

"*Friends?*" He frowned. "I thought you didn't like *Friends*. You were scathing when I brought home those videos."

"Nessa and Bree came over and we were supposed to be watching something else," said Cate. "But we got stuck on *Friends* and then you came on. It threw us a little."

"I'm sorry," he said. "For the show. My producer told me afterward that it was not the thing to have done."

"Might be good for your ratings, though."

"She said that too."

"Why did you have to blab all that stuff on television?" she asked. "It's private between us, Finn."

"Because I wanted to make a grand gesture," he told her. "Carol said that women didn't really need big gestures but . . ." he faltered. "She was probably right."

"It was certainly big," said Cate. "And of course she was right. Gestures are only gestures. They don't mean much in the end."

"It got you here though," Finn said. "I didn't think anything else would. You didn't phone me back."

"Why should I?" asked Cate. "You didn't leave a message."

"Your office said you were on holiday," Finn told her. "I thought you might ring when you got back. I could hardly believe you were away. You were always difficult to persuade that you needed time off."

"I went with Nessa and Bree," said Cate.

"You didn't!" For the first time his tone was entirely natural. "How on earth did you three manage to spend a whole week together?"

"It was surprisingly good fun," said Cate. "They got drunk a lot and I watched them."

"What's the story about Nessa and Adam?" asked Finn. "Have they sorted out their problems?"

"It depends on what you mean by sorted out," said Cate. "They've separated."

"Oh." Finn's looked uncomfortable. "I'm sorry to hear that."

"It was the right thing for her to do," Cate told him. "He was cheating on her with at least two other women."

"No!" Finn's expression was shocked. "I never would have believed it. He seemed such a home-loving sort of man."

"He loved home all right," said Cate. "But he also wanted to play away. At first Nessa didn't believe it—that was when she thought there was only one of them. Then Bree found out about a second woman. We told Nessa on holiday one night when she rang home and discovered that he was allegedly working late. Of course he was actually with one of them. She flipped. It was a case of straws and camels' backs, I think."

"It's a pity all the same," said Finn. "They seemed to have so much going for them."

"*C'est la vie*," said Cate lightly.

"Do you want some more water?" asked Finn.

She nodded. "But it runs through me," she told him. "I'll be in the bathroom in five minutes."

He smiled at her and returned with another glass. This time he'd floated a slice of lemon on the top. The lemon was ancient, he'd found it in a bowl on the worktop. "I suppose we should talk about things." He looked uncomfortable.

"You've said it all, haven't you? To everyone who'd listen. You think you love me?" Her tone was cool.

"I do love you," said Finn. "But I didn't say the right things."

Cate shrugged and rubbed her finger along her empty glass.

"I suppose what I really should've said is that I'm sorry." The words came quickly and she looked up at him, startled. "I *am* sorry, you know," he said. "I was horrible to you Cate."

To her dismay she could feel a lump in her throat and tears prick at the back of her eyes. She said nothing.

"To say that I was shocked isn't an excuse. I mean, I *was* shocked, but that doesn't make any difference. I treated you very badly."

She gulped her water. The bubbles got up her nose and made her eyes run. She wiped them with the tips of her fingers.

"When Tiernan Brennan phoned me, I couldn't believe what he was saying," Finn continued. "He told me that he'd met you in the restaurant of the airport hotel and that you were having a meal all on your own and that you were supposed to be getting the last flight to London but he reckoned that you'd missed it." Finn took a deep breath. "I asked him was he sure you were still in Dublin because I thought you'd caught the flight and he got very flustered and said that maybe he'd spoken out of turn."

"You hadn't heard from him in months but he rings you up to tell tales about me and pretends to be flustered?" Cate looked disdainful.

"I know." Finn rubbed the back of his neck. "He'd had a few drinks, had Tiernan. He wanted to know if I'd meet him for some more in town since both of our girlfriends were clearly having better fun without us."

"Trouble-making shit," said Cate.

"I said I was too busy. I rang your mobile but I got your voicemail and I couldn't think of what to say. I thought you might phone me. But I knew there was something seriously wrong. You'd told me already that you were in London. You'd lied. So I assumed the worst."

"Understandable, I guess," said Cate.

"I thought you might ring me the next day. I'd have said something to you then, to let you know that I knew something was up. But you didn't. And I thought that you were clearly having too good a time to ring me."

"I wish," muttered Cate.

"So I got really furious then. And I decided that I'd throw you out."

"Thanks," she said crookedly.

"Then when you came home and told me . . ." His voice trailed off and he looked at a spot in the ceiling. "I couldn't believe it. And after all the time I'd been thinking that you were having an affair with someone I suppose I believed that the baby couldn't possibly be mine. Every time I thought that it might be, I was consumed with rage that you hadn't told me. And that you were going to get rid of it without telling me. I couldn't believe that you'd do a thing like that without telling me, Cate, I just couldn't."

She stared into her glass of water, watching the bubbles rise to the surface and break around the thin slice of lemon.

"You told me you didn't want children," she said finally, not looking up at him. "I was going to tell you one night when we were having a takeaway only you started talking about not going down the suburban route and having kids and so I just couldn't. Especially whenever I thought of what it would be like with you and the TV show and the radio shows and everything. You'd be so busy and I'd be the one who'd have to do all the nappy changing and getting up in the middle of the night and everything. You were moving onto a different level of success, Finn. I didn't want to destroy that by dumping the whole notion of a baby on you."

"But you didn't have the abortion after all."

"No," she whispered. "In the end I couldn't." She looked up, her eyes swimming with tears. "I didn't want the baby, Finn. Not really. But it was there, it was part of me, and I couldn't just . . ."

He watched the tears slide down her cheeks. He'd never seen her cry before. He reached out and put his arm around her shoulder. "Cate—"

"I'm sorry." She sniffed. "I think the crying is a hormonal thing. I kept doing it earlier on in the pregnancy but I've more or less gotten over it now."

"Cate, I'm really, really sorry."

"For what?" She took a tissue out of her bag. "You were right to be mad at me. For all the reasons you gave. If you'd lied to me I would've been mad at you too."

"I didn't give you a chance to explain," said Finn.

"I told you what happened," she said. "You only half believed me. Fair enough. You wanted me to leave. I understood."

"Cate stop being so bloody understanding," said Finn.

"I said I understood," Cate told him. "It doesn't mean I liked it very much!"

"I was ashamed of myself," said Finn. "Even if the baby wasn't mine, presenting you with a packed suitcase wasn't exactly a nice thing to do."

She sniffed and said nothing.

"I thought about ringing you almost straightaway but I couldn't. I was hurt and annoyed and embarrassed and all sorts of things."

"And busy," said Cate.

"That too," admitted Finn. "But not so busy that I couldn't phone. Only I didn't know what to say."

"It doesn't matter," said Cate. "It was a difficult time."

"I do so absolutely hate it when you're being rational," Finn told her. "It makes it very difficult for me to appear hard done by."

She gave him a watery smile. "Why should I help you feel hard done by?" she asked.

"No reason," he said. "But at least that way I don't see myself as an utter bastard."

"You're not," she said.

"I tried to be," said Finn.

"Look, I'm not going to keep pandering to you," she told him. "You *were* a bastard but I wasn't exactly great either so we're quits."

He grinned at her. "Oh, Cate, I love you the most when you're bossy and commanding."

She looked at him. "Oh?"

"And when you do your icy, always right kind of thing."

"I don't feel very icy or even halfway right," said Cate.

"How do you feel?" asked Finn.

She looked at him and bit her lip. "Different," she said eventually. "The last couple of months have been so different for me. I found out that there were other things in life besides sports shoes and sales graphs. I found out that I couldn't exist on just a lettuce leaf and cup of herbal tea. I found out that my two sisters have become good friends as well as family."

"And I found out that I love you more than ever," said Finn. "And that I was a complete fool to tell you to go."

Cate said nothing.

"I know that I made a fool of myself tonight too," he said. "And that dragging our lives into the public gaze wasn't the cleverest thing I've ever done. I know that I was difficult to be with because I was so caught up in my own life. I know that I made the TV show into the biggest, most important event in my life. I know that I sometimes treated you and your job as secondary to my own so-called brilliant career. But, Cate, it'd be different if you came back. I promise you. If you want me to give up the TV thing I will because it means nothing without you. If you want me to get a job as a—"

"Stop," she said.

"Stop?"

"You talk too much," she told him. "You get carried away trying to make each sentence more meaningful than the last. It's probably your chat-show persona."

"It's how I feel."

"Oh, Finn." Tears spilled down her face again but she didn't bother to wipe them away. "I sometimes thought that you were only with me because I looked nice and because I had my own career."

"Don't be so bloody stupid," he said. "I was always with you because I loved you."

She smiled through her tears. "Actually, that sentence was probably the most meaningful yet."

"So you'll come back?" He looked at her hopefully.

"Of course I'll come back." She rested her head on his shoulder. "I never ever wanted to be away."

It was a couple of minutes later before she raised her head again. Then she stood up.

"Where are you going?" asked Finn.

She walked into the bedroom, turned on the light and opened the window. He followed her, surprised at her actions.

She leaned out of the window and waved. Below them, in the car park, he saw the door of Nessa's Alfa open slowly. Bree, Nessa and Jill got out.

"Everything all right?" called Bree.

"Couldn't be better!" cried Cate.

"You don't need any moral support?" Nessa asked.

"I think I've worked it all out."

"Sure?" Bree and Nessa spoke at the same time.

"Absolutely certain," said Cate.

"Are you still in love?" asked Jill.

She turned to Finn who moved into the space beside her.

"I hope she is," he told Jill. "Because I'm sure as hell in love with her."

Bree and Nessa looked at each other and grinned.

"Are you?" called Nessa.

"Actually, I am!" Cate smiled down at them.

"But I'm going to be really nice to her now and make her a cup of hot chocolate before she goes to bed," said Finn. "She's had a hard day."

"Treat her right," warned Nessa. "You'll have us to answer to if you don't."

"Oh, I will," Finn promised. "I will."

He closed the window. Cate waved at them again and then moved inside the apartment with him.

"That was fun," said Jill as she climbed into the backseat of the car and then yawned widely. "And I'm out really, really late."

"I'm glad they've sorted it out," said Nessa. "I'm glad you have too, Bree."

"Oh, I haven't sorted it out," Bree said. "But I'm ready to give it a whirl. What about you?"

Nessa smiled. "My horoscope for tomorrow said that I should look out for advantages in new situations. But to take things as they come. It's probably the best advice I've ever seen in one."

"You're back reading them, then?"

"Only when they say something sensible." Nessa got into the car and started the engine.

"They never say anything sensible." Bree slid into the passenger seat beside her.

"Oh, I know that," said Nessa. "I always knew that really."

And she smiled as she put the car into gear and headed home.

Up Close and Personal
with the Author

ARE YOUR BOOKS AUTOBIOGRAPHICAL?

I think every author is asked that at some point and no matter how hard I try to explain that I make it all up, people always believe that it's based on fact. I very rarely put actual events that have happened to me or people close to me in books, though I made an exception for the car-getting-stuck-in-the-mud scene in *He's Got to Go* which is based on a real event that happened to me and a couple of close friends while we were in Spain. It was a total nightmare and I felt I couldn't waste the experience! Everything else is complete fiction.

However, I know that there must be something of my life in the characters of my books because our personal experiences color how we feel about everything and my novels deal with feelings and relationships. So although the plots are totally invented I suppose I have experienced the emotions that the characters go through, although in a completely different context. I've lain in bed and wondered if the man I loved was cheating on me—but in a very different way and very different circumstances, for example, to Nessa. I've also experienced the feelings of pressure that Cate does in her job as a sales executive, although in my bond trading job. And I think there's a bit of Bree in me too. I like fixing things.

Writing is a little bit like acting, without being on stage, because you do get under the skin of all of your characters and there are times, when I'm deep in the novel, that I start behaving like them too which can be a bit disconcerting for people around me. Actually, although I don't have children myself, when I wrote about a pregnancy in one of my previous novels (*Dreaming of a Stranger*) I used to feel bloated and uncomfortable whenever my character Jane felt that way. And I had sympathetic back-ache too—though that might have been because I wasn't using a very good chair at the time!

The other great thing about writing is that you can be the kind of person you aren't in real life. I quite liked the idea of having my own motorbike but when I dated a guy who had one I was utterly hopeless. It was so heavy I could hardly hold it upright let alone ride it. I'm fairly short (5' 1") so I get a kick out of making my heroines taller. I'm not the world's greatest cook either and it was fun to write about a chef in a previous novel (*My Favourite Goodbye*). The thing is, when you're writing, you have to be every character and believe in every character—even the less pleasant ones. Generally I like to think of my characters as close family or friends and I believe in them totally. If I didn't, I wouldn't want to write about them. Besides, they're with me for a long time when I'm writing about them, a lot more than my actual family.

DO YOU HAVE SISTERS OF YOUR OWN?

Well, yes, two of them—which is why many people assume that *He's Got to Go* is about us and why I specifically mention them in the acknowledgments to say that it's not. But I am fascinated by the dynamic that goes on between family members and how, at different times, each one can be up or down or be the strong one or the dependent one. At the same time you never lose the tag you had as a child—I was always the academic one because I had my nose stuck in a book all the time!

YOU WERE A BOND TRADER? HOW COME YOU'VE ENDED UP WRITING BOOKS?

I got into finance by mistake. Honestly. My mother accepted a job for me while I was on holidays because I'd already turned down a couple and I think she was afraid I'd spend my life loafing around. And then I discovered that I was quite good at managing other people's money (much better than at managing my own). Also, I like to do whatever I'm doing to the best of my ability so I kind of threw myself into the whole dealing thing. But it certainly wasn't what I expected to do with my life and career.

DID YOU ALWAYS WANT TO GIVE UP TRADING AND WRITE BOOKS?

It was certainly always my ambition to write books because I was a big reader myself as a kid. Whenever I had any money I'd buy myself a book and I used to walk a couple of miles to our local library once a week too. Reading is still very important to me and I suppose I've always wanted to bring that same enjoyment to the people who read my books now. But I enjoyed working in finance too and I guess it's given me an understanding of the business side of writing; like when the publisher is screaming for you to meet a deadline it's not because they want to make your life a total misery, it's because there's a whole team of people—editorial, production, marketing, booksellers—waiting to get your book on the shelves. Knowing that people are depending on you helps the motivation!

SO WHAT MOTIVATED YOU TO WRITE *HE'S GOT TO GO*?

I wanted to write about sisters but also about women whose lives aren't going exactly as they planned because, let's face it, nobody's life goes exactly how you planned it. The thing is, though, a lot of people look at what goes on in the part of your life that they see and think that everything's fine, whereas things might not be so fine at all. And that's the case with the three sisters in *He's Got to Go*. They each envy each other for specific parts of their lives but they don't initially see the unhappier sides to them. It's probably a case of the grass always being greener as far as they're concerned. But at the same time, their feelings are colored by their experiences as children together—so that both Nessa and Cate still see Bree as a flighty baby, for example. I enjoyed writing the parts when two sisters call each other to complain about or discuss the third but I hope the reader can see that even though they're being bitchy sometimes they're also deeply concerned for each other. Both Bree and Cate are worried about Nessa's fairy-tale marriage falling apart, even though they've mocked her about it in the past. Cate and Nessa are concerned about Bree's lack of boyfriends (and then the man she chooses) while Nessa and Bree are anxious about Cate's high-pressure life.

WHAT'S THE ASTROLOGICAL STUFF AT THE BEGINNING OF THE CHAPTERS ALL ABOUT?

Whenever I read a magazine I always look at my horoscope. I forget it almost straightaway but I can't help myself. I know there are people who believe that their horoscopes can help them in their lives and Nessa is one of those so I thought it would be nice to give an astrological heading to each chapter. Of course in her case when things go wrong her stars don't really prepare her for it. Interestingly, though, I do think the main characteristics of star-signs are uncannily accurate. I didn't allocate the sisters signs at the start but as I wrote about them I knew when their birthdays would be.

DO YOU BELIEVE THAT A MAN WHO BETRAYS YOU HAS GOT TO GO OR SHOULD HE BE GIVEN A SECOND CHANCE?

That's a million-dollar question. I think when trust has gone it's very, very difficult to repair a relationship no matter how hard you try. At the same time people are a lot less willing to work at relationships these days and perhaps that's a bad thing. Whether you stay together or split up depends on a whole range of issues but you've really got to think hard about what you want and what's good for you. Sometimes we make decisions and then try to justify them afterwards. It's worth trying to think things through before you make that final choice. But it's much easier to make the hard choices for someone else, for yourself it's not at all clear-cut.

ARE YOU IN A RELATIONSHIP OF YOUR OWN?

Yes. I live with my partner and we've been together for double-digit number of years! It scares me when I think about it sometimes because the time has passed so quickly. And we've had both good times and bad times together. So far we've always managed to work through the bad times but maybe that's because we try not to take each other for granted and because we both make compromises! (I reckon I compromise more than him. I think all women do!)